The Fearfully and Wonderfully Made

Diamond

The Fearfully and Wonderfully Made

Chizellé T. Archie

First to my Daddy, Jesus Christ, who always saw the best in me when the world could only see the worst in me. Thank you for loving me so much that you would die to save a sinner like me.

To my husband John, "Snoop", thank you for loving me the way you do. Your love has meant everything to me. I'm blessed to have you in my life, you've been my friend, and my love.
I love you.

To my joy, my light, my energy, my Freedom, everything mommy does is for you. You are the greatest gift I could have ever hoped for.
I love you.

To my Pastor, Craig L. Oliver, Sr. Thank you for letting me take a seat in the theatre of your mind, the best seat in the house.
I love you.

...I will praise thee; for I am fearfully and wonderfully made.
Psalm 139:14

What is a Diamond?

A Diamond is the ultimate gemstone, having few weaknesses and many strengths. It is well known that Diamond is the hardest substance found in nature, but few people realize that Diamond is four times harder than the next hardest natural mineral, corundum (sapphire and ruby). But even as hard as it is, it is not impervious. Diamond has four directions of cleavage, meaning that if it receives a sharp blow in one of these directions it will cleave, or split. A skilled diamond setter and/or jeweler will prevent any of these directions from being in a position to be struck while mounted in a jewelry piece.

As a gemstone, Diamond's single flaw (perfect cleavage) is far outdistanced by the sum of its positive qualities. It has a broad color range, high refraction, high dispersion or fire, very low reactivity to chemicals, rarity, and of course, extreme hardness and durability.

D   **I**   **V**   **A**
(Divine)   (Inspired)   (Virtuous)   (Annointed)

Foreword

Imagine receiving this phone call one day after coming home from work.

"This is Dr. Robinson calling. How are you? I'm calling about your lab work from your recent visit. It shows you have DIABETES. Can you come in for a follow up visit tomorrow?"

You can agree that this would be distressing but not the end of the world. You probably know several people with diabetes, and there are countless cookbooks, TV advertisements and talk show segments aimed at people diagnosed with this disease. People share recipes, tips and stories like diabetes is an old friend.

Now imagine the word in capital letters was HIV. Who would you tell then? No more TV time, no more Oprah, no more conversations over cappuccinos. For most women, having HIV becomes their dirty little secret.

In 2007, for over 110,000 U.S. women living with HIV or AIDS, this dirty little secret was a harsh reality. I have been fortunate in my practice as an HIV physician to meet some remarkable women, who have struggled and overcome so much to get to where they are today. No other disease has the power to strip women of their dignity, their sexuality, and their self-worth like HIV. Many became infected by a spouse or partner to whom they'd pledged fidelity and expected the same in return. Some were raped. One woman I know became infected through an injection with a dirty needle overseas when she became ill while visiting family. When she found out her status, her husband divorced her, though she had done nothing wrong.

Why does such stigma still exist 25 years after HIV's discovery? After all, HIV is the *Human* Immunodeficiency Virus, not the intravenous drug user's immunodeficiency virus or the gay man's immunodeficiency virus. Yet the general U.S. population still perceives HIV as a disease confined to these non-mainstream groups. In actuality, over 80% of women contract HIV through heterosexual contact. The public face of HIV still seems to be that of the prostitute, the drug user, or occasionally, a rape victim. Rarely do the media portray an HIV-positive woman who is a teacher, a lawyer, a flight attendant, or an accountant. But HIV doesn't discriminate, and success doesn't protect against infection. I have met HIV-positive patients in all of these positions.

As you read Chizellé Archie's "The Fearfully and Wonderfully Made Diamond", I challenge you to start breaking down any stereotypes you have about HIV. As women, and as society, we need to start destroying the taboos surrounding HIV and start *talking* about it. There are women out there struggling with isolation, loneliness, betrayal, violation, and so much more. They feel they have no one to share their pain with, because doing so would mean disclosing the one thing they don't want anyone to know. By making it alright to talk about HIV, we bring healing and support to women whose lives have been shattered into a million pieces by something no one deserves. It saddens me when I hear a patient tell me "I feel so alone. I bet I'm the only one that cries at every appointment." The truth is, that woman usually isn't even the only crying woman I've seen that day, let alone ever. If only they could all get together and share what they're going through, and find out they're *not* alone. In fact, they probably all know someone who is HIV-positive, but that person doesn't want to say anything either! You likely know someone who's positive as well. Or are you the one with the secret?

On a final note, I want to impress upon the readers what a long way we have come in the treatment of HIV infection. While we still don't have a cure, long-term successful control of the disease is a reality. With the currently available medicines, and a strong dedication to taking care of one's self, the survival of an HIV-positive person in 2010 is not much different from that of the normal population. While not minimizing its seriousness, having HIV is much like having heart disease or diabetes. It requires a significant lifestyle change after diagnosis, but HIV is by no means a death sentence. People can live long, healthy lives and even have healthy HIV-negative children under proper medical supervision.

I have been inspired by the strength and spirit of my patients, and on many occasions we have shed tears together. I am privileged to be their physician, and the relationship we share truly makes medicine worth it for me. To them, and to those who will come after them, I am grateful.

Melissa Osborn, MD
Emory University Hospital

Atlanta
February 2010

All statistics from the Center for Disease Control, HIV/AIDS Surveillance 2007

Chapter One
Victoria

Louis Vuitton, Gucci, Prada, Ferragamo, Chanel, not to mention the others, but unlike my husband, they have never let me down. No matter how lonely my marriage seems, or how much I long for him to want me the way he used to, somehow, someway, they always seem to bring me comfort. Here it is seven o'clock on a Saturday night, and I am standing in my oversized closet getting ready for the "supposed to be party of my life", with a fake smile plastered across my face in hopes the world will continue to get the idea that all with me is peachy cream.

Staring into my 19th century French antique mirror that stands every bit of seven feet and five inches, I glance at the woman who to the world seems to have it going on. Dressed in a white Donna Karan pantsuit, I look as though I am on the cover of this month's issue of Vogue, however, I can't help but admire my collection of designers hanging in their prospective places. I gaze as each hangs according to color, fabric, and even season. My shoes, also are placed in order according to designer, if it is a round toe, square toe, peep toe, or a pointy toe season; I know exactly where to find them. This is my haven; my place of retreat, the one other place besides Fifth Avenue I feel secure. Praying this will be a perfect night, I'm beginning to wonder when and how did my life get to this point …

Hello, my name is Victoria Diamond Jean-Pierre, but to my daddy and friends it's just "Diamond". Today, I turn 33 years old; seventeen years ago today I turned sweet sixteen and it marked the day I received all the elaborate gifts I asked for. I grew up in a middle-class home in Brooklyn,

New York. Thanks to my father, I never knew what it was like to want for anything. I went to the best private schools; I also graduated from The Modern Day Finishing School. We weren't rich, but we did well. I guess you can say I was spoiled; at least that's what I heard from my friends in the neighborhood.

Back in the day they said I looked a lot like Vanessa Williams, the ex- Miss America, maybe it was because of my light complexion, oval face, and high cheekbones that made me look like my smile was always on automatic. My features have pretty much remained the same over the years, all except the unexpected pounds I've put on. Lately, I've been wearing my hair in a body wave that gives the illusion that I have "good hair". A couple of months ago, I colored it a golden brown so it would accentuate one of my best features, my hazel green eyes. Since I have been working out on the treadmill, my hips have become more defined and my butt has grown from a seed to a full-grown apple. I've been told my body is a combination of Janet Jackson, Halle Berry, and J.Lo, so I've got the coke bottle shape that the Commodores sang about, and because of this, it has been a blessing and a curse at the same time.

I'm employed with a notable Investment firm, Rucker, Banks, and Norris in Manhattan. I started out as an intern during my last year of college. They were so impressed with me they offered me a position after graduation. Every day is a new challenge, and I'm very blessed to be in the position I'm in. I started out delivering mail, running errands, and today I am the only black female at junior partner level. Currently I am up for the position of senior partner, pending this case I am now working on. But every job has its ups and downs. Come Monday morning I will find myself rushing to greet my clients with the daily woes of where to and not to invest their prized assets.

These days I've been so stressed out, there are days when I'm not sure if I'm going or coming. I love my job, but there are days when I feel like I should've made another choice. Even though I have the luxury of managing my own hours there are nights when I'm so beat. I go to bed without fulfilling my wifely duties. With both of us working the day shift, it's hard to keep up. Nevertheless, if I had to choose my career over again, I wouldn't trade it for the world. I must say when I look back over my life and see where God has brought me from, I can't help but say "thank you!" And of course my job allows me to do the one thing I love to do most of all; Shop! I'm a shoe fanatic, when I see a pair of shoes that look like they were made for this petite size six and a half, whether they're vintage or new era, I have to have them. I can say this has been my addiction. I have been praying that one day I will be delivered from impulse buying. So in saying this Kate Spade, pray for me.

Growing up, I always dreamed of living the life of luxury, I had it all planned out. One day I'd work on Wall Street for the Stock Exchange, drive the most expensive Mercedes that Daimler would make. I would be the richest girl to come out of Bed-Stuy, next to Lil' Kim of course. In class I'd find myself daydreaming about having a 5,000 square foot home in the Hamptons, gated entrance, Belgian block driveway, 3-car garage, 7 bedrooms, 6 bathrooms, cathedral ceilings, marble and granite throughout. I'd throw the most fabulous parties for the upper echelon and their entourages. Versace tableware would cover the 10 seat antique dining table, 24 karat gold place settings; it had to be the best, and I was going to get it at whatever cost.

I'm the baby of the family, besides my older brother Julian. After me, my mother was pregnant with a baby boy named Miles, after the famous Miles Davis, but he died at birth due to a genetic defect. My father is still hurt over that, and to make light of it, he says, "Miles was the couldna, wouldna, shouldna baby, because after me they were done." After that, they never tried again. My mother had a hard time dealing with the idea that someone she carried and nurtured for nine months didn't live to be a part of this world.

My mother, Delores, is a proud, classy and sold out for Christ woman, whom to everyone is known as "Mrs. D". She's a retired educator for the New York Public School system, she majored in English, and you best believe she'll correct you for speaking incorrect grammar at the drop of a dime. Once during church, my mother took notes of the Pastors sermon, critiqued every word he said, and had the audacity to stay after service just to point out the words he mispronounced. So needless to say, around her we make it a point not to use ebonics, everyone except my father, he could care less.

Mom being the proud woman that she is would always tell me, "Because you do not have a million dollars, that doesn't mean you should not act and look as if you don't". To this day I constantly play that thought over in my head, but I've changed it around a bit to suit me. I tell myself now that you've got the million dollars; you had better look and act as if you do. It's all about the way I think about the situation. My mother has taught me a lot, although she is not a woman impressed by "things", she says, "*things are temporary, but Jesus will last forever.*" That stays dear to my heart, but on another note ... it sure doesn't hurt to carry a Hermes bag with a cute pair of Jimmy Choos.

Ever since my mother retired, she has been spending most of her time volunteering down at the church, helping cook meals for the homeless and the elderly and helping to clean up the poverty stricken areas. She tells us all the time, if she would not have gone to college for education, she would have pursued a career in Social Work. She has a natural knack for helping people, maybe it's because she didn't grow up in a wealthy home like most, she grew up very poor, and she definitely knows the value of a penny. Even though she does all these wonderful things, I still say she missed her calling; becoming an evangelist, because she's always reminding us of God and His goodness, just how blessed we are and we are to never forget it. "Preach, Mrs. D., Preach!"

My father on the other hand, Winston Xavier Jean-Pierre, known to us as "Daddy", is known as a strong hardworking, loving man, of which whom can become pretty hard to deal with at times. Daddy stands 6'2", and commands attention whenever he is in your presence. He is of Creole descent, born and raised in New Orleans, Louisiana, the city that never sleeps, and I do mean never. In Nawlins', as daddy calls it, you can get all the Creole/Cajun food you want, and just in case your man/woman, significant other has done you wrong by any means, you can pay to be rid of them. All you need is a candle, some oils, a needle, toothpick, a little doll, etc ... I don't know all the ingredients; it's just what I heard. But from my understanding you may not see them again, or better yet they could possibly be the chicken you have for dinner tonight. Since he and my mother have been together, obviously my fathers' culture has worn off on her, because she's known for whipping up a good pot of gumbo that'll send you running for cover on any given day.

Since he moved here with his family at the age of fourteen, he hasn't gone back to visit that often. When we were kids, we used to go a lot for Mardi Gras, but since we're all grown up daddy says once you've seen the Zulu's you've seen them all. Anyway things just ain't the same, he says. He does make mention that growing up he was the young man in the neighborhood that watched out for all the young ladies; he was their hero, their protector. Of course momma doesn't care, because he protects her now, and that is what I admire about daddy, his boldness, he's the type of man that will build you up, and tear you down in the same breath. He doesn't tolerate much of anything; you can cross him if you want to. We always knew when and when not to play with him, he had this look that said don't mess with me today. Today ain't the day, and tomorrow ain't looking too good either. As a matter of fact, I can remember him telling us his Aunt Marie was a voodoo priestess so there's no telling what he might cook up, make him mad enough.

Daddy owns three car dealerships, he recently sold two of them, but he remains in control of the one over on 41st Street. He taught me everything I know about cars, especially the Mercedes; the first thing he taught me was that once you have purchased one, you have finally arrived. By the time I was five years old I could tell you the very first Mercedes that was made, a "motorized tricycle." On my fifth birthday, I received my first Mercedes Toy Car. As a child, I could tell you all about them, what make and model by the details in the structure and design. My personal preference has always been the S class, and this is why today I choose to drive a custom S550, it's classy, sleek, and demure, just like me, and those massaging seats sure make good for a hard day at the office.

Daddy's first career was very promising, he almost made it to the NFL, he was drafted by the NY Giants, and he got as far as to receive the sign on bonus, but unfortunately while at a block party my mother had given him, he decided to go for a ride with his now ex-friend Uncle Clarence. Little did my father know Uncle Clarence was well over the legal drinking limit, and due to him failing to stop at a traffic light, the car they were riding in collided with a huge truck, in which it left my father's left leg severed, shall I say that injury was the end to his career in football. As the saying goes, "almost isn't good enough". They survived the accident, but daddy has not been able to forgive Uncle Clarence for over 30 years now, he still comes by to see my mother from time to time, but daddy doesn't really talk to him much, he calls him the "career killer", because he was the one that killed my father's dreams.

He was also due to sign a million dollar contract, but thanks to the advance money, after all the medical bills were paid, he was able to stash away $250,000. After everyone realized he wasn't going to be "the superstar", they left, no where to be found, everyone except my mother, and they got married just before she finished college, and one year later there was my brother Julian. Let my father tell it, Julian was going to grow up and become a Supreme Court Judge, save the world, make daddy proud.

Between the both us, Julian was never the stronger one, to most people I was the one calling the shots, even though he always took up for me when the children in the neighborhood picked on me. I could tell he wanted so badly to play with us on the block, but my father was very strict on him, because he wanted him to be the best. He was my big brother and to me he was the best; he made the better grades, went to the better schools, drove the best car, and got the best girls. None of the guys liked him, because even though he was a nerd, he was still pretty cool. He never tried to be more than what he was; he didn't care if the guys made jokes of him. He wasn't going to compromise just to make friends. He kept his head in the books, and maybe this is why he graduated top of his class.

We were very close growing up; I could talk to him for hours at end. He could relate to the things I was facing at home and at school, he cared about what I thought, and how I felt. We used to play this game that he would one day grow up and be a judge, making a lot of money, and I would be the cute little girl in the cute little shoes handling his money. He would make the money, and I would decide how to spend the money.

We were a team, until he went to college, fell in love, got married, had a beautiful baby, got divorced, and fell in love again.

Outside banging on the door is one of my closet girlfriends from college, Noëlle. Noëlle is a very beautiful woman, almond colored skin, big brown eyes, tall, thin, long straight black hair; she kind of reminds me of Aaliyah by the way she wears her hair over one eye.

All of the men love her, why not, she's sexy, bright, attractive, and most of all she is PAID!! The girl's game is tight. She is CEO of a major music production company. I met Noëlle while in my senior year of college; we hit it off from the beginning. We had a lot of things in common; we both had high expectations of our future, and our future men as well, we both pledged the same year, even though she was swayed to pledge Alpha Kappa Alpha, there was no doubt in my mind that I wasn't destined to adorn the Crimson and Cream, Delta Sigma Theta. She and I have remained tight every since. I was the accounting major, and she was the one to get the MBA. To my knowledge, we have never had any reason to argue, just the usual tisk-tisk girls do, although there is that one time, but I can't seem to remember, so it must not have been that important. Thinking back, I do recall what brought us closer, she introduced me to the love of my life, Malcolm. One day she said she had a friend that had a friend and he was single; well say no more ...

Malcolm was the epitome of my father; he knew what he wanted, and how he was going to get it. He had a plan!! He had his mind set on becoming president of a prominent banking institution. At the time, he was an intern at the Federal National Bank of New York, and I kept saying to myself, "he's the one; he's going to be your husband". He also met the qualifying requirements, he had his own apartment, drove his own car, (not his mother's), also he had GOOD CREDIT with a bank account that actually had money in it. And most of all he had his green card from the health department, stamped, "Clean Bill of Health". Best bill I have ever seen.

Malcolm never stayed out late, he wasn't the partying type; he only wanted to study. I used to think he was sooo square, back then his motto was, "you will never get a promotion unless you are in motion". Making it to the top was his main priority, but don't let me forget, the boy was fine too, and oh could he dress! He was always draped in the finest attire, Ralph Lauren, Hugo Boss, Perry Ellis, the list goes on. Above all else, it was the way he treated me, as if I was his special prize. Wining and dining me was his forte'. Back then Junior's was our favorite restaurant, but the more I think, what intrigued me most about him was that he was saved. He was a God fearing man that in his quiet time could be found reading the bible, on some nights he would challenge me on scriptures that were discussed in Bible Study.

I never understood why Malcolm wasn't interested in making out with me, who wouldn't want to? I thought it was me, every other guy I ever dated wanted to jump my bones from the start, but he never grabbed me and kissed me, he never made love to me. I later found out Malcolm was waiting for his bride; he was waiting for me! I was used to the guys that only wanted you for two things, what they could do for you, or what you could do for them, but thanks to my father who taught me what to look for in a man. He showed me how a man was supposed to treat a woman. Daddy used to say sex wasn't everything, back then I couldn't see what he meant, but now ... I wish I had waited for Malcolm like he did for me, because he was so gentle, and compassionate, and I loved him so much. I think between his faith in God, and the teaching of his parents, Malcolm learned to be a great man.

We fell in love instantly, we were married three years after college, and no doubt, I had to have the fabulous wedding, besides my father would not have had it any other way. I had the Romona Keveza, six bridesmaids, flower girls, the whole nine yards, and I also got the Platinum 3.5 karat emerald-cut Harry Winston. We were so much in love, and I still don't know who has spoiled me the most, my daddy or my Malcolm.

Noëlle says, "Girl what's taking you so long? We've been waiting for you for almost an hour."

I snap back into reality, and remember there are guests waiting to help me celebrate my birthday, so I throw on a pair of white satin Giuseppe's and we're on our way.

"Tonight is going to be the best night of my life." I say, as she drives me to my soiree. As we pull up to the Four Seasons, my heart is beating from all the excitement; I have waited for this night all year. Malcolm has gone way out to make this night special for me. I feel like a celebrity, destined for Oscar glory. The men at valet even look good; their uniforms are a replica of the soldiers from *An Officer and a Gentleman*, clean, crisp, and pristine. I'm feeling so good; I slip one of them a hefty tip. I might need to write it off on my taxes.

Noëlle mumbles, "Girl I got your back tonight, just enjoy yourself, and in the words of your father, *"Laissez Le Bon Temps Rouler."* Which means, "Let the good times roll." My daddy is teaching her French on her off time. It only makes him feel good, it's like he's keeping in touch with his heritage, teaching French makes him feel connected.

Walking inside the ballroom, I'm speechless. Malcolm has hired one of the best event planners around. He really deserves whatever his cost is; he has transformed it into a place fit for a diva, a place fit for me! The décor consists of bold reds, oranges, yellows, delicate handmade linen tablecloths, dramatic centerpieces that capture your attention at first glance. The exotic flowers were flown in from Hawaii, because we fell in love with them when we were there on our honeymoon, so I had to have them. Walking to the table that is set aside for me and Malcolm, I notice the cake; it looks as if it came right off the pages of a Martha Stewart magazine.

The deejay realizes the honoree has made it, and throws on my jam, Frankie Beverly and Maze, "*Before I Let Go.*" Everyone is having a ball, dancing, mingling, sampling appetizers, and drinking. Malcolm orders me a Cosmopolitan, so I know in about a few minutes I am going to be ready to get this party started. As I get settled into my seat, I see a friend from college, she looks a little bit on the chunky side, makes me wonder what she has been doing all this time. She comes over to speak; only to be nosy, she was always good at being in other peoples business. I don't remember putting her on the guest list; so she must have been someone's plus one.

"Hi Michelle, long time no see."

"Victoria this party is all that, and I love that outfit."

"Thanks girl, glad you could make it. Are you here with someone?"

"You didn't think I would miss the party of the year now did you? As a matter of fact a friend of mine and I came together."

"Where is he?" I ask.

"Not he, she. She's around here somewhere; you'll get the chance to meet her."

"Well I'm looking forward to it."

She hugs me, and says, "You can't miss her."

Returning the hug, I thank her again for coming, and tell her to enjoy her night.

"Wouldn't have missed it for the world," she says.

All while in school Michelle was the person with inside info on everything from what man was with your girl or even what man was with your man. She knew everything about everything. It's amazing she graduated, last I heard she wasn't doing that well. An old school friend said she had some disease called Sarcodosis, it's where you have to take a lot of steroids, and this could be the reason she has gained so much weight.

Sitting at one of the tables across from us are my parents and some of their friends from the church, some old ladies that probably don't even remember who I am, they're just here to be nosy, get the latest for Sunday's gossip column.

"Happy Birthday," mother says, standing up to give me a hug.

"Thanks Momma."

"We were almost late, because you know your father; he could not decide what to wear."

Daddy breaks in and gives me a huge kiss, "That's right baby, you know I had to look good for my princess on her 33rd birthday."

"Daddy, I love you and I know you had a hand in planning this party too."

"So what if I did?"

"Well, if you did thank you."

He says he just wants me to have a good time.

If it is the last thing he does, daddy is going to make sure I have nothing less than the best. Even though I'm married, he still feels the need to take care of me in some way or another. Malcolm has reassured him many times that he doesn't have to, but he says, "as long as he has breath in his body, his Diamond will always be his Diamond."

As I walk over to my best friends table to say hello there's a bit of hesitation, because let him tell it, I've been kicking him to the curb lately, therefore I need to give him some TLC, but before I can get to the table I get a glimpse of the chick Michelle must have brought along with her. She's leaning against one of the columns alone as if she is casing the place.

I'm tripping; it's like every man in here is peeping her out. Even Malcolm ... Who is she? I've never seen her before, and I don't believe she had the nerves to come wearing the outfit I've wanted since the Dolce & Gabbana spring and summer collection debuted. The gold sleeveless charmeuse dress, with the high waisted belt, and to top it off she even has on the Leopard print Christian Louboutins, the ones I had Jermaine at Saks order for me. She does have an eye for fashion. Snap! Her hair is pulled back in a tight chignon, with a white gardenia in her hair; she's a girl after my own heart. Onyx polish on her nails, looking like a Playboy Vixen. I gotta say hello to her before the night is over.

Continuing to press my way through the crowd, I finally reach the table. Lucy's screams over the music, "Diamond, you are wearing those shoes tonight Diva!"

I hate tooting my own horn, but I must agree.

"They are bad aren't they? And I do appreciate you."

Lucy's real name is Luciano. Since I can remember, he has been my best friend. He is one of Brooklyn's fiercest queens, and you had better not tell him otherwise. Jet black wavy hair, that he's currently letting grow, it's long enough now to pull back in a pony tail. He uses it as his bait and hook. He's tall, dark skinned, and has legs resembling stilts, but his greatest asset is his butt. I have questioned God on occasions and asked how he could give that perfect gift to a man wanting to be a woman instead of a thoroughbred such as me. Shall I say, He didn't answer; and this is why I am constantly doing squats.

His parents were never married, because his mothers' family didn't approve of his father. I was told his mother was a strong, gorgeous black woman that fell in love with a Puerto Rican man, and apparently, his father wasn't the only thing his mother was in love with, because she died when Lucy was nine months old from a heroin overdose. After that his father has been incognito.

"I see you brought a friend."

"Yes Ms. Thang, and as you can see, he is fine too."

Standing with his hand on his hip, as if this man is Denzel or something, it's taking everything out of me not to laugh. Instead of Denzel, it's more like what-the-hell.

He says, "I met him about a month ago, and he treats me right in every sense of the word, and if you would call me more often, you would know all about Mr. Gavin Jackson, Esq."

Should I be impressed?

He whispers in my ear, "Girl he has long money, and he lives in Long Island, practically a millionaire."

"Well I hope he's the one for you this time … because lately you have been moving faster than the Metro Transit Authority, but as long as you're happy, so am I, but I gotta catch you later, looks like Noëlle has had one too many drinks already."

I hope it's not too obvious that I'm trying to let him down softly, I love Lucy, he's like both the brother and the sister I never had, but recently his choice in men leaves much to be desired.

"Alright Diva, you can go for now, we know it's your party, but don't forget about our appointment we have scheduled on Wednesday, you are gonna be there right?"

"Lucy, did you think I would forget? Ok don't answer that."

I get another look at the woman who is trying to show me up. Do you believe this? And on my birthday! But I'm not the least bit worried, it's evident who the center of attention is.

People will be talking about this party for a long time, although I am not sure how the invitation read, I'm beginning to think it said "80's flash back party", because some of the people here look like they stepped right off of a New Edition Album.

Everyone's enjoying the party, but it's not official if the Soul Train line isn't done at some point. My father looks a hot mess trying to boogie down, and do the Mash Potato, and Julian looks even worse. I can tell the bartender is on his job, everyone is toasted, but it's not complete until the Cha-Cha is done to the point the weave goes from Beyoncé to Cher. By judging some of these hairstyles, the Asians must have sold out of Yaki #2; I know I'm buzzing, but it looks like Ms. Veleeta couldn't decide what style she wanted, because she has a crimp on the left, flip on the right, and a French roll in the back. She's wrong for that.

I guess time really does fly when you're having fun, because people are starting to leave. I scan the place to see if Ms. Lady has taken off, could I be that lucky? Right before the deejay plays our favorite song, "*Nothing Even Matters,*" Malcolm asks can he be excused to tell some people goodbye. I take advantage of this and introduce myself to the Diva in Training.

"Hello, I'm Diamond, nice to meet you."

"I know," she says. "I've heard a lot about you."

I feel the need to question her, but I'm not sure if I want to know.

"Michelle's told me all good things about you. This really is a nice party; your husband did a wonderful job."

I'm wondering how she met Malcolm, knowing him he's the gracious host and he has been meeting and greeting all night, and he does appreciate a beautiful woman.

By the sound in her tone, it seemed as if she was surprised he would do this for me.

I say, "Yes, he's a sweetheart."

Skipping to another subject she says, "Nice outfit."

I reply, "And so is yours. We must trade secrets."

Laughing hysterically she adds, "That would be good, maybe we can have lunch sometimes."

Malcolm interrupts by asking me to dance, I immediately say yes. I tell Michelle and Jane Doe, "Goodnight."

They both tell him, "Goodnight."

He nods.

"Baby thanks for this party tonight. I feel so loved, the way you used to make me feel. I know a lot is going on at work, and hopefully the stress will be over soon."

I notice he's a little on edge, even though he's trying to hide it. It seems he's close, but distant from me at the same time. Where is he?

I sing, "Malcolm, Malcolm where are you? This is our song."

Sighing and taking a deep breath, he says, "Victoria, not now, not tonight. Why do you wish to start this here? That's why ..."

"Why what Malcolm?" Trying to hold back tears, because whenever I think back to the way things used to be, it makes me real sad. He acts as if I have said something wrong. He's back with me now ... "Never mind, nothing baby, let's just enjoy tonight, we will talk about it later."

"You know what Malcolm; it is so funny that you never used to act this way. What changed you?"

"Life and marriage has changed me, some things are not always what they seem."

No he didn't. He would say this trying to make me feel guilty, playing on my intelligence, but I already know he has plans to smack it, flip it and rub it down tonight I'm sure, although lately it's all about sex, new positions, new places; he forever has something new for us to try.

"Victoria, you never seem to have a problem as long as you are getting what you want out of the deal." He says.

"I feel the mood changing and I don't want to ruin a perfect night so in saying this, baby let's go home, suddenly I feel like thanking you in a special way."

I gather up my things, as we say our goodbyes. I notice Noëlle helping the caterer put away some items left over, maybe if she would cook sometimes she wouldn't have to carry food out wherever she goes, but that's Noëlle. Malcolm hugs her and thanks her for her help. Even though I'm leaving to go home and make love to my husband, I can't stop thinking about HER. I know there's no reason for me to feel this way but ... the thought of her. The thought of her smooth chestnut colored skin, chinky eyes, and toned firm body, just looking at her makes me want to hit the treadmill a couple of more times.

While Malcolm showers, refreshing himself from the love we've just shared, I'm lying here thinking this is the best we've made love in a very long time. What is this? He's never kissed me with that much passion before; it was as if he had something to prove. I've never seen him take charge like that; my legs are actually numb and trembling from just the mere thought. After a work out like this, I could walk the catwalk in my birthday suit for Valentino at Fashion Week.

Out of nowhere Malcolm's cell phone rings, which in this case, more than usual means he is about to come up with some cocka mamey story about having to go somewhere.

Here it goes ... 1, 2, 3

"Baby, that was Nate, obviously he's having a problem with the truck again. I keep telling him he needs to just break down and get another one. I have to give him a jump start, so I'll be home as soon as we can get him going again."

"Can't he just call AAA or something?"

"Victoria, that's my brother, he would do it for me, so don't wait up."

Judging by past experiences, he'll probably come home late again; whenever they get together it's always a late night. My heart tells me it's not Nate he's going to see, but I'm sure that if he suspects I'm going to question him, he'll do what he does so well. It never fails, whenever he stays out real late, I always receive an assortment of Orchids, which happen to be my favorites, and like clock work, he leaves a blank check on the counter stating "Enjoy yourself at Saks." This is his way of getting rid of me when he's not in the mood for 21 questions. Regardless, he knows no matter how good he puts it down; my ultimate climax is cash, check, Visa, MasterCard, or American Express.

I wonder if Noëlle's up. She's probably tired like me; it's been a long night. I should call her and let her know how Malcolm just scored some more brownie points. Two rings, she's not answering, code for do not disturb, M.O.P. (Man on Premise).

Yada, yada, yada this long drawn out message she has on her answering machine is way too long, she sounds like a 900 phone sex operator.

"Hey girl, where are you? What are you doing this late? Or shall I say who are you doing this late? I was just calling to tell you what just happened. Malcolm just made love to me better than ever, aahm, you remember when I told you that he didn't have it in him anymore? Well I lied. He still got it. This is all I've been wanting, for him to show me he still cares. I'm always saying he doesn't love me the way he used to, and he doesn't do this and that, but I do love him, even though he makes me soo mad sometimes ... How about I'm talking to the darn voicemail, anyway ... but as always I'm lucky to have a friend that listens to me, one that never says anything, never judges me. Oh yes, you were rocking those Manolos tonight; girlfriend you did that! They could not have looked any better as if I had them on myself. This is why we're girls; we're cut from the same grain, Lord and Taylor."

Rolling over to pick up the book I've been reading, *Twenty Five Ways to Happiness*, only reminds me of my quest of pursuing total happiness. Can it happen? Does it really exist? Sometimes it seems as if I'm headed in the right direction, even though there are days when I question can I truly be happy and successful at the same time. I could stand to read the next chapter "Believe in Yourself" but it's late, and I need to look over Mr. Bouviér's file, read up on him a little more. If I plan to help Rucker get his file, I need to know something about the man. Hopefully he'll choose our firm. Reviewing his bio, it says he is an alumnus of Howard, majoring in business and marketing of course. He is also the proprietor of several businesses around the city, and he even has a couple located out in California. Charles Schwab is currently managing his portfolio, although I'm confident that we'll be able to establish a relationship. Just a quick glance it looks like his liquid net worth is an estimated $2.5 million, but with all of his businesses, real estate, combined with stocks and mutual funds his net worth appears to be somewhere in the neighborhood of 7 million. I'm beginning to see why this file is priority. Prayerfully this is it for me, this could be the file that helps me make partner. I need to read some more, but I can't keep my eyes open long enough.

Chapter Two
Victoria

Pulling up to my parent's home in Park Slope, I notice my brother's car in the driveway, my niece Melanie is here too. This must be their weekend together. She, her mother, and her stepfather, live around the corner, this way my brother still gets the chance to see her. She loves visiting her grandparents, and more than likely, she'll stay the night. I think between her mom remarrying, and she having a set of twin brothers now, spending time with them assures her that she's still the number one grandchild. She is, I guess, since it doesn't look like I'll be having a child any time soon.

I notice my father drinking his favorite planters punch, hopefully he's in a good mood today, that way he and Julian won't get into it.

I can tell mom is here too, she is probably cooking Sunday dinner. Ever since I can remember Sunday dinner was always ready on Saturday, I stayed in trouble many nights sneaking food before anybody else. I used to blame it on Julian until I got caught red handed taking red beans and rice to my room.

"*Bonjour le papa*" I say to my daddy.

He replies, "*Bonjour ma princesse, mon Diamant.*"

This is how we greet each other in French. He was adamant Julian and I learn it fluently. He always said, "How can you know where you are going, unless you know where you've been." Of course, he is teaching French to my niece Mel too. She's taking it in school, and I don't think it's one of her favorite subjects, but I bet she won't tell daddy that.

Mom yells from the kitchen, "Hello, my baby!"

Yelling back, I say, "Hi mom!"

Heading towards the kitchen I can smell the aroma of stew chicken, lightly steamed cabbage, and to top it off she's baked my favorite; bread pudding with whiskey sauce. I miss the days of being in the kitchen with my mother when she prepared meals for us, they seemed to take us through the whole entire week, I would get so sick of left-overs I could scream. I promised myself when I got out on my own, it's later for that. Of course she would say thank God for the left-overs because there are people out there starving every day, and there I was praying faithfully for one of the starving people she was talking about to come and eat this last little bit of whatever it was we were having for the week. I was so glad when someone wanted my food at school; this was a chance for me to swap what they had, and by me doing that, I soon found out everybody's mommas cooking don't taste like mine.

Sitting at the table I ask, "Momma how did you do it? How have you made yours and daddy's marriage work so long?"

She replies, "It hasn't been all me, it's been God in this thing. It's been Him who has kept us all of these years, and— a whole lot of prayer. You know your fathers no piece of cake to live with. He's a good man, but a stubborn one too. Where is all of this coming from? I sense some hesitation in your voice."

She always knows me so well, I never have to tell her what's wrong, she can read my face.

"Oh nothing momma, I just wish my marriage could be like yours and daddy's. I know Malcolm loves me, but sometimes I feel like he's not happy with me anymore."

"Honey what do you mean by that? That man just gave you a beautiful party; you should know he loves you, and that he cares about you."

"I know momma, but ..."

"But what?"

"We don't spend enough time together, it's either he's away at work, or on a business trip, and me, I have been so busy lately trying to make partner, I don't get a chance to see him that often."

"Well baby first you must know your first priority is God, then your marriage, that's what's wrong with you young couples today. You put everything before marriage, and with you and Malcolm, I see you've also been putting work before the Lord."

Why did I even start this conversation with her? Whenever we talk, it always winds up that Malcolm and I don't go to church that often anymore.

"Diamond, don't you realize that without Him none of your success means anything, you can have everything and still have nothing."

"You're right momma."

"Oh, I know I'm right."

At this point, we hear loud voices coming from the porch, I go to stand by the door hoping they don't hear me; I overhear my father and Julian talking.

Dad shouts, "Son, why couldn't you be a real lawyer?"

My father has never really liked the field of law that Julian chose, he said if anything he could have been the one defending criminals. He thinks Real Estate Law is some kind of cop out, way too soft, whatever that means.

Julian says, "Dad I am a real lawyer."

"Well it's a long way from Supreme Court Justice," daddy says.

My father was always so hard on Julian, he held him to some pretty high standards. He did with me too, but he wasn't as strict on me.

"So what's on your mind son? Lately I see you been acting a little strange when you come 'round me. I don't see it with your momma, just only me."

Julian bursts out and says, "Dad, why didn't you play sports with me? I always tried to make you happy. Graduated Magna Cum Laude, member of Delta Theta Phi, pledged Kappa Alpha Psi, so what more would it have taken to make you proud of me?"

He answers, "Julian, I just wanted what was best for you and your sister."

"But Dad ... do you realize you never let me do what the other boys on the block were doing; they were having fun, playing wall ball, going to Coney Island, going on dates, missing curfew, I never got the chance to do any of that, because I was too busy trying to become YOUR Supreme Court Judge."

"Julian I was there for you as much as a father could have been. I was working trying to make a living for my family. I was the provider; I needed to make sure you had what you needed, so no one would neva haf to say they did anything for you, your sister, or your mother."

I hated the fact my father was never at home when we were growing up; he was too busy working nights on end at the car lot. I don't know how my mother did it all those nights. At first, it was just him, and Mr. Clyde. I remember having to stay home with momma while he closed, because she was working on her Master's degree, Julian would have to go to the dealership with him books in hand. Momma did all she could to make sure she never missed a PTA meeting, or a teacher parent conference, but my father couldn't make it, he was always working.

From out of nowhere, Julian stands up and says, "I wonder if I was born this way."

"What way! Dammit boy! You are my son, I have a boy and a girl, contrary to what you may think, not two girls, and when you realize that, then you will one day walk the way God made you. Like a man."

No matter how upset my father gets with him, I believe Julian still needs his approval; He needs my father to be proud of him. Everything he has done has been to make him happy.

Angrily, Julian says, "I am a man ... that just happens to be in love with a man."

I could feel the tension, and I'm sure my mother doesn't want to have any part of this, and maybe I should not be listening but ...

"Son it has not always been that way. Did you have those feelings all along?"

Daddy always knows how to get him in a corner. I wonder why he's asking him all these questions. Especially now!

Clearing his throat, hesitantly Julian replies, "No dad, not until college. I always loved women."

"My son, why did you even marry Kai, why did you put us all through that? You came to me, told me that you were in love, said you neva felt that way before."

My father is good about bringing up the past; I can only imagine what Julian is feeling.

Shrugging his shoulders, he continues, "Dad, I thought I was, well ... I know I was."

"So what went wrong? What changed your mind?"

I see the pain in my fathers' eyes every time he looks at Julian. Julian once told me he felt like a disappointment to both of my parents.

I get a text message from Malcolm, asking me where am I. I respond that I'm at my parents.

"Cool, call me on your way home." He says.

"Where are you?" I text back.

"On the 278."

Remembering what my mother said, I write and say, "I love you".

No response back. After a second it doesn't even matter, I'm too busy trying to listen to Julian and daddy's conversation. I tip back to the door. I hear Julian saying.

"Dad, I will never forget the day I met Kai, she was so beautiful. Before her, I hadn't seen another human being as beautiful as ma'. She was my soul mate, if my heart stopped beating so did hers. She was my friend, she never criticized me, and she always let me be myself. I felt like a king with her, it was as if there was nothing in this world we couldn't do together."

My father becomes very quiet, like he's dazing off into la-la land. For a minute it's like he's not even listening and he thinks this is all a lie.

"Keep going," he says.

"Dad, Kai didn't want to be married anymore. She wanted out. She said I was more in love with the idea of marriage more than the actual commitment itself. More and more she began to complain and say my job was more important to me than she and Mel, but that wasn't true. I loved her more than I loved myself, and I would have stayed for Melanie's sake, but it was over, and I could not understand where these other feelings were coming from. Once I met Trenton, I knew what I was feeling was real."

Moments go by before my father says anything else. Maybe he's trying to process all of this. If I know my father I'm sure he's counting from one to ten, in order not to say something that could to turn this into a get ready to rumble episode.

"Julian, my son," he says. "You could have stayed to make your marriage be what God wanted it to be, what He ordained it to be. You see that little girl out there; she ain't nobody's mistake. She was an angel sent down from heaven. Yeah, I know marriage ain't always easy, it ain't always like a good portion of beignet's, it can be more like a dirty rice concoction, all mixed together, but see that is your good and your bad, and to make a good marriage work you got to suffer the good with the bad."

Has daddy been listening to my heart?

Julian goes on to say, "Dad I know, but sometimes it's like I've made my bed so I have to lie in it."

"Always remember son, 'the hand of God won't lead you, where the grace of God can't keep you', son I love you, and I still want what's best for you, and that Trenton fella ain't it. Your momma says all the time until you and your sister get right with the Lord, Satan, he gone stay on your trail. Got that my boy?"

"Yes dad got it."

You can never win with my father; he always has to have the last word. I don't know who's worse out of my parents when it comes to the Lord.

Lastly, my father says, "this Julian is going through, it too shall pass."

My mother asks standing over the stove, "Jules are you coming to church on Sunday? I have a speaking part in the Mother's Day play, and your sweet Melanie is going to serenade us with her flute selection."

"Not sure ma'."

"You know that girl has really taken a liking to that church, maybe if you would come and see her more often, better yet, come get the word more often ..."

"I know ma' but ..."

"But what son?"

Momma has this way of saying whatever it is in a way that sounds as if she is chastising that little ten-year-old boy she remembers him as all over again.

She shakes her head saying, "Jules I have told you time and again, there is nothing you can do to ever make God love you any more, and ultimately there is nothing you can do to make him love you any less. He paid that price for us a long time ago, and speaking of that, you weren't in church this past Easter, and why was that? I was sure you would have come on Resurrection Sunday, you know like the ones that only come three times a year, the CME members."

We both look very afraid to ask what that means, but we're quite sure she's going to tell us anyway.

"Think about it, Christmas, Mother's Day, and Easter, now which category do you fit in?"

Does she really think we're stupid enough to answer that?

Julian says, "Mom it seems like every time we go, we don't feel comfortable."

"Maybe if you wouldn't treat the church and the people in the church like they owe you something, then baby you wouldn't have to feel that way."

"Alright ma' I will think about it."

The doorbell rings, and by the look on Julian's face, I can tell it must be Trenton. I remember him mentioning to me he had some papers for him to sign, and if they are financial, he wanted me to look them over. Whenever he comes to my parents' home, things never go well. If my father has anything to do with it, it will be like World War II.

Melanie says, "Daddy, Mr. Jennings is outside."

"Oh good Lord", my mother says. "Let me get the door, you know how your father can be."

She's pushing chairs over as if Mayor Giuliani has issued a Code Red. With my father here, Trenton was really better off not coming, Julian should have warned him, but how does the saying go? If you like it, I love it. Trenton tries to act as if the way my father treats him does not bother him, but of course I know better. My father can make the strongest man feel and look like a punk.

Mom says, "Hello Trenton, nice to see you. How's your family?"

"Hello Mrs. 'D'. Everyone is fine, and you?"

He barely speaks to me; our history has not been that good. I just put up with him because of my brother.

"I've been well, just still working down at the church aiding our YoungEns Ministry."

At the church they called the senior citizens group YoungEns, they say, "they will forever be young in the Lord. Never grow old, because only houses and cars get old."

"Glad you could stop by to see us today."

"Well actually, I needed to stop by and give Jules some important papers."

Mom takes a deep breath, because if it is one thing that bothers her about their partnership, it's the fact Trenton calls my brother Jules. Momma has called him that since he was little, and Trenton calling him that is in straight violation, but I bet Julian has never gotten the nerves to tell him she hates it.

"So ... what are you doing this Sunday Trenton? You know that offer still stands about coming to church with us; you know the Lord's doors are always open, and we would love for you to visit us at Brooklyn Tabernacle."

"Uuh- uuh", daddy bursts out and says, "Now 'D', you know darn well that boy ain't going to nobody's church, he's too afraid that something gon' get hold of him and neva let him go."

"Well, Winston that is what we all need, and Mister I keep telling you, ain't is not a word, no matter what Webster says."

She spends more time correcting my dad, knowing good and well if he has said ain't all these years, what is going to change now? Maybe it is just that she knows that the one person she can correct, that will not rebut against her.

Trenton says to her, "No, Mrs. 'D'. I don't think I can make it this Sunday."

My father blurts out again, "The next Sunday either can you boy?"

"Winston stop it!" she yells.

Trenton continues, "The last time I went to church, I got really funny looks."

Laughing hysterically, my father says with no regret, "Did you say funny? What did you think the Pastor was checking you out?"

"Oh no, Mr. Jean-Pierre, nothing like that, I just felt everyone was staring at me as soon as I walked through the door, and most of all, I just don't think God is ready to save a man like me."

Hoping my father would lay off the jokes, Trenton holds his head down as if he has just told a childhood secret.

Tapping her fingers on the counter, I could see my mother's temples beginning to flare, and this usually means she's angry, or she's in JESUS mode. Ready, get set, go!

"Baby, did you say God is not ready to save you? Child don't you know God can save anybody, and that means you too. It was his assignment to save the lost, this is why He died; for our sins. He knows all about you, more than you could ever know about yourself. He made you. So don't you let **NO** devil in hell make you think that God doesn't love you. He's waiting with arms open wide."

Getting caught up, my mother has never been able to deny the goodness of the Lord, but somehow, I knew she wasn't done. In her last attempt to get him to church, she continues.

"And son, just remember, if God saved Mr. Jean-Pierre, He can save anybody! And just so you know I haven't always been saved, I was once lost too my dear."

Dad says, "Alright Reverend 'D', since we've had our sermon for the day, why don't you pass the plate over here so we can take us up a collection, the bible does say, "Give and it shall be given unto you."

I guess that's my fathers' way of saying time for the benediction.

I realize it's time for me to head home. Malcolm and I have plans for date night.

I tell my parents I'm about to head out, and I'll see them later. I call Malcolm to let him know I'm leaving also, but he and Nate are still at the car shop. I know I shouldn't feel this way but I'm real tired of his brother blocking our plans. But me being the nice wife I am, I say go ahead, I'll see him later this evening. The one good thing about it is I can stay and eat dinner.

I over hear Julian telling mom they're about to leave as well.

She replies, "No don't go just yet, I was about to put the food on the table, and I know Melanie would like it if you stayed."

Just when they thought they'd broken free of this "holy place", she wants them to stay and break bread.

Showing off those beautiful brown eyes Julian has never been able to say no to, Melanie ask, "Daddy won't you and Mr. Jennings please stay and eat with us? Auntie Diamond is going to stay."

"We will stay just for a little while, and then we must go." Julian answers.

There's a lot of tension in the air, Trenton is eating as fast as he can, not coming up for air. The brother looks like he's swallowing his chicken whole. Whenever my father and Trenton are in the same room, nothing ever goes well. He's forever saying Julian is going through something; he acts as if Trenton stole his virginity or something.

Trenton says, "Thank you for dinner, Mrs. 'D'."

"You are welcome, anytime you wish to stop by for some good home cooking, feel free. No invitation. Just come by.

Now I know my daddy is swallowing his chicken whole for sure.

"Well mother, we really are leaving now, but thank you for everything as always."

Melanie says to Julian, "Daddy, I really hope you will come to church on tomorrow to hear me play, because I always see a lot of ladies that don't have a boyfriend, and you don't have a girlfriend, so ..."

Julian confides in me and says, "I don't know how much longer I can do this without my baby girl knowing. Every chance she gets she is trying to hook me up with the first thing smoking. When we're at the park, and there's a lady there without a man, she automatically assumes this will be her new stepmother. I wish she was old enough to understand, but I thank Kai for being such a good mother, not bashing me, not making me out to be the no good father."

Dad hollers out from the kitchen, "Yep, there will be plenty of fine women at the church, please come, so I can see which one 'em you will wind up with."

You would think he was a comedian by the way he cracks on any and everybody.

On the way out the door, Julian tells me, "Girl, I know you've got that husband and all, but you can still call me sometimes. You don't have to be a stranger. Remember how close we used to be? Also, don't forget, I will be leaving out for the Annual Lawyers conference in Atlanta next week."

I do realize that we've grown apart; in spite of it all, I do miss my big brother.

"You know your sister has been working real hard lately, putting in a lot of hours at the firm. It's been hard trying to make partner, but it does look promising."

"Don't worry about it. Like momma says, if God brought you to it; He'll bring you through it."

My heart flutters. We hug goodbye.

Before I leave, I must go to my old room. It's so funny how things have changed. I'm all grown now. I used to have sooo much fun in this room that used to seem so little at one time. I can still see some of the tape that momma removed from my old posters. My favorite was L.L. Cool J, the one with him and the boom box on his shoulders, with his then baby chest. I laugh because that was going to be my husband. He wasn't supposed to hook up with that Simone girl, but I guess the better woman won. It's probably better that way; I don't think I was cut out for the entertainment world. And let's not forget my girls Salt-N-Pepa. I give thanks to them for my first real haircut. The asymmetrical bob! With the big gold earrings that looked like they weighed fifty pounds, but in reality no weight at all ... had to have my name inside of them, *"Diamond"*. Oh my goodness, every time I come in here it trips me out to see that momma kept my "Beat It" jacket, the red one with all the zippers. I should've put it up for sale on Ebay. I saw one going for $799.00, the other day. That's hilarious they called it "vintage".

Those were the good ole' days; I had no stresses, no worries, all I had to do was wake up, go to school, learn, make good grades, and my parents would take it from there. When I look back over my life I can really say my brother and I were blessed. Listening at daddy talk to Julian earlier made me realize all he did to sacrifice for us to be in this house. We moved from Bedstuy when I was nine, and yes things and the people around here were different. Back in the Stuy my friends were just cool, but over here in the Slope it seemed like the game changed. Daddy started making more money, momma got a promotion, and my friends changed. All except Lucy, he has been my best friend since forever. When we moved, he was always over here. I remember how we used to sit up and plan our clothes for the week. Even then the boy had a sense of fashion. You just don't find many boys that are that particular about white after Labor Day. Still today if he sees someone with white on before Easter, that is three snaps and a fashion police fine. I will never forget the time Lucy and I were at a Winter Fling, and a girl named Latrice Mahann came dressed to the nines, so she thought. So then my boy walks in, and sees her in a navy and white sailor dress, with a pair of white opaque tights, and to set it off a pair of white chunky heeled sandals. OPEN TOE at that ... I believe Lucy almost lost it. He called her out as the biggest fashion mistake to hit William Alexander. Although we didn't go to the same school, Lucy and I were as close as could be. He introduced me to my first "true love", Darrell Walker. Ooh that thang was so cute; the only problem was he knew it. Back then I was too slow for him, even with my big dreams and plans, I still wasn't enough. He was already experienced enough for the both of us. At fourteen years old, I just wasn't thinking about doing it. Yet and still a lot of my friends were, but I was too scared my father would find out, and there was no way I would destroy his image of his little princess.

Time has flown; I can stay here forever reminiscing on the past. Now I have to go and face reality, a husband, a home, a job, a big girl's life.

Chapter Three
Malcolm

Victoria looks so peaceful lying there. I'm sure this will wind up being another piece of cake day. I've got to chill though on coming in so late. It's getting a little overrated, dishing out forgive me checks on a regular basis. Last night my cell phone didn't ring off the hook for a change, maybe she turned in earlier than I thought.

"Good morning sweetheart how was your night; sleep well?" I say.

"Malcolm, it was fine; lonely as usual. I really wish you'd take into consideration that you're not the only one in this relationship, because I'm getting a little tired of sleeping alone, you know."

"You were not alone, I was here baby."

"Yeah right." And what time did you really roll into bed last night? It had to be way past three o'clock."

"Nah, it wasn't real late, maybe around two."

Sitting straight up in the bed, Victoria yells, "Two?" You know what they say about that time."

"Yeah I know Vic; there is nothing open past two, but legs."

"Yes, you are right, legs Malcolm, and for your sake you had better not been in sniffing distance of anybody's legs but mine."

Lately, Victoria has been on this trip about me staying out late. She knows I'm a business man, and there're times when associates invite me out to dinner, which includes some strategical planning of the minds.

I love my wife; at least I think I love my wife, but things just have not been the same lately. With all the pressure of my settling into my new position at the bank, we haven't been on the same page.

I stand here grinning, "Victoria, you know I'm only in love with you. I've told you that on several occasions, and for some reason my word isn't good enough."

She counters, "Like I said the other night, you left saying you had to go help Nate with his car, and last night you left going to the store, and I know for a fact the milk man doesn't run past twelve."

"Baby listen, I ran into a couple of my friends that live on the Upper East Side, we hung out for a while, got a few drinks, shot the crap about the old days and when I realized it, time had passed."

She mutters, "Whatever."

"Vic look, today is going to be good day. It's Monday, a new week, and new possibilities. Let's just focus on that. We both have to work, and I have to go make the money, so you can take the money, then spend the money, then we come back and do it all over again."

"Aahm, well in that case ... Malcolm do you remember this is a big week for me? I'm not sure exactly what day, but we're meeting to discuss the details of the file. This could be the week your wife makes senior partner, and frankly I don't need any distractions, such as your making me feel guilty again that you have a problem with me spending OUR money. Remember I told you in the beginning 'don't start what you can't finish.' When you met me, it wasn't a problem then you doing nice things for me, so why start now?"

As she continues to get dressed, I can't stop thinking about the last six months of my life. Regardless of what's been going on at home, I haven't been this happy in a real long time.

Spraying on the one perfume that reminds me of our love, "Chanel Allure", she kisses me goodbye, grabs her briefcase, picks up the last muffin, and darts out of the door, ready for the world.

I holler out of the door that leads to the garage, "Have a nice day, and don't forget, tonight I promised Nate I'd go with him to his AA meeting!"

The look on Victoria's face reads, "Remember John and Lorena Bobbitt."

I probably want go in to the office until later, I really need to catch up on my over due e-mails, the Blackberry's been blowing up, and I have a pretty good idea who it is. New picture mail; got to be more careful. I must learn how to use this function, could be sending Vic the wrong picture one day, and I'd hate to be on that receiving end. That's one of the reasons I love her, for her tenacity, she's got a lot of her father in her, but I must say ... although she acts all tough, she's really an innocent little girl on the inside. This is why it's not that hard to tell her what she wants, and needs to hear, because she loves me so much she can't see herself without me, so that makes it that much easier, and plus I've got it like that.

Sitting in the Mayfair recliner, checking the messages on my laptop, all I'm getting is junk mail as usual, offers that need to be deleted, and sent straight to spam. More than likely it's some idiot in pursuit of stealing my identification online; can't trust anything anymore. I see so many complaints that come through the bank of people with fraudulent identification, this day in time; no one or no thing is safe.

I see the travel agency's sent the confirmation for the trip. By now everything should be set; all I have to do is find the right time to let Victoria know that I'll be out of town this weekend, but first things first, just as I'm about to sign out, an instant message pops up.

LadyChief69: Hey handsome, late night? Rekindling vows?

SmoothVP: Nope thinking bout you. Last night was the bomb!

LadyChief69: Still on for tonight?

SmoothVP: As far as I know. It's out there she's gotta receive it. They left in foul mood, under pressure.

LadyChief69: I'm guessing u have pressure 2?

SmoothVP: For sho', need to work off some steam. Can u help me out?

LadyChief69: That's why I'm here, to help you feel better. Smile.

SmoothVP: If all goes as planned, it's on. Can't wait for our trip.

LadyChief69: Me either, I need it ... and I need u☺

SmoothVP: Same here, my nature's rising as we speak.

LadyChief69: What about her, did u play doctor last night?

SmoothVP: LOL, had 2, but thought about u the whole time.

LadyChief69: Keep that up I'ma have to come over there.

SmoothVP: Wish you could, but I'll C u 2 nite.

LadyChief69: xoxo

Today's going to be a long day; there are so many files I need to catch up on. I wonder if Cherish put them on my desk like I asked. We're nearing the end of the month, and I feel we've done rather well considering it's only the second quarter. From judging by the last Board Meeting, my department has done really well, and I've only been VP of Credit Management for three months. I think I'll give Cherish a call, and have her send my favorite girl some flowers, a brother feeling really good. Looking at the way my manhood is standing at attention, I feel real, real good.

Cherish has been with me from day one. She started at the bank as a part-time teller, while working on her degree. While I was in the transition phase of becoming VP, I noticed something in her. She wasn't like most females, she had class. This is what I liked in Victoria when I first met her, but Cherish never went out her way to make herself noticeable, she had skills and drive. When I first approached her about being my assistant, she wasn't to keen on the idea, originally she wanted to become a loan officer. She was sold on helping unfortunate people attain loans that somehow otherwise they couldn't get on their own.

When I look at her, she makes me proud. She cares for other people, not just herself, not like Vic. Before I came in contact with Cherish, it was my plan to become Senior VP of investments, but she steered me in another direction, and this is how I got here. I'm now overseeing the entire loan process, ensuring that all risks have been assessed, basically making sure that the person who approves the loan has verified all the necessary documents, and making sure no loan that is not worthy gets through the cracks, and speaking of that I need to give my father-in-law a call.

Every time I call the dealership, that same honey asks me who I am, every single time, as if she doesn't know. Victoria swears she is one of the girls on my to-do-list, let her tell it every chick is on my to-do-list, but Ayana is not one of the top ten, although I would love to tap that Ethiopian beauty a couple of times.

Pops says, "Hey dare my boy."

"How's it going Pops?"

"Oh, just making another client happy. So what can I do for you my favorite son-in-law?"

"Does the name Nader Sameer ring a bell?"

"No, can't say it does."

"Well he's a partner of mine that I have done business with in the past and he's looking for top of the line so of course I had to send him to you, and he's paying cash, so hook 'em up pops."

"Thanks son, actually just got a new shipment in today."

"Well I guess this is perfect timing then."

My father-in-law is really a cool guy, most people prefer to think other wise, but I think deep down he is a softy, especially when it comes to that daughter of his. When I started dating Victoria, he told me up front that if I could not step up to the plate, be a man, take care of his daughter like she should be treated, then I was going to have to keep it moving. For the most part, I have kept my end of the bargain. I really hate it that Vic and I got married so soon, I should have waited a bit longer, but it's alright, I still got it, women checking for me left and right.

Me and Pops end on a good note, anytime I send him a referral it's always good, I'm just not sure for whom. To me Victoria seems to get all of the perks and more, even when she hasn't contributed to anything. I have a new text message and I would suspect it is Cherish, being it is already 10:00, and I haven't made it in yet.

Cherish: Your appointment will be about fifteen minutes late, traffic is bad.

Me: On my way, if they get there before I do just have them complete the financial profile.

Cherish: Ok sure.

Me: C u in a minute.

I could've had Cherish a long time ago, but I think she was afraid of Victoria finding out. I kept trying to convince her that wasn't a problem but she wasn't hearing it. Maybe that's why I respect her so much, because she didn't give in to the feelings I know she had, but one day—she will, and when she does ... The girl gives the America's Next Top Model's host a run for her money, she's just that fine.

I don't understand why my scheduled appointment couldn't see Raheem, or Daniel. I usually don't meet with the client until after the loan has been approved. Cherish said they only requested me, so who am I to let a potential customer down.

"Cherish, you can have them come in now."

"Yes sir, Mr. Cartiér."

There she is, standing in my office looking as if she's been run over by a truck. Words escape my mouth, because I'm not used to seeing her like this.

She says. "Hello Malcolm, why have you not returned any of my calls?"

"Excuse me, after what you pulled at wifey's party, showing up uninvited like that, what was I supposed to do?"

"Well how else was I going to get your attention? I have left numerous messages on your voicemail. I've tried to contact you on several occasions, but you act as if I'm a leper or something."

"You are."

"Malcolm please. We really need to talk."

"About? There is nothing we have to say to one another. We said it all six months ago."

Sydney was never the type to take no for an answer. Things fell apart with us when she decided she wanted more than what I could offer. When she realized that I wasn't going to leave my wife and sacrifice everything we had built at that time, she couldn't deal. She started sending me text message after text message, with crazy notes, saying that if she couldn't have me, no one could. It began to get out of control. It was not what I had bargained for. At one time I really thought I loved her. In my heart I wanted to leave Victoria, start over, with someone who loved me. At least that's what I thought.

"Malcolm, lately I haven't been myself, I haven't been feeling that well."

I mumble under my breath, "That's your problem; you need go to the doctor."

She turns around to me quickly and says, "I am afraid to."

"Well."

"Why are you treating me this way Malcolm, what ... you must've found someone else? Because you are never going to be the faithful husband your wife thinks you are."

Trying not to create a scene, in a harsh tone I say, "That is none of your business. You need to leave, now!!!"

Looking at me with both fear and anger in her eyes, she says it ... "If I am pregnant, you had best pray that this baby doesn't make it, because if I am you will live to regret every moment of it."

Sidney was famous for making threats, but I never took her serious, because I knew that they were all a plot to get me to destroy my happiness with Victoria, and this latest threat— I ain't sweating it because I know she is just on another trip again. I did not want to be that harsh, but she had caused enough harm in my life. Just when I thought I was free from her, she shows up out of the blue. Yeah she has tried to contact me, but I feel the more I ignore her attempts, the better off I am. I woke this morning in a very good mood, and I can't let my day end up like this. Dealing with her problems! But why do I feel this is going to come back and bite me sooner or later. Maybe I should have heard her out, but whatever, she'll be alright.

Cherish chimes in on the intercom, "Mr. Cartiér, are you okay?"

I pick up the phone just in case what she's about to ask me, I don't want the entire office to hear.

"Yes Cherish, I'm fine. Why you ask?"

"The way that lady stormed out of here she didn't look so happy."

"She'll be fine, she just really needs this money for a big project and by judging her past credit history it's not looking that good."

"Isn't it something that we can do? Don't you know her? I saw her at Mrs. Cartiér's party."

Here is Cherish again; turning into Wonder Woman trying to save the day, but this is one she can't help me with. I've done a pretty good job keeping Sydney's and I affair undercover. Thanks to the Player's Handbook. I always made sure she never came to my office, in case anyone became suspicious. Victoria is a well known lady, and I don't want to start any confusion. I always have to stay one step ahead. I learned some of my best techniques from *"Two Can Play That Game."* Vivica Fox was bad, but that Morris Chestnut was an even badder. The master should never let their guards down.

I tell Cherish, "No, there is nothing we can do to help her."

"But—"

"Cherish that's it. Enough about her, she'll probably have to go to a Credit Union or a Finance Company. That's her best out."

"Are you aware that they may charge her anywhere from 18 to 24% interest on a loan?"

"Yes I'm aware Cherish, but I can't jeopardize my position here at the bank. Remember I just made it to this point, and thus far I have prided myself on managing with integrity."

Hold up, what am I saying? I've been talking to Cherish about that psycho broad too long, for no reason. That's not even why she was here. She's got me lying over some dumb bull that has nothing to do with a loan. I won't allow myself to get caught up in her drama, not now, not ever.

We finally end the saga, but I can tell by the sound in her voice that I've upset her first thing this afternoon and having her upset with me is not what I would prefer to do. I may need her later on for something or another. Heading towards her desk, in desperate need of kissing up, she looks at me with those pretty brown eyes; here I am finding myself saying I'm sorry.

I ask, "Are there any more appointments scheduled?"

"No, we just have to go through that stack of files I put in your chair earlier this morning."

Remembering that stack, I know this can take the rest of the day.

She asks, "Are you hungry?"

"No I'm fine. I'll get something later tonight; I need to have a big appetite."

"How's Mrs. Cartiér?" she threw out at me from nowhere.

"She's fine too."

I'm wondering what made her think of that. I know women have that 'women's intuition', but could she think ... nah ... she doesn't have a clue. She never questions who the flowers are sent to, typically she thinks they are to Victoria. I keep it real simple on the card, words like, "Thinking of you", "Can't wait to see you", "Missing you", all that girly stuff they like to hear. But I always seal it with a "Love, Malcolm". That gets 'em everytime. So there's no way she would think otherwise. And speaking of that, I have to set things up for tonight. This is the last night before our trip, and I'm well overdue for some relaxation.

"Cherish, do you think you can send some flowers for me today, now that you brought Mrs. Cartiér up, I need to make sure everything is set for tonight. She's preparing for a difficult case, and she needs some encouragement letting her know I'm thinking of her, and I can't wait to see her. Just put on the card, "Hot and cold goes good together. Love, Smooth VP."

"Yes I can do that Mr. Cartiér, anything for that beautiful wife of yours."

"Thanks."

I can't believe Alan left this many files to review. I feel bad he had to move down south to help his moms and all, but it's good for me that I was chosen for this position. I've worked so hard to get to this point. Too bad my mother couldn't be here to see it. I haven't spoken to my father in a while; I regret things between us haven't been that good lately. He always tells me that now since I have gotten to the point where I think I have a little something; I think I'm better than everyone else. I don't look at it as being conceited I feel I am confident. If it wasn't for my being able to go to college, work hard, keep my head in the books, I wouldn't be where I am today. You determine your destiny.

Aunt Colleen helps by keeping me grounded though; she's been a big support system in our lives. She adores Victoria and she's constantly asking when we're going to give her either some grand nieces or nephews. When my mother passed, my aunt threw herself into fulltime motherhood. She's been like a mother to both Nate and I; by the way she keeps up with me, one would think I'm still a little boy, but I appreciate it. I miss my moms a lot; she would be very proud of me right about now.

Ultimately, the thought of having children never crossed my mind before today; right up until the train wreck ruined my day. What if ... no she can't be! As much as I don't want to admit it, there is a possibility, but I've gotta stop thinking about it.

Come to think about it, I haven't talked to Auntie in a couple of weeks. I do need to talk to her and let her know I'll be out of town on a business trip this weekend. She gets upset whenever I take trips or whatever, and she doesn't know where I am. I try to make sure she has a way to contact me at all times. I'll give her a call on my way to the restaurant.

Before I can get focused on all of this catch up work, Cherish alerts me that Mr. Jamison wants to speak with me. I wonder what this could be about. I've only been over this department for a couple of months and things have been going well so far.

"Malcolm have a seat," Mr. Jamison says.

For some reason I'm nervous sitting here, especially knowing that it isn't time for my review yet. He asks his secretary to hold his calls. This doesn't sound good.

He proceeds to tell me that I've done a wonderful job in my department, he's gone over the numbers for this quarter, and he's very impressed. He also says he's proud of the work I've done in such a short period of time. Then he does something that is so out of the ordinary for Mr. Jamison.

"Malcolm, do you golf?" he asks.

I reply not knowing where this is going, "Yes sir, I do a little bit, I wouldn't say I'm Tiger or anything, but I can hold my own."

He laughs and says, "My son is a member of the Saticoy Country Club in California, and myself and some other colleagues are flying down this weekend, if you're available I would be honored if you would join us. I have the cost of your ticket and the itinerary."

I don't want to pass up this opportunity, but I know in my mind that this is the weekend I have planned for the get away. Although ... this is a good way to let Victoria know I'll be out of town, since I haven't quite found a way to let her know just yet.

I have to let him know that this is a great offer, but I have prior plans with my wife this weekend.

"Maybe some other time, you just have a good time with the wife, that's very important in this business; to keep family first, because we have to keep so many crazy hours."

I was grateful for that piece of advice, sorta made me feel guilty, sometimes I wish things with me and Vic could really be that way. Looking at my watch, I realize I haven't made reservations yet ...

"Hello this is Malcolm Cartiér; I need to reserve a table for tonight."

"Good afternoon Mr. Cartiér. Would you like your usual table?" the female voice asks.

"Yes, actually I would, but can you make sure there's a little something extra tonight. I want to make a good impression."

"Red or Pink Roses?"

"Pink, it's her favorite color."

"Say about seven?"

"No better make it more like eight."

"You're all set Mr. Cartiér, and if I'm not here, have a wonderful night. Mrs. Cartiér is a lucky lady."

"Thank you, and yes she is."

I've got to give it to myself, if I didn't know any better I would think I was up for the best leading male actor category in a daytime drama. Sometimes I think I should've majored in fine arts and pursued finance as a back up. Now I just need to finish off the deal by calling Victoria.

"Hey baby."

"Hi Malcolm, how was your day? Miss me, I hope."

"Yes I did, it's been busy, that's why I wanted to take a minute to stop and call you before I leave the office. I'm on my way to Nate's AA meeting. You didn't forget did you?"

There was a silence that left me feeling a little unsure about this one. Maybe I shouldn't try this tonight.

"Victoria, are you there?"

"Yes Malcolm, I'm here. What time will you be home? I hope not your usual time."

"It shouldn't be that late. His meeting starts at seven so give or take a couple of hours. I'm sure we'll probably get something to eat afterwards, so no need to leave anything out for me."

"Fine Malcolm. But may I talk to you real quick about something?"

"Yeah, go ahead."

Whenever she has that tone in her voice, it always means she's been feeling neglected, or she's been talking to some of her unmarried friends getting marriage advice from them. Whether I like it or not she's going to say it anyway.

She begins, "Malcolm, I have been doing some thinking, and I feel we both should start going back to church more, we haven't been in over six months."

"Who put that in your head? Oh yeah I know, your mother. She's been spitting that church talk to me too, and so has Aunt Colleen, what's this, Save Malcolm Day? Every time I go by your moms it's 'you need to go to church Malcolm, the both of you need to be affiliated with a church home Malcolm', so I feel you, but right now baby my schedule is way too hectic. As much as I'll be traveling, it'll be difficult to be in church every Sunday. And speaking of that ..."

She begs, "Malcolm, I'm serious, with everything happening for us lately, we need to give thanks to God. It's like we both have gotten too busy to thank the one person who has enabled us to do all the things that we do."

"Victoria I get my share of church on Sundays. I watch the "Potter's House at seven, send my tithes, and then get a glimpse of the man in the shiny suits."

"You're silly, are you talking about Bobby Jones?"

"Yeah him, he has all the gospel stars on his show, Kirk Franklin, Yolanda Adams, and my boy Ty Tribbett. Now dude gets it crunk! And after all of that, I don't have to go church. I've had the choir, the offering, and the word all within an hour and a half."

I hear the beep on the other line. It's her. I feel like a giddy school boy.

"Hey babe, its Nate calling on the other line, can we finish this later?"

"See you later Malcolm."

This sensual voice on the other end says, "Hi there my Smooth VP. So I take it we're on for tonight?"

"Glad to hear your voice, how was your day? I was about to call you to let you know where to meet me."

"Where?"

"Where else? A.J.Maxwell's. I've got chef Jean-Christophe cooking a nice meal especially for you."

"Yeah right."

"No kidding, everything's set, so I need you to meet me there within the hour."

"So what about her? Is she cool with it?"

"I got this. I'll see you in a little while, wear something pretty."

"I love you Malcolm."

"Same here."

Oh yeah, I forgot to call one important person in this thing, Nate. Gotta let him know what's up before he talks to Vic and blows my cover. He's not answering his phone; hopefully he'll get the message.

Man, this woman got me tripping; I still didn't get to those files at the office. Between Sydney and her madness my whole day has been messed up but I'll make up for it.

Walking to the table, I notice her wearing a sexy pink dress that reminds me my day hasn't been all that bad after all. She sits down not saying a word, and I'm really not sure how to take it. She takes notice to the roses, and gently places one behind her ear.

"You look beautiful."

"Thank you, and you look good yourself."

"Hopefully you enjoy your meal, because he's one of the best chefs around."

She doesn't waste anytime, "Have you gotten the tickets yet?"

"Yes I have, my flight leaves at 8:30 Friday morning, and yours is scheduled to leave at 8:40. Sorry I couldn't get them leaving at the same time, but I thought it would be better this way, we'll still arrive about the same time."

She says she's packed and ready to go. I bet not as much as I am, I have been waiting for this all month long. After we complete our meal we head to the closest hotel around, to finish off our night. What a perfect finish.

I never enjoy leaving her, because she always looks so sad when we go our separate ways. I don't know how long I can keep doing this. I believe I'm starting to fall for her. As much as I want to, I just can't bring myself to go inside of her uncovered. She's wanted me to for a while; she keeps saying she wants to feel all of me. She's expressed to me several times how I can't possibly love her, because if I did, I would make love to her condom free. She constantly says there is nothing standing between us; that she's not worried about my wife, because she knows if I care enough about her not to take home anything, I'll do the same for her. Unbelievably I feel the same way. I trust her enough that I don't think she would cheat on me, so I don't know why I've been trippin'? I'm going to surprise her on the trip and give her what she's been wanting, me, all of me.

Driving home, I'm thinking of Victoria, and how she's probably sitting up watching the clock, pretending to be asleep. If I had enough energy I would go home and make love to her. I've just got to be on my best behavior these next couple of days if I expect to pull this off. The trip with Mr. Jamison, I'm getting excited thinking of how good of an excuse this will be. She'll never find out 'bout this one.

My last thoughts before I go inside are of her, and what we've just shared, as I take one last sweep of the car, making sure I have no trash that would give me away, I go into my coat pocket, and I find a letter that she had written to me. She must have snuck it in my pocket before we left.

My Malcolm,
*   Not a day goes by that I don't think of you, and I would be lying if I said I'm okay with the way things are with us. At first it was cool to share you, but I don't know how much longer I can stand you going home to another woman. I lie in bed at night crying myself to sleep, because I want so badly to be next to you. I know you have asked me to be patient, and I am, but I just wanted to let you know how much I love you, and how much you really mean to me.*
*   You are the best thing that has ever happened to me. In my life I have come across many men and none of them can compare to you. I respect you not wanting to up and leave her without any notice, but as I said, it's getting real lonely. This trip we are taking, I know it will only confirm what we both feel for each other. Our love is true.*
Yours Always,
LC69

Just reading this puts my heart into overdrive, makes me want to count down the days until we leave. It's sad to say but I would kill Victoria if she was doing some bull like this, anyway I know that I'm the only man she's ever really loved, and there will never be another like me.

Chapter Four
Victoria

*V*ictoria, I will need those files on my desk by 9:00 tomorrow. In addition, there is a meeting scheduled around lunchtime. If you have anything planned, you may want to reschedule that, because this is the final meeting to strategize our plan. I know by this time on Friday that Mr. Bouviér will be our newest client. This is why I trust you to always come through for us. And by the way, Victoria, when you close this deal you know there will be great things ahead for you."

Something told me I should've checked my voicemail earlier this morning, but I figured it was Lucy reminding me again for the umpteenth time about that freakin' appointment of his. That reminds me, I haven't listened to the messages on my cell, and the red light has been blinking for the longest. Seven missed calls ... and I bet they are all from Lucy.

You have **five** unheard messages.

Message 1: "Hey Vic, it's me, haven't talked to you since the party. Hope you haven't forgotten about the appointment tomorrow. I need to be there around 4:30 to fill out paperwork, and the appointment is actually at 5:00. It is the new clinic between Nostrand and Utica. I get off around 3:30, I'll catch the 4, and meet you there. Thanks Boo for being my girl."

"Oh yes Ms. Lady, I forgot to tell you that I saw Malcolm in the store earlier today, looked like he was shopping for something FABU. You must have been real good to him last night. Honey that thang had the little Ms. Shoe girl running around like a chicken with her head cut off. Work it Strange' work it."

Message 2: "Hello Mrs. Cartiér, this is Jermaine from Saks, those shoes you ordered are in. If you wish I can go ahead and put them on your account, but we did not get those Leopard Loubou's in yet, but as soon as they come in I will give you a call. By the way, the party was fabulous, and yes the Giuseppe's were on point."

Message 3: "Hey sweetheart, I'll be home late. Very important meeting this evening, and I am guessing the fellows will go out and get something to eat later, don't wait up. I'll call. Be sweet. I love you."

The nerve of him, he didn't even ask if I had something to do, but it's all good, 'cause I don't need to be bothered anyway. Hopefully he's setting up something good for me like Lucy said.

Message 4: "Chica, its Noëlle. Inviting you to the best and by far the hottest party of the year. Just got the details on Diddy's white party, of course it's in the Hamptons. Yes girl, nothing but A-listers will be there. You just may get the chance to hob-nob with the Donald himself. Oh yeah, got your message the other night. It was a late night, was having my own after party. Hit me back."

Message 5: "Hello baby, it's your mother. I know you've been working very hard, but I just wanted to call you to say I love you, and also that I am praying for you. I put your name in the prayer box on Sunday, and I asked God, if it is his will to let it be done. We believe God that you will make partner, it is all you've ever wanted besides owning your own firm, and no one deserves it more. Your father says hello as well, and that he loves you the same. By the way, Bishop Michaels says he misses that smiling face of yours. I told him you have a lot on your table now, but one thing he said was, 'don't ever get too busy that you forget God'. Okay baby momma will" ...beeeeeeeep.

Mommy just can't get it right; she doesn't realize you can't leave a long message like that all willy nilly. I need to change my greeting so that it says, "If you will leave a SHORT detailed message," hopefully she'll get the picture.

There was another message but they didn't say anything, they'll call back.

Since Malcolm will be home late, I'll read over my presentation then try to get some rest. I hope this meeting doesn't last that long, I need to stop by Saks to pick up my shoes. Hopefully I can find that jacket for his birthday, and swing by Bergdorf's to find daddy's Father's Day gift. I know the perfect gift, I saw them in the catalogue; the Paul Smith winged tips. That'll make him happy.

From the looks of it, Malcolm's already been home, I can always tell when he's been here; the Issey Miyake follows him. It's been a long day, and it's now that I could use a good Diamondtini, that'll relax me. As usual nothings on television but Christian programs, but with everything that's going on lately, we need as many of 'em as possible. I hope Jakes is on; he always has a word for me. He might as well be my Pastor, because I find myself tuning in to him more than I do my own Pastor, and looking at the checkbook, my money goes to the Potter's House more than Brooklyn Tabernacle.

Listening at him is making me think; am I really spending my time with the wrong crowd, am I giving my time the way I should? I think I do, although I don't go to church as often as I used to, it's not written that everyone has to go to church to be saved. They have even made it to where you can watch your church in real time on the computer. I haven't gone in six months and I'm doing fine. Malcolm has a successful career, I have two degrees, and I'm about to make partner, (I hope). Everything is going well, me and my girls are tight, Lucy's okay, my parents are fine, and my brother ... well I don't know about him since I haven't seen or heard from him in a while, although I'm sure that conniving Trenton is okay, so Julian must be okay. I still should give him a call. I will later this week, but now I'm calling it a night, but can't do that without saying my prayers.

> *"Lord it's me Victoria, I know I haven't talked to you in a long time, but I really need your help on tomorrow. Yes I know I shouldn't ask you for things all the time, but this one is a little different. Lately I've been real busy trying to get this promotion so I can better myself, and oh yes have more time to worship you. God I know I'm not the best Christian and I don't always do what you ask of me. I don't read my bible like I should, but, Father if you find it in your heart please help me. For the first time in my life I feel like I've done something by myself, I realize you've helped me get where I am now, but it would mean the world to me if I could become partner at the firm. I'm also praying for my husband, my family and my friends. Before I close I ask that you will condition Mr. Bouviér's heart, in that he will make the choice to let us represent him. This prayer I ask in Jesus' name Amen.*

I wake up this morning to a plate of fresh strawberries over a stack of waffles, with a rose on the side, being serenaded by my husband. "Good morning sweetheart, how was your night? Sorry I didn't call, it was late, and I didn't want to wake you." The song goes.

I tell myself today I'm not going through the motions, I'm feeling better than I've felt in a long time, so I answer in a loving voice, "It was fine ... lonely as usual, but I wish you would take into consideration that you're not the only one in this relationship, because I'm tired of sleeping alone."

I find my self saying this so much, and in his defense, I wasn't alone. I guess he thinks that'll make me forget just how late he came home. I know one thing; I can't keep playing this cat and mouse game.

"Exactly what time did you roll into bed?"

"Maybe around two."

Taking a deep breath I pause, "Two? I knew it was well past that and anyway my mother has always told me ..."

Malcolm interrupts me by saying, "Yeah, yeah, yeah, I know Vic nothings open past two but legs."

"Sho you're right Malcolm!" for a second I forget I'm trying to be the sweet loving wife and say, "you had better not have been in between another woman's legs but MINE!!" At least I hope he's not as dumb as other men I know, but there are times when I'm not so sure. To me we have the same conversations over and over.

"By the way, Malcolm don't you think that's too late for a married man to come home, even if it is related to his job?"

My gut feeling is telling me that his job was over much earlier last night.

"Baby listen, today is going to be a good day, this afternoon you'll be partner, something we've both been working on, and it's all about to pay off. I want to take you somewhere very special to celebrate; it's your choice."

Suddenly I can't hold it anymore and I say to him, "Malcolm, I know we talked about this briefly the other day, but I really think we need to start going back to church."

"Where is all of this coming from?"

Lying across the bed, I say to him in hopes that he will hear me this time. "Malcolm you are not that "church boy" I used to know, you've changed."

In a very sarcastic tone he says, "Change is always good. See you tonight baby, and break a leg."

He's such a jerk; he was trying to be funny about the whole legs thing, but I meant what I said.

Mr. Rucker just stopped by my office and asked to meet with me. To my recollection the presentation went well. I feel I did a good job convincing Mr. Bouviér to sign with us. I must admit I was actually nervous at first. Most of the time I'm not nervous about prospective clients, because I usually make sure I'm well prepared, but this one was a challenge.

"Please sit down."

Could this finally be what I have worked so hard for? My knees are shaking, I hope he doesn't notice. I should've passed on the double espresso; I can hear my stomach bubbling as we speak.

"Victoria, as you may know for the last nine months both you and Tyler have been in close consideration for Senior Partner. I have watched you grow from being the quirky young girl that started out running errands for us as an intern, to the poised, confident, eager, woman you have become. Over the past several years you've shown us that you have the will and drive to succeed in order to make things happen. You possess many technical skills and you have been the go to person for many cases, and not to mention you've brought in a substantial amount of business. Every task you have been assigned to, you've completed without complaining, and although I'm sure that there were many times you felt you were getting the brunt of the cases, you still handled them in stride, and this is what we have been searching for. Both you and Tyler were our top candidates because you both share similar qualities, but we want the person that is going to represent us with integrity, and we want someone that will not compromise on the basis of trying to snatch and grab a client depending on the amount of money they may have. Here at Rucker and Associates our philosophy is built on the whole human, we wish not to single out anyone. Everyone we represent is equal."

I guess he's noticing by this time I'm about to pass out in my seat, so he gets to the point, finally!

He continues, "On behalf of myself and the other partners, we would like to extend you the offer as Senior Partner of the Business Advisory department."

I'm not hearing anything else; it all seems like a blur. The one thing I could think of is to say, "Thank you Jesus!"

He goes on to say, "There is a very lucrative package that comes with this offer. We are prepared to offer you an annual salary of $525,000, along with quarterly and annual bonuses for production and recruiting, which the profits will be shared throughout all partners and within the company itself. You are entitled to no weekends, a company spending account, along with an executive office equipped for you as you desire. And for your hard work, you may have the week off with pay."

When I set out to get to this point never could I have imagined that I would be doing something I really love. If I had to do it all over again I would not trade it at all. I know from this point, one may think my stress is going to level out, but now that I'm over this department that makes me responsible for so many under me. The firm has now a total of eight partners, with eighty individuals consulting, and not to mention my fifty current clients, but Lord I thank you, I'm not complaining.

"Thank you Mr. Rucker, you will be very happy with your choice, I won't let you down. I promise."

"You earned it, now make us proud," he adds, "But you may want to personally thank Mr. Bouviér."

Walking to my office to get my things, I'm feeling like a new woman, one that's on top of the world. I head to the waiting area to look for him.

"You are welcome Mrs. Cartiér," says the man standing against the fountain impeccably dressed in a navy pinstriped Armani suit, silk white shirt, and a pair of Gucci moccasins, but who noticed?

"Thank you again, you made a great choice going with Rucker."

Praying he doesn't notice me adding up the cost of that suit in my head, and not to mention those shoes, but if I had to guess I would say he spent well over two grand on the suit alone.

He says, "Must I say, you were one of the contributing factors. I needed a woman with not only your beauty, but your mind as well to manage my funds. Just as you were researching me, I was researching you.

I'm smiling as if I am the girl chosen on the Bachelor waiting for my rose. Only one thing ... I'm not single I'm happily married. At least this is what I keep telling myself.

He asks, "May I walk you to the elevator?"

"Yes that'll be fine."

I love his accent, reminds me of my father's. I can't help but ask where is he originally from, and he says, France. Why did I know that?

While we're waiting for the elevator, he looks at me as if he wants to ask me a question. I pretend to be oblivious in that I don't want to give any impression that I want him to. When the door opens I notice a FedEx carrier heading toward the office, and it looks like the package has my name on it, but I'm in such a hurry to get home, it can wait until I return next week. It's probably some papers from another client of mine.

"Well this is the end of the road Mr. Bouviér, I'm looking forward to working with you, if you need anything further, please let me know."

"I sure will Mrs. Victoria Diamond Jean-Pierre Cartiér." He states.

"How do you know my entire name?"

"I told you I researched you as well, I had to find out about the woman who knows even more about my money than I do."

I smile, thank him again, because obviously he has no idea how important he is to me at this moment. As long as I can remember I have played this day over and over in my head, and it's because of him; Mr. Marcel Armand Bouviér.

Passing so many restaurants on my way home, I can't figure out which one I would like to go to. Listening to Kirk Franklin playing in the disk player, only gets me pumped up for church on Sunday, so I can get my praise on. Malcolm hasn't answered his phone since I left the office. I hope he's feeling okay; he's been coughing and sneezing all week. I didn't check to see if he took the medicine I left out for him on the counter. While I'm thinking about it, I need to call and schedule my annual exam because it's past due. I haven't been able to keep up with my schedule, because lately everything has been so crazy.

I'm glad the doctor could see me on Monday, especially since I don't go back to work until later next week. I realize my phone has not rung once; maybe it's because I still have my phone on vibrating since the meeting. As soon as I switch it to ring, there is an alert, Please Call: Momma. I'll wait and call her after I speak with Malcolm, but since he's no where to be found, I guess I'll give her a call.

"Momma!" I scream, waiting for the light to change "I did it, I made partner! Where is daddy?"

"Baby," she says.

"Momma you should have seen me, I worked it like a pro."

"Baby."

"I didn't seem nervous at all, I had it all under control."

"Victoria!" she shouts, "Listen, I called you earlier to let you know we rushed your father to the hospital, he began complaining of shortness of breath, so we didn't want to wait."

Right here everything inside of me is numb, and everything around me has become obsolete. I can not begin to imagine that my father, the man I've always looked to as being invincible is now at a point where he has to depend on someone else.

Hesitantly I ask, "Where is daddy now?" Of course I'm not fully ready for the answer, but it seems like the only sane thing that will come out right now.

"He's home now," she says.

A sigh of relief comes over me, because I know if he's home maybe it was just a false alarm. My mother assures me he's fine, she mentions something about angina, and him needing rest. I don't really understand all of this medical terminology, all I know is that my daddy is my hero and if anything ever happens to him, I don't know what I would do.

I finally get the chance to tell mommy my good news, and of course she is proud of me, she says that I should definitely be in church on Sunday. She also tells me that Julian and Trenton were there and he had already told her the news. I wonder how she already knows. Need I guess? My brother's boy toy for sure. Sometimes I regret he works at the firm with me. Let him tell it, he's responsible for my becoming junior partner. She mentions Julian will be in Atlanta next week for that conference, and the good news is Trenton isn't going. He's moving to California. FOR GOOD!

It's six o'clock and traffic is still horrible on Lexington, I thought for sure I would get home faster this way. I need to call Lucy to tell him the news. Oh snap! It's Wednesday, his appointment was today and I totally forgot. Lucy has been talking about this appointment for weeks now. I'm getting his voicemail, and my call is interrupted by an unknown caller. I answer, but there's no one on the other end. If it's important, they will call back. A couple of hours later Malcolm and I get to Tavern on the Green, good we were able to get a last minute table. The couple ahead of us had reservations, but there was an emergency, so lucky me.

"Baby I'm so proud of you, I knew you would do it, also I'm glad you chose this spot, we haven't been here in a long time."

I can't resist the urge; I order the East Coast Oysters and the Spring Salmon. Whenever we come here this is what I order. Kinda feels like we're dating again. Malcolm has the waiter bring out the best bottle of Moet. As I sit here staring into his eyes it reminds me of old times.

"I can't believe it, you a Vice President, me a partner, it's like all of our dreams are finally coming true." Before the waiter brings our meal, Malcolm has this funny look on his face.

He says, "There's more to come, I have something special for you."

You would think he's about to propose to me all over again. Then he pulls out a perfectly square box with Stephen Dweck written on it.

"Oh my goodness, a silver and pearl bracelet, you must have read my mind."

"No, I just know you and I didn't read your mind, I read your heart."

"Well thank you, it's beautiful."

Malcolm always knows what to say to make a woman moist in more places than one. If there is one thing he has, its game, and he's laying it on thick. We toast to our success, meanwhile, he looks at me as if he can't wait to get me home, and I'm doing the same.

I say to him, "Malcolm, I was hoping we could go to Montreal this weekend to celebrate, its perfect timing, now I have more free time to spend with you.

He makes this distraught face as if I've just said lets move to Montreal.

He says, "About this weekend, I want to talk to you about that. Mr. Jamison and a group of his friends invited me to go with them to California for a golf tournament this weekend. He said he wanted to invite me because of the good work I've done since I've been in this position. I couldn't say no."

The other me would tell him hell to the no, he can't go, but how would that look. So the new me wants him to know I can trust him, even if he has been acting strange lately. In addition, this will give me some time to spend with daddy. All of a sudden, he complains of a headache, so I ask if he's taken the medicine from earlier, and of course he says he doesn't feel the need to, because it's just a cold and that he'll get over it.

His phone is vibrating, I try and act as if I don't hear it, but it is irritating me beyond belief.

"Malcolm is that your phone?"

A dumb look comes across his face as if he heard me, but he doesn't want me to know he did.

"That had better be Jesus calling you; tonight it's all about you and me."

He asks can he take the call, and who am I to deny him of answering his phone. I sit waiting for him to return sipping the last of my champagne; I'm beginning to get a little tipsy. I want to go home, and finish what we've started. We leave the waiter a more than generous tip, considering I'm making more money than ever. Baller Status!

When we get home we can't wait to get to each other, it's like we haven't made love in ages. I see the light blinking on the answering machine, but that's the farthest from my mind. Tonight Malcolm's a different person, if anyone has ever said there is no difference between making love, and just having sex, they lied. I can tell the difference. Malcolm's just plain ole' having sex with me and it's what I want ... In every way possible and for once I like it.

Again, I don't know why Malcolm has been treating me so nice. I hate he's going to California; I wish there was a way to surprise him so that we can have another night like tonight. Nah, I'll let him have fun with the boys, who knows before you know it, he'll be on the board of directors.

Oh my goodness, it's Lucy calling me, do I really want to deal with this now?

"Oh Miss Thang, you must have lost your mind, you got your nerve standing me up today."

"Lucy, I can explain."

He goes on and on, "Diamond you know I needed you to be there with me, and to think you didn't even call. Some best friend you are. I bet if I was that shady Noëlle, you would've been there before time. You're always kissing up to her. 'Yes Noëlle, how much Noëlle, how high Noëlle.' I can't stand that—!"

Right about now I want to say something, but it may be something I'll regret tomorrow, and I did forget the appointment, so I'll let him curse me out for as long as I can take it, and that's going to be sixty more seconds.

After about one hour of pure drama queen action, I'm able to apologize. I explain that today was my big day, and I finally got the opportunity of a lifetime. This has been the reason for my being so tired and stressed out lately. I hope he understands. It's going to be hard making this up to him.

Ever since he was fifteen he has been on his own. Daddy has held a special place in his heart for Lucy for as long as I can remember. When I told him daddy wasn't feeling good, he all but hung up on me. Lucy honestly believes Daddy can't stand him, but that's not true. He treats Lucy as if he was Julian, if not better. I did ask Lucy to go to church with me, he didn't say yes, but he didn't say no either, so that's a first.

I enjoyed catching up with Lucy, it's been a while. After all the fun we had, he told me he rescheduled so that I could be there with him. That works out perfect, now I can go with him tomorrow since I have a few days off and while we're out, we can go see daddy. After talking to Lucy I fell asleep. I was so tired I don't remember when Malcolm came to bed.

"Daddy you have to take care of yourself."

"Diamond baby, your father is going to be just fine. All I need is a little rest, and a little help to give up the cigars."

This is the habit he's had forever. My mother's been trying to get him to stop, but it has been a losing battle.

He continues to say, "Baby your daddy ain't going nowhere no time soon."

Here he was lying on the sofa, the one he refuses to throw away, trying to be strong for us. Lucy laughs as he thought of all the nights he fell asleep on that sofa. After his father suddenly became unavailable, there were many nights daddy would let him stay over.

"Mr. Winston, what are they testing for?" Lucy asks.

"Their checking my lungs," he slowly replies.

"Daddy I think you need to consider selling the other dealership."

He shuts down any thoughts of that happening, which lets me know he plans to be around for a long time.

While Lucy and I are headed to his appointment, Noëlle calls.

"Hey Diva, how's it going? I called you on yesterday; Malcolm told me it was a big day. I called both office and cell. Alexis said you had already gone for the day."

"Yes ma'am, I have the rest of the week off, because that's one of the perks of a senior partner."

I turn the speakerphone on to concentrate on where I'm going. I'm not too familiar with the new office we're going to.

"Turn left," Lucy says in the background. I can tell he's mad as all get out by the way he's poking his mouth out and rolling his eyes. Lucy has never cared much for Noëlle, he says she has the looks and walks like a two faced horse, not sure what that means.

"Congratulations girl, I am so happy for you. I knew you could do it. Also tell Lucy hi. I hear him, oh excuse me, I hear her in the background."

That's one way to make Lucy go off, is to reference him as a Him. I think I'm the only one besides my father who can still call him by his given name.

As Lucy signs in at the desk, I began to notice so many young faces in the office. I'm not sure if this is a pediatric clinic or what. Since the sign on the wall says no cell phones or laptops allowed, I put my phone on vibrate so I won't miss Malcolm's call.

I had the impression this was a Family physician, walking over to the pamphlets, everything I see is concerning HIV. The pamphlets read, "Should I Get Tested?" "HIV and Treatment", "How Can I Get Help?" It's so many it's dawning on me we're in an HIV clinic. It's unbelievable that it's mainly younger people here than anything, and from that they're mostly young girls between the ages of 13-19, and the ones I'm seeing are primarily black young women. This can't be. How is it that so many of our young girls are becoming infected with this deadly disease? Furthermore, why is Lucy here! Is there something he hasn't told me?

Waiting for Lucy to come out, I focus on what's before me. One young girl who looks to be no more than sixteen, must've gotten her results today, she left very upset. Seeing this makes me even the more grateful that I've been careful. As Lucy comes out, a handsome young man is behind him in a white lab coat; he tells Lucy that his results will be available in 2-7 days. I grab a few pamphlets on my way out; it doesn't hurt to read a little more about this.

The drive home is a fairly quiet one. All Lucy does is look out of the window.

"You want to talk about it?" I ask.

"Not sure what to say, but I'll be glad when the test comes back."

The look on his face is reading, "Scared as Hell."

"You know it's okay to be afraid, but you don't have to worry because you're not alone, I'm here for you no matter what the out come."

Out of nowhere Lucy says, "You know Diamond, it wasn't until recently I became a bottom-feeder, I'm usually the jaw queen. Ever since I've been with Jackson he's had me doing all sorts of stuff, it doesn't bother me, I just hope that all I've done is not catching up with me."

It's rare that Lucy and I talk openly about his sexual encounters; mainly we just beat around the bush. He leaves a lot to my imagination, and its better that way. I've always felt he was forced into this lifestyle. Now my brother Julian on the other hand, that's a different story. I don't know how that happened. Let him tell it, he's always known.

I'm glad Malcolm left something out to eat; I also see he's left my mail on the counter. The books I ordered are here, "*Good to Great*" and "*The Millionaire Next Door*". I've got to stay ahead of the game. I once heard a

Pastor on one of those Christian stations say; in order to have something you've never had before, you must be willing to do something you've never done before. Ever since then, I've been on the path of finding true purpose. I know one day my dreams will come true. Although I've accomplished my goal of becoming partner, that is just one part of my plan, I still want to own my very own Investment Firm. Every time I've shared it with Malcolm, he blows me off; if he thought I was serious about it he would find a way to shoot me down. He's fine as long as we're both comfortable in white collar jobs working for white collar people, but not me; I want to be my own boss. Ever since I was a little girl I had big dreams. My parents constantly drilled it in my head that the sky was the limit, they would also remind me that I could be any and everything I wanted to be and not to let anyone or anything stop me.

Not a day goes by that I don't imagine my name on the marquis of a beautifully constructed building, designed to my liking, where I can call the shots. Don't get me wrong, I'm grateful to have the job I have, but that's not it for me, I want more, and I am going to get it by any means necessary.

Chapter Five
Victoria & Lucy

I wish I could've taken Malcolm to the airport, but I just don't feel like myself today. I thought I'd be better by now. I keep saying I'm going to schedule an appointment, but I haven't gotten around to it. At least now that he's gone I can do something around this house like clean up for instance. If it was up to me, we would hire a maid named Olga to come in twice a week.

It's funny, I've been so busy the past few months I haven't had anytime for myself. It's a stack of unread magazines with pages waiting to be opened, new fragrances waiting to be tested, quizzes that need to be taken. Maybe they will let me know if I'm in love, or if I'm in lust. Better yet, I can take one that reassures me I'm satisfied with me. When I think about it, doesn't look like I'll be catching up on any of these anytime soon. Safe to say this is trash.

I'm glad daddy's results turned out to be good. After this scare hopefully he'll start to take more time off, start letting some of the other men handle it for a change. I can't recall the last time my parents took a vacation. That actually sounds good. I think that's what I'll give daddy for father's day, along with the shoes. They need this.

Maybe Noëlle can recommend someone; she has a beau in every industry, why would this one be any different. It's still early, she's probably not up yet, but I'll try her anyway. Of course voicemail, reaching her lately has been almost impossible, but I'm not mad at her, being owner of your own record label can be a hassle. Good days and bad days. When she gets the message she can call me back some time today.

Lucy should've gotten his results by now, haven't heard from him in a couple of days. If I know him, he's laid up with Jackson somewhere. He's still my BFF after all these years, but I still pray one day he'll have a change of heart and secretly I believe he wants that too.

My baby calls to let me know he's made it. He sounds so excited. I hope he has a good time, hopefully when he gets back we can have some us time. Didn't think I would miss him this much, so soon, but I do. Now that things are somewhat back to normal, I'm prayerful things are going to change for the better.

I see Neiman's is having a sale, now that sounds like a plan. I can treat myself to a long overdue shopping spree, and I'll even call Ming to see if she can fit me in. I deserve it, a day at the spa, even better I'll bring momma along with me. What better person to share in my happiness besides my husband, and he's not here so there it is ...

From the looks of the trunk, you would think Samantha from Sex in the City owns this car. A girl wasn't feeling any mercy. Out of all I've bought, the Kimono is my favorite, and without a doubt the Loubou petal sandals win hands down. I don't think momma will be coming shopping with me anymore; she's still trying to catch her breath back at the register. None of this fazes her; she could care less about Manolo or Polo. Give her a pair of nice slacks, a blouse, and casual pumps, she's good to go, but don't get me wrong however she puts it together you best believe it's going to be classy. I wouldn't say I have any regrets, but ... if I wasn't so good with numbers, I definitely could have been an alumni of FIT. Fashion is truly my passion.

It was good Ming had availability, which is strange, you usually have to book her two to three weeks in advance, but I wouldn't have anybody else do my mani/pedi. I just would've had to wait. She works the balls of my feet so good makes me feel like I'm walking on clouds. It's no question momma is going to love Mandisa, because after being massaged by him, I wouldn't be surprised she leaves rethinking her marriage vows. He has the muscular build of Dwayne "The Rock" Johnson, the beautiful and sultry smile of Lamman Rucker, and the hands of Djimon Hounsou. Lord Have Mercy!

At the restaurant, we also get something for daddy. He loves it when momma thinks about him, even if he doesn't eat it, it's just the thought. Just before we leave, an exquisitely dressed man comes over to the table and says, "Hello Mrs. Cartiér." I recognize the voice.

Shoes: Ferragamo Mocha crocs, I'm guessing 10 ½.

Suit: Sand Etro Linen and paisley shirt.

Watch: Cartiér (the white Pasha), but again who noticed. It's him,

Mr. Bouviér.

He asks, "Who is this beauty that graces the table with you?"

Momma looks up and smiles, extends her hand and says, "Delores Jean-Pierre."

"This is my mother Mr. Bouviér, she and I are having a girl's day out."

"Well I see where you get your striking features from. You both are very beautiful women; it's a pleasure to be in your company, but don't let me interrupt your dinner. I just happened to see Mrs. Cartiér, and thought I would come over to speak, and let you know again how excited I am to be represented by your firm."

"Again you're welcome, and we're excited to represent you also."

"*Au Revoir* and you ladies have a nice evening, and once again the pleasure is mine."

"*Même ici,*" momma says.

He looks surprised momma knows French, but interestingly enough gives a smile, and hands me his business card and tells me I can call if I need any assistance with anything. Even though we represent him, he's invested in a number of companies. There could be a number of things to call on him for, but what? I do know the man has long money though, but that's neither here or there, I can't worry about that now; the only thing on my mind is digesting this food I've eaten.

On the way to my parents' home, Lucy calls to see what I'm up to, he convinces me to make it a ladies night, being that Malcolm's out of town. My first reaction is to say no, but we haven't hung out in a while, and I'm anxious to hear about the results.

I help momma with her bags, daddy just shakes his head and says, "Better be something in those bags for me."

"Daddy you know there's no way we wouldn't bring you anything back. I think momma got more for you than she did herself."

He laughs, as if to say he's surprised momma let me buy her anything, especially from the places I shop. This is why I'm a daddy's girl; we're built the same way. We have Barneys, Saks, Neiman's, Bloomy's, and Bergdorf's flowing through our veins, and it bleeds "GREEN". He's partially responsible for my addiction. As far back as I can remember my father was always a well-dressed man. Always on point, I guess it's due to his line of business.

I don't realize how late it is, if Lucy's coming he had better be on his way now, because instead this may turn out to be a ladies morning. Although I woke earlier in a groggy mood, this has turned out to be a really good day, I've been having so much fun with momma today, I haven't thought about Malcolm as much as I would've normally. By the way, its 9:45 here, and there's a three-hour difference between us, he hasn't called since this morning. I hope he's okay. But I'll give him a call anyway just to say goodnight. No answer. I can try back later.

The house seems so quiet; it needs some noise. I've been asking Malcolm for a puppy, but he claims I need to learn how to take care of one first, which simply translates into a NO!

I can tell Lucy's outside, Gwen Stephani is blasting on the radio. You would gather he was going camping with all this stuff he's brought with him.

"Boy, what is all that you've got?"

"You know me boo, ding dongs, ho ho's, Little Debbie's, Crunch-n-Munch, and most of all a bottle of Hypnotic. Gotta have it. What's a girl's night without the treats? Oh yes, and I had to get my movie, *Waiting to Exhale*.

"Not that again—how many times have we looked at that? And how many times can Bernadine burn that man's stuff up?"

"Uhn-Uhn rudeness, if you were in her shoes, not enough. That Bern is a bad mutha shut yo mouth. And that haircut is fierce! And let's not talk about how she holds that cigarette in her mouth while she's watching his stuff burn. Now that's a DIVA!"

Before I know it, our heads are tight, we're here lying on the floor, laughing and crying at the same time. When you're drunk Loretta Divine looks soooo good walking away. Now I know how Gregory Hines musta felt.

Just when I'm about to dose off, now he wants to talk. Why now? Couldn't he wait until my head was clear and I could at least think straight? All I can focus on is that God forsaken wig Whitney is wearing, wondering what was on those people's mind.

I don't know what makes a woman think that a married man is going to leave his wife no matter how much he says he loves her; you best believe that wife is going to always be first priority. There are the holidays, birthdays, and the so-called anniversaries, that's made up to pacify her into believing that's their special day. Anyway!!! If Malcolm ever got to a point where he wanted to leave me for somebody else he can go. I don't want anybody that doesn't want me.

Out of the blue, Lucy asks me, "Do you ever think about dying?"

"What? How'd you come up with that? Is there anything you need to tell me?"

"First off, so you'll know, I'm negative, but ..."

"Yaaaah! But what Lucy? Just say it."

"Vic, I'm scared. For the first time in my life I've never been this frightened. At first I was unsure what the results were going to be. It so could have been me. I've done all kind of stuff, with all kinds of people, and I haven't always done the right thing, I just said it couldn't happen to me."

I know I told him I was here for him, but honestly, my head is killing me, and I've heard all I needed to hear. He doesn't have it, so really that's all that matters. He's got to recognize I'm a little distant, but he still wants to talk soooo here it is.

"No seriously Vic, that was my first time ever being tested, and at first I didn't think that much about it until the nurse swabbed my mouth, then it became a reality that I could be infected with a disease that has no cure. Something I could have died from. My life actually flashed before my eyes."

"But Lucy you don't have it, and you shouldn't beat yourself up about it, the one thing that's for certain, you must be more careful from this point."

He sits up and clears his voice, and says the words I never thought I would hear him say.

"VIC, I WANT TO GO TO CHURCH."

I'm speechless, here I am supposed to be the saved one, drunk as coota brown, now is the time I should be giving him the Come to Jesus speech. I have nothing. I feel so bad. The only thing that I can do is say, "the doors of the church are open."

"Vic did you hear me?"

"Yeah I heard you, but I'm not sure if you're saying this out of fear or this is something you really wanna do."

"I'm serious, when you asked me the other night, I thought about it, and it won't hurt for me to at least go."

"You're right Lucy, and I'm sorry for not taking you seriously, I just well ... okay ... aah man I'm drunk! Can we please finish this in the morning? I haven't been like this in a long time, and I honestly don't feel right discussing this now, and look at us we've got bottles of beer and liquor all over the floor."

"If I'm not mistaken, I heard a Pastor say on TV one night, when you're sinning that is the perfect time for Jesus to be invited."

No he didn't just call me out like that. A heifer! Put me on Front Street like that. The unsaved is schooling the saved. I guess satan and all his little satans are down there having a big ole' party right about now.

"No it won't hurt, and you're right, and just like Donnie McClurkin says in his song, I think I'll sing it ..."

"No Vic don't, please that's okay."

"But a saint is just a sinner who fell down and got up. We fall down, but we get up, we fall down but we get up, oh yeaah—"

"Go to sleep Vic, goodnight, I love you."

I head to my bed searching for my phone because I realize the time on the clock says 3:30, and Malcolm still hasn't called me yet. I need to check my messages. There's no mailbox, no texts, but I do have two missed calls from an unknown caller. Even for Malcolm this is a first, he always calls, no matter what. That must be a real good golf game. He acts like he's Tiger or something. Malcolm Woods, yeah right. A lying so and so!

I'm lying here trying to get myself together, as sleepy as I am I want to call him. I need to call him. I know I say I trust him, but I just want to hear his voice. It's only 12:00 there. They're probably out partying. He's never been to California before, so that can be another one of our vacation spots. Hollywood here I come; they'll probably give me a star on the Boulevard. If I know me, I'll do some real damage in L.A.; Rodeo Drive hasn't seen anything until I stroll through. Oooh I'm so drunk ...

I just remembered Malcolm was supposed to leave his hotel information and the itinerary on the counter for me. I don't think I have enough energy to go in there and look. My bed is so lonely, I'm so toasted. I know I'm going to have a horrible headache in the morning, can't go to sleep without saying my prayers.

Dear Lord,

Now I lay me down to sleep, I pray the Lord my soul to keep, if Malcolm's with another woman tonight, please give his soul to Satan to keep!

No for real, I really need to pray tonight before I go to sleep, my best friend wants to go to church, and that's a good thing.

First God let me say please forgive me for coming to you under the influence of alcohol, but you know my heart. Thank you for this day. Today has been a day of promise in more ways than one. Lord I'm asking you to come into Lucy's heart, and give him the love that he so longs for. I have prayed that he one day finds you, I believe that with you anything is possible. I believe he knows you, but he's afraid to accept you. Please remove the spirit of fear, and let him know that with you he's more than a conqueror.

God I also pray for my husband Malcolm wherever he may be. Keep him safe, let no harm come upon him. Guide him in the right path that he will not stray. And if it is your will bring him home safely to me. I trust you, and I trust him. This prayer is answered in Jesus' name Amen. Good night Malcolm.

My head feels like I have been hit by a 747. That's the last time Lucy will get me to drink like that. We're not spring chickens anymore, at least I'm not. That party life is old. I guess since I've gotten married, settled down, I've become a boring person, but I wouldn't trade it for anything, especially after hearing Lucy last night. If I had to go back to being single,

I would just have to stay single; it's too much out there now to have to worry about dying.

My phone's beeping, it's a voicemail alert. Malcolm called at five this morning, and I missed the call. That's what I get for being an a-ka-haw-lic. From listening at the message, it sounds like he's just gotten in, or just tired; he's talking so low I can hardly hear.

1 voicemail. "Hey Lady, it's me. Just giving you a shout to let you know I had a good time today, and I miss you ... a lot. I saw where you called, sorry I didn't call earlier, but you know we got real tied up with the game and all. I'll call you later on tomorrow to check on you. I love you Vic."

I know he's probably sleep by now, but I'll still call him. It's going straight to voicemail. Either it's off or it's dead. Now which one am I going to let my spirit believe? For his sake, it had better be dead.

"Malcolm, hi, I'm guessing you are asleep by now, just wanted to hear your voice, see how things were going. I hope you're enjoying yourself, but not too much. I miss you too and I can't wait until you get home. You'll never guess what ... Lucy's going to church with me Sunday. Call me when you wake up. Love you too."

So early in the morning, and I hear Lucy in the kitchen, he must be cooking breakfast. That's one thing I miss. He would always cook when he stayed over to our house. I always said he'd make a fantastic chef. The boy eats like a horse, but only weighs 150 pounds. He's yelling for me to get my so and so up, to come and eat. I'm starving, but my stomach feels like I need to throw up.

"Good morning Bernadine."

"Same to you Savannah."

"Thanks for breakfast, I need to put something on my stomach, but it's all balled up in knots, although I can't pass up these crepes. All I need is some blueberries."

"I got you boo."

"Lucy I know we were tipsy last night, so I want to be sure I was hearing what I thought I was."

"Yes, Vic you heard right, I said it! I want to go to church."

"Just making sure, now you do know service starts at 9:30 in the morning?"

"Now you're pushing it. What time are we getting out? You know it's been a while, so I don't need to be in there all day, I might not come back."

"You'll be fine."

I don't want to tell him, but it's first Sunday, and we usually take the Lord's Supper on that day. It's been a while for me to, so we'll be in there together. Once I went back, I really wanted to go with Malcolm, but nows a better time than any, no need to wait around on him. Both Lucy and me in church at the same time, momma is going to have a fit.

Lucy helped me clean up, now I don't have as much to do. I can really rest today. I'll use this time and get things ready for next week. It's still hard to believe that I'm a full partner, it's like my life and finances have changed over night, which reminds me I need to work on my parents' vacation , and Noëlle still hasn't called. It's best anyway, I'll just use the one Malcolm and I always use.

That bath was just what I needed. I can tell just how stressed I've been because it's in my shoulders, even though Mandisa hit some good spots yesterday, I could have used another 45 minutes on top of that hour. I know Momma sure left feeling good. I don't remember the last time I've seen her so relaxed.

Malcolm's Aunt Colleen stopped by to check on us. To her surprise Malcolm is out of town, and he knows how she gets if he leaves and goes anywhere without her knowing. She's livid. Too bad, he should've called her; it's not my responsibility to let his family know every time he makes a move. She says she's getting ready to go on a trip herself. I gave her our agents name and number through the airline, Laila will get her a good deal, that's why I enjoy working with her, she goes over and beyond to make sure all of her clients are happy. I need to call her for myself.

Shuffling through the rest of the mail, waiting for Laila to come back on the line, the phone keeps beeping on the other end, unknown caller again, maybe I should see who this is, and they've called several times already. I answer, but all I get is silence. Then a voice says softly, "Hello is this Diamond Cartiér?" My first reaction is to hang up, because no one knows me as Diamond except my family and close friends.

"Yes this is Mrs. Cartiér, and to whom am I speaking?"

Then the phone goes dead. What the ...

I click back over to make sure Laila hadn't hung up. Good, she hasn't.

"Hey, Mrs. Cartiér," she says with such excitement in her voice as if she already has the Rates of the Day plastered over her screen.

"Hi Laila."

"How's it in St. Thomas?" she asks.

I'm saying to myself, does she know who she's talking to. I'm not in St. Thomas, last I checked I was standing in the middle of my kitchen in Harlem.

"Laila, this is Victoria Cartiér, you know Malcolm's wife, your banker."

She goes on to say, "Yes I know which Mrs. Cartiér this is, I thought you were in St. Thomas."

For a moment I'm truly knocked of course, I'm not sure if I should lead her on to get more information, or should I just let her hang herself. I can't resist.

I say, "Well no, I couldn't leave out just yet; I had some last minute details to tie up first."

Then she says, "According to my log, I have scheduled two round trip tickets under the name Cartiér."

I know fully she has to have the other name of the passenger listed, because there is no way they could have checked in without it. I go out on a limb.

"If you do not mind, what names are on the actual reservation?"

I can sense there is hesitation in her voice, and she sounds as though she's stalling, perhaps she sees another name that's not mine and doesn't want me to know.

She continues, "Mrs. Cartiér, this reservation was made two weeks ago, and I wasn't here, at that time, I was on vacation."

I want to say to her so badly I could care less; all I need is a name! She puts me on hold and comes back with some lame story about the computers are going down. Does she think I was born yesterday? She asks if she can call me back once they're up and running again. What am I suppose to say, no, don't call me back, but I need her. So I can't act too surprised, I just need to keep my cool, so she'll think its okay. She reassures me it won't be long.

These are the longest minutes ever. I am pacing back and forth trying to get my thoughts together. My heart is racing, my head is pounding, and my fingers are tingling, all because of the unknown. I know Malcolm did not just lie to me like that. Go out of town with another—Ugh, I'm so mad I can scream! I knew it, something inside of me said it wasn't right, but I wanted to trust him. Unless ... maybe the other name is Mr. Jamison, but ... no that can't be, because he would have paid for himself. Why would Malcolm pay for both of their tickets? And anyway what am I thinking, she didn't even say California. She said ST. THOMAS! He hasn't even taken me to St. Thomas. She must be a bad girl.

The phone rings, I pick it up without taking a breath. I remember I must stay calm, because if she feels any way that I'm prying her, she won't cave in and give me what I need. It's not Laila, it's her manager, Mr. Somebody, all I know is that he's saying stuff to me like, passenger's confidentiality, because I'm not the one who purchased the tickets, and I can't prove I'm the second passenger, so they can't release that information to me. I say in a mellow tone, "Well can you at least let me know what card was used to pay for them?" He tells me, with cash. Before I know it, I hang up without saying goodbye.

I take a deep breath; I look in the mirror at the women that looks back at me. Tears flooding my face, I can hardly breathe. I can't believe he would do this me. I've got to call Noëlle; she would know how to deal with this. Before I call, I try Malcolm's cell again hoping there is some mistake, and we'll get it all cleared up, and he'll put Mr. Jamison on the phone and this will be over. Still the voicemail, the cheapest cell phone would have charged by now. I hang up. I call Noëlle, she answers. Finally!

"Hey chica," she says.

There's a lot of noise in the background I can hardly hear her.

I say to her crying, "Noëlle, where are you?"

"Girl, I'm in Vegas this weekend. Remember I told you I was trying to sign this new group." I've been here since Thursday. You don't remember?"

Right now, I can't remember anything; I'll be surprised if I can remember my own name.

"Yeah I remember, but ...When will you be back."

"Monday afternoon. My flight arrives at 6:30."

"Can you talk?"

"Yeah I got a minute, what's wrong?"

I'm trying to hold it together, because I'm not sure if she has anyone around her. So I make it brief.

"You won't believe this, I think Malcolm is cheating on me, and I can't prove it."

"Diamond, why are you saying this, Malcolm is a good man; he wouldn't do anything to hurt you. You're just probably tripping right now. You've been stressed out lately and you just need to get some rest, and anyway, what makes you think that?"

"First of all I have reason to believe he's not where he says he is, in California. I've called him and his phone goes straight to voicemail. My heart is telling me he is somewhere else, and if I'm right he's with a woman."

"Diamond stop!"

"No, I'm serious. The travel agent thinks he and I are in St. Thomas."

"Girl please, that's ridiculous. I thought you said that's where you wanted to go for your next anniversary."

"And?"

"Well Vic, I really don't believe Malcolm is cheating, I see the way he looks at you, that man loves you. On another note, girl I'm getting ready to head into the restaurant so I'm going to call you back, and please Vic give him the benefit of the doubt. You know, innocent until proven guilty. And you know Malcolm knows if he trips, it will be the *coup de grâce*."

"Okay girl, I'll talk to you when you get back Love ya."

"Back at ya."

My heart is still aching, and I wish he would just answer his phone. I can't wrap my head around this. I know if I call Lucy, she'll be ready to go find him, and I don't need that right now, and I definitely don't want to call momma, there are some things I can't tell her. She'll only tell me to pray, and I don't feel like praying right now, and I will never let daddy know, if I did, Malcolm won't live to see the next day. I think the best thing for me to do is to just lie down, when I get up I'll go out and do what I love best. Think I did damage yesterday, I only made it to Neiman's. I've got Jermaine's number on speed dial.

Chapter Six
Victoria

My first day back at the office is like a welcome home party. I never knew so many people were pulling for me before now, at least that's the affection I'm getting today. I'm not that stupid to think EVERYONE is happy for me. I heard someone say, if you got haters be glad, because they're the one's to let you know you are doing something right.

The furniture I ordered has not been delivered as of yet, so this leaves me to my makeshift desk and chair. It's hard to think a couple of weeks this time I was so excited to put Malcolm's and my pictures all over my desk, but now it's difficult for me to even look at him.

After these past weeks, he's still walking around as if everything is fine. We've gone round and round about him lying, and why, and his only excuse is that if he would have told me he and NATE decided to take a brother's retreat I wouldn't have understood. I must look like I have a big "S" on my forehead for stupid woman. And of course the part about the reason he couldn't answer his phone was because the *battery was dead.* Spare me, but I will say, I've got a surprise for Mr. Cartiér.

I know I'll regret this in the long run, but Mr. Bouviér told me to call him if I ever needed him. A man with connections such as himself must know of a well-qualified private investigator. Neither do I have the time or the energy to play Malcolm's games. Whatever the outcome, I'll have to deal with the consequences.

Since my doctor's appointment is tomorrow, maybe she can prescribe me something for the constant tiredness, I thought it was just stress, but lately I'm so out of it, I can hardly keep my eyes open most nights.

Our first meeting as partner went well this morning; it felt good to be sitting at a table that consisted of mostly men, and to think I am now the first female partner of the firm.

Reviewing my schedule, I can see it has increased drastically, just this afternoon I have an appointment with a couple that was fully vested in their 401k, but to both of their surprise they were laid off due to the economy. I'm guessing their plans are to discuss more retirement options.

The one thing I can't sit on though is finding a new assistant. Not quite sure if it's going to be man or woman, one thing for sure, they need to be someone that has both mine and the company's best interest at heart, someone who'll keep me on my toes. I really wish I were able to keep Alexis, but she's needed more in my last department. She was great, but I've got to step my game up. No longer in the minors, we're playing with the big boys. I'll have human resources contact the temp service, but the good thing is I'll still have Alexis until I get a replacement.

She sends a call through, it's Malcolm. What the heck does he want? Whatever it is, we can discuss it later.

He says, "Vic, do you think we can have dinner this evening after you get home?"

I don't respond.

"Hello."

You would think a brother would get the picture, but I guess he knows he's way—past credit card makeup. Well let me rethink that. Only if there is a "black card" I don't know about ... No seriously, I got my own money now, so later for that.

I say quietly, "Malcolm, I'm at work can we talk about it when I get home?"

"Yes we can, just as long as you promise to hear me out."

"Goodbye Malcolm."

I can't let him upset me like this. I've waited too long for this moment.

Before I can hang up the phone Alexis comes in with the most beautiful flowers. Immediately, I ask who are they from. She reads the card: "To my sister, my best friend, I always knew what you were worth. Love, Julian."

That was sweet, I wasn't expecting that. I haven't spoken with him since I left moms. I hope his trip went well. I should call and thank him.

This day has gone by so fast, maybe because I've spent most of it in meetings, returning calls, responding to e-mails and what not.

One thing I can't stand is when it rains, we New Yorkers drive even crazier, I promised myself no more road rage, that I would remain calm, but ... this cabby just peeled out in front of me, one more inch and my beautiful S550 would've been going for repairs. And if he knows like I know, that's a no-no.

Today Frederick Douglass Blvd is booming, it's something about living in Harlem that gives me a wonderful feeling. Everyday I look forward to the drive home; all except the traffic, but I find myself falling in love all over again.

It reminds me of when Malcolm and I decided to move to Hamilton Heights, there was no availability at first; this is how I know it was God who allowed us to get the brownstone we have now. I didn't think I could ever be as happy living outside of Brooklyn, but I was wrong. Sometimes I wonder what will happen if we go our separate ways, we've had so much fun here; at first I believe we ate at Sylvia's practically everyday. We would spend the bulk of our date night at the Lanes for happy hour. Everything seemed so good back then, now we hardly take time to schedule a fifteen minute meeting, and oh yeah we're down for dinner tonight. If I know Malcolm it's probably take out.

I'm so tired as I walk in, I'm rushing to get these rock climbers off my feet, I promise the shoes they make now are strictly for fashion, not comfort, but as I always say a DIVA never lets her guards down, don't let 'em see you hurt.

Looks as though Malcolm has prepared a full course meal; he's in full make up mode. Candles lit with the aroma of Lavender and Jasmin traveling, and if I'm not mistaken the boy has Kem playing in the background. He must know I'm about to jack him up, or he's just feeling guilty as oh get out. Either way it doesn't matter right now, I'm so hungry I can eat for days.

"Victoria, I hope you like your food."

"I do."

"Well I was hoping we could talk about what's going on between us."

I keep eating. I don't stop to even look up.

"Malcolm please don't spoil this for me, I haven't had anything but a sandwich all day, and this is by far the best squash casserole you've ever made."

"I have something for you."

Oh goodness I can't take it, not another gift, and no he didn't, he pulls out a picture of us when we first started dating on campus, we look so goofy back then, but we were happy, all we had on our minds then was graduating and becoming the successful people we are now.

"Do you recognize this?" he asks.

Although I do, I act as if I don't.

"Yeah, what about it?"

"Vic, this was the day you and I made it official that we were a couple, there were going to be no others, just us."

"Just us huh? Well you have a funny way of showing that."

"Baby please let me make this up to you, I'm trying so hard. I know I messed up, but ...Vic, I promise there won't be any more lies."

As much as I want to hate him, I can't, it's like he has some hold on me. My heart is telling me to trust him, but my mind is telling me to go with my first thought and call Mr. Bouviér. I do miss Malcolm, mainly in a physical way, so I gotta do what I gotta do. If you ask me it's a set up, he knows I can't resist him, especially when *"I Can't Stop Loving You"* is playing in my ear.

Filling out all these personal questions on the patient registration form is getting on my nerves. They want your whole history, new insurance, address changes, occupation, etc. What is this a doctors appointment or a national survey?

Problems/Issues: Check up, tired a lot

Allergies: None

Current Meds: None

Date of LMP: April 29th

Normal or abnormal? Normal

Last pap smear: a year ago

Normal or abnormal? Normal

Discharge: No.

Last Mammogram? N/A

Ever diagnosed with any of the following:

Pelvic Inflammatory Disease: No (not as I know of)

Endometriosis: No (not as I know of)

History of STD: No (thank God).

Before I can complete the paper physical, the nurse calls me back. Looks like she's been doing this for a while, so I can trust her, she asks me to get on the scale, and I'm not sure if I'm reading this right but looks like I should've passed on the second helping of casserole last night.

The doctor comes in, and it's not my usual doctor, they tell me she's on call, so I have the great opportunity to be checked out by the practitioner. Don't know much about the medical field and all of its titles, but I do know the first word in that says "practice", so she had better be good.

SHE'S REAL GOOD!!! Just my luck, the day I get the practicing physician is the day I find out I'm about to be a mother ...

If I would've known I was about to urinate a future seed in a cup, I would have waited. I guess this explains a lot. All I know is she says I'm ten weeks. I wonder when did this happen?

Just as they're drawing the remaining blood I have in my body, my phone is vibrating.

The nurse tells me it's called a prenatal profile; she says they're checking for all sorts of things, big words I don't understand, incompatibility, certain diseases like hepatitis, HIV, diabetes, and other things. All I know is that she's taking enough blood from me to check for everything.

I really can't believe this; I just regret Malcolm is not here to share this with me. The most exciting part is seeing this little image inside of me, so perfect, although looks more like a little spot. They send me on my way with all sorts of goodie bags, with coupons off for this and that, never figured formula into my budget. My next appointment is four weeks out.

Walking to the car is all a blur. What about my new job? What about my figure? What will I tell Malcolm? Malcolm, the adulterer! How could he? Just when he pulls some mess like that trip, now I'm faced with this. What am I saying? I'm acting as if I just got the worse news ever. This is actually what I needed. A baby! Me a mother. If only I could start the car, but I'm limp from head to toe. Mother, me, baby, all of that in the same sentence sounds crazy, but I just got a jump start, what if it's a girl, then I have a shopping partner for life.

Rescheduling my early appointments until this afternoon was a good idea, being that I waited two hours to get the news of my life. The whole drive back to the office I was planning how to tell Malcolm, my parents, and family. Momma is going to be so happy, and Daddy is going to freak out. He has spoiled Mel uncontrollably; I can only imagine what he'll do now. Lucy is going to lose his mind. That's all he talks about is having a little nephew to dress up. NOT! And I know Aunt Colleen is going to be ecstatic.

It sounds like Grand Central in here, obviously the market has gone up, and of course I have a meeting at one o'clock.

There's a note on my desk, human resources didn't waste anytime getting a temp. Her name is Melissa. I remember a girl named Melissa in finishing school who was straight west coast. You could definitely tell her parents were making her go. Learning proper etiquette just wasn't her thing. She only wanted to find out what fork was what, because she always had some little cute rich boyfriend whose parents she was trying to impress.

Ten minutes later, a charming young woman, around the age of twenty-three, with sandy brown, chin-length hair, dressed in a modest gray two-piece suit, comes in to greet me. With a beautiful smile, and delicate voice she looks as if she could be me in a later life.

"Mrs. Cartiér, hello I'm Melissa."

"Hello, nice to meet you."

"Alexis has shown me around, I've gotten somewhat familiar with the way things work."

"You will do fine, just relax, and rely on what you know. I'm pretty laid back, but since I ..."

"Yes I know, you've recently been named senior partner, in which you have been a great asset to Rucker, Banks and Norris. In your first year, you made well over a half a million dollars for the company, graduated top of your class, also completed your internship with RBN, and you worked your way up from runner to where you are now. You're the second child born to Winston and Delores Jean-Pierre. Also you're happily married to Mr. Malcolm Cartiér; the both of you have no children. Hobbies include; shopping, reading, traveling, and shopping."

"Okay Ms. Lady, you've done your research. Where did you hear all of this?"

"No, I've just admired you since the day you came to Columbia University and spoke for our Students in Business Week."

A part of me tells me to get her out of here, because if I wouldn't have cut her off, there's no telling what she would've gone on to recite about me, but there's something about her. She's special. Can you say stalker? Hopefully she's up for the task. We both have a long road ahead of us. I think more than anything she's just a bit nervous.

She gives me a list of names that have been on backlog, clients that haven't been contacted in over six months. She has alphabetized them, arranged them according to salary ranges, complete with updated phone numbers, addresses, and emails. Where has she been all my life? To top it off, I notice she's wearing the cutest pair of Jessica Simpson flats, sorta reminds me of me when I was younger.

The more I try it's hard to concentrate, knowing that I have this little person growing inside of me. It hasn't really hit me yet though. Maybe Malcolm will change his ways, come around, and begin to act like a father, opposed to a single married man. In saying this I hope and pray he'll begin to go to church now more often, now that he has a little a little one to raise. What am I thinking, I haven't even told him yet, who knows he may not accept it the way I want him to. He may trip out, and do just the opposite, but I can't make myself believe that. He does have some great qualities that will make him be a wonderful father.

Its 2:30 and I have a client scheduled in about a half an hour that gives me time to get a snack. Something light, I'm assuming it should be healthy, nothing fattening. Not much I can get like that out of the vending machine, so chips and M&M's it is.

I can barely reach my office before Mrs. Helena interrupts me. Some days I stop by and chat with her. She's the firms lead receptionist who's been here for about as long as I can think of, well before I started. She's the lady that always has a positive word for you, even if you don't want to hear it. I can say there have been days where I really wasn't up to hearing the Jesus Jargon, nor the catchy Christian clichés. Most of the time she's busy, but today she's just like chatty Kathy. We walk together and the entire time she's saying "what God has for you, it is for you," and so on. I try and derail her, but she persists. She also says something that catches me completely off guard. She usually says I look nice or something of that nature, but today, she says I'm actually glowing. Could she know already? Is it that noticeable?

"Thank you Mrs. Helena," I say.

"Just make us proud."

"I'll try."

She smiles and walks away. To know her is to love her, yet I've always wondered with the different religions and cultures we have here, no one has ever complained about her boldly proclaiming her faith in Jesus. She's a breath of fresh air.

Mr. Hunter, my 3:00, never late, comes to see me just for the conversation. He never has any major issues, except today he wants to cash out his retirement fund in which he has saved a substantial amount. He is interested in investing in a condominium that he feels is very marketable. Although he was in the 25% tax bracket last year, I advised him that withdrawing out a sum of $250,000, may hurt in the long run, because if his income rises into the 35% bracket, this will make the taxes on the retirement funds $25,000. I try to convey to him that I would want him to avoid as much as possible those type of unnecessary purchases and wind up paying the costly consequences later.

I feel Mr. Hunter left rethinking his options. After talking with him a little more, I find out he saw this condo on a whim, and believe me those are the worst purchases one could make. I never try to make the client go on my feelings; I always take their wants, dreams, and goals into consideration before I advise them on their savings. It is their money, but this is why they trust me, because more than some, I am going to do what's in their best interest.

I thank Melissa for such a wonderful job she's done, tell her I expect her to be here tomorrow. She smiles, and says she hopes I want her back. I feel she and I are going to work well together.

For some strange reason I can't wait to get home, I've been wondering how I should tell Malcolm he's going to be a father. I've practiced my expressions; all of them are void of the current disappointment I've been carrying around. If I can hide this I can hide anything.

Before leaving for the day I Google upscale maternity boutiques in Manhattan, I come across a Pea in the Pod. It's a sign from heaven, they have brands like Juicy Couture, Diane von Furstenberg, it's like the mother ship has landed. Nowadays they have all sorts of stylish wear for mommy's to be, and just because I'll be bare foot and pregnant doesn't mean I have to look as though I'm straight off the plantation. They even have Tru Religion jeans, I must say, this is going to be perfect.

Malcolm calls me to see if I have any plans tonight, this time I'm going to be cordial, I've heard people say babies can sense confusion, so in that case, it's woo-saa from here on out. Anyway I'm too pumped to think about what's been going on. Maybe I need to forget about it, and concentrate on the future, our future ... as a family. All of a sudden, my tone shifts.

"Hey Malcolm, how was your day?"

"Good, I've had better ones. Just letting you know I'm going to be a little late tonight, meeting at the office. If you want, there are some leftovers from last night."

"Ok fine, I'm pretty hungry so I can eat anything."

It's the woo-saa working overtime! I don't want to laugh but the Lion King's song jumps in my head ... hakuna matata, no worries for the rest of my days. Malcolm will no longer stress me out.

My cell phone rings, it's a number I don't recognize. I call it back, and it's Melissa on the line.

"Mrs. Cartiér, I just wanted to thank you for making my first day special. I really hope that this will be the beginning of a new relationship."

She had me a little nervous, because Alexis is the only one that calls after hours to brief me.

"Again you're welcome Melissa; you did a great job, looking forward to tomorrow."

She goes on to say, "In the madness of the day, I forgot to give you an important message; a Mr. Bouviér called and said he would appreciate it if you would call. He left his number."

"Thanks."

I give it a few minutes and call. I'm wondering what is it that he wants with me. Was he reading my mind about the private investigator? I call only to get a message that states. "Worries are for the faithless, if you're going to pray why worry, and if you're going to worry why pray. Today is the tomorrow you worried about yesterday."

How do you follow up with a message like that, I leave him a message that it's me whose calling and that he can contact me either tonight or tomorrow at the office.

Just as I hang up a call comes through from a 310 area code, it's him.

"Marcel Bouviér returning a call."

"Hello Mr. Bouviér, Victoria Cartiér, I apologize for my slowfulness in returning your call, it's been a hectic day. How may I help you?"

"I have a business opportunity for you. I'm sure it will be very beneficial to both you and your firm."

"And what is that may I ask?"

"Yes you may, but I would prefer if we meet at your office, I understand your schedule is tight but if you could pencil me in that would be awesome."

"Well I don't have my book in front of me, so it's difficult to say at this time, but I can go over it in the morning with my assistant and have her give you a call."

I'm stopped by the light, must not be as fast as the person ahead of me. He hears me honk at the car ahead.

"Mrs. Cartiér, let me guess, you're in traffic?"

"Yes, I'm on 57th and Lex."

"Really? I'm on 59th."

"That's wasn't you ahead of me that ran the light was it?"

He laughs out loud.

"No not this time. I don't usually do this, but have you eaten this afternoon?"

"No I haven't to be exact; I was on my way to—never mind."

I forgot, can't let the cat out of the bag, especially if I haven't told Malcolm yet.

"Well would you like to meet me at Park Avenue on 63rd?"

"I don't have a problem with that, a friendly business dinner with a client, there's no harm in that."

"Great see you in a bit."

Oh my, this place is so *trés* chic. The décor in the main dining area is very seasonal, being that we're in summer; the colors, yellow and white, are so bright and vivid. A nice woman named Shirley greets me; she has a hostess direct us to our seats. The steel walls are very impressive, not to mention we have a seat directly by the mirror, which only illuminates the room even the more.

As the hostess seats us I overhear Mr. Bouviér request a table for three, but I wasn't aware that someone else would be joining us.

A man dressed in a pair of khaki Dickies and a crisp white polo shirt comes to the table. I speak, and he returns the gesture. Mr. Bouviér introduces him as Carleton Le'Fleur. He takes his seat and we proceed to order drinks. I order a sweet tea light on ice, Mr. Bouviér, the same; Mr. Le'Fleur orders a glass of water, but also requests a bottle of Chardonnay to have along with his meal. I'm not a big wine girl, but just because I'm not sure what I can have or not, just the thought of it sounds good.

We order, and while we wait for our meals, I notice Mr. Le'Fleur is interrupted several times by the constant ringing of his phone. He makes a call to a Patricia, and asks that she have all his calls forwarded to his machine. You can certainly tell he's a busy man.

"Mrs. Cartiér, I see you've been with Rucker, Banks, and Norris for several years."

"Yes sir, I have."

"And I also hear that congrats are in order."

"Well thank you. It comes with a lot of hard work."

"I hear you are one of the best in your field, and I've been contemplating switching my portfolio for some time now, just haven't found a planner or advisor that I was satisfied with."

"Mr. Le'Fleur, I thoroughly understand your concern, having a trustworthy planner is very important, I have been heralded for being as honest and upfront with my clients as I can. It never pays to make raspy decisions that cause you to wind up paying more later on."

He shocks me when he says he has researched the company and also he has done a check on me as well. What are these people Googling me or something? I'm nervous because I feel as though I'm being interviewed, maybe he is interviewing me.

Mr. Bouviér interrupts and says he and Mr. Le'Fleur are business partners, and that I come highly recommended. I'm honored, although I'm not so sure why we're meeting like this, to me this could have been handled in the office.

"Mr. Le'Fleur continues and asks, "What are your firms total earning assets?"

"We have $15 billion in assets under management firm wide."

"That's impressive, for a firm such as yourself, but I feel I could be a great asset to your firm. My last review stated my net worth was 3 billion, mostly due to inheritance; it also includes oil and banking investments."

I keep an annual copy of *Forbes' Top Billionaires*, but I can't recall his name, although that doesn't matter, my job is to ensure his assets are exactly where he wants them to be.

"Mr. Le'Fleur, I can assure you that if you choose to have RBN represent you, I will do all in my power to make sure you are always satisfied."

He says, "I believe that, and this is why I'm here now, Marc is my closest confidant, we're closer than brothers. To be exact, we grew up together back in France, and when we both moved to the states, we've remained close ever since."

I go on to say, "I'm elated to have you think so highly of me Mr. Bouviér ..."

"Call me Marc," he says.

"Well Marc, you can call me Victoria."

"Ever since I read your profile, I felt the name Diamond suited you perfect," Mr. Bouviér, (Marc) says.

"Diamond it is."

We all laugh, complete our meal, in which I am stuffed. That was the best herb grilled chicken I've ever had, although I really wanted the Salmon, but I remember the "practice doctor" telling me not to eat any Salmon. I can't wait until my next appointment on Monday. They'll do the ultrasound, and necessary lab work she was talking about. My doctor will be there and she should be able to answer the rest of my questions.

Before we wrap up, Mr. Le'Fleur pays the ticket, and leaves a very generous tip, and to my amazement, he asks to meet with me first thing next week to set this in motion. I'm stunned, never in my wildest dreams could I ever imagined I would bring in a billionaire my first week of being senior partner. Once again, thank you God!

Mr. Le'Fleur proceeds to head out, but I'm shocked because one would think a man of his statue would be picked up by a limo, however he gets into a black Honda Civic. Here I am with a liquid networth of $1 million, and I drive an S Class, although this man with more money than David Rockefeller is driving a regular ole' car, but sorry the Benz stays, it's paid for. Shortly afterwards Marc walks me to my car, and thanks me for representing his partner, I notice him leaving in a Silver Cayenne, from what I can tell, the tag reads VVS1.

I'm so excited I can't think straight. I'm like that little girl on Christmas morning that has just opened her first Easy Bake Oven. I've got to tell Lucy, he's going to pee in his pants.

"Lucy, guess what."

"What, Ms. Thang?"

"You'll never guess who I just had dinner with."

"No I want, spare me the details and tell me honey."

"Carleton Le'Fleur."

"Ooohkay."

"The Carleton Le'Fleur! The man that happens to be richer than Oprah and Donald Trump."

"So what does this mean?"

"Lucy, it's like my dream come true. He wants my firm to represent him, in particular me being his advisor."

"Wow!"

"Yeah I know, can you believe it?"

"Diamond I can, growing up girl you always dreamt big, you were the only girl on the block with a Ferrari Big Wheel customized with jewels. You remember that?"

For a minute he takes me back to that Big Wheel, and it makes me laugh so hard, because I had daddy put special stickers all over with my name in glitter.

"Thanks Lucy, you have always been my best friend."

"Even better than Noëlle?"

"Even better than Noëlle. I keep telling you there is no comparison between you two. She's my girl for different reasons; there are no reasons why you're my girl. That's just fate."

"Well since you put it like that. But I still don't like her."

"But I love you Lucy, be good. Oh yeah, what are you doing this weekend? I want to have a girls get together with all of my best girls, haven't gotten all the details but I'll send you an evite once I square everything away."

"So the Robin Givens wanna be is going to be there?"

"Lucy stop, you know she'll be there."

"I'm out, and by the way, do you boo."

Lucy has never liked any of my other girlfriends. He feels he's my exclusive. My one and only. When I would bring a girl home from college it was always "she has an alternative motive." Like I was a charity case or something. He always felt the need to protect me; he thinks people always want to take advantage of me. Keep in mind Lucy stands about 5'7", and I would say 140lbs wet, but I guess it's because I'm the only family he's ever known.

I was going to wait, but I believe tonight is the night I'm going to let Malcolm know he's going to be father. I have it all planned, a night he'll never forget. I think I'll stop by Victoria's Secret, get something special, pick up some fruit, get some rose petals, and oh yes, what better way to let him know besides some cute little baby booties, can't leave out the Jodeci CD. I'm pulling out all the stops tonight.

Talking to Lucy reminds me I need to see if Noëlle is going to be in town this week. The industry has been so hot lately, all these new stars coming out at one time, I can't tell one from the other. I wish we had more of the TLC's, and the less of the one hit wonders. It's all about image, the more you show the better. I'm glad momma raised me to have a level of respect about myself, and daddy always taught me about class. He says a lady is a lady at all times, even when she's being bad, she's being good.

I can't believe it I get her on the phone and not her voicemail for a change.

"What's up DIVA?" she answers.

"Nothing too much, just riding cloud nine, where are you?"

"Actually, I'm headed to meet with my staff; we're doing a big promotion for my artist I recently signed. I was over by the office today, but couldn't stop by, deadlines pressing like crazy ... so what up witcha?"

"I wanted to know what you have planned for this Saturday afternoon, maybe around brunch?"

"Believe it or not, nothing. I'm so beat all I need to do is rest, it's like the more I go, the more tired I feel. I'm about to stop and get me one of those energy drinks now. I'm going on strictly adrenaline."

"I hate that, but it's good you're free so I will send you an evite with the details, and yes it's short notice but it's all good."

"That's what's up ... did you ever make up with that man of yours, I told you to never go on a whim. You were trying to crucify the man, before you even gave him a chance, by the way what did he say anyway?"

"Some tired mess about him and Nate on a brother's retreat, whatever!"

"Girl you need to stopppp, Malcolm will be stupid to leave you."

"I hope so. I'll talk to you later."

Home never seemed so sweet. The first thing I do after placing my goodie bags on the counter is rumble through the mail. Sales papers are the devil to me now. Victoria stay away! Like I said Satan is always busy, when you would do good, evil is always around. Why is it when I just had a major splurge, I get Nordstom's fall catalogue. Evil I say.

I resist the urge to browse, but oh yes they must have a maternity section now??? Just my luck they don't see the necessity to advertise stylish fat belly women this particular season. I guess they reserve that for the hot and steamy months, when they're tired, restless, and most of all hot! But I'm sure they have a maternity department, I just never paid any attention to it. Before now, pregnancy was a bad fashion statement. Now it's the new vogue.

Stepping into the shower, I take a glance at my now beautiful silhouette that over time will grow to look more like the hunchback of Notre Dame. But when I think of the women in my family, we have all aged well and triumphed over pregnancies well. It's the genes. I'll snap back in no time.

I get the mood started by listening to Jill Scott, a little Prince, mixed in with some other artist. I burn some sage to ensure everything flows right. I don't want anything to interfere. I'm glad I have candles, because I forgot to pick them up.

Smelling like a blend of casaba melon, plum, and freesia, this pure seduction is sure to mess him up. I think I have enough candles to start a two-alarm fire. The last time I used all of these is when I was trying to persuade Malcolm to buy me those outrageous Dior platforms that I've only worn once. Some things are only to be seen at that event and that event only.

It's starting to get late, good I ate earlier. I call Malcolm to get an idea of how much longer he's going to be. No answer, fast busy. I try several more times. He hasn't called me, and I'm starting to get worried. I call Nate just to see if he has heard from him. Nate says the last time he spoke with him was yesterday. No luck. Aunt Colleen hasn't seen him, neither has he talked with my parents. I'll give it some more time.

Before I realize it, it's daybreak I roll over, and to my dismay NO

MALCOLM! Where could he be at 6:22 in the morning? He has never pulled anything like this. I don't know whether to be angry or afraid. Right now I'm both ...

First I try all major hospitals in the area, I call the local jails, and I turn on the TV to see if there have been any fatal accidents over night. Nothing. I get myself together; I try and calm down, because it's no longer about me anymore. I quickly throw on some clothes to go out and look for him, despite the fact momma would always say NEVER leave your house, especially looking for a man. He knows where he lives, if that's where he wants to be that's where he will be. Later for that momma, I'm going to find my husband this morning.

Just as I begin to pull out Malcolm pulls in behind me. For that one moment I am relieved. He looks a mess, tie all loose, jacket half-buttoned, suit looks like it needs to be dry-cleaned more than once, and he reeks of some expensive cologne. Women's cologne that is. As I get out of the car, and the closer I get, it smells like Gucci. Lets me know she ain't no cheap so and so. The only thing I think of is to hit him with all of my might, but I can't.

The first hour is complete silence. When he does decide to speak he only says, "Vic, I know this looks bad, but please know that I love you, and no matter what you think I was not with a woman. Well, I was with a woman, but not how you think."

I do the one stupid thing, I have him explain in his own words.

He says, "When I last spoke to you, we were planning to have a meeting, all department heads were to attend. Afterwards they, meaning Mr. Jamison decided we were going to go out to a bar. Of course all the guys wanted to go to a strip club ..."

Clenching my teeth, "Is that what you've gone to now, women who sell themselves on the regular?"

He stops me, "Vic, let me finish."

"Okay Malcolm."

"Vic please, I can have them back up my story."

"Yeah right, like some man is going to be honest for your no good, cheating ..."

I'm asking God to be with me now, I can't go there.

"Ok Vic, if you must know, I did get a lap dance, well I got two or three, a young woman and I started talking, she seemed so much more than the woman shaking her body for a few dollar bills. It was never my intention for you to find out, but I didn't anticipate being there so late, after an entire bottle of Hennessey, I didn't make it pass the car. I fell asleep in the car. Too drunk to drive. Next thing I know when I woke up, I was parked in the same spot. No lie Vic, I promise."

"A promise is a comfort to a fool, but not this time."

Chapter Seven
Malcolm

Just when I stop tripping, try to do the right thing I mess up like this. I didn't think it was going to go down like that. Any other time she would've still been screaming and yelling, but she was calm, almost as if she didn't care. I've got to fix this. I hate ole' girl won't get it through her head it's over. I guess I brought this on myself. I should've known better than to get involved with her.

I'm supposed to be at work at eight, not going to make it, that's if I go in at all. This is bad. I've never seen Vic so hurt. There was a time I probably wouldn't have cared, but now it's different. Nate told me I was too far gone, and this was going to come back at me.

Several missed calls from her, why won't she take no for an answer. The word love gets you in trouble every time. How can she expect me to leave Vic like that? We talked it about in St. Thomas, and I thought she'd gotten it then but out of no where she's making demands, and not to mention the bull about she's pregnant. Why do females feel they have to get pregnant to keep a brother?

My phones ringing now, we squashed this last night; and I ain't up for it today. I wanna turn it off, but Vic may call. Out of pure disgust, and hesitation I answer.

"Yeah, what's up?"

"Why won't you talk to me?"

"I thought we were done with this?"

"No, you were done. I thought you said you loved me, that we were going to be together."

"I know what I said, but things change."

"How you gonna change your mind like that?"

"Things change."

"You don't love her, you love me. You're staying for convenience."

"I don't have time for this."

"For this! That's not what you've been saying for the past year."

"Noëlle look, it was fun while it lasted, but nothing good is coming out of this."

"I betcha if I'm pregnant your sweet little Diamond won't like that too well will she?"

"Girl stop tripping you're not pregnant, and you wouldn't tell her anything like that, that's supposed to be your girl."

"You don't get it do you? I care nothing about her, it's time The DIVA wannabe gets what she deserves."

"I can't keep doing this, I'm sorry if it didn't turn out how you wanted, but you knew from the beginning what this was. We got caught up and ..."

"And what Malcolm? You love her! Negro please! If she knew half the things we've done, you would be paying her alimony for the rest of her life, on top of child support to me. Which one do you choose?"

How could I get myself tied up with this woman? Obviously she never cared for Vic, but she ain't crazy. Vic will never forgive me; also Mr. Winston will kill me.

"I got to go, I'm about to get ready for work."

"And I'm about to go and buy a pregnancy test, Mr. Cartiér."

I keep calling Vic she won't answer. Who is this Melissa person? Every time I've left a message for her to have Vic call she stresses she's not in. She left home as though she was dressed for work, but I'm not sure. This is the first time I'm scared I'm going to loose everything.

I do the one thing I haven't done in a long time, I pray. But I know God doesn't want to hear from me now. I've messed up so bad that I'm the last person he'll listen to.

...this prayer is answered in Jesus' name. Amen

Hopefully, after a prayer like that He hears me. I feel better; maybe I will go in today. It's the one way I can get mind off of this.

I walk in and the first person I see at the teller is Aunt Colleen. That lady is forever getting funds out for some trip of hers. She's always traveling, she said once she raised me and Nate, she was going to see the world, and she's doing just that. I'm not really up for seeing her today, but she notices me heading to my office. She walks in behind me and the one thing she says out of her mouth is "Son and where you last night at heaven thirty?"

I laugh because that was always her little term to let us know we had passed curfew. She doesn't laugh back.

"Aunt Colleen, how do you know I wasn't at home last night?"

"Well, if your pretty little wife hadn't called me, I wouldn't have known."

"Auntie, it's fine, it's all straightened out, it was big misunderstanding, just went out with some of the fellows and it got a little later than I expected."

"Alright, you and the fellows are going to have your stuff outside the door if you don't start acting like you're a married man. I keep telling you, ya'll need some children running around that house, maybe your behind will grow up then. They'll make you grow up real fast."

Not the baby talk again, I've had one too many talks today about babies, that's the last thing I need to hear. If it was up to Aunt Colleen, me and Vic would have a kitty litter by now.

She gives me a few more words of wisdom, tell me she's on her way somewhere, I can't even remember. My mind is so far away right now.

Cherish fills me in on a client that's in need of a loan for $1,000. I wonder why they couldn't just go through the regular credit app with the bank, interest rates are real good now, 3.2%.

I soon discover Mr. Mitchell from the old neighborhood is who the loan is for. He says he remembered I worked here and he hoped I could help him. Mr. Mitchell was my mentor back in the day, he was like the father I used to have, I used to look up to him. I loved his wife, she always treated me so good. Every day after school, she would have cookies baked for me; she said that they were my "brain food". It's funny how I believed her, maybe that's how I got so chunky in middle school.

After 42 years of marriage, Mr. and Mrs. Mitchell divorced. He told me he was one of the men who had to have it all, the wife, the woman on the side, and the little cutie around the corner. Everyone knew what was going on except Mrs. Mitchell. He said after so long of fighting it, it was over, she couldn't do it anymore. Later on she passed from heart failure, he lost the business, the cars, and now he does whatever he can to make ends meet. This loan is to help him with a down payment on a room at a rooming house.

I can't bring myself to let Mr. Mitchell get a loan from the bank, although it's my job, I find it in my heart to give him the money, I write him a check for five thousand from my personal account, tell him to find himself a better place, and we'll work on trying to get him a job. I have a couple of friends that owe me.

Doing this for Mr. Mitchell makes me feel so much better, maybe it's God's way of letting me know it's time for me to get it together. Vic has been talking a lot about church lately, and that's probably what I need.

It has been a long time since I've been to church, and the way things are going lately, there is no better place I should be.

I try Vic on her phone and her office line again, still can't get her. I know she's been a lot busier now that she's in another position, but I'm not used to her being unreachable. This is strange. I throw myself into work, if I focus on the clients I have today, maybe, just maybe, I won't think so much about me and Vic's problems.

It's around four o'clock, and the lobby is about to close, I have no more clients this afternoon. A part of me wants to go to the firm to see Vic, but I'm not sure if she's just in meetings today or what. I know one thing ... I plan to be home before she gets there today, I got a lot of making up to do.

Just as I get my things to head out, Nate calls, he wants to meet down in SoHo, says he has to talk to me about something important. I take a rain check, I need to head to the crib, but before I do, I need to stop by the drug store to pick up some more Tylenol; I thought I was feeling better, but I just can't break this. Vic keeps stressing for me to make an appointment

I jump in the Range Rover throw on my favorite CD, "The Best of Luther", push track 5, "*A House Is Not a Home*", and ride out. That Luther was a smooth cat. He always knew exactly how to make a woman feel right just by saying woo, woo, woo. Too bad I ain't Luther. I know it may not change anything but I gotta stop and pick up some flowers for Vic, she says she's not impressed, but I know her, she loves it when a fresh new bouquet of flowers come, no matter what they brighten her day. Why not, it won't hurt.

My phone is vibrating off the hook, forgot I left it on while I was at work. Turn down the music. Of course, it's Noëlle. What is it now? Maybe she's got the results back from her pregnancy test, yeah right. Same ole', same ole'. Only this time I try and be a little more descent.

"Hello, Malcolm."

"Hey Noëlle, what's up?"

"Not much just thought I would give you a call to apologize for earlier. I was out of line."

"Yeah you were, but it's cool."

"Do you think we can start over and put this behind us?"

"I don't see why we can't."

"I was thinking ..."

"And?"

"How about you meet me at my house later, and we can come to some conclusion that will be best for the both of us."

"Noëlle, I don't think that's a good idea ... I"

"You have plans with Diamond, is that it?"

"Not exactly, but ..."

"So what's the problem, don't you want to see me at least this one last time. Don't make me beg."

"I know I'm going to regret this later, but let me see and I'll call you back."

"Thank you, I promise I won't do anything stupid."

Something about that scares me. But one thing I thought about earlier, there is no way she can be pregnant, because I have always wrapped it up. So she can't put that on me. Although if Vic isn't going to be home, in which she'll probably go over her parents, or call Lucy or something, so this won't be long.

I make my way to get the flowers for Vic, still no answer. This time I leave a message.

Hopefully she gets it. I really want to do right this time, and this is why Noëlle and I need to discuss this rationally. And somehow see how we can remain friends in this whole thing.

I call her back. And she's expecting me in about an hour. I decide to kill time, so I let Nate know I got a few minutes if he still wants to hook up.

My brother has never been the type to just lay it out on the line, and this was the first day he point blank told me I am making a big mistake if I continue to see Noëlle. Actually he said he's tired of the lying, after Vic called him last night he said that was it. NO MORE! He respects her too much for that. I told him I was headed to talk to Noëlle now to officially break it off, and make her understand I am going to make this work with my wife for a change.

As I drive to her house, I think back of the many days and nights I've spent here away from the one person that trusts me with their life, and to imagine how many times I've hurt her, lied to her, looked her in her face and told her I loved her knowing I had just left her best friend. Man, I wouldn't be surprised if God never forgave me for that. I hope after today she understands that the best thing for everyone is for us to just be the way we used to be before we crossed that line.

I head to the door and it's already opened, the sounds of Jaheim playing in the background, the aroma of incense, exotic oils burning. It looks like a séance in here. Something told my behind not to come here. From out of nowhere, she steps behind the door in an outfit that resembles next to nothing, with a long stemmed yellow rose in her mouth. From what Vic has taught me about the colors of flowers, yellow symbolizes friendship, and nothing about this says friendship.

My first mind tells me to get out of here as fast as I can, but I have to finish what I came here to do no matter how much she doesn't want to hear it. I immediately find the remote, turn off the music, follow the smoke circles of incense, put it out, and blow out the oils. I'm determined nothing is going to stop me from getting my life back to normal.

Just then she stops and looks at me as if I had done the most unforgivable thing ever.

"Malcolm, what is wrong with you?"

"Noëlle, what is this?"

"I knew you were coming and I wanted to make our last meeting together perfect."

"This is not what I meant when I told you I was coming."

"So what did you mean?"

"Noëlle, please sit down!"

At this moment I detect a slight rage in her tone, she's very upset. This may not be as easy as I had hoped.

"Noëlle, like I explained earlier, this between us is over, we can't keep doing this. I'm not going to leave Vic; I have too much invested for me to walk out like that."

"Why now? Just several weeks ago, you had it all planned out, you were going to tell her that you were unhappy, you didn't want to be married anymore, what made you change your mind?"

"My heart."

"Is that it?"

"Yes."

"I can't accept that, and I won't accept it, especially when I know how much you love me. Your feelings for me are real."

The more I talk to her the more I realize I've created a monster! When and how did she get to this point? This is not the Noëlle I know. It's not the same person I thought ... Wow, just at this moment I think back on some of the things we've talked about, the things we've shared, and if I was her, I would think it was love too. I knew it was love with Sydney, but this ... it was only physical. I told myself it was more because that's what I wanted to believe. It made the sex even better, but that's not what it was.

My phone rings, and its Vic. She must have gotten the message.

"Hey, I've got to take this."

The look she gives me is death defying, but I answer anyway. Today I'm going home to my wife, and nothing is going to stop me. I go into another room so she won't here the confusion.

"Hey baby, where you been? How was your day? Get my message?"

"Malcolm, yes I got it, but that's' not why I'm calling, I had a lot of time to think today and ..."

"And, you want to start over?"

"No Malcolm, I don't. I'm tired. I'm tired of the lies, the heartaches, the p-p-ain."

"Vic are you crying?"

"No, it's just air blowing in my face."

"Where are you?"

"That doesn't matter."

"Yes it does, Vic I will come wherever you are."

I can suddenly hear the music come back on, louder than before, this chick is crazy.

"Malcolm that won't be necessary, I'll just see you later."

"At home right?"

The phone goes dead. My heart is hurting, and it's beating fast. For once, I get it. I head back into the room only to see her now standing naked. She's relentless. Nate told me, but I wouldn't listen. He told me the worse thing I could do now was to entertain her. He was right.

"Hey I'm out! I thought that if I came over here we could sit down like two adults, discuss this and walk away as friends, but I see ..."

"What did you think I was going to let you go like that? I told you I care nothing for her."

"Noëlle you have your career to worry about, you don't want this to go any further do you?"

Right then she gives me the worse sucker punch since Ali and Frazier. I try and stop her, but she's coming at me from every which way. All I can think about is my baby somewhere crying, and I'm here dealing with this.

Before I do something I will live to regret, I break free, head to the door determined more than ever to get home. My face is burning, lips bleeding, and my neck is scratched unbelievably. How will I explain this?

I push voice dial on the phone to call wife. It rings three times before she answers.

"Vic, it's me, listen I'm on my way home, please be there when I get there."

"Malcolm, I'm not staying at home tonight."

"What do you mean?"

"Just what I said."

I beg her to please come home tonight we have to talk. At first she hesitates, but I know she wants this as bad as I do. I've definitely got to stop by the store, first to get medicine, and now something to help clear up these scratches, and oh yeah a shirt that will hopefully cover them at least for tonight.

My phone is ringing nonstop. I can't answer it. It's over. I don't think we can repair it. Just then a text comes up. I'm PREGNANT! Tell her that ...

Right at that moment, my head goes blank. I don't know what to feel, but I know I can't deal with this now.

When I arrive at the house I see Vic is here, I rush upstairs to see if she's okay. She's lying across the bed as if she's in another world. It's quite disturbing, because of the calmness that she has. I'm feeling dead inside. I don't like to see her hurt like this.

I lean over and try and give her a kiss, it's useless, she turns her head.

I go to the bathroom to clean up, and hopefully she'll feel better once I'm out.

I can hear her on the phone; wonder who's she talking to? I know it's not Noëlle, like I said she ain't crazy.

I feel a lot better now that I've freshened up, now I want smell like I've been in a boxing match, or better yet look like it. Once she's finished on the phone I go into our room to try and comfort her, and that is the last thing she wants from me right now. With her back still facing me, she says that she wants us to take some time apart. I'm caught off guard, because I really am not sure what this means. I ask her to tell me exactly what she's saying. I can hear in her voice she's been crying for a while. Could this be the end of my marriage? Just when I'm trying to make a change, I once heard Mrs. Jean-Pierre say *"when I would do good evil is present with me"*. And this is so true right now.

I refuse to accept this. I have to show her just how much she means to me, but I have hurt her so I don't know how. The only thing I can think of at this time is to have her get down on her knees and we pray together.

I feel that made her feel much better. It's been so long since we've prayed together, although it was me doing most of the praying. God has got to help me with this. I'm not sure if I'm more afraid of loosing Vic, or just being alone. She's all I know.

Thinking back on all the women I have cheated on Vic with, Kelly, Amina, (ooh Amina) she was Jamaican, and not to forget Paris, Brett, (the investment banker), and Sydney. Sydney was the best of them all; I just knew we were going to be together.

Okay here I am, just got finished praying and I'm already reminiscing on the past, but that's what it is starting now, the past. From this day forward, it's me and Vic. No more lies.

I convince Vic to order in and I notice there are rose petals under the bed, not sure where they came from. I question her about them, she tells me they were for me last night, but since I decided to go to the peep show instead of coming home that's where they ended up.

We wind up watching a movie, talking about us and the future, talking about our plans. She asks me do I ever think of having children, and the first thing I say is not now. Although I don't mean it, it's just that the baby topic is really getting to me now. What is it today? Did I miss the memo? "Topic of the Day with Malcolm, B-A-B-Y."

I try and clear it up with her even though I can see the disappointment on her face; it's as if she wanted me to say I wanted a baby. Right then my phone vibrates again; I act as if I don't hear it. Vic picks it up and hands it to me. I can see the words PREGNANT again. Oh, my God please tell me she didn't see this. I turn the phone completely off, tell her no more calls, tonight it's only about us.

Last night was perfect. We really had a great talk; it's been a while since we've just talked. It didn't even matter to me if we went to bed with out loving each other, although I'm sure that won't be happening for quite some time now. In all that, I think there's a chance she'll forgive me. She says she has a doctor's appointment Monday around noon, but I have a meeting, therefore I'll have to go with her some other time. Anyway it's just her girly appointment.

By the way I need to schedule myself an appointment; in all this excitement I didn't even take my medicine. This headache won't go away, and I know the drama hasn't made it any better.

Vic left out for work this morning in a better mood. Praying helped. We prayed again this morning. We plan to make it a habit, to pray every morning before we go to work and before we lie down at night.

I turn on the computer to check my e-mail, 64 messages, some of them from business contacts that I have yet to return, and the rest from LadyChief69. I delete them all. Block her from all future contact, but there is one important message from someone I don't know, it's marked urgent. I open it, it says, "Last chance." Not sure what this means, but I'm not stressing it.

Turn the phone back on, and of course there are 5 messages. Need I guess who they're from? I immediately call Vic to see if she's made it in to work, she has and she's fine. Good, today is going to be a good day. I even tell her I'm going to church Sunday. She laughs.

Even though I have a hectic day ahead of me, it's all good. Looks like Vic and I may make it after all, I called her to let I know I made it in, she sounded happy.

Mr. Jamison calls me in his office and briefs me on today's tasks. I have a major credit analyses that's due by next Wednesday. Looks like I'm going to be locked in my office most of the day. I've got to prepare my quarter compliance and review, and I know there're a lot of loans that'll need to be placed on the "watch list", so I may have to work from home. I'm sure Vic won't mind. He informed me the Board of Directors will be here on Wednesday, and this is my first time having to prepare the big quarterly review. I guess this means we'll have to have fun at home this weekend, but we'll make the best of it.

Cherish is aware I'm not taking any calls today except from Mrs. Cartiér, so she's activated do not disturb on my line. With all the craziness of the economy there are more people applying for loans than usual, the problem is we can't approve as many as we would like. Hopefully, that will soon change, especially with the new administration in office. Even as I look out of my window into the lobby, lines are long, but people just don't have the income they're used to.

When I decided to go into Banking and Finance, I admit, it was all about the money, making the six figures, having the bulging bank account, but now I see so many people hurting its like does it all matter. As Vic would say, my quest for fame and fortune helped turn me into the man whore that I have become. One thing I'm glad about is I believe God gives second chances; this is why this time I'm going to make it right.

I had to take a break get out of there for a minute. My stomach is telling me it's time to eat; I guess I'll head to Nobu; I have a taste for sushi. I ask Cherish if she wants anything, of course she says no. If I didn't know any better, I would think she never eats. Could be that guy she's fooling with. Lately she's not herself, it's like she has a lot on her mind.

I get my favorite table, thanks to Kim; she hooks it up for a brother. Don't have much time today, got to get back to the bank to get some more of files generated. While waiting for my order, I take the chance to call Noëlle back, just to check up on her, it's funny but I still would like to her friend. Can't believe it there's no answer, must be a good sign. I try and give Vic a call since she's usually at lunch around this time. Umm, second time today she's taken my call.

"How's it going babe?"

"Hey Malcolm, it's good, just a little busy. Melissa and I are going over some portfolios."

"And who's Melissa?"

"She's my new assistant."

"Oooh okay, you're doing it like that huh?"

"Yeah, you know how I do."

"Well you do you; I was just on lunch, thought I'd call and say I love you."

Complete silence.

"Vic you there?"

"Yes I'm here."

"Did you hear me, I said I loved you?"

"I love you too Malcolm."

That was strange. She never hesitates to tell me she loves me. Maybe she was just busy like she said. I'm glad she has another assistant, one of her own, this way she'll be able to get done faster, and we can have more time together. To hear me say these things is even unbelievable for me. I've been such a bad husband for so long, I've forgotten what it's like to care about the simple things.

Just as my food comes to the table I notice Mr. Winston walks in. I beckon for him to come over. This is one man that makes me cherish what I have. I see how he and Mrs. Jean-Pierre have managed to keep their marriage strong for so many years, and all he sacrificed to make it happen really makes me appreciate just what Vic and I have to look forward to.

"Hey dare my boy, how's it going?" He says.

"Trying to make another day Pops, you know who I'm married to."

"Don't I know, she's still the Diamond in my eye."

"Pops, what are you doing over this way?"

"Well you know I'm at the dealership at least three days now, 'D' and the children have convinced me to scale back some. I think this last episode scared us all."

"They were right you know. If it's up to you, you'll go down like the captain of the ship, last man standing, but you've got to let some of those other men you've trained handle it. If you trained them ... then you know they're capable of handling it."

"Son you're right. That's why 'D' and I are going to take that trip you two gave us. Get away, enjoy ourselves. You two need to do that also you know."

"Pops, I'm glad you brought that up, because that's exactly what I was thinking. I wanted to surprise Victoria with a trip. We need some time together; she has a little more flexibility now, so we're free to travel more."

"You know I'm not the type to pry, but everything's good right?"

"Yes sir. We're good, but it never hurts to replenish."

"That's it my boy. How you think me and the wife been in this so long, it ain't because I've been so good."

"What you mean Pops?"

"Oh don't think it's always been crème de la crème, we hit some bumps along the way. Trial and error, but if you remember God is the center of everything then you'll find your way. Just don't hurt my baby no matter what you do."

"Got ya Pops."

"I need to get back son, so you have a good one. Stop by and see me sometime other than "gumbo day"."

"I'll keep that in mind."

It's good to know that it ain't all green on the other side. Other people go through too. This only makes me know we can make it, and I believe this trip will help do it. Remind Vic of why she fell in love with me in the first place. I just need to figure out where is it I can take her to do this. It can't be any ole' place ... somewhere nice.

Right away I get Laila on speed dial, set up reservations for one of the most romantic places on earth, somewhere neither Vic nor I have ever been. I tell her this has got to be special. She books us at the Occidental Grand Aruba. I spare no cost. This is going to be a second honeymoon for us. Soft white sands, blue seas, lagoon pools, I even requested the Romance package. This is going to be sweet. I know after this Vic will have no choice but to see how much she means to me.

Time goes by so fast, before I know it, I've spent well over my hour, good I'm not being held to it. It's one of the perks.

Just as I'm heading inside, my phone rings, I glance at it, and it's Noëlle. Can't take it now, she's gotta wait. I send it to voicemail. That's what I must learn if I'm talking about being a changed man.

Today was a pretty good day; for once I can't wait to get home to my wife ... my wife, it feels good to say that and have no second thoughts. I give her a call and let her know I'm on my way, she's good.

Usually I throw on something smooth for the ride, but today I need to hear the word. I sort through my collection of CD's and tapes, and I come across a CD that was given to me a while back. I never felt the need to listen to it, maybe because I wasn't ready at the time, but after going to church yesterday, and listening to the Pastor, I'm in a better place. The title of the CD is, "The *Anatomy of an Affair: the Scandal of a Secret Lover.*" Go figure.

Proverbs Ch.7.

Being where I'm from, it's hard for me to even think a Pastor would tackle a topic like this from the pulpit, it must be good, and to think there were people in the bible that had affairs. Now that's funny ... The sermon goes on ...

First, the Pastor recites some lyrics from the song *"Secret Lovers"*, then he quotes another writer and says, "Life is a game, and nothing spoils the game except the one that takes it too seriously." He goes on to talk about a man that goes by a woman's home (a harlot), late at night creeping. This man, obviously, is man with no understanding or wisdom. And this woman is obviously a woman who goes around looking for men to be with.

As the story goes on the woman goes up to the man, tells him she has peace offerings, which she is willing to give him. She tells him she has decked her bed out with the finest of linen from Egypt. Sounds like those Egyptian cotton sheets to me. She also has put perfume on the bed, with oils and aloe. She goes so far as to ask him to go with her in her bed because her husband is not home; she said he's gone on a long journey. Now that could've been anywhere.

This woman must be a smooth talker, because she was able to flatter him with the way she walked and talked. (This is how I got caught up with Amina). He decides to go with her like an ox goes to the slaughter. Reminds me of the way I fell for Noëlle. I knew she was Vic's friend, even in college there was a time before I started dating Vic when we tried to get together, but it just didn't happen then, but the man in the bible didn't realize what he was getting himself into either.

The Pastor then states that an affair is not an event, it's a process; you just don't fall into one. Now that is true ...

He breaks down the different phases of an affair. (I didn't even know there were phases; I was just going through the motions.) He names them, first it's, ...the *Entertainment Phase*- which starts the process, it's usually simple and innocent, then there's the *Enticement Phase*-this occurs when the flesh is stimulated through verbal expressions, and visual antics, next it's the *Encroachment Phase*- this is the intrusion or for a lack of a better word trespassing. It's when you go beyond the limits and boundaries; it's when one runs the risk of getting caught. Like when I decided to have Sydney in my wife's bed. I never thought it was that serious. I never got caught. I always made sure that my game was tight.

He continues, "There's also *the Encouragement Phase*- this is when I would keep going in spite of knowing what I was doing was wrong. Then there's also the *Endorsement Phase*- This is where the man in the bible agreed to be with the woman." And this is the same thing I did with the women I was with. I never thought of how Vic would have felt. I only was thinking of myself, and then the *Environment Phase*-this is when we would put on the music that was sure to take us where we didn't need to be.

There's more, there's the *Enactment Phase*, the *Enjoyment Phase*, the *Engorgement Phase*, this is the phase where I got too involved, I had to have more, no matter what the consequences. The *Enslavement Phase*,- this hits home with Noëlle , I felt enslaved, it had gone so long I had convinced myself it was okay. I was a prisoner of Sin. Finally the *Endangerment Phase* - just like the man in the bible so was I on my way to the slaughter house, to hell. My life was in danger and I didn't even know it.

The Pastor ends by telling me the punitive consequences to my affairs, he says they are definite, although they may be delayed, our sins will find us out, we can run but we can't hide. Wow! Lastly he says the consequences are detrimental and deadly, they will cost me my life!

I thank God I have repented for my sins, and I pray that God will find favour with me, and forgive me. I'm glad that I have come to myself, and never to return to those ways again. Victoria is the best thing that has ever happened to me, and if I ever lost her I don't know what I would do.

Before I realize it, I have pulled over into an empty parking lot, I notice tears streaming down my face, I'm overcome with emotion, and once again, I'm so glad God gives second chances.

I just may be ready to be a daddy after all.

Chapter Eight
Victoria

Today I greet my baby again. Too bad Malcolm's not here, I can show him the picture later. This time things are going to be different, although he shocked me the other night. When I asked him about children, he seemed like he didn't want any now or ever.

It's also a good thing that Noëlle couldn't make it Saturday either, now I can let them all know by way of my little sonograms. I'm so excited, but I do wish I had someone here to share it with.

She's beautiful! Even though we won't know the sex for another eleven weeks, I know it's a girl. Malcolm would probably be better off with a boy then he can train him to be just like him; well no that's not a good thing.

I ask what is it that I really can eat now, because my appetite has increased a lot, and of course it's a generic answer like ... just make sure you get a balanced meal from all major food groups. Now to a person that is hungry as Jack himself that could mean anything. I keep hearing words like protein, folic acid, but I can't focus on that now, this baby is telling me to go the nearest Mc Donald's.

Going by my week-by-week book, I'm almost at the 12 week point, this is considered as the "Announcement Stage," this is to say I've made it through the rough part, and so has the baby. I can't wait to get back to the office so I can take a better look at my little sweetheart.

Traffic is out of control, but it's all good, although I could use a little India Arie to get me through on the ride back. Nothing can get me down today, not even Geneva the Diva. Ever since she's gotten to junior level, she's been unbearable. If I didn't know any better I'd think she's made it this far by kissing up to junior management, but it doesn't fly with Mr. Rucker, he sees through her charades all day long. It's so noticeable though; can you say desperate?

I still can't believe Malcolm and I went to church yesterday. He's trying so hard, maybe a little too hard, but I give him an "A" for effort. He's actually acting like the Malcolm I used to know, but it's too early to tell. We had fun this weekend though, even if he did have to work.

Lucy hasn't been answering his phone all day, wonder where he is. There's no telling, knowing him. Oh yeah, I forgot he told me he's about to start volunteering down at the clinic. Next week is National Testing Day, and it seems like ever since he got tested he's been a different person, he's even started going to church, I guess it took something to scare you to death, but I'm proud of him. He's still Lucy, and that's not going to change, but he's not as promiscuous, thank God. At least something good came from it.

Momma calls me on the way in, and I can tell in her voice she's excited, as if she has good news.

"Hey momma."

"Hi sweetie. I called your office and Melissa said you were out, so I just thought I'd try you on your phone."

"How's it going momma?"

"Just fine baby. Momma was just thinking about you and felt like calling. You know I don't like calling you at work unless it's important, but today I just felt like hearing your voice."

"Well here it is ..."

"You're silly."

"I know momma, can't help it."

"There is something I wanted to tell you that I know is going to knock you off your feet, but don't say anything to your father yet, I'm the only one that knows."

"Knows what?"

"Do you remember when your brother went to Atlanta for that conference?"

"Yes ma'am."

"Well, he brought a friend back with him."

"You mean he's not seeing Che' la Trenton anymore?"

"No—better than that."

"What he brought another man home?"

"Young lady stop playing, but yes he did, and HER name is Reese Campbell. She's an attorney as well, and she's from guess where?"

"Not the NY?"

"Yeess—"

That can't be. How can you just be in love with a man one day, and then a woman the next? Can you even do that?

"I'm speechless momma."

"But like I said, don't say anything to your father. Jules wants to tell him. And by the way I think he really likes her."

"Well I'm happy for him; I know Mel will love that. She's probably picking out herself a flower girl dress as we speak. I left him a message to thank him for my flowers, but haven't heard from him, maybe because he's been busy."

"Not sure if he's told her. I believe he wants to make sure this is going to work out first."

"I understand."

"I love you Victoria, and don't you forget that."

"I know momma, I love you too."

As soon as I get in Melissa has a stack of messages for me to return. I thought the rest of the day was light, but looks like I'm going to be on the phone for the remainder of the day.

Ever since Mr. LeFleur has become one of my clients people here are acting as if I'm a rock star or something. To me it was fate, but I really do thank Mr. Bouviér for sticking his neck out for me like that, plus he was very helpful in getting me the private investigator's phone number for "my girlfriend". It's unlikely he suspects I'm the client. He thinks I'm happily married and all is well, and I'm sticking with that. A small part of me is beginning to regret I even hired her, but he says she's worth it, so it can't be that bad, and as much as I pray Malcolm isn't cheating, my heart would like to know the truth.

I just got off the phone with Mrs. Hawthorn; she's one of my faithful clients whose children are trying to have her declared incompetent, only because she's gotten a little older and her steps have become a little shorter, they feel the need to put her away. She's in her right mind as far as I can tell; she just wanted to make sure there are no changes that need to be made to her current life policy. For some time now, she and her husband (may he rest in peace), have been my clients. I've never understood why when a person is over the age of seventy, the children can't wait to have them committed, especially when they have a policy of its magnitude. In the event of her death, she's worth a million. And there are only two remaining beneficiaries. You best bet they are counting down the days.

That's one thing I'm glad my parents have taken care of. Julian and I won't be fighting over the "leftovers." All of that is squared away. I think it's so tacky when a family member dies and during the funeral other members start hollering and crying, some even trying to jump in the casket, for what? It's not because they're just that sad, it's because they have been left

PENTILESS AND BROKE! Now they're left to pay the funeral home, the doctor bills, the regular bills, the car notes, the remaining mortgage, and oh let's not forget, the balance on that funeral outfit, because we have to look good.

Malcolm calls to see how my day has been; I let him know that everything is good. It seems like he really wants to make this thing work. For the first time I can honestly say, I'm excited about what lies ahead. Melissa hands me a manila envelope addressed with my entire name on it. There's no return address so I'll have to deal with that later. It's probably a document from a client I was expecting.

I continue to go down the list to touch bases with my regular clients. Although they don't need me right now, it's good for me to stay in contact with them just to make sure they're okay.

Mr. Rucker comes in to invite me and Malcolm to a dinner party that he and his wife are having this weekend, sounds like a good idea. This will be good for us. We need to get out and mingle some. It's been a while since we've had a fun night out.

Melissa asks if there is anything else I need from her today because she has a meeting with her wedding planner. It's beautiful thing to see couples so in love. Makes you believe again. I glance over the schedule and tell her that's fine, only if I am allowed to tag along. She's in total disbelief, as if she can't imagine her boss wants to hang out with her, but I'm feeling so good today; I just want to be surrounded with people that are happy and in love.

After her meeting, I treat her to dinner, and of course she's a vegetarian, just my luck, because I'm ready to eat every kind of meat that's on the menu. I take one look at the steak and immediately my eyes become bigger than my stomach, and this little person inside of me is screaming get it! And those mashed potatoes too!

Now that I'm about to be a mommy, I find myself desiring foods that I never ever thought I would want. I realize that it's not just me I'm eating for, so I've got to be kind to my little friend, in hopes that he or she will be kind to me. No indigestion, you hear ...

I'm really enjoying this outing with Melissa. The more I talk to her, the more I get to know her. She's a bright and intelligent young lady, she has that passion and drive that I had when I first graduated college. It's funny how much she enjoys children, but wants to wait until later to have them, which also reminds me of me. Always on the "career path", I remember when Julian had Mel, I was so excited to baby-sit, but I was even more excited to see her GO HOME! She never looked as cute as she did leaving out of that door ... but I still get the #1 Aunt of the Year award.

Somewhere in between our meals we get into the conversation about love and what it really means. I will say she has some great points; I'm surprised coming from someone that's still "wet behind the ears", as momma would say. Listening to her talk about her relationship with her fiancé makes me think about how Malcolm and I used to be. Just seeing how happy she was about planning her wedding and their future together, it really gives me hope. I know Malcolm and I can survive. I believe it and I know that God would not have brought us to this, to not bring us through this.

"Mrs. Cartiér, how long did you and your husband date before you were married?" she asks.

"Five years total."

"Well that's about the same for us, we've been together for four years, and to be honest, I was getting a little antsy."

"Yeah you were wondering when that ring was coming, huh?"

"Yes, but finally on Christmas Eve it came, and I still can't believe how he took a Barbie doll and placed my ring on the inside and asked me to marry him."

You can tell the Piña Colada is starting to get to her because she has this look on her face as if she can't wait to get home to see the love of her life.

I ask her why does she love him so, and she simply says, "It's his personality and the way he acts around people. I love the way he genuinely cares for them, also the way he treats his mother, and other family and friends it makes me happy to be with him. My mother once told me, you'll know how a man will treat you by the way he treats his mother. If he treats his mother badly that's a sure sign how he'll treat you."

For some reason I'm sitting here picturing how Malcolm treated his mother or better yet Aunt Colleen. He doesn't treat her bad, but he doesn't treat her good either, and also that isn't his mother, even though I do recall her telling me that when his mother was alive he treated her wonderfully. He treated her like the queen of his world. When I think about it, and I outweigh the good with the bad, he's treated me like a queen as well. Taking into consideration I've never caught him with anyone, I've only gone on my intuition, but above all, I know he loves me, and I love him, that's why I've got to make this work.

Before we leave, I ask her one last thing. If she could have one thing what would it be? She answers, to live happily, be comfortable, that everyone she loves is safe and free from all harm. With an answer like that, that lets me know I have made the right choice. I'm glad I've decided to bring her on as my assistant permanently. She takes the last sip of her drink, looks at me, and asks, when am I due? How does she know? Right then, something comes over me, and I suddenly say January.

Finally, I'm able to say it, and no it wasn't my husband that I told first, and technically I didn't tell her, she told me. So there it is the cats out of the bag. It just feels funny, because I've always pictured sharing this moment with him and my parents first.

Now that she knows, there are all the questions; she's already planning the baby shower. I need her to slow down just a bit, at least long enough for me to catch my breath. She says things like ... what did your husband say, and then I remember, he doesn't know!

After leaving the restaurant on one of those four types of clouds we learned about in fourth grade, I now know there is no waiting, tonight is the night. I'm going to tell him no matter what, although this time I want be doing the sexcapade charade, he's going to find out he's about to be a daddy.

I give him a heads up to let him know I'm heading home, he's just leaving work, but has one stop to make first, therefore, I will more than likely make it home before he does. He sounds so happy to hear from me. Before we get off the phone he asks me to say those words he loves to hear, and just because I know what he's thinking, I catch him off guard and say, COLOR, CUT, CLARITY, and CARAT WEIGHT! He laughs uncontrollably. I miss that laugh. I miss him.

I'm in the mood for a good laugh, so I put Tyler Perry's "*Why Did I get Married*" in the DVD player and ride it out until I make it home. My favorite scene is when the song "*Giving Up*" comes on. It's something about the powerfulness of it, how she asks, "Did I kill him?" It's hard to imagine that you can love someone that hard until when they hurt you and you can't come to grips with it, so you do the first thing that comes to mind, you hurt them back.

There have been times I've contemplated hurting him, but I've always asked myself what would come of it? Who would hurt the most? This is why I pray he's not doing anything that'll tear us apart, because I don't know what I'd do, especially now. I heard someone say before; it's a thin line between sane and insane.

I'm so caught up thinking about us until I forget the movie is on. I ask myself, why did I get married?

Thinking of how happy Melissa is now, and I thinking of how happy I was when we were dating, those were the good times. I remember how he used to walk me to class, and wait on me to get out of class. He would open the door for me, both in and out of the car, never let me walk on the outside of him, he would protect me, he would take the time to listen to me, he cared about my dreams, he wanted the best for me. We would spend countless hours talking about our plans for the future, how he never wanted to hurt me, never make me cry.

I never paid for a meal; he always made sure I didn't go without. Even though I had daddy to take care of me, Malcolm made sure I had the best. He would even pay to get my hair done, which was a first, because daddy always did that, and yes Ms. Genevieve kept my hair tight ... that's it—I got married because I found someone who cared for me just as much as I cared for myself.

I'm glad Noëlle got us together. It's hard to believe she never tried to get with him. Maybe it's because he just wasn't her type. She likes 'em to cater to her every need and want, the ones that stroke her ego, makes her feel way more important than she already feels, but that's my girl, if it wasn't for her, I would probably still be with "pretty boy Terrance".

One hour and fifteen minutes later due to the wreck on Amsterdam, I finally make it home. I'm desperately in need of a bath; sitting in that car for so long has worn me out. Malcolm's still not here, I have time to get myself together.

Rummaging through the mail, I come across the usual bills. I check the voicemail, and there's a message from Sister McMillan asking if I'm able to speak at the upcoming Financial Seminar. I think it's a great idea, all churches should consider some form of biblical financial teachings. I can call and confirm the details.

It's a good thing I've already eaten, hopefully Malcolm has too. It feels so good to plop down on the sofa after a day like today, maybe I can catch up on my favorite shows. I still haven't decided how I'm going to tell him, I guess the best thing is just to come out and say it.

Right when I get comfortable, Lucy calls to check in, he must knew I was getting worried. I haven't talked to him in a couple of days and that's not like him. He asks if I have the number to a Mr. Cartwright that he referred me to a few months back. I look in my briefcase only to run across the envelope Melissa gave me earlier; she must have put it in here for me.

As Lucy is going on an on about what's been going on at the clinic, I open the envelope and see it's not a document, it's a DVD that reads, "WATCH ME". I walk over to the player and put it in, as its loading I hear Malcolm pulling up in the garage.

I tell Lucy I'll call him back later; got some work I need to take care of. Then unexpectedly a woman appears on the plasma. First I'm thrown off because I don't recognize her, then as it becomes clearer my heart begins to pound, because at this point I'm well aware that this has nothing to do with work.

She's positioned in front of the camera as if she is sending this to me purposely. As much I want to place her face my mind is drawing a blank, then she begins to speak and it becomes painfully clear. This is the woman from my birthday party. I turn up the volume so that I can hear exactly what she's saying. She clears her throat, and says these words ...

"Hello, I know you may not remember me, but yes you and

I have come across each others paths. After I left your party it had become apparent to me that we had not been properly introduced, so let me start out by formally introducing myself. My name is Sydney Blair, and I do apologize that we haven't gotten the chance to do lunch yet, but there are much pressing matters at hand.

I have tried contacting you several times, but to no avail. By the time this reaches you, all three of you should have a copy of your own. I especially hope Malcolm has had the chance to view his copy by now.

Three years ago Malcolm and I were intimately involved for over two years. During that time we made some heavy promises to one another, one being that we would never hurt or lie to each other. One day he decided that he no longer wanted to be in a relationship with me. This was after he declared to me he was leaving you and we were going to be together as man and wife. It's funny how I had begun to look for wedding dresses during that time, because I believed him. He told me things like he wasn't happy, that you were not what he wanted, that he no longer felt connected to you anymore, so I trusted him, so much that I allowed him to make love to me without a condom, time after time after time. Don't panic, I'm not pregnant, but it gets better.

I paid a visit to Malcolm right after your party in hopes that he would give us another try, but it seemed as if he really wanted nothing else to do with me. At that time I had been very ill and I didn't know why. I had been to the doctor several times, and they couldn't find anything wrong with me. They kept saying it was just a cold that would eventually get better. I was admitted to the hospital with a mis-diagnosis of the flu, my glands were enlarged, and I just couldn't break the flu like symptoms. Labs were drawn, and I got a call back from the doctor telling me I needed to come back in for more labs. I did that, and the results came back. At that point I was asked to see my doctor so that he could tell me more about my labs. I could have never prepared myself for this.

Once I got there all I remember were them saying things like CD4 count, viral loads, and none of that made any sense to me until I asked what it all meant. He explained that my T cell count was 141, and my viral load at that time was 400,000.

I recognize these words, and I'm getting a flash back of the pamphlets from the clinic, my head is beginning to throb, and I'm getting hot, but she goes on ...

> **... Never in my wildest dreams would I have imagined that at 31 years old, I would be diagnosed with HIV nevertheless full-blown AIDS!**
> **I know you're wondering why did I go to this limit to let you know, and my answer is ... why should I go through this alone? By the time this sinks in, Malcolm, you, and his sweet little Noëlle will be reading about me in the Death section of the New York Times. Pay back is something isn't it?**

And this is where my life ends.

The screen goes blank, and I all of a sudden hear Malcolm drop everything in his hands. He's standing behind me like someone I don't know. Who is this man? He's a stranger in my home, a man that has possibly robbed me of my future. Robbed me of me. I look at him and I don't recognize him. Out of the blue he looks sweaty, worn, confused all at the same time. He stands there with nothing to say.

Once I'm able to take a step, I get a jolt to my head that is like nothing I've ever experienced before. Next thing I know I'm laying in the back of an ambulance. I hear the tech asking me is there a possibility I could be pregnant, and at this moment I remember my baby, my baby, my innocent baby. Oh my God, my baby, could she be?

Could I be? My heart is pounding faster and faster, I can't catch my breath, I'm struggling for air, there is none, Lord Help me! Don't let me die! Not like this.

I wake only to see Malcolm leaning over me, he then asks, "Vic why didn't you tell me you were pregnant?" I muster up a breath to say it really doesn't matter.

I ask the nurse to please have this man removed from the room, then I hear him arguing with the nurse, I asks them to get security, then I hear daddy at the nurse's station asking where am I.

I don't have enough energy to answer questions right now, all I want to do is go to sleep and hope that I'm dreaming. Momma rushes in like they've already pronounced me dead, then there's Julian, what is this? I must be on my way out; I haven't seen this many people hovering over me since I don't know when. I can even hear Lucy's big mouth out there telling some nurse off because they won't allow him back.

Momma keeps asking me where is Malcolm and why don't I want him in the room. I can't face her now. It only reminds me of ...Again I remember why I'm here. That— I can't even say it. Right now I don't know what to feel. I do know the only person that I want to see is my brother Julian. He should be able to recommend me a good divorce attorney right about now. Too bad the PI wasn't a little faster; I don't think she would have even found this out.

Huumpf! They diagnosed me as having an anxiety attack. You think? If only they really knew. All I keep thinking about is what my life was like six hours ago. I can't bring myself to get any sleep, I should've asked for something to knock me out; then maybe I wouldn't have to wake up and face the unknown. Malcolm didn't come back to the house since he left the hospital, if he knows what's good for him, HE WON'T! This is one time I want to go and get Pookie for his—nevermind. Knowing Malcolm, he's probably somewhere trying to come up with an answer to make this all better. No amount of money, flowers, any of that can make this better.

Thinking back on the night of my party, I said to myself that she wasn't who she said she was; my heart kept telling me different, not to trust her, but me being the nice sweet person I am, I go along with natural instinct. And look where I am now, pregnant with a man's baby who has cheated on me, no telling how many times, with God knows how many women.

What do I do?
What do I do when it's not me he needs?
Regardless of my tireless begs and pleas,
He looks straight through me only to see
Another woman's inner beauty.

What do I do when it's not me he craves?
Not my touch, not my warmth, not even my taste.
I've tried to be the woman that he needs,
Just to find out that I will never be.
The one that truly has his heart,
The one that has torn it all apart,
At the drop of a dime, one phone call,
The one that has made him risk it all.

What do I do when I realize I can't win?
Knowing I've given my all through thick and thin.
My heart hurts and my mind can't rest.
After eight years, my results are I didn't pass the test.

It is 12:30 at night and I'm staring at a computer that stares right back at me, words escape me, but this is what I find myself starting to write. It's therapy for me right now. I can't wrap my head around what has happened, and I don't even want to think about my so called friend Noëlle. I never would've thought she was one, if anybody, Malcolm was cheating with. All the times we all spent together, the times I left her here in my house alone with him, the many times we've gone out as couples, laughing, having the times of our lives. To think about how I was actually trying to hook her up with some of Malcolm's friends is mind boggling to me. That would explain why they were never a good fit, or maybe why she just couldn't feel for anybody in particular, I guess not, because she was too busy feeling what and who wasn't hers. I remember once we had the conversation about the forbidden. Wanting what you can't have and my being gullible and naïve I never would've imagined my husband was *the* forbidden fruit.

My mental wants to replay the DVD, but the physical is telling me to throw it as far as I can in the Hudson River.

Hopefully, sometime tonight I can drift off to sleep. My mind is flooded with so many things until my head is hurting uncontrollably. This seems like an out of body experience I've heard people talk about, but never thought it was real. Having to feel like this is not something I would wish on my worse enemy.

Chapter Nine
Victoria

wake this morning, take my horse of a prenatal pill; perform my daily routines and then its breakfast for baby and me.

Being that I'm not quite showing yet, I step inside of my closet in search of an outfit that I can still wiggle my hips into, and at the same time one that will still keep me on the top of this week's Best Dressed List. Amazingly, I come across a cute coral and black tunic dress that I can wear post-pregnancy, if need be. I shower, pull my hair back, slide my dress on and throw on a fierce pair of black Burberry sandals, spray on the Chanel #5, grab my bags, and head to the car.

It's a beautiful day outside; the sun is shining ever so brightly. I've never seen the sky as blue as it is today. Not a cloud in the sky. All is calm, even the usual hectic traffic seems as if it has come to a screeching halt. All I can think about is the results of my entire test. I've prayed so hard that I don't even think I can pray any harder to God.

Lucy calls to let me know he and momma are on the way, he's always been an early bird and if I know him, he didn't sleep last night either. I didn't want to tell momma but I would have preferred Daddy come with me, right now he hates Malcolm just as much as I do. Momma keeps saying, "God says we should forgive those that have spitefully misused us." That sounds good and all, but I don't think I have much of a forgiving heart. That turning the other cheek thing just isn't me, I'm more like eye for an eye, tooth for a tooth, now that's more like it.

We're here and its quiet, which is out of the norm, the sweet little receptionist is away from the desk. I never paid much attention to the pictures on the wall, nor have I ever cared so much for the office aesthetic appeal. Never really mattered I guess. Just sitting here waiting and anticipating is driving me insane and I can say the same for momma. She's trying to act as if nothing's wrong, and all is well, but I know she's tripping on the inside, scared to death. And poor Lucy, look at him, if the boy could just drop dead for a little while he would. One thing does take my mind off of things though, is that there is a lady here in a pair of hideous five inch stilettos, with the most unattractive toes ever. I know her feet are hurting, because looks like she has blisters on the toes. The price we women pay for beauty.

The nurse calls me back and I take one last breather before I come face to face with what can be described as the worst day of my life.

It's Wednesday July 10th, 11:24 am, and the look on Dr. Lewis' face leaves much to be desired. She asks me to take a seat in her office along with the nurse and a Social Worker. She's begins to talk about things I'm not familiar with, she says something about T cells, and ask me have I ever heard of this, and of course I say no. She proceeds to break down the results, but none of it makes any sense, and at this time she says according to my results I am HIV positive! WHAT!!!!! I glance at the Social Worker and she has tears streaming down her face, in which I'm not understanding this, because if I'm not mistaken she's the one that should be comforting me, and oddly enough she can't stop crying. All I can hear are those words that change my whole everything. She can't be telling me this! I cry out, "Why me Lord! What did I do to deserve this? I was faithful to my husband; I did most of the things you asked of me. Why?!!" I'm wailing from the depths of my belly, this can't be real …

I'm both cold and hot at the same time, I know people are around me, but I feel sooooo alone, I can't feel anything. I'm numb. I hear my heart beating louder than ever. I take small fast breaths as the nurse tries to calm me. The room is going round and round. Everything is dark, I had this same feeling when I saw that DVD! Oh my God, it's happening again! My fingers are tingling and I'm sweating profusely. I actually feel like I want to throw up. I want to throw up everything, every part of me; they hurry to take my blood pressure, in fear that I will harm the baby. The nurse ask if it is okay that they bring my mother in, and I give them the best nod yes that I can, at the same time the nurse is trying to explain to my mother what's going on, now she's freaking out. Dr. Lewis is breaking down the lab values to my mother, as if she understands anything she's saying. All she knows is her baby is hurting and there is nothing she can do. Feels like an hour has gone by, but they somehow succeed to calm me, but I'm soon reminded of just how my life will never be the same.

The doctor is calling out medicines like AZT; she mentions another medicine called Combivir, which she says, is a combination of AZT and another drug called Epivir. All of this is just too overwhelming. She goes on to say there are other drug choices, but because I'm pregnant a drug named Sustiva is not even an option. I can't focus on any of this, and there is no way I can take this medicine. It seems like I will be taking medicine all day, several times a day, I can't do it, I totally refuse.

She refers me to another physician that she says can better manage this. I've never even heard of an Infectious Disease doctor. Who knew that a few months ago I was wondering if Lucy had it, but it was me all the time. I'm the one that has been given the death sentence. This isn't fair to my child, how can I subject a baby to this? This baby did not ask to be here, nevertheless suffer from a disease given from its mother by way of a LYING, CHEATING FATHER! I must make a choice. I know if I have it so does my baby. I hope one day I will be able to live with myself.

We leave headed towards home, the car is so quiet, Lucy doesn't say a word, momma's trying to hold back her tears; she's always tried to be the strong one. Cell phones are buzzing like crazy, I know its Daddy wanting to know what's going on. It's funny, but when I left to come here the sky was so clear, now I'm looking out of the window, head pressed against a cold piece of glass, blinded by drops of rain. God did you already know this was going to happen? You must have, you sent the rain to go along with the clouds over my head.

When I realize that I'm home, I began to look around at the memories that remind me of a once happy marriage. I still have not been able to bring myself to taking down those wedding pictures, the ones where family and friends share in our happiness, although one day in one of my rages I somehow took my anger out on the beautiful black and white of me that gave me a flashback of how much time and energy I put into making myself beautiful for the *pre-wedding photo shoot ... WHATEVER!*

Momma and Lucy must've left because there are no signs of holy water, anointment oil, or joy juice in sight. Seems like I've been asleep for sometime now, and for some odd reason I keep having this dream. I keep having this dream where I'm standing in front of Jesus and it's judgment day, he begins to tell me of all the things I've ever done wrong. To my knowledge I thought I was a pretty good Christian, but listening at some of the things he calls out begins to make me scared, the list grows longer and longer, and the more he reads the farther I get away from him. It begins to get hot, I feel a sudden heat wave around me, and then out of nowhere appears Lucifer. He looks the way I've always pictured him,

UGLY!, but something's different about him, he has younger Lucifer's with him, all dressed in black, and they're carrying these outrageous picket signs with expressions like "HIV got ya!", "You got It", "Take Her Out," and I look up, and there's a baby on the floor crawling dressed in white, but his sign says "YOU KILLED ME!" I wake in a sweat praying this is not my life.

My throats so dry I can drink this entire pitcher of water. I don't think I'm crazy, but I know I hear a faint knock at the door. I knew it wouldn't be long before Lucy came back, he's been acting like my guardian slash bodyguard, feels like we're stuck at the hips. I hate to admit it, but I really don't want to be alone, I don't think I can keep having these strange dreams, because every time I close my eyes I'm freaking out, I'm scared I'll be faced with my biggest fear. Dying!

I guessed it right; it's Lucy at the door with enough luggage to stay forever. He must know that I don't want to be here by myself.

"Diamond, I'm back sweetness."

"Well I can see that, looks like you never plan to leave."

"No honey it's not that, just can't let my sister be alone tonight."

"Looks as if I've been alone for a long time now."

"Now don't go there suga, you ain't never been alone. I've always been here, and I ain't going nowhere."

He is dropping things in the middle of the floor, not even taking a minute to look down, and he's going back to the car for more. I didn't realize this boy had so many clothes, I guess that's one of the benefits of being a personal shopper; you get first dibs on the good stuff. His M-A-C caddy is better than mine.

Before I know it, Julian is walking through the door with bags in hand, does Lucy have THAT MANY things?

"Before you ask Vic, these are my things." He says.

"Hold up, what's going on? Why is everybody barging their way in here tonight, I can understand Lucy, but ..."

"So what about me, I'm your real brother."

"That's true but ..."

"So I'm not good enough to stay over?"

"It's not that, it's just ..."

"Just what?"

All the while we're having this conversation; I can't believe I'm seeing this, it's MOMMA and DADDY! What the ... I ask, "Did Lucy go and recruit the whole family?"

"Sure did," Lucy says.

"And why?" I ask.

They all say it's because they love me, and there is noooo way they would never let me be here tonight alone. It's so hard for me to not think about the word alone, because no matter what, its how I feel. The whole time I've been married, my husband has never loved me just for me, apparently it's always been someone else. So as I say, I'm alone, I've been in this marriage all by myself. And look what it has gotten me. Once again, I find myself with tears running down my face.

Out of nowhere, my daddy comes over and hugs me, as if he had not seen me since I was a little girl, he looks as if he has just seen a ghost. Like his little girl is gone far away. Suddenly I break down into tears, I can see my mother trying to hold herself together, and unbelievably Julian is shedding tears as well, but my Lucy shouts out and says, "Look we didn't come over here for a pity party, we came to be with her, help get her mind off of this." Daddy gives him a look that says, boy if you don't back up off of me … And he does. I try with all I have inside of me to get it together so that this will not be a night of sadness, because I don't want to feel bad, I want to feel the way I felt before all of this happened to me.

Walking to the kitchen, I notice my father has a bag stashed with old home movies, resembling the ones when I was growing up. Oh my goodness, I hope he's not planning on going down memory lane, I don't think I can handle that right now, but if I know Daddy he will insist, it's something he used to love to do anyway, he said it made him appreciate life even more.

Momma's already getting the popcorn ready, it's been so long since I smelled the aroma of popcorn in this house, Malcolm never liked it, so I eventually decided that it was no need to have it since it made him sick. But if he was here right now though, I would crank up a whole popcorn machine, like the one at the movie theatres. It's a shame I'm in such a revenge mode. I know I shouldn't say this, but I HATE him. I never thought I would feel this way about my husband, but I do. I can't believe he did this to me. If I had grown up in Marcy I would be playing that Jazmine Sullivan joint, "*Bust the Windows Out your Car!*" Too bad I didn't, because a brother would be messed up by now.

"Diamond, do you remember when we recorded this?" Daddy asks.

In the back of my mind I'm saying no, but I know better so I say the next best thing.

"Yes sir."

Julian is over there laughing as if he was the one holding the camera.

He says, "Vic, you were headstrong even back then."

"And what does that mean?"

"It means you didn't take any mess."

"You got that from your father." My mother says.

"That's right." says daddy.

But why does it seem like I've been played, it looks like I let him walk all over me, but I didn't, all I wanted was for him to love me, and ONLY me, I never thought it would turn out like this.

My family is trying so hard to make me feel better but it's not working, I can't stop thinking about my life, and what lies ahead. It's just 10:45 pm, and I'm still afraid to go to sleep. Daddy shows one last video, and this is the one that I remember most of all. I was twelve years old, and I was first runner up in the school pageant. They asked me what my idea of my dream job was, of course I said; my dream job is to have my own company. It's funny how some things never change. I never looked at it that way, but I have always been obsessed with the idea of having my own.

I look around the house and catch a glimpse of the picture Noëlle and I took in Cabo San Lucas on one of our vacations. I can't seem to bring myself to take it down either; it's a reminder when everything was good. Lucy constantly asks me why do I still have it up, but I tell him in some strange way it helps me. But even in my own mind I wonder what am I thinking. She probably was in love with Malcolm then, and look at her cheesing as if she was really my best friend. Yeah right.

We finally decide to call it a night at 1:00 in the morning. I can tell Julian is worn out, but I thank him for being here with me, we had a good time tonight, like when were young, only that I know we are not those children we were back then, we're all grown now. If I could only turn back the hands of time.

Daddy insists on tucking me in like he used to when I was younger. He comes in just as I am getting in the bed, sits on the side of the bed, turns down the lights, and leans over me, and says to me he will always love me, there is nothing I could ever do to make him stop loving me. I hold back the tears, but they force their way again.

"Daddy, why did this happen to me?"

"Baby girl, first you must know you did nothing wrong."

"I never would have done this to him."

"I know that baby, but sometimes we have to suffer things for reasons unknown, only God knows what's in store for us."

"Why do I feel as though this is punishment from God?"

"God chastises us, but He doesn't punish us. He loves us unconditionally, in spite of all the things we do to hurt him."

"But daddy, I've always tried to do the right thing."

"I know baby, but we can't question God about he way He chooses to go about things, we only have to accept and believe that He loves us, and He will never put more on us that we can bear."

"But daddy."

"Shhhh, you are my Diamond, and you are the greatest gift that I've ever had, besides your mother."

"Thank you daddy, but I can't understand why if I did everything right, God chose to give me HIV, if He loved me, he wouldn't have done this to me. The same with Malcolm, if he truly loved me, he would have never put me at risk like this."

"I can't speak for Malcolm, but I do know, that ever since you were a little girl, you were destined to be something special."

"I don't feel special, right now I feel like the lowest person on this earth. This wasn't supposed to happen to me."

"You're right sweetheart, but I know God is going to see us through this, and you will come out of this better than ever."

He kisses me on my forehead, and turns to leave, but I stop him to ask, "Would you have felt the same if this was Julian?"

He turns to tell me, "You are both my children, no matter what, I will love you the same. You both are apart of me."

Just when I think I'm asleep, my mother comes in and asks if it is okay that she sleeps with me. There is no way I can turn her down, believe it or not, it's the one thing I know for sure, yes I want my mother here with me. She lies with me, holds me, and shields me through the night, helps fight off the boogieman, who keeps invading my dreams.

I woke only twice through the night. Each time I looked over at momma she had this look on her face as if she was protecting her newborn infant so many years ago. I sometimes wonder how often she thinks about Miles, now that's hilarious, because I 'm quite sure I will be joining him sooner than I had expected. Just the other night, I caught a peek of one of those HBO specials where they were talking about it, and how many people have survived, I'm sure that's all to get the people like me who's newly diagnosed hopes up just to tear them down.

You can tell daddy is up and at it, because I'm greeted with the pleasant smells of couch-couche, and his famous ham and egg soufflé. Julian is still not up and it's already eight o'clock, he was never a night hawk, I could tell last night he was barely hanging on. And there's no doubt that Lucy is in the kitchen aggravating him to death trying his hardest to get his hands on his recipes; yes daddy's threatening to beat him if he as much comes within a square foot of him.

I always looked forward to getting up on Saturdays. There was just no other day like it, no school or homework, just a day of fun, except later that afternoon is what I dreaded; the almost 2 hours of getting my hair washed, combed, and platted, just so Ms. Genevieve could hot comb my brains, at least that's what it felt like. No matter what else was going on, every Saturday at 3:00 p.m., there momma was calling for me to come inside for the weekly ritual. There were days where I just wanted to cut it all off.

My cell phone and my house phone are ringing; I miss all the calls, maybe they'll call back. Before I can say it, my cell rings again and I so know who it is, of all days she wants to decide to reach out and touch. Should I or should I not? Okay, I do.

As to not alarm anyone here I quietly answer the phone.

"Good morning."

"Hi Victoria, can you talk?"

The voice on the other ends sounds like death! Maybe it has come to knock on her door as well.

"Yeah what's up?"

I head into my bedroom where no one can hear me, because more than likely this is not going to be good.

"I don't know where to start, so I guess I'll start by saying I didn't mean for things to turn out like this."

"Well I bet you didn't."

"I haven't had the courage to come to you and talk to you about what's happened."

"It's all good."

"No it's not; I've destroyed our friendship—"

"Let me stop you there, we are not friends now, nor have we ever been and nor will we ever be."

"Victoria listen—"

"Girl look, there is nothing you and I have to say to each other."

"Yes it is, there's a lot we have to say. I feel both of us have been caught up."

If I didn't know any better I would think this chick has lost her everlasting mind.

"Noëlle, you did the most unforgivable thing to me. I would never have expected YOU, of all people, my best friend. You even went as far as to say you loved me, we were thick as thieves, but this is what you did to me, you and Malcolm deserve each other."

"There is no me and Malcolm, this is why I want to talk to you."

"Aren't you talking now, spit it out."

There is a silence on the phone, and it sounds as if she's talking to someone else.

"Hello."

"I'm here, but I was talking with my nurse. She was going over some other information that I need."

I can't help it, but I ask, because I don't think it's fair that I go through this by myself, I want someone else to suffer just like me, might as well be her.

"What are you sick? Oh my ..."

She gets quiet again.

"Victoria, I really would like to talk to you face to face."

"Why are you doing this? Haven't you done enough?"

"Victoria, please."

Daddy is calling both Julian and I to come and eat, and there is no way I would dare let him or Lucy know who I'm talking to. I rush her off the phone; tell her I will see her later in another life. All I hear is, "Can we meet somewhere?" I hang up.

By the time I make it to the table momma can tell there is something wrong with me. Lucy has set the table about as pretty as the Four Seasons without all the fru-fru stuff.

Momma asks do I mind if she has invited someone over for breakfast, and I'm like first of all this isn't even her house. Lord if it's the Pastor I'm going to scream!

I had better get to screaming. Now here it is almost 10:00 a.m. on a Saturday morning, what business does Pastor Michael's have, especially at my house, and isn't it a sermon he needs to be preparing for? I so graciously welcome him in. Daddy sets another place for him. I know this was already planned. Here I am in my around the house clothes, momma in her not so ready for the outside world clothes, daddy in his usual morning attire, Julian in an old pair of jeans and a white t-shirt, and Lucy, my sweet Lucy, the marvelous host, is all dressed up as if he was about to be photographed my Nigel Barker. I guess it's true what they say, a DIVA must never be caught off guard, should be ready at all times.

He sits down hungry I suppose, and the first thing he says is…

"This is the day that the Lord has made, we will rejoice and be glad in it."

All you hear is momma and daddy in the amen corner. The last time I remember having the Pastor at our table was when he was trying so hard to recruit daddy into becoming a trustee. As far as I know of it must've worked, because when I went to church this last time daddy's name was plastered all over the order of service.

"So how are things with you and that baby, Sister Cartiér?"

Ugh! I never thought that name would make me so sick to my stomach.

"Everything is good Pastor, and you?"

This is so uncomfortable. I can't believe momma did this to me.

"All is well in the land of the living; you know I'm blessed and highly favored, I'm the head and not the tail, and I'm more than a conqueror."

All I did was ask him how he was doing, and I'm getting a mini sermon.

"And you, Brother and Sister Jean-Pierre?"

"Absolutely wonderful Pastor."

I don't hear Julian saying anything; he probably hasn't been to church since well before I have.

"I know you're doing pretty good yourself Mr. Jean-Pierre."

"As a matter of a fact Pastor, I am." Julian says.

I swallow because it's like a frog is in my throat.

"Good Morning Passa."

Lucy is crazy; I knew any minute he was going to put his two cents in.

Julian goes on to say, "I really enjoyed last weeks message, it helped me so much."

Okay, what is this a make Victoria feel bad moment?

By the time we've all finished I notice everyone putting away the dishes, and I'm left with the Pastor, I frantically start putting away any and everything that doesn't reflect a Godly household. He asks if he can have a seat on the couch, and I tell him no problem, although I'm scrambling to make sure that I don't accidentally hit the play button for the CD to start bumping sounds of Bone Thugs and Harmony. Every now and then a girl has got to have her Rough Rider music. Once upon a time, I really could have seen myself as being someone's as they say, "ride or die chick," but not anymore. I don't ever see myself being in love ever again. Life for me, as we know it, is OVER.

It's a good thing that this is a big enough house for the whole family, seems as though they've all disappeared. It's a set up ...

"This is a lovely home Sister Cartiér."

"Thank you Pastor."

"You're welcome."

"At first I thought it was a bad idea your being here, but it's kinda nice."

"So you don't mind having a stuffy old Pastor in your house."

"Actually no, I don't mind."

"I believe I mentioned how excited I was about your promotion at the last service."

"Yes sir, you did, but thank you just the same."

"The thought ran across my mind to talk with you about being the church's official planner."

"Wow, now that's an honor."

"Yes, we are in the process of revamping some things at the church, and it's my desire we are represented by a reputable firm such as yours."

"That sounds like a great opportunity, and thank you again for thinking of us."

"No problem, I'm just blessed to be amongst people in our congregation that we can utilize to that degree."

"I'm glad to help out in any way I can."

"Thank you."

"So, is that the only reason you graced us with your presence this morning?"

I'm laughing so hard on the inside it's not funny. I know good and well he came over here to see how long I have left, as if momma has not already told him what's going on. He shifts on the sofa, and pauses.

"To be exact, no that's not the only reason for my visit. One reason is that you've been on my mind lately; I recognize you're not as active as you used to be. Neither you nor Mr. Cartiér have been in a while. Really miss you in the services."

"Well ..."

"Yeah, I know you've got a lot going on, busy with the everyday stressors of the world, that you just can't make time for God. Remember your job is not your source, God is your source, and He is the source behind all of your resources. Like I always say don't ever get too big for God."

"Well Pastor I wouldn't say I was too busy, it's more like I've become comfortable. When Malcolm ... and I ... aahm"

"Go ahead."

"Well, we previously decided we were going to change things around and start coming more often."

"Then what happened?"

"A lot happened, Pastor."

"No one died did they, because that's the only thing I could think of and even then you're still going to have to come that way."

"Malcolm and I are separated Pastor."

By the look on his face he looks rather shocked to me, but you can't tell, that just could be the "oh didn't know that" preacher look.

"Have you seeked Christian counseling?"

"Don't think that's going to help."

"Have you tried?"

"Honestly, no."

"You do still love each other?"

"Well I can't say for him, but as for me ..."

"Do you even want to work it out? You realize there is a baby involved in this equation."

"I don't think we can make it work Pastor; there is too much hurt, and anger there, at least for me."

"What could be that bad, that you feel God can't work it out?"

I hesitate, take a deep breath, ponder if this is something I'm ready to share, but against my first instinct it rolls off my tongue.

"Pastor, it hasn't been 24 hours yet that I've just been told I'm HIV positive."

I immediately expect him to be thrown completely off guard, instead he doesn't blink, he continues.

"Is that the worse thing in the world?"

"Yes, to me it is."

"Like I stated earlier, you're in the land of the living aren't you? That's reason enough to praise God right there. There are many that didn't wake to see this day, and God has allowed you to wake and see the dawning of a new day."

It's strange I never pictured having this conversation with anyone let alone my Pastor, and he doesn't seem to sweat it one bit.

"Pastor, I thank you for being so understanding, but I'm really not in a good place right now. There are so many things going through me head, I'm angry, confused, ashamed, embarrassed, all at the same time, and I know momma already told you what's going on."

"Sister Cartiér, one thing I will say is your mother hasn't told me anything of that nature, she just felt it would be good for us to fellowship and your house just happened to be the place."

"Do you mind if I ask a question?"

"No, go right ahead."

"Does God approve of divorce?"

"Sister Cartiér, God does not condone divorce, particularly between two Christians, but He does allow it under certain circumstances, the first being adultery, where there has been unfaithfulness on the part of a spouse in a marriage. And keep in mind, God does not command it, He only allows it. The next being where there is an unequally yoked relationship, where one spouse is a believer and the other one isn't, but it is also commanded to stay in this relationship unless the other one leaves. Does this help you?"

"More than you will ever know. Thank you Pastor."

"You're welcome, but I will also say before you do anything you may regret make sure you have prayed about it, and have made peace with it. God bless you my Sister, and no matter what, God loves you, and so do I."

I sit here staring at a blank wall trying to decide my future, not sure of what lies ahead, but one thing I am sure of, the last chapter will not read *... and they lived happily ever after.*

After everyone leaves I crawl in the bed, get under the covers, roll over and find a pen, before I know it I'm doodling names for my baby.

Zora
Ashby
Rylee   CARTIÉR
Marley
Gabrielle
Faren

All of these are nice but only one really jumps out at me. Just wished the last name was different.

Chapter Ten
Malcolm & Victoria

Three months later ... I can't believe today my divorce is final. Thanks to help of Julian and Reese. I'm surprised Malcolm didn't give me any problems, no hassle, although I haven't heard much from him since that night. He called to see how I was, but of course I didn't want to talk; to be honest I could care less what happens to him at this point. If I'm not mistaken Noëlle tried to call me at my office the other day, but Melissa intercepted the call thank goodness. Now is not a good time.

The Social Worker called to check on me, I told her I was fine, although I don't know what fine is anymore. Everyone is calling, especially daddy; he hasn't taken it too well. As bad as I want to, I want to go shopping, but I'm just not in that place to do any of the things I used to love. I'll just be glad when, if ever, I get back to my old self.

I still can't believe it's a girl, imagine that. I haven't thought of a name for her yet, but I'm sure before long something will come to mind. It's been so hard developing a bond with her, I hope she doesn't know how hard of a time her mother has been having. This is why I try and remember to take the meds right because I don't want to take any chances that she will have it. I couldn't live with myself.

Momma calls, and I need to talk to her, because I've been avoiding her for the past week. There are days when I don't feel like talking to anybody, I just want to go to work do my job, get it over, and come home and get under the covers. Lately, I feel like I'm putting on the face that the world wants to see, as the saying goes, "you see my glory, but you don't know my story." If only they knew.

"Baby, are you okay?"

"Yes, momma I'm fine."

"And the baby?"

"She's fine too."

"Victoria, you know I'm here if you need me."

"Yes, I know momma."

"What about your medicines? Have you taken them like you're supposed to?"

"Yes momma, I've taken the medicines, if not for myself, for the baby. I've got the routine down, Combivir in the morning and again at night; Reyataz, I only take once a day, and the Norvir, I take it once a day as well."

"You know I talked to Pastor Michaels this morning."

"Momma please, not another person you've talked to and most definitely not the Pastor. I just don't feel like hearing all that God loves you, and he knows what's best for you speech. I appreciate him coming to the house, but I still want to hate Malcolm, and it may take a while before I get over that. You know today it's final, didn't take long at all. I kept most of everything; the only thing he really wanted was his car. He can have that extra bill.

"How do you feel?"

"I'm okay, better than I thought I would be. I'm glad it's over. I just hope God can forgive me, although he's the one that has allowed this to be. And momma please don't have the Pastor call me or anything like that, I'm not in the mood for a heart to heart.

"Baby, I'm only trying to help."

"I know, but momma you can't help me, no one can. I have HIV and thats it."

"Victoria that's not it!"

I know she only wants what's best for me, but I'm not ready to talk about this as if everything is going to be fine. It's not going to be fine. I'm HIV positive with a baby on the way. She has all but frustrated me; I make up some silly excuse to get her off the phone.

For some reason I thought I'd feel more like celebrating my emancipation, but I don't. I only want to lie down and wish this day would be over. Any other time I'd whip myself up a mojito, but not this time; it's plenty of water for me these days.

I burn the last pictures that the PI gave me of Malcolm and Noëlle, its strange how at first I couldn't see the signs; they were right under my nose. Soon after the DVD I found e-mails on the computer that he had undoubtedly forgotten to erase. All that time I had access to his account, but never wished to use it, in fear of what I would find, but even he wasn't smart enough to delete the content of his secret rendezvous, but now everything is clear. Noëlle had this planned from the beginning, but I'm guessing she didn't think this would be the outcome. I can see it now, headlines read: *CEO of record label diagnosed HIV Positive resulting from an affair with best friend's husband*. Wonder if she'll make a blog about that, or better yet, if she'll tweet about it. I know I'm supposed to forgive, do the "Christian thing," but right now I hope she gets everything that's coming to her and more. Maybe I should call Lucy, then we can have a Everyone Hates Noëlle party, I know he'll love that.

I'm glad that the nausea has subsided, but this little girl is really doing a move on me. I'm not sure, but when I was looking through old pictures of Malcolm and me, right before they became fiery pieces of Kodak paper, I believe I felt her move. It's unbelievable, a feeling that I can't even explain. I always imagined me being pregnant with my husband by my side every step of the way, and never in a million years did I think I would going through ... everytime I think about it, I find my self crying. I'm crying all of the time, even when I look at my growing belly I cry, and this should be the happiest time of my life. It's not that I don't love my baby, although when the doctor first told me I was infected, my first thought was to ... Oh my goodness, just the thought of THAT makes me cry. I don't believe I even considered the thought of not bringing my baby girl into this world, but so many things were going through my head. Even now I wonder what if—my doctor has reassured me that as long as I continue to take my meds, it's a good chance my baby won't have it. It's just the medicines I'm getting used to.

The doorbell rings and something inside tells me to ask who is it, in which a faint raspy voice says "Me". My initial reaction is who can this possibly be at a time like this? I slowly pull open the door and to my dismay it is the last person I would want to see right now. It's Malcolm, and he's standing here in front of me as if he has spent his last days under a rock. I guess the saying is true that people can really look like they crawled from under a rock, and right now he is making that statement seem way underrated. I have never seen Malcolm look this bad. There are dark spots under his eyes, he's smelly, his lids are swollen, face ashen, skin ugly and dry, lips chapped, just a hot mess!

"Hello, Victoria."

At first I'm speechless, because I can't get over this figure standing in front of me.

Nastily, I say, "Hello."

"May I come in?"

The ugly side of me wants him to stay out in that hard and ruthless world he's been in, but another part of me wants him to come inside so I can hide him from any neighbors walking that might mistaken him for a broken down robber.

"Victoria, can we talk?"

"About?"

The depth of my anger towards him scares me. He's about as bad as my worse enemy. Didn't think I could dislike someone so much, except Noëlle, now she's another story.

"I've been trying to find the words to come up with to explain—"

"Explain what Malcolm, you cheated with another woman, and here we are."

"No, I need to let you know—"

"You don't owe me anything, today is satisfaction enough for me, today I'm totally free from you, no more lies, no more disappointments."

"Vic, please let me get this off of my chest."

Everything inside of me wants to knock the last breath out of him, but I'm scared that he looks so bad that if I hit him it'll just take him out.

He continues, "How are you and the baby?"

Now this boy has the unmitigated gall to come in here and ask me that.

"It's a fine time to ask that don't you think, as far as we can tell you don't care and never did."

"Victoria please don't think I never loved you, I always have and always will."

Who does he think I am? Not this time.

Standing in the middle of the foyer I curtly say, "Malcolm get on with it, I really don't feel well, and I believe we have said all we needed to say in the divorce decree."

"Vic, I don't know what to do, I thought I could handle this, I thought if I set you free, then you could go on and live your life."

"What life! You've taken whatever life I had away from me. You put our unborn child in harms way."

"Vic, I'm sorry."

"That you are."

"Okay, I accept that."

"Please say what you came here to say."

"I know there are no words that can ever make you trust me, or even like me again, but I want you know that I never meant to hurt you. It all started out as fun, I saw a way to do those things and I did. I felt if you didn't know, it couldn't hurt you, so once I realized it, I was too far gone."

My heart really needs to hear this but my head wants me to get him out of here, but somewhere in my soul I feel the need to listen to what he has to say. Therefore I ask him to sit down, and then I switch the player to Coltrane number 6, because this is going to be a rough night and I need the smooth sounds of *"Naima"* to hypnotize my mind. As I listen to him do his thing as he did it so well, I breathe and take in the bluesy, melodic, yet romantic tune that is paired, coupled as a perfect pair, sort of like a marriage. Ironic huh? A perfect marriage. Please, give me a break. Today is evident that there is no perfect marriage.

"Vic, how are you feeling?" the oppressor asks.

"Well I'm doing just peachy cream Malcolm, and you?"

He pauses, looks down at the floor, as if to say I deserve that.

"How's the baby?"

"The baby's good too. She's going to be just fine, in spite of."

The look of shame crosses his face.

Disgusted I ask, "Malcolm, why are you really here, isn't there some other women that you could be infecting right about now?"

He looks up at me as if he has lost a friend from way back when.

"Victoria, I've been to the doctor, they have decided a regimen for me, and they have reassured me that if I do what I'm supposed to, then I can reach undetectable status."

"Yeah they've told me that too, but I still feel it's a bunch of crap, especially because I'm taking THREE different meds Malcolm."

"Vic, do you mind if I ask what are you on?"

I'm saying to myself, SELF, now why does this dude even care what medicines you're taking, he needs to be worrying about himself.

Sharply, I ask, "And why do you care?"

"Vic, regardless of how you feel about me, I will always care for you."

Then for one minute this place in my heart travels back in time, where I like him, where he was my friend, and I find it to delve into his life for this time.

"I'll act as if I didn't hear that but ... because of the baby, YOUR baby, I have been put on Combivir, Reyataz and Norvir, and because Reyataz leaves stomach acid, when I take an antacid, I have to take it two hours apart."

As hard as it is for me to do this, I go ahead and ask.

"So what about you Malcolm, what are you taking?"

I really hate to do this.

"They've got me on Atripla, it's a once a day dose, so far it's been pretty good, I haven't had any major side effects, although the first couple of weeks I had the usual nausea, vomiting, and of course the diarrhea. But I'm good now. What about you? Is the baby adjusting well to the meds?"

"Yes, same here, but I had the same little things too, I guess you can say side effects. It was hard for me to tell at first with the nausea, because of the baby, I wasn't sure if it was just being pregnant or was it really the medicine."

By this time the sounds shift to *"Every Time We Say Goodbye."* That Coltrane is a bad boy, and the way Reggie works those keys, magical. Just takes me to this place, a place where I feel so free. I grew up listening to Jazz; at that time I would go and hide from the rest of the world. Daddy taught me all about it, it's all inside of me, and every time I run from it, it finds its way back to me. It was never Malcolm's cup of tea; he was always more of an R&B lover.

Although Malcolm is my truest nemesis, something in me still wants to know how bad off he is, I guess somewhere in my heart there will always be a place for him.

I hesitate for a while. Not sure what else to expect. He breaks my thought, tries to find me in that space, and begins to tell me what I so want to, but really don't want to hear.

He says, "Victoria, the day the video came, everything inside of me was lost. I couldn't believe that I had been subject to the most feared disease. Me, Malcolm Cartiér, this couldn't be true. It took me about a week to get my thoughts together, especially when you wouldn't take any of my calls. Then I decided to go in and get tested, of course the screen and the Western Blot were positive. Once I found out, my T cell count was 225 and my viral load was 150,000. After three to four weeks of waiting for the results of the genotype in which it showed no resistance, they decided to put me on Atripla. I will say at first, I was reluctant, because I was afraid, and I'm still afraid, I guess I will remain afraid. Every 3-6 months I have to go and get my labs rechecked, prayerfully, next time my values would've increased."

I look into his eyes and I no longer see the laughter of a man who so once upon a time, seemed to have everything at his feet.

He continues, "Victoria, I'm going to beat this thing, I'm not going to let it get the best of me, but I will tell you this, I feel I owe it to you. The day the video was playing, so that you will always know this; I was coming home to tell you I wanted a fresh new start, I had decided to put all of those things behind me. I didn't want to hurt you anymore. I had made up in my mind, finally I was going to do right, and I was going to be the husband you needed me to be."

I interrupt him, and say, "It's too late now!" He never stops, he finishes his thought.

"Everything that has happened to me, I deserve it ... I've hurt so many people, mainly I've put my unborn child in harms way."

He reaches over to place his hand on my stomach, and I hurriedly push him away. I can't allow him this. He gets a whiff of my hurt and despair. Yet he still goes on ...

"Vic, you were right, yes I know God, I've known him all along, but I was determined I was going to do my own thing. It all happened over time, the affairs ... they started off very innocent, and I didn't plan for anything like this to happen."

Has he and that so called human being Noëlle prepared the same speech for me? It's sounding real familiar here.

He places both of his hands on his head, and takes a breath, I don't believe that he's trying to explain this to me now of all days. Today I'm a free woman; I've been set free of all of this. Does he not know what today is?

He's relentless, he keeps it coming ...

"I knew God was going to catch up with me one day, I felt it. He was going to do something to make me believe that I wasn't in this thing by myself. You tried so many times to get me to see that, but I guess I was too caught up."

I can't believe I'm asking this, but I can't help myself.

"Malcolm, why did you have to tell them you loved them?"

"Vic, this may sound sick, but I really thought I did."

"But how..."

At this moment I loose my composure, and the ruthless Victoria rears her ugly head.

"How can you love, not one, not two, maybe not three or four women at the same time, who do you think you are?"

"Vic, wait!"

"No you wait. I've heard enough!"

He reaches out to grab me to pull me close, but I pull away.

"Vic, I love you!"

No he didn't. After all of this he still manages to fix his mouth to say those words, I thought I asked him not to say that to me.

"There's no way you can love me, you don't even love yourself."

"No, that's where you're wrong ... I do love my self, and I give thanks to you for that."

HERE IT GOES ...

"Vic, I've been going to church."

I clap my hands to the beat of the music, and say, "Well good for you!

At least somebody sees the good in HIM, because I see none! If He was this PERFECT JESUS then why ... why would He do this to me?"

I lose it, I'm screaming and yelling to the point I want to hurt him. I want to make Malcolm feel the pain he's made me feel. I stop for a minute, take a look at my growing stomach, and then I look at him; he's crying. WHAT FOR? HE HURT ME!

"Malcolm please leave, I can't handle this."

"Victoria, today is the day our marriage is over as it says to the legal system, NO, I didn't pressure you, because I want what's best for you and the baby, and I realize that I can no longer give you that, but ... how can you say those things about GOD?"

"Why not?"

"Vic, listen to yourself, why are you saying these things?"

"Don't you get it, for me life is over. I will never be the same, no one will ever love me, no one will ever want me. I'm no longer a woman anymore, you've taken that from me, and your GOD has allowed this to be. I hate you and I hate HIM!"

He stops in his steps, as if He can't believe I've just said something like that.

"Malcolm you not only cheated on me, but you cheated on me with my best friend, so I thought."

This is when he says the stupidest thing ever.

"Vic, that meant nothing to me. That was something to do. Every time I've ever gone out and committed adultery, it was not that I didn't love you; it was because I felt I could. This is why I made the choice to stop, stop trying to be the man, and become a man. I just regret that it has cost me my life and my family."

"You said that right, but you don't have to worry about that anymore, we are no longer your responsibility, and you got a death pass on that."

I amuse my self; suddenly I burst out in laughter, because for once I realize that there is a chance we all are going to die …

"Furthermore, Vic, if there is one thing that Lucy was right about, it was the fact that Noëlle never cared for you. She never told you that we were together in college before you, did she?"

I stumble, although I will not give him the benefit of the doubt, and say, "Yeah she told me." Why am I lying to protect her, that's all she did to me was lie to me. She's on my list too. Lucy never trusted her from day one, said she looked cock-eyed, and somebody who had funny eyes couldn't be trusted. Sneaky she calls 'em amongst other things, but I'd rather not say now. My phone is ringing off the hook, whoever it is will just have to call back.

I say to him in a very nasty tone, "It's funny, you knew she didn't care anything about me, and yet you laid with her time after time. What does that say about you? I hope she dies from this too, that's even if she has it."

I was hoping at this moment he would reveal it to me, and just like a sucker he does.

"She has it too. She's not as bad as me though, but because she's newly infected she doesn't have to take meds."

"Lucky for her. So what about your other love slave? Who is it, Sydney? Oh yeah how can I forget her, she made it plain and clear."

"As far as I know, the last time I talked with her, after the video, she said she was pretty bad off. She actually has full blown AIDS, and then her viral load was in the 750,000 range. She says she chooses not to take meds, so she's just going to ride it out."

"If it wasn't for this baby, I probably would feel the same way. What's the purpose? You're going to die somehow."

Not paying any of attention, the disk has changed and now I'm listening to Fantasia, and Lyfe ask the question, *"Hypothetically."* Fine time for that huh? I immediately push the stop button.

I ask him one last time can we stop this song and dance we're doing, because in all reality none of it matters.

He puts his hands in pockets, sighs, and gives me a tireless "Yes." Then his phone rings, and of all things he has the ring tone, *"Never Would Have Made It."*

Once again I laugh, because I needed that, only for the humor, and I say, "They say when you get in trouble, you find JESUS."

He snaps back and says, "He found ME!" then gathers his keys and heads for the door. Looks back at me, and says, "He will find you too."

Tonight is not like any other night; I still can't go to sleep, because my heart is troubled. I'm fighting with this repulsion I have for Malcolm. It won't go away. This dark side of me will not let me feel for him in any other way but disgust. I'm surprised I stomached him for as long as I did today, it's a good thing I'm pregnant, because I'm sure I would have done something I may have later regretted.

I sit up in the bed, turn on the night lamp, and move the Bible over, only to get to a scratch piece of paper where I can jot down some thoughts. I've never felt like this before, but I feel like the devil and I are partners in crime, and the only thing on my mind is revenge. I want to make those who have hurt me, hurt just the same.

Reasons to Hate Malcolm
   1. He cheated on me.
   2. He gave me HIV.
   3. He had sex with my best friend.
   4. He gave me HIV
   5. He got me pregnant, and left me alone.
   6. He gave me HIV.
Reasons to Hate God
   1. He lied to me, He said he loved me.
   2. He gave me HIV.
   3. I gave Him my heart, I trusted Him.
   4. He gave me HIV.
   5. I loved only Him.
   6. He gave me HIV.

Looks as though they are neck and neck, I trusted both of them and both of them hurt me. Both of them have seen to it that I will not be here to see my daughter grow up. They have taken everything from me, and because of that I will never love again. This is a fine way to celebrate my divorce; with the person I got the divorce from.

Chapter Eleven
Victoria

Lucy has talked me into going to a party in the village tonight. Can't remember the last time I've been out. Need to find the right outfit though, and since I haven't been to Neiman's in a while, I suddenly feel a shopscapade coming on. Being the weather has changed, Fall brings out so much more beautiful clothing, so there should be even much nicer things in the maternity department, and the best thing about this is I can definitely wear some of them again, like the Bolero jackets, they're my favorites.

This will be my first time out as a single woman, got to look fly, but not too fly because I don't want to bring any attention to myself. How would that look? I can picture it now; he says, "Man there was a fine woman in the club tonight, but oh yeah, she was already pregnant, and by the way she's got HIV too!" Now that would be a good start out of the gate, and now that I think about it—don't think it's such a good idea anymore. I'll just call Lucy and get an I-O-U, still not comfortable being in huge crowds right now anyway. The only place I'm at my best is here at the office. When I'm here and in work mode I'm in my element, some days I even forget I'm positive. One good factor is my workload has picked up a lot, and if ever there was a time I needed Melissa, it's now. I'm so grateful to her, she's been such a huge help especially on these days I just can't get it together, where I don't feel like doing anything or being bothered with anyone. It's like my hormones are going crazy, I wake sick as a dog, overly tired, and most of all there's days when I don't feel like putting on the "pretty face". I can count the times Melissa has asked "where's the makeup, are we going Ah-na-tu-ral today?" To me I looked good; at least that's what I tell myself. Like today, my hair is pulled up with wood chopsticks to ensure it's secure, also I've put together a fairly cute ensemble I think; an Asian Kimono wrap dress, with a pair of wedge Jimmy Choo's, cute for a mommy to be, I would say, but I didn't go as heavy as usual on the face, just a little foundation, eyeliner, and of course the clear lipgloss. Gotta have it.

I got an email from Melissa, looks like Mr. Rucker has called an impromptu meeting; wonder what about, we just had a partner's meeting Tuesday morning. He mentioned something about expanding our market to another city, but all the details weren't confirmed as of yet. Lord, I'm so tired I can hardly keep my eyes open, but I wake real quick like when he alerts us to another filthy rich prospect. Her name is Mrs. Delaney Sinclair; she's an heir to the famous Randall Sinclair of Sinclair Architectural and Design. He passed away a few years ago, and she was his only living survivor. They're noted for building some of the most beautiful landmarks from highrises to Hotels and Resorts. Last I checked they were on Forbes' Top 100, not sure of the rank.

Out of nowhere, Mr. Rucker states she exclusively requested that I be her personal planner for her business affairs, as well as her private ones. I'm shocked, happy, but shocked. He goes on to say Mr. Bouviér is partly responsible, because he told her how pleased he was with our firm, so he recommended she use us as well. There's no way I can think of sleeping, I've got so much work to do. Good! Maybe this will keep me busy, busy enough to keep my mind off dying for a while.

Later on in the day I get a call from Mrs. Sinclair. She wants to meet this evening for dinner. Of course I'm up for that, it's been a while since I've eaten at a good restaurant, even though its business, this baby won't know the difference one way or the other. She requested we meet around seven, so that gives me time to get a brief update on her. I have Melissa come in so that we can go over the basics. I love being prepared when I meet with a potential client, there's nothing more I hate worse than not knowing anything about the client, and this is one lady I would like to make a good impression on. I never thought by having Mr. Bouviér as a client would prove to be even more profitable than ever. He really knows a lot of people; a lot of wealthy people that is.

I have the waiter bring me a glass of iced tea while I wait for Mrs. Sinclair to arrive. About fifteen minutes later a gorgeous woman about 6'2", honey skin tone, short cropped haircut, walks in wearing a purple two piece suit with a jeweled neckline, topped off with the most fierce pair of silver metallic peep toe platforms, that are to die for, with the accessories to match. With all that, she can leave the Chanel bag with me. She also has with her a woman around my age that she introduces to me as her daughter. Her name is Zoe; she's actually the president of the corporation. She looks to be a very poised young lady, intelligent, with a kind of wit that would sure turn you off if you were not use to the brash type. Unlike her mother, she doesn't come dress to the nines, she looks more like your everyday hardworking blue collar woman, if you didn't know she was a millionaire you wouldn't guess it by the way she's dressed. Also she doesn't smile much either, you can tell she's strictly business. Mrs. Sinclair breaks the ice by asking, "Where're the drinks?" We both laugh, and say after a day like today we need one. My guess is she can't tell I'm the size of a house underneath this table, so later for that.

My phone is blowing up, it's Lucy, I forgot to call and cancel. He'll be alright; he just wants to go to some lame party where any and everybody knows you, and I can't handle that right now, tonight I'm focused on Mrs. Sinclair and her assets.

All the while we're eating not once do we talk about why we're here, it's like they've asked me to come here to inspect me, find out what I'm all about. Although I'm enjoying dinner and all, it's like this is more of a meet and greet, perse'. Right before they bring the entrée's, Zoe bursts out and asks, "So how long have you been in this business?" After so long of laughing and chit-chatting about this and that, I'm suddenly put on the hot seat, needless to say, you would think she was the CEO; her mother on the other hand is so laid back it's ridiculous.

I say, "I've been in the business well over ten years."

She's not impressed, not that I would expect her to be anyway.

"You look so young, how old you are?" she asks.

It's a good thing I don't mind telling my age, so I oblige her.

"I'm 33 years old."

She doesn't respond. I'm not quite sure what it is about Ms. Zoe, because she's nothing like her mom. Mrs. Sinclair is having a ball, laughing, telling jokes, really enjoying herself, but Zoe; now that's a different story.

Just when it looks as though the evening is coming to an end, Zoe suddenly changes her disposition.

She says, "I really trust mom's decision to hire, you, I think she's made a good choice, and with all of your qualifications you should be a great asset to our company, and Marcel also spoke very highly of you."

Now that's a switch. She has hardly said twenty words, and now she wants to talk, go figure. The question is, do I want to work with her. Mrs. Sinclair is no problem, but I don't think I can handle her attitude.

While we're waiting for the tickets, we settle that we will meet at my office on Tuesday, and at that time all of the necessary documents can be presented. Although I caught a glimpse of what's to come, I notice

Mrs. Sinclair is a laid back woman, but she doesn't play when it comes to business, so I need to have my game face on, especially if she's coming with her sidekick. I am a bit perplexed though, most times I get referrals it's probably the case where they were unhappy with their prior consultant, but Mrs. Sinclair made it clear there was no discourse between her and her previous consultant, she just felt it was time for a change, and once again I have Mr. Bouviér to thank for that.

What a surprise, traffic's good tonight. I look at my phone and I have several missed calls, mostly from Lucy, I wonder if he's still home or has he already left to head to the party.

"Lucy, what's up?"

"Not much, just putting the finishing touches on this ever so gorgeous face of mine."

Already I can tell his pisstivity level with me is at an all-time high, his voice is down low, and his answer is short and dry.

"I got your message, but I couldn't call, because I was in a very important meeting with a very influential high net-worth individual."

Complete silence.

"Lucy, did you hear me?"

"Yeah, I heard you."

Here we go again, every time I'm busy or can't get back with him at the drop of a dime he throws a man fit.

Hurriedly he says, "Don't patronize me with your rich people lingo, is that all you wanted was to let me know that, ok I got it, but I have to go, me and some of my friends from the store have a party to go to; remember the one you were supposed to be going with me to. And you know this is the kick off of Fashion Week, so ta-ta, this diva has to go."

"Lucy, I told you I was busy—"

"Vic, don't go there, you've known about this at least a week. It's like since you've gone back to work, you don't return any of my calls, until you decide to, and actually I never thought I would say this but—"

"What?"

"Nothing just forget it."

"Lucy, hold on I've got another call coming through."

"Whatever!"

This is a number I don't recognize, but I answer it anyway.

"Hello, Victoria speaking."

The female voice on the other end clears her voice and says, "Hi Victoria, its Zoe Sinclair, is this a good time?"

"Yes, its fine. How may I help you?"

"I don't want much, I only wanted to first apologize for the way I acted back at the restaurant."

"Oh, there's no problem."

"Actually it is, I left feeling like I came off in a shallow way."

"It's okay."

"I'm not always like that, but I'm always protective of my mother and myself, we've both been through a lot, and there are not many people outside of business that we allow into our circle."

Where is all of this coming from, just a few minutes ago, I would have made her a close relative of Omarosa, but now she's a total different person. I try to reassure her that everything is fine, but she insists that I know she's not this cold hearted person she comes off to be.

She goes on to say, "I don't have many people that I associate with, and it just caught me off guard when Marcel told us about you, he was very impressed, so I needed to see who was this Victoria Cartiér."

"And."

We both giggle.

"You're cool."

"Well thank you."

"And mom thinks you're cool too."

"Again, I thank you."

I don't notice but I've forgotten all about Lucy (again). He's really going to kill me now, but whatever, I'm tired of he and momma always trying to make me feel like everything in my life is A-okay. They're not the ones that are living with a monster inside of them that they can't get rid of. Just as I say this I feel her kick with a force that's truly to be reckoned with. I wonder if she thinks I'm talking about her. While I patiently wait for this light I gently caress my perfectly round belly to make sure she knows that no matter what mommy loves her. She gives me another kick as to say she loves me too.

Time has flown I can't believe I've talked to Zoe the entire way home. She's really pretty funny. The one thing I do know is that she knows her craft, and by listening to her, I know her mom made a great choice, and anyway she's been groomed for this from the beginning.

Once I'm home all I want to do is relax, take a soothing bath, calm my nerves, but this thought is interrupted by a knock at the door. I know this time it's not Lucy, because I'm sure he's leaning towards giving me the silent treatment, and I don't expect him to give up on that anytime soon. I open the door only to be greeted by Judas. I always imagined what it would be like if we ever came face to face. What would I do? How would I react? But right now I'm at a loss.

"Victoria, hello, may I come in?"

Growing up Daddy used to tell me to go with my first mind, never second guess yourself; right now my first mind is immediately slam the door as hard as I can. So I do, and darn she catches it right before it comes head on with her dreadful face. What would I give for Lucy to be here now?

She asks again, "Lucy, may I come in?"

I say nothing, just pull back the door and step aside. She makes her way in and I automatically say, "No need to take a seat, you won't be here that long."

"Victoria, I have tried calling you numerous times, but you will not accept any of my calls."

"Should I?"

"I'm not here to get into a cat fight with you. I only want to make peace with what has gone on between us."

"Look, this is the deal, you and I have or never will we be that way again. As a matter of fact you are that person I love to hate."

"I respect that."

"So why did you come here, you could have told me that over the phone?"

"Because I need to let you know that you are not the only one that's going through a rough time."

If she really knew me, she would know that this is my daily wish for her, that everything she touches will fail. Not a day goes by that I'm not consumed with her anguish. Not only did she make me think she was my friend, she cheated with the man I called my husband. That's lower than low.

"So what, you got it too, I hope."

She pauses to take a breath.

"Yes, I do."

"You deserve it; you deserve everything that you get. It couldn't have happened to a better person."

"Victoria, I didn't mean for it to get to this point."

Laughing I say, "What did you expect Malcolm to leave me, marry you, and the both of you live happily ever after? I thought you were smarter than that. You of all people know the married man never leaves; he stalls but never leaves. And let me ask you this, in that sick little head of yours did you not one time think that if he left me, he wouldn't one day leave you too. He told me you got it too, and that you're lucky enough you don't have to take the medicines. Well good for you, as you can see I have to, I'm responsible for another life."

"Victoria, I'm sorry."

"Please leave, but before you go, I have one more question for you, did you really love Malcolm?"

I ask a question I really don't want an answer to.

As she heads to the door, she looks back at me, and says, "I always did, and in my heart I know he loved me too, it was just he couldn't leave you, because of the commitment he made to you. He once told me, he was only there because he knew if he left, he would disappoint so many people he loved. So he stayed, and Victoria, you said it yourself, he wasn't happy, and neither were you. You told me all the time that he didn't satisfy you anymore, remember there were times you wanted out, you no longer wanted him, so I guess he felt that."

"And I guess that's when you stepped in, huh?"

"No, I was always there; I just needed to see how far it would go. You never loved him, you were in love with the idea of him, he was your knight in shining amour. You were so caught up in the life, the fabulosity of being Mrs. Cartiér that you failed to love a man that gave you everything. You even stopped going to church because Malcolm didn't want to anymore."

This is unreal, I can actually feel my heart racing. I know if she stays here one minute longer this will not be good for either of us. I take a glance at my stomach, and realize that I'm not in a position to do anything crazy so I tell her once more to leave.

I'm left standing in the middle of the floor, looking and feeling like a complete idiot with tears streaming down my face. I'm not sure if I'm more embarrassed that the other woman has just read me like a book, or if I know what she said was true and I don't want to admit it. How could I let this happen to me? I feel like everyone that has ever told me they loved me, besides my family, was a liar. It's my promise that everyone that has hurt me will pay.

I look at the clock, and it's not too late, I grab the phone, dial Lucy's cell, let him know I'm on the way. I'm on a rampage, and I'm ready to party. I need to get this off of my mind. I don't believe I let her come into my house and not only tell me she didn't plan for this to happen, but she loved him, better yet by the way she sounded as if she still loves him! Tribeca Grand Hotel, here I come.

After a warm shower I dab the pressure points with the Panthere de Cartiér, and head to the closet to find the little black dress, topped off with a pair of Kate Spade exotic pumps. Never thought being pregnant would prove to be so fashionable. For once I forget I'm HIV positive, and there's nothing standing in my way. I glide into the S550, activate the surround sound, command the player to disc 3, Mary J, *"My Life"*, open the panorama, and ride out.

I feel like that teenager who has just gotten her first whiff of freedom, there are goose bumps in my stomach, because I'm both excited and afraid at the same time. The city is jumping as usual, and the Avenue of the America's is no different, it's by far the spot to be, and 6th and White are tight with cars, so there's no doubt I'll be using valet. Lucy said this was a big to do, I believe I underestimated him, didn't think it would be this off the hook. There are Bentleys, Ferrari's, Lambo's, the whole nine crowding in to get first dibs to be parked. A very handsome gentleman with a gorgeous smile hands me a claim ticket and flirts with me as if I really need that. I promised myself I wasn't going to do that. Tonight it's all about fun; I'm here to have a good time.

I finally spot Lucy dead center of the crowd dressed to kill. I swear if the boy wasn't gay, he would be a heck of a metrosexual. Eyebrows waxed and on point, goatee trimmed just right, ponytail pulled back, and he even decided to sport his new glasses. He's such a diva, anything that interferes in his image goes against the grain.

"Well la-ti-da, look who decided to grace us with their presence, if it isn't Ms. Victoria Di-a mon Jean-Pierre, herself."

At this moment I feel like a complete idiot, he still hasn't forgiven me, even after I've pressed my way to be here with him, therefore I smile and laugh it off.

"Hi Lucy."

"Hi yourself."

I can tell he's already had one too many chocolatini's already, his head is tight and it's only eleven thirty.

He musters up enough dignity and says, "I'm glad you're here, but you still owe me one."

Just like a man, never satisfied, but don't say that to him.

He takes me around, introduces me to some of his clientele, and I must say, I'm quite fascinated, can't believe I'm partying with some of New York's finest, if I didn't know any better I would say that Betsey Johnson, and Zac Posen are over at the bar. Lucy said he had some heavy hitters, but sometimes he tends to over exaggerate. I've gone to parties with him before, but never have I seen this many designers in one setting. I've gotten several compliments on my cute little number. Although this was a last minute decision I've learned a girl must always have a Chanel ready to go at anytime, that way you'll never go wrong.

Now that I'm here, Lucy doesn't have much time for me, he's too busy mingling with the fashion world who's-who's, but its okay. On top of that, a gentleman sporting a leisure suit comes over and starts a conversation, one that I'd rather not participate in to say the least, but he is very attractive, and I did come here to enjoy myself so maybe I can be nice for a change. It seems like an hour has gone by, and he's only talked about himself the entire time. I try so hard to act as though I'm somewhat interested in knowing where he lives, what he drives, how much money he has, blah, blah, blah; like I don't have my own money, heck I drive a $90,000 car, so what makes him think I really care. He finally gets it that I'm not interested and eventually keeps it moving. Thank you, I did everything but yawn, can you say boring! The only other thing was for me to pass out; now that would've been a sure way to say leave me alone.

It's something about house music that gives me a feeling of wanting to let loose, as Noëlle would say, let go. There I am again, tripping over her. I hate she came to my house tonight; I know the only reason I'm here is to free my mind of all that madness. Right when I take a seat at the bar to rest my feet, a young lady comes up behind me and says, "Boo, guess who?" I should have guessed it, but its Zoe, the girl really has her grown woman on tonight, a total different person from earlier today. Black one-sleeved mini with patent leather trim, leggings, and, oh my goodness, she's pulled out the open toe platform booties. This is definitely not the same woman that sat across from me earlier dressed as if she was on her way to photograph for People's Worst Dressed List.

As to seem as if she has not thrown me for a loop, I say, "Hey lady, how are you?"

"I'm good, and you? I didn't expect you would be here."

"I wasn't at first, but I changed my mind at the very last second."

I can't stop eyeing those boots, it's like she could have come in here without anything on, except those boots, and she still would have been a showstopper.

I hesitate and ask, "I'm usually on top of it, but I must know who are you wearing?"

She says in one breath, "Gucci."

I knew it ... being pregnant has done something to my brain cells, I should've known that at first glance. I can't let her know how much I'm willing to trade my 5th grade rock collection for those shoes. I thought her mom had on something today, but right now Ms. Zoe has her beat.

I change the conversation, "So what brings you out tonight?"

"Believe it or not, I usually don't frequent these functions. As you can tell earlier that I don't have to have the designer clothes or shoes, although I like to dress up every once in a while, but this is Fashion Week, so why not, and also we did some work for Tom Ford once."

"Well, I'm having such a good time; it's been a while since I've been out. I feel like I need a drink."

"Why don't you? We're here at the bar; I don't think one drink is going to hurt you."

"As bad as want to, I shouldn't, the doctor says that that's a no-no, but ... one Cosmo won't kill me, and you should know, I need it, I haven't had one since ..."

"Since when? Please don't say before you were knocked up."

I pause, and say, "Yes and no."

"Honey, I know you don't believe all that about drinking will harm the baby. As long as you do it in moderation, you should be fine."

My sentiments exactly, where has she been all my life. This is such a refresher from my family, Lucy, and now Melissa has even jumped on the wagon, telling me what's good for me and what's not. I do have my own mind, so I believe I will have a drink.

After two Cosmo's I feel so much better, I should've ordered right when I got here. I hope my sweet baby want think bad of me, but mommy's been in need of this for a long time. This is my kind of party, the one that goes on and on, and on. The last I saw of Lucy was when he was on the dance floor grooving to *"Green Light"*, with his new beau; and this one is fine. I'm dying to ask Lucy does he swing both ways, because he's too cute to be set aside only for the male species.

I'm starting to feel the effects of my sinful ways, my head is getting light, and the music is somewhat drowning my thoughts. I can barely hear Zoe over the noise.

Zoe says, "Are you far from here?" I guess she notices I'm feeling pretty good right now?"

"Nope, I'm in Harlem, not too far."

"Are you okay to drive?"

How is she going to ask me that when she's the one that helped convince me to do this, nevertheless, I don't regret anything.

"Yes, I'll be fine, if anything, my friend Lucy is here, he'll make sure I get home."

"Lucy Lucy?"

"Aahm yes, since you put it like that, he's my best friend since childhood. We've been through a lot, he's the reason I'm here. I wanted to support him as usual. Do you know Lucy?"

She laughs hysterically, "Yes I do, and I've known him for a while. I met him through my mother, of course, he started out as her stylist, and from there is where our friendship began. He's a trip."

"I take it he hasn't read you the riot act in regards to him being referenced to as a him? It's embedded in my cerebellum so, that I dare not make that mistake at least not in a public setting."

"Oh yes, he tried, but I wasn't hearing it."

We continue to take turns ragging on Lucy not knowing he's standing behind us. I wonder how much did he hear?

He barges his way in, and says "Oh yes girlfriends if you wanna know did I hear, darn right, Lucy don't miss a thing baby."

We both look at each other and burst out laughing again.

"So what's so funny?" Lucy asks.

"Nothing, you're just such the drama queen." I say, looking away.

"Oh no Ms. Thang, you're not gon' sit here and laugh about me in my face."

I want so bad to stop laughing, but the more I laugh the funnier it gets. Tears swell in my eyes; I can't remember the last time I laughed so hard. Zoe is so funny; she has him down to a science, his mannerisms and all, if I didn't know so I would think she's the missing piece to our puzzle.

I'm so caught up that I forget to hide the last drink I've had the bartender conjure up. But before I try and slide it over towards Zoe, he recognizes that's one too many drinks all at once for one person.

Loudly, he says, "What are you thinking?"

Suddenly I feel I'm being chastised by my mother, almost just not the whole package. This is part of the problem why I need a breather. They hover me as if the man has shared with them my expectant departure date, but the only thing is that He didn't share it with me. So until I get to the point where my CD4 is below 200, I still have time left, and since I'm doing good so far, that doesn't seem too likely.

We go on for about another 45 minutes, until I realize I'm just not going to make it. People have started to clear the place and it's time I make my way towards 125th. I gather my purse; check for the keys, but shockingly there not where I placed them. Zoe asks that I check thoroughly, still no keys.

She says, "Where are you parked?"

For some reason that's a distant memory, I stand to make sure they haven't fallen in the midst of my courtship with the bartender. I stumble, and this is when it dawns on me just how much I'm not in condition to drive. By now Lucy is doing farewells, waving as if he's this year's homecoming princess. After several checks through the bag, I get a brain boost that I'm in valet. Zoe looks at me and laughs.

Lucy heads over to see if I'm fine. I tell him that instead of him having to get me home, along with my having to come back to get my car, I decide I'll get a room, wake up in the morning, and head home. Of course he says he can stay, but in my drunkenness I say no. I'm not up for a lecture tonight; I just want to lay my head down.

The woman at the front desk checks me in, tells me all the specials they have, but my head is hurting so badly I can't process one thing from the next. I feel nauseated, where's the nearest can?

It's a good thing I stayed the night, because I don't think I would've made it. First thing, I check my phone for any missed calls; eight out of ten are Lucy. I still don't understand how he can party so long and still find it to make it to work without ever complaining. He has to be tired, because I am, and he started way before I did. I only check one of the voicemails and delete the others, I'm sure they're all the same.

Before I can make it home daddy is calling, says he came by this morning and I wasn't there, and he really needs to know where I am. Last I checked I was grown. He stresses that he has something for me, today is the 15th of the month, and every month this time he always has me deposit $1,000, into my account; it's been my allowance since I graduated college.

He wants to make sure if anything ever happened I'd be okay. This is why it wouldn't have been an issue if Malcolm tried to take anything; I've got money that I've put away for years. Sometimes I think this is what made him stay, because I didn't need him for anything, daddy made sure of that. He and momma both said that a woman should always have her own. I think it's crazy when a woman is left with nothing if the man leaves. That's a cardinal rule, a woman should have three things; Jesus, her own money, and a fierce pair of shoes to be ready at any time.

Looking back on last night I must say I really had a wonderful time, although I did have more than I anticipated, it was great. And I can't believe that Zoe is totally not the prude she presented herself to be.

I'm slowly reminded of the old days from this pounding headache, along with the queasy feeling in my stomach that forces me to pull over and bring up everything I've eaten the last two days. I haven't been this sick in a while, even though I accept my punishment, I would gladly do it again. It's a swap from having to take three medicines a day ... and that reminds me, I've missed this morning's dose already and I didn't take the last dose last night either; too upset. I don't think missing a dose here or there will hurt.

Lucy calls again and I feel responsible to answer being that I haven't talked to him since he and Zoe made sure I was checked in.

"May I ask why you're not answering your phone?" he asks.

This is where I lose it, and snap back with vengeance.

"I didn't answer because I chose not to, what's up?"

"So, what you go out one time and this is how you act?"

No matter what he says I can't focus, because my insides are doing flips. I'm in no mood for his desire for control at this time, so I don't dignify the question with a response. I can hear him breathing, but I could care less. He doesn't leave it alone, obviously he wants to upset me.

"Vic, are you ignoring me?"

I'm waiting to see just how long it'll take for him to realize I'm not entertaining him, if he wants to trip he can do it by himself. It's taking all of me not to get sick anymore.

"Oh, so you're not talking?"

Right here is where I can't take it anymore; I bring it up again, the rest of whatever is left at the pit of my belly. He gets quiet, and finally asks if I'm okay.

Barely I say, "Yeah, I'm fine."

"Good." he says.

There's a sudden calmness over the airwaves. What I long for, finally peace and quiet.

Chapter Twelve
Victoria & Zoe

really enjoyed the party last night, I'm glad Zoe asked me to go. The only thing is, it could have lasted a little longer. The best thing was I got the chance to mix and mingle with some other people besides the normal bourgeois crowd I'm used to. I'm still pumped about our trip to Vegas next month; I'm surprised she asked me to go with her. More than likely she'll be busy talking contracts, while I'll be busy on the strip. The last time I was in Vegas, I was with the get fresh crew, Malcolm, Nate, not to mention his fly by night girlfriend Giovanna, Julian, and Kai. Thinking back that was a while ago, that was when everything was smooth sailing, no divorces, or no HIV to tend with.

What's today? Sunday ... if anything I know, is momma has cooked a good meal, and to say the least I'm up for that. Especially since I haven't had time to go grocery shopping much, it's basically been fast foods, but this little girl doesn't care as long as it's food. Church should be out in about an hour, I guess I'll throw something on, and make my way over there.

I've noticed things have been a lot quieter since Lucy hasn't been around. Momma asked me the other day when was the last time I spoke to him, and when I thought about it, I realized it's been over a month. He was already mad at me before the party, and now he's still mad at me, but I don't care. I'm not going to call him up and beg for his forgiveness, especially when I did nothing wrong. I wouldn't be like this if he wasn't always trying to act as if he's my keeper. Plus, for the past couple of months the conversation have only been "did you take your meds", "have you eaten the right stuff", and oh let's not talk about the water; if I don't drink another bottled water it want be too soon. As far as the meds, I've read where people like me have the virus and they're not taking any meds, and they're fine. As long as I have gotten enough in my system the baby will be fine.

On my way out the door, my cell rings, my hands are full so I miss it. Once I'm inside the car I see it's Zoe, she's probably tripping over some gospel show on TV and wants to make jokes. Since I've been talking to her we haven't really gotten into whether or not she goes to church. We've just only had fun and that's what matters. She's cool; she doesn't let much of anything bother her. It feels good to be around someone that doesn't know my status; they just like me for me.

"Hey lady, what's up? Sorry I missed your call."

"Too bad, I didn't want much, just laughing at these people that call themselves Christians."

"What are you watching?"

"I flipped through the channels and ran across a show where different people get up, sing a Holy Ghost spirit filled song as they call it, and the audience chooses who sings the best."

"Oh yeah I saw it when I was home, funny huh?"

"People trip me out when they get the Holy Ghost and start jumping around and dancing everywhere."

This is perfect timing, I jump in and ask, "What church do you go to?"

She gives me the loudest laugh as if I've just cracked the funniest joke.

She responds, "Holy springs and mattresses."

At first she catches me off guard because I only hear the word holy.

"Come again," I say.

"You heard me right the first time; church is no place for me. That's just like the club. At church you meet the adulterers, drug dealers, woman beaters, wanna be pimps, alcoholics, everything; it's like they do everything their bible says don't do, then they've been out all night. Yet as soon as they get in church, they're the main ones praising the Lord, shouting all over the place, 'thank you Jesus this, thank you Jesus that,' but the first ones to turn their head when something they aren't familiar with hits him head on. So why would I go there? I can stay at home for that. Don't tell me, you're one of them?"

Before I know it, no has come out. It's because I'm so mad at Him right now, I might as well not be one of them. He really let me down, and there is no way I can forget that.

I feel the need to explain, so I say, "Naw, I used to go to church, but I don't anymore, I feel like you, they're all liars. That's all I heard as a child, how good He is, and that He will never leave you or forsake you, but all

I've gotten from Him is problems and heartache."

She says, "I'm with you on that."

We continue to talk about just how much we don't like church folks, but I'm quickly reminded that where I'm headed is the house where the poster children for Jesus Christ lives.

As soon as I hit the door I'm greeted by my father wearing a shirt that says "Jesus Freak," like I said, poster children. He hugs me and tells me how glad he is to see me, kisses my belly with both his hands, and says, he can't wait for his baby girl to arrive, but he doesn't hide the fact he has no grandsons. I break in to say that's Julian's job, then Daddy turns and yells out to Reese, "You'd better get busy girl." She laughs, and gives Julian the I'm ready so what's up look.

I head to the kitchen, and as usual momma is in her Sunday garb, along with the apron we gave her for a gag Mother's Day gift. We even had it personalized, "D's kitchen, No Axcess." She didn't wear it for a long time only because we misspelled Access. You'd think she would get it; not momma. I'm so hungry, and she's got it smelling so good, I don't think I can wait for the bread. I walk into the den hoping no one will start up with me. This is partly the reason I don't visit that often.

I can tell my family's pissed with me, but oh well. The air is so thick you can cut through it. Julian is sitting in the recliner laid back watching the game, chest puffed out like he's Simba, and Reese is Nila, but too bad because Mufasa still rules the throne. I slowly settle into the comfort of the new leather sofa, last time I was here they were still rocking the green and grey furniture from back when. I soon discover it doesn't sit the same, because my back is getting an unwanted pain that I definitely don't need. I mainly feel the pressure on my diaphragm, so I ask Julian if we can swap, you would think I asked him to do something out of the norm. One thing I didn't take into consideration is the fact the chair sits a lot lower, and the depth is unbearable, but I somehow manage to nestle into it. The problem is going to come once I have to get up, but we'll deal with that when the time comes.

Before I can lay my head back, Julian jumps in and asks, "So Vic, where have you been? I've called, left several messages and you haven't returned any of them. What's up with that?"

"I got them, but I've been busy."

"How busy can you be that you can't find the time to return any of my calls? I just stopped calling, and said if you wanted to call me back you would, so I see you didn't, because you haven't."

"I didn't come over here for this. All I wanted to do was get something to eat, see momma and daddy, hang out, and go home."

Reese gets up to go into the kitchen, praying momma needs her to help set the table, but to her dismay, momma already has it done. She sets out to look for my dad, but only to find he's making his way towards us. She's the only one that's made me feel welcome since I got here. Even daddy's hug wasn't the same, and momma's hello was as dry as a bag of Mahatma Rice. I guess I'm supposed to call and check in everyday with everybody. Sorry.

Daddy makes his way into the conversation by asking, "Baby you haven't been around much for anyone lately, and why is that?"

I'm so starting to regret I came over here. Something told me to ask Zoe if she wanted to go get something to eat.

"Daddy, like I told Julian, I've had a lot going on, my client database has increased, and so when I get home in the afternoon, between dealing with being pregnant, and the stress of everyday life, I don't feel like being bothered."

Both of them say at the same time, "Bothered?"

Julian says, "Now we're bothering you?"

I suddenly get the desire to get up and walk out of here, but I forget I'm stuck in this oversized piece of cow hide. And if I wanted to get up now I would surely need someone's help, therefore I'm trapped so I have to stay and listen to this.

To top it off Momma yells from the kitchen once again, "So who is this Zoe person? I've heard about her, you've had plenty time for her, that's all you have for her, is time. So much partying is not good for you sweetheart."

And where did that come from? Let me guess big mouth Lucy. I think I'm set free from him for a while, yet he still manages to tell my mother on me like I'm some little girl. I'm over this. These people are crazy, I don't need this, and anyway I've got too much other stuff to deal with. It's like they all are against me, the only person missing is Lucy. I ask momma for a plate to take with me, I can't stomach being here one minute longer.

I hop in the car, call Zoe up to see what she's has going on, it's a good thing I did, we've settled it that we're going to meet at 21. I'm glad I look half way descent, wasn't prepared to eat out today. I can't believe momma is calling already, and I haven't been gone ten minutes.

"Victoria, you should not have left like that."

"Momma its fine, I really didn't feel like being put on the hot seat."

"You weren't, we're just concerned. You know we all care about you, and want what's best for you."

"It didn't seem that way; I'm tired of being treated like a child. Yes, I know I have HIV and I need to be careful, but I would like it if all of you, including Lucy, would just leave me alone!"

The silence is death defying; I know she's looking at the phone saying what the—.

"Victoria Diamond Jean-Pierre, never in all of your 33 years of life have you ever talked to me that way; what is your problem young lady? Obviously you have lost your mind!"

"No momma, I'm in my right mind, there's nothing wrong with me. I just don't appreciate it when grown people try and treat other grown people as if they were a child. I can take care of myself, I don't need a personal nurse, or a social worker to help me through this, me and my baby will be fine."

"Alright then Victoria, if that's how you want it then fine. From now on your father and I will not hover over you, we will let you do as you wish, but just please know, that if you think for one minute that God is pleased with the way you are acting think again. He knows all, and He sees all."

"Yeah, yeah, yeah, there you go again, with your Jesus jargon, why is it that every time something out of the ordinary happens every one brings up Jesus? He has not done anything for me so spectacular lately that I have to completely depend on Him. He has shown me that by doing that you get hurt every time, so please don't come to me with that."

I can tell that I have totally thrown her for a loop. She is furious. I don't remember the last time my mother has been this upset with me, but it's a first time for all things, and this is one time I'm not going to apologize. I don't need them for anything; I've got everything I need. I don't need to ask for money, I've got all of that. I don't need clothing or shelter; I've got more than enough. So why should I expect Him to do anything else for me. He has already stricken me with a death sentence, what more does He want?

We never say another word to one another, from there all I hear is. "Goodbye Victoria, but don't forget we love you."

As soon as I make it to the restaurant, it seems as if my pressure is up; I'm steaming. I can't remember a time when I've ever said these things to my mother, never the less my father. I guess they think I'm the problem child, but I'm sorry I can't be perfect like Julian, always has it together, I'm not Julian. I'm me and that's not going to change any time soon.

Zoe says, "What's up girl, you look upset about something."

I don't say anything, all I want to do is just get through this meal, and call it a day. She's already been here at least fifteen minutes before me, so she's already sipping on a glass of wine. I try to ward off the desire, but I can't help myself. After what I've just been through, I owe it to myself. I have the waiter bring out a bottle of Chardonnay; this should help me.

Now that I'm a bit more comfortable, I say, "Thanks for meeting me. Since I talked to you last, I've been on the phone going back and forth with my mother."

"I know how that feels."

"Girl, why do parents feel that no matter how old you get, you will never be old enough to them?"

"I guess it's the whole parents' thing. Moms is like that with me too, now that my father is a permanent non-fixture in our lives, she's stepped up her game; it's like I don't even have my own place."

"What's up with that?"

"You're saying that now, but once you become a mother you'll be thinking the same way."

"I doubt it. I plan to give this baby freedom."

I mumble under my breath, as long as I'm alive.

"You'll still keep tabs." she says.

I giggle, but I also say, "It's funny but my parents have just recently become like this. When I was married it wasn't this way."

"Marriage is for the lonely and deprived."

"It has its perks, but I don't think I'll ever do it again." I say.

"And why is that?" she asks.

"Men don't believe in being faithful, I don't think it's in their DNA; at least it wasn't in my ex-husbands."

She holds her head down, looks away, and says, "I was engaged once upon a time, and there was not a happy ending."

"Did he cheat?"

"That and some."

"Well don't feel alone, I try not to think badly of all men, but right now, I don't like any of them. It's hard looking at my own brother; he cheated on his wife, for a man."

She takes the rest of her left over wine down as fast as she can, and asks, "Are they brothers?"

"Who?" I ask.

"Your brother, and my ex-fiancé," she says.

Awkward as this may be, I ask her, "Did he leave for a man?"

She's always so on point, but this time, I can tell I struck a nerve.

She burst out and says, "Hell yeah, and this is why I hate men to this day."

Wow, someone that shares my anger.

"Do you mind me asking, what happened?" I say.

"No, I don't mind, it's simple as this, I was in love with a man that also loved to be with men, but when I found out it was too late."

" Too late, what do you mean by that?"

"Never mind," she says.

By this time our meals have arrived, and I'm not holding back a thing. I'm starving, and if I leave anything on the plate, it's only because my stomach can't hold it. We continue to men bash, although I haven't done this in a while with any one. Come to think of it, I have no girlfriends, all except Melissa, and she's about to take the plunge in less than three months. It's cool she's having a holiday wedding though; this will mean most of her family will be in town.

While we're laughing and wishing our men could be more like Will Smith, all of a sudden I hear this loud voice behind me; it's no one but Lucy. Why me? And not only is he fabulous, but the boy has cut his hair, now he's sporting a short curly afro. It's about time he did away with that long stuff, granted it was beautiful, but it was too much, and he couldn't do anything but pull it back. This look is good for him, but I will not let him know it.

He says in a very loud and boisterous voice, "Oh Chica, so this is who's been occupying your time?"

I slowly turn my head to give him a quick glance, and say, "Whatever."

"Hey Ms. Zoe, haven't seen you at the store in a while, where you been?"

"Apparently not at the store." she says laughing.

"Oh so this is how it is?" Lucy asks.

"No," I say, "we're just out having a peaceful lunch."

"Whatever sweetness."

He's standing over me as if he's ready to get something jumped off, but he knows better, he may act crazy, but he's not, anyway, he would never go off in a setting like this.

"Lucy, why are you acting like this? What's wrong with two people having a nice meal?" I ask.

"Nothing, when both of them are responsible people, and there is no risk to them and their unborn my child, more importantly, my niece."

Disgusted, I respond, "What harm am I doing?"

He comes back, "Look at you, in here with your wine, and your fish, doing everything the doctor said not to do; you call that responsible?"

"I'm my own woman."

"So I guess you're taking this Savannah thing a bit far, huh?"

"No that's the problem, this is real life, I'm not Savannah, I'm Victoria."

"Well go ahead Ms. Victoria, with your bad self; you don't ever have to worry about me caring again. And to you Ms. Zoe, I'll see you later; you'll need some Prada sooner or later."

"Boy I tell you, he's more than you know." Zoe says.

"You're telling me, I've dealt with him all my life, this is not the first time he's been mad, and I'm sure it want be the last."

We finish our meal and she tells me she has tickets to Jay-Z's show at the Garden tonight; now that's a date. Lucy doesn't care too much for him; she says he's love sick with Beyonce'. Truth be told, it's because he want give him the time of day. I tell her I'll need to go home, rest up, clear my head, and freshen up. To know that these tickets are not easy to come by, I'm glad she asked me to go with her. A part of me feels like she's the other half of me, but I know it's not like that; we're just two wondering souls in need of companionship.

The show starts at eight so that allows me time to get some much needed sleep, and then I can wake up ready to go. I need to figure out what am I going to wear, you just don't go to a Jay-Z event any kind of way. I wouldn't be surprised if I ran into Noëlle tonight, this is her element, so I'll be prepared for whatever comes my way.

I pander the idea to stop by Barney's on my way and of course yes always wins, and since I haven't done much shopping lately, I splurge. It only takes me a minute to settle on the grey cashmere knit dress, and the ever so fierce peep-toe, grey Manolo booties, let's see Zoe's face when I show up in these. I can only hope she's not on one of her I didn't feel like dressing up kicks. Before I realize it, I've dropped a fast two thousand dollars. I haven't sent any tithes to the church in a while so that spares my bank account at least an extra four to five thousand a month. Might as well spend it where it's welcomed.

By the time I make it home it's already five o' clock, I had planned to rest, but later for that. I've got to do something with my hair. I need to wash it, but I just don't feel like the hassle. This is something Lucy would have loved to do. Sometimes I really do miss him, and this is one of them.

Once I'm done transforming myself into a fabulous diva, I call to check with Zoe just to make sure everything is still on, and it is, so I take a quick cat nap, this baby is requiring it. I hope she lets me enjoy myself without me dosing off. I pass my dresser, look into my pill counter and realize I haven't taken any meds all this week. I'm good to go, I feel okay, and as long as I eat, keep my strength up, it shouldn't be too bad. I can make those doses up next week.

I don't know what I was thinking; Zoe did mention this is a benefit concert Jay-Z is putting on. So it may be a while before he takes the stage, I'm so tired I might not make it until then, and to think I have to drive home. To perk myself up I get a drink from the bar before we head in. I didn't plan on walking this far, this is one night I chose the wrong shoes. We've got great seats, we're in section 3 row 3, dead center, in front of the stage, which this is a good thing on one hand, but on the other, hopefully my bladder doesn't start working overtime.

I've always enjoyed Jay-Z's music, maybe it's because we are both New Yorkers, and just maybe because his lyrics are the truth. I haven't sat down the entire show. I loved it when Mary J joined him on stage, and it was a given that Beyonce' would be here. He has a great line up, so I'm sure this will pay off for all of those involved.

I take another look at Zoe's choice of clothing, and I can't help but wonder, what was on her mind, this is why she's so interesting, she always keeps you guessing. Looks like tonight is bohemian night, here I am all glammed up, and she's looking like one of the Olsen twins, a pair of skinny jeans, a Roc-a-Wear t-shirt, a scarf, and those Uggs. I've never understood the craze for a pair of boots that make you look like you've walked out of the house in a pair of oversized house shoes, just with a little more sheepskin and there you have it. Oops! It's that time, time for a restroom run; the mojito is running through me like water. I have to press my way over at least ten people just to get out to the main floor, finally I make my way to the nearest restroom. I'm so wanting a major refund on these booties, and although I am going to pay for this later I can't wait to make it to the car, I'm driving barefoot the whole way home. If I'm not mistaken, I feel a blister rising on my pinkie toe at this moment. Just as they have a shoe shine booth, they need a foot soaking booth, my feet are being brutalized, and the worst part is there is a line!

I never thought I would be so glad to come and to go, but it doesn't take that long for me to realize I'm in no shape to make it home. Before I was pregnant, I could hold my liquor a lot longer. Zoe suggests that I stay the night at her place since she's closer, its times like this I wish I lived in Tribeca. Right before we head for the car, I have to make one more pit stop, this is not good. This little girl is feeling no mercy for me. This is another one of those times where it would've been a better decision for me to be made a man, then at least I could make some diversions, but since I'm a woman looks like I'll be running for the nearest restroom.

It's 12:45a.m., and I'm on the phone calling Melissa to make sure she reschedules my clients in the morning, there's no way I'm going to make it like this; my body is tired, my mind is tired. I've been going nonstop for the past three weeks; I'm entitled to some personal time. She doesn't answer, I leave her a message, a groggy one, but otherwise a message she can interpret.

I don't notice I've taken off the shoes of horror even before we're out of the parking facility, my feet have never felt so good. I hope all of this is from the pregnancy at whole, because I've never had any problems with platforms until recently. At my last weight check, I had gained a few pounds, but I wouldn't think my being heavy would cause this kind of pain, it's been said there is a price for beauty, and tonight I've paid a large one.

Zoe so kindly allows me to bunk in the guest palace. I am very impressed; she has a true knack for decorating. The place is not too overly done, it's just right, for her anyway. She's chosen a well-defined earth-toned pallet, corals, greens, browns, splashes of yellow. Her style is a balance between eclectic and modern, overall I would say it's quaint and chic, but I love the goose down pillows, they make well for a night like tonight. It just would've been so much better if I didn't have to climb a flight of stairs; it's equal to adding fuel to the fire.

She comes in to make sure I'm settled in, and that I don't need anything. I tell her everything is fine, if only she knew that anything is good now, I'm so broken down. As she turns out the light, she pauses, and softly says, "He gave me HIV."

What! I sit straight up in the bed. I know I didn't just hear her say what I think I heard her say, so I ask that she repeat it.

"Yes Vic, he gave me HIV, my ex-fiancé had sex with a man, his now lover, and after all of that I'm left to fight the demons of HIV."

I'm completely in silence mode. It's as if I've seen my life flash before me, but only one thing, it's not me. For the first time since I was diagnosed, I haven't been in the company of anyone except me that has it, outside of the patients at the doctor's office, and I don't see myself sharing anything with them. I'm stunned; I don't know what to do. I do know it has completely ruined my buzz.

I shift in the bed, and look down at the floor, and for once I forget the place I'm in, and say, "Me too." She stands there in a far off land, we both stare at each other as if we've known each other forever, but we've just met, yet the only thing that separates us is the date of our diagnosis. No other words are said, our eyes say it all, tears running down like rivers of waters that have no end. Some things are better left unsaid.

I arise to a rainy and gloomy day; time has passed so that I've missed all five of Melissa's calls. I immediately return her call. She answers on the first ring.

Frantically she answers, "Good morning Mrs. Cartiér."

"Hello Melissa, did you get my message?"

"Yes I did, and I've rescheduled, but for the most part they said they would rather cancel and schedule later on their own."

"Oh well, that's fine we can go over the book tomorrow to verify my lightest days."

She adds, "You did have a potential client call wanting to meet with you as soon as possible."

"Did you get the prelims?"

"Yes I did."

"Good, well I'm going to rest up today, make sure I'm ready for in the morning, and you hold down the fort. No one has asked where I am have they?"

"Actually yes, Mr. Rucker inquired on your whereabouts, but I told him you weren't feeling well."

"Thank you. I don't know what I would do without you."

"How's the baby?" she asks.

"She's fine, just kicking up a storm."

Quietly she asks, "Well are you okay?"

I chuckle and say, "You know me so well, I'm fine, but I had a late night, and I knew I wouldn't be good to anyone if I showed up with a last nights leftovers."

She too laughs, and says, "Just get some rest, it's covered here."

This is the third time I've canceled appointments, it's out of character for me, but like I say, there's a first for all things. Those people have been with me for a while, I don't think they'll leave just because I canceled a few times; look at me, I'm pregnant. I'm not going to wake up everyday, and it always be a good day. She says she'll call if anything comes up.

As soon as her feet hit the floor she's up and at it. How does she do it? She's moving around as if time is not her friend; she's rushing to get dressed. She grabs a cup of coffee, and asks if I'm ready. No hello, good morning, nothing. It's like last night never happened. I'm still stuck on the last thing we said, I want to finish the conversation, because I never thought I would meet someone like me, different scenario, but same outcome.

On the way to get my car, the ride is quiet. All of a sudden she says, "Are you still tripping about what I said?"

In my heart I am, but she's seems so distracted, I'm not sure if this is a good time to elaborate.

I say, "I wouldn't call it tripping, just thinking about it, a lot."

"Why? Now you know my secret, and now I know yours. No big deal."

I continue to ask because I really want to know, "How long have you known?"

"If you're asking when I was diagnosed, it's been 3 years ago today."

I look at her and wonder to myself, 3 years, and she's still alive, what is it she knows I don't.

"Were you afraid?" I ask.

She turns the corner and says, "Never was I afraid, it's been more like angry."

I can't resist the urge to ask, "Are you on meds?"

She responds, "I was at first, then later on I was like what the hell, I'm going to die anyway, so what's the use."

"When was the last time you took any?"

"I really don't remember." she says.

Before I get out of the car, I ask, "Do you ever plan to take them?"

She looks at me square in the eye and says, "Not if I can help it. Look at me, I have HIV, and you can't tell it, if I wouldn't have told you, you wouldn't have known. Plus, I'm not taking any meds, and you're silly if you put all of that in your body."

My mind immediately goes to my baby, am I harming her, or will she really be fine if I take them or not. We say our goodbyes, and head to our different lives, with similar situations.

This now explains the degree of her anger, along with mine. Now I ask, if there really is a God, why he would allow these things to be?

Chapter Thirteen
Victoria

Sleeping has become increasingly difficult, I seem to spending the bulk of my nights sprawled out on my side, or better yet my back, in which this is causing me to feel more pressure up top. I've lost count of the times I tee-teed last night. It's like she's sitting so low I can have her any minute now, but too bad I'm only 34 weeks, so I've got a little more time.

Once I finally roll over, rub last night's crust from my eyes, my swollen feet make their way to the floor, and slowly I glance at my belly that has blown up over night, which could all be due to the all night taco fest. It's hard to believe some of the foods I've taken a liking to, and that could also explain the burning in my chest. As the mirror greets me, I realize there is no way I can ignore how much my nose has widened since yesterday. I struggle to make it in the shower; it's like everything has become a challenge lately. The simplest things such as walking from one room to the next leaves me in search of my breath.

As fabulous as I desire to be, today is just one of those days where I don't care to be in diva mode. I don't even feel like meeting with Theodore McCullough, the client that has been trying to meet with me for over a month now. I've already bailed on him twice, so I should at least grace him with my presence. Melissa texted me about an important meeting once I get in. I've got a pretty light day so I can manage that. I just hope it's not too long and drawn out, because I need to meet with the decorator about the nursery. I've chosen the colors, but I'm still not sold yet, but I'm sure it will definitely include the color pink.

It's almost been three days since I've checked the mail, I failed to notice there's a beautifully crafted invitation addressed to me. When I open it, I realize it's the invitation to my baby shower. Judging by the way I've been ostracized it's amazing someone would even take the time to host one for me. I must say it's adorable, and the theme so embodies all that is me; "A Fairytale Winter in Wonderland." The lux design is set on a heavy white custom bristol stocked paper, with silver embossing that reads, 'Please join us as we celebrate the royal arrival of our princess, Baby Cartiér, the fairest one of all.' The front is monogrammed with a beautiful "C" on it to add a special flare. I just wish I wasn't in such a funky mood. To be honest I haven't thought much about a baby shower, it's enough just getting through the day. It's good that I've mustered up enough energy to focus on where she'll lay her head. The one thing I can do is to ensure that her homecoming is special, even if she is coming home to a one parent home.

Walking into the office is a little different today, on any other day this place would be jumping, but not today. It's peaceful and quiet, somewhat like the calm after the storm, even Ms. Helena is not her usual talkative self, she doesn't have much to say. I pass Jerry's desk, the office gossiper, thinking that on the way to my office he will offer up the news for the day, but to my surprise he's mum. I waste no time settling in, by this time Melissa is urging me into the big conference room, I ask, "Can I at least get my pen and paper?" She tells me they have been waiting for me for at least twenty minutes.

When I make my way in there's only a couple of people here.
"Hello Victoria", Mr. Rucker says.
I return the gesture, "Hello Mr. Rucker."
"The others will be here shortly." he says.
I'm thinking what's this about?
He asks, "Has everything been going okay for you lately?"
Perplexed, I answer, "Yes it has, and what about you?"
Plain and simple he says, "All is well."
In walks Mr. Banks, Mr. Norris, and Warren, all in their Armani power suits. I'm not sure what sort of meeting this could be, especially since I've just learned of it less than a couple of hours ago. There's always a message in my company's inbox, but not this time.
Waiting I notice the room is much colder than normal so I ask to be

excused to get my sweater. By the time I return they're all sitting around the table staring at me like I have the plague. Right before I take my seat, Beth from Human Resources, and Preston Lagerfeld the company's attorney both walk in like they've been best buddies since preschool.

Mr. Rucker says, "Now that we're all here, we can get down to the business at hand. Victoria we've called you here because there are some rumors that have been circulating around the office that we would like to get clarification on."

I ask, "Are these rumors regarding me?"

Mr. Banks breaks in, "Actually they are, and we, the partners, felt it would be necessary to get a better understanding of what they are about."

"May I ask what they are pertaining to?"

Out of nowhere Preston says, "There has been some very important allegations brought against you, along with Tyler Keith. According to my records both you and Mr. Keith have been accused of undergoing illegal and deceptive practices."

At this point I'm speechless, because first of all, I don't recall being involved with Tyler on any other cases except the one he called me in on a year ago. I don't know what to say, but I do know there is no way I should be having this conversation without my attorney present. I take a long and deep breath, because when I woke this morning, this is not how I expected my day to turn out.

I ask, "Can you elaborate, what kind of allegations?"

He calls out a list of things that send my head into overload. Things I never would have ever thought my name would be tied to.

"Mrs. Cartiér some of the accusations listed includes fraud, theft by deception, negligent misrepresentation, coercion, only to name a few."

I feel as though I'm being railroaded. What is this?

He goes on to say, "These are some heavy accusations, and it is my responsibility as the firms' attorney to make you aware."

I'm looking around at this room full of powerhouses, and I'm thinking is this a joke. I would never do anything that would jeopardize my business ethics, nevertheless get myself involved in something that could cause me to lose everything I've worked so hard for. Furthermore, where is Tyler in this whole thing? Why isn't he here?

"Where did these come from, and how long has this been an issue?" I ask.

Mr. Banks breaks in and says it was brought to our attention about a month ago, but we downplayed it, because we refused to believe this could be true."

"Well they are not true, and I feel this isn't fair that I haven't had any time before now to hear about this."

Mr. Rucker says, "Victoria, do you recall the client you and Tyler consulted on together? He was torn between investing in a mutual fund versus the hedge."

Thinking ... He was left a very large inheritance and Tyler wanted to build a relationship with this client badly. He felt the need to call on me so that I could go over with him all the details involved in starting a hedge fund. At first glance he appeared to have a lot of reservations about the whole idea of investing period.

Preston goes on to say, "the claim reads as this: The client, a Mr. Bailey Coleman, claims that you and another advisor persuaded him to invest his inheritance, and insurance proceeds into a hedge fund, although instead of the funds being invested into the market as promised, the money was used for personal expenses. Also it is stated, that the client did not agree to have the monies transferred although his signature was on the documents created in order to put this deal through. Finally the client claims that since he has been under our representation the returns on his investments have been grossly misrepresented to where it has caused him to lose well over 500 million dollars."

This is really a joke ... but I can't help after hearing all of this to ask, "Where does this leave me with this company?"

All is quiet, and for one moment, it feels like I'm in a time capsule, because I know this isn't happening.

Before they can conjure up an answer they hit me with one more thing.

Out of nowhere Mr. Rucker says to me that there are some rumors floating around the office and to be sure he would like to find out if they are true.

He says, "We've had a couple of clients questioning the fact whether or not you have been diagnosed with AIDS."

My heart drops to the floor, and it moves so fast until I can't move fast enough to catch it. After sitting here listening to all of this nonsense I immediately say, "If you're asking if I have AIDS, the answer is no."

I'm confused; I am both angry and disheartened. How did they find out? I remember Beth was the only one I told, only because I was concerned about an increase in insurance premiums, and I had other questions regarding adding the baby as a rider for a life policy. She reassured me this was confidential information, and that I was not obligated to disclose this to any one that I chose not to. At the time I didn't feel the need to let them know, first of all because I was afraid, and next I had been told by my doctor I didn't pose a direct threat to myself, co-workers, or my clients, so why should I tell them? This is my personal business, and how dare them question me. First they accuse me of fraud, and now this.

I look over at Beth and she looks as if she wants to drop dead for a little while, and she should.

Mr. Norris gets his turn in and says, "Mrs. Cartiér we're not trying to make this difficult for you, but you must understand our position on this as far as the company as a whole. We're thinking in the best interest of our clients."

I'm sitting here in a silent rage, completely blindsided, not knowing where my future lies, and here he is telling me about the clients' best interest, what about me? I'm the one that's suffering here.

Mr. Rucker states, "Due to the nature and severity of these allegations, we the Board, feel it is in the best interest of this company to terminate your tenure at this time."

Then by a unanimous vote in one second they decide to let me go from a place where for the last ten years I've only given them my best. Once again I feel so alone, I'm left here with no one to defend me. After all of that, in an unusual move, they hand me a stack of papers to sign setting me free from this place, along with some other riff-raff that probably clears them from having to pay me. It's so many of them it's tiring me out, seems like I've signed my name a hundred times looks like they all say the same thing.

I'm livid, I storm out of the office repeating every four letter word that there is. While I'm on my way back to what I thought was to be my office for at least the next ten years, it is now just a big space of nothing, the room of unfulfilled dreams.

As I pass Melissa sitting at her desk, she holds her head down as though she knew today was the day I would come to blows with my present and my future. She runs towards me calling my name. "Mrs. Cartiér, are you okay?"

"I'm fine."

"Is there anything I can do to help?"

Quietly I say, "No thank you, I'm cool if you will just close the door behind you."

I don't mean to come off as rude, but from my understanding I've just lost my job, so this is no time for casual conversation.

I have no desire to stand here and try to figure out my next move, all I can think of is my baby. I turn around and glance over the office, the plaques, awards, certificates all that I've gained over the years I've been here. If it's anything I know, I've been a great employee. I've helped to bring in record winning figures for this company, I have brought with me some of the most notarized high profile clients, and there is no way I'm going to take this sitting down. I take one look up at the ceiling and say, "If you were such a good God, why didn't you see this coming?"

I gather some of my things and head for the car; I take the walk I've always feared, the walk of defeat. I pick up the box that holds my most prized possessions and prepare to face the world as a divorced pregnant woman with HIV, and I can now add unemployed. I cusp my stomach to let her know that momma has this; we will be just fine.

I speed out of the lot, and I try to hide the fact I'm really afraid, because I'm not sure of all of this, it's like I've stepped into a time capsule and it's not moving. And worst than that, now that I'm on the outs with my family they're the last people I want to talk to.

I immediately begin dialing Grant's number. I only get the voicemail. He's probably in a deposition. It's been a long time since I've talked to him, never thought I would need him to get me off some bogus junk as this.

I don't know where this is headed, but I'm quite sure once the media gets wind of this everyone will know. OMG! This is one of those Johnny Cochran moments; I'd pay whatever it is to clear this up. I'm not even sure that I even want my job back; I just don't want the world to find out my status. What about my clients? What will they think? Will they stay or will they follow me? That's even if I plan to continue to practice. My life is a mess, and to think I still have to go through labor pains and delivery.

I finally reach him and he doesn't believe this as neither do I. I give him a brief overview, and all he asks is one thing, "What am I looking to gain from this?" I stop and ask myself what I really want, it doesn't take to much thought, in another bout of anger I say, "I want it all, everything including the toupeés on their heads." That gets him to laughing. He mentions that he feels they let me go out of fear and bigotry. I say, "I agree." He lets me know he's definitely up for it, and he'll take the case, because they are going to have to prove I was involved, and as far as my having AIDS, I didn't lie, I don't have AIDS, I have HIV.

Grant believes that beyond a shadow of a doubt I'm covered under the American Disabilities Act, whatever that's all about, but one thing is that I must become comfortable with the fact people will know my status, because this has the opportunity to become really ugly. I say to him, "Let's make it happen."

An hour later, I still can't focus, I'm not sure where to go from here. I'm in a daze, driving in circles. I find myself headed towards Central Park, not sure why here. I cop a spot where I sit and let my mind go, I cry, I get angry, I cry some more. A little girl passes me and says, "Don't cry, your mommy will be here to get you." I want so badly to tell her my mommy is mad at me, and so is the rest of my family. Oh to be young again. It's crazy how as a little girl, I couldn't wait to get older, not knowing that I had everything then, the only thing I had to do was wake up, and my parents would do the rest.

I go back and forth about should I or should I not call Lucy. These are the times where I really need him. I've never been without him in my life this long. I guess he really is getting his point across that he's tired of me and my madness, but no one understands what I am going through.

I don't know how I'm going make it through this shower, maybe if I knew the gracious host, I could find some way to get out of it.

I've been so distracted since I left the office, I have totally forgotten about the meeting with the decorator. I don't think it would be good for her to see me like this. Maybe I can reschedule, and this will allow me time to figure out what am I going to do about this situation. With all of this going on, no one can make me believe that a God that says He loves his children would let these sorts of things happen to them. I have to ask myself, where is that God momma used to talk about? If I didn't know any better I sound like that man in the bible; Job. Nothing in my life is going right, and the only thing I'm guilty of is trusting someone so much and allowing them to hurt me, but never again.

I haven't slept all night; I've been lying here trying to think about how this happened. I still don't remember doing anything that could involve me other than what I already know.

In the midst of me hoping to fall asleep, I make my way into the one room in this house I haven't been in a quite some time. I open the door to Malcolm's old office, it's really cold down here, I've never had a reason to come in here since everything happened in fear that I would run across some more trails of his infidelity.

I can't even pick up the phone and call him; I know he would have some grandiose words of wisdom. With him everything was always over the top, he made it so much bigger than what it was. I do come across a book he left in the wake of him cleaning out the place. I find a book titled *"The Power of a Praying Husband."* Now that's hilarious. Why would he have that? The funny part is I have the other part somewhere around here; *"The Power of a Praying Wife."* I remember I got it when I was so sure I could make my husband be what I wanted him to be. I've seen what prayer can do for you. Every time I prayed, either the prayer was not answered, or the total opposite of my prayer happened.

I look over and notice over in the corner some papers that were left; maybe he was trying to get out so fast he missed them. Old balled up papers that carry on a conversation, looks like he printed them but forgot to get rid of them.

The date reads June 16th 2008.

SmoothVP: Missing u.

LadyChief69: Same here. R U by yourself?

SmoothVP: yeah she's asleep, what's up?

LadyChief69: u I'm guessing. ☺

SmoothVP: want to go for another round?
LadyChief69: laughing ... I'm tired from last time.
SmoothVP: u told me u can handle it.
LadyChief69: every girl needs her rest.
SmoothVP: I'm all rested up.
LadyChief69: meeting tonight, meet me at the spot.
SmoothVP: how about a quickie?
LadyChief69: u know there's nothing quick about me☺
SmoothVP: I guess I can wait.
LadyChief69: why don't u play with your barbie doll next to you?
SmoothVP: why should I, I got u.

The end of the paper is torn, and I can't make out the rest, must have been one of those cheezy conversations with Noëlle. Funny how she named herself Lady Chief, and how I know it's her, is because that was always her favorite call back number back when pagers were in. The secret code for the booty call. Typical.

You would think I would be over that by now, but I have to admit seeing that still upsets me. It's hard to get pass someone bold faced betraying you right under your nose, and I know the baby can feel my pain as well, because she's working overtime tonight; she hasn't stopped kicking since I got here. The pains feels like what they describe as Braxton Hicks contractions, it's a little soon, so she's going to have to make herself comfortable. That's the last thing I need right now, to go into labor and her room not be prepared. I tear the remaining paper up; throw it in the garbage, to think no more of it. I get a warm glass of tea, lie in the bed, and put the earphones on my belly in hopes that the classical sounds of Beethoven will soothe her.

I can't believe that this is the first day I haven't had to go into the office voluntarily in I don't know when. It feels strange to not have anything to do. I can't wait for Grant to get all the facts needed so we can show them I had nothing to do with it. I'm hoping this can be over with fast. I don't need the drama that comes along with being a notable advisor gone awry. I've come too far to let this destroy me.

Fired ... I've never been fired. If anything I would have wanted to resign only because I was opening my own firm. This is not how I planned any of this. I wonder what's next? Can it get any worse?

I see that I've missed a call from Zoe. Haven't talked to her in a couple of days, hope everything is okay. I hope the news hasn't spread that fast.

"Hey girl, what's up?" I say.

"The question is what's up with you?"

I act as though I don't know where this is going.

"What do you mean?"

"So you're acting as if I haven't heard that RBN let their most prized jewel go."

In some strange way I needed to hear that.

"Something like that." I say.

"They didn't find out did they?"

"Find out what?"

"What is this, are you smarter than a fifth grader?"

I laugh something I haven't done in twenty four hours.

"I'm really not sure; all I know is they came at me with some story about myself and another advisor having been accused of all kinds of bull."

"You're not stealing are you?"

"Why, so you can fire RBN, and get someone else?"

"Well since you put it like that. We might need to."

This is part of the reason she and I have become friends, we can joke and it's okay, joke, laugh, and keep it moving. With Lucy, everything is so straight forward, no in between, unless he wants to be the comedian, then you had better laugh or else.

"I've already talked to my attorney, and we're working out the details."

"You didn't answer my question, do they know?"

"Not sure, but they questioned me about it."

"And what did you say?"

"I said no ... I don't have AIDS."

She says nothing.

"What was I supposed to say?"

She still says nothing.

After a minute she says, "I hope that is not the true reasoning behind firing you, if so, you have a really great case."

I never thought about that, all I want to do is prove I'm not a criminal, never did I consider the AIDS thing is the real issue, and for their sake, I hope not.

I change the subject and began to tell her how much I'm not looking forward to this baby shower. How can I concentrate, and to make matters worse, who will show. I have no friends, only business associates, unless you count some of my girls from college. I ask if she's up to hanging out, and of course she says she's busy, but she can hang out with me earlier tomorrow to help get my mind off of things. She suggested the one thing that'll make me forget. Shop! And I did get my quarterly catalogue for Nordstrom's this week; nothing like a serious shoe sale. I tell her it's a plan, but I just need to figure out how to spend the rest of my day today.

I call Melissa on her cell so that in case they see my number they won't think I'm asking for inside information. I would hate for them to dismiss her as well. I just needed to talk to my assistant no matter what she will always be my assistant. I invite her to dinner tonight, as I would love to hear the final details for the ceremony.

Tonight she can't make it, something about a date night. What's that? I don't think I have to worry about that ever again. I'll just have to make the best of my day. The decorator calls to see if I'm free this afternoon, there was a sudden cancellation, and she's looking forward to starting the job. I don't have much on my plate so it shouldn't be a problem. I need to get this squared away anyway, couldn't forgive myself if I didn't.

She has awesome ideas for the nursery; I'm sure when she's finished it's going to be beautiful. We've decided on a fairy theme, a lot of pinks, purples, and glitter. I think she's going to love the canopy over her bed with the jeweled-scalloped-corniced crown, accented with faux gems and jewels. I love it, I only hope once I'm gone she will know how much I loved her and I wanted the best for her.

During my meeting, I've had several clients try and contact me, but I've refused to answer or call back. I really am in no position to explain anything; also Grant has asked that I speak to no one at this point. I know once this thing gets out every one will start calling, I wouldn't be surprised if Wendy Williams hasn't already gotten her info squad on standby.

A couple of hours later, to keep my mind busy, I go through some of the things I've already chosen for the baby. It's so hard to decide what the right size is. At my last visit the doctor assured me she was growing and her measurements were accurate, so I'm hoping that she'll at least get the chance to wear most of these. Although I'm not excited, I am interested to see what type of gifts she'll receive. Then I will have some idea from that point what I need and what I don't.

As much as I don't want to admit it, I'm missing Lucy like crazy; he's been with me through every important moment of my life, and although I don't talk to Julian as much as I should, I miss him too. Even though Reese called me again to check on me, it still doesn't erase the fact that they have all called me unreasonable. Nevertheless, I do think she's going to make him a good wife, but never did I think within a year's time, he would go from having a male partner to falling in love with a female. A really good one at that. Momma likes her because she's all in the church scene. My old sister-in-law was the best, but my brother couldn't give her what she deserved. He called it being confused; I call it being greedy, wanting the best of both worlds. That's one thing I don't think Lucy will ever do is fall in love with a woman, he's too much like me.

Four days later, and the day is here, I am requested to be at the Westminster Hills Country Club at four o'clock. Of all days I've had the hardest time choosing an outfit, nothing I found would do, maybe it's because I can't bring myself to act like I'm excited when I'm really not, and more so because I feel like a stuffed baby doll. My feet let me know up front, later for the platforms, because when I woke they were the size of casaba melons. So I finally settled on the winter white cowl-neck sweater with the woolen pants to match, which are fitting so closely over my belly, and between the tights and the stretchy material I'm thrown into an itch fit. Since its cold out, I threw on the cashmere Pashmina, complete with the buttery-soft fringe suede moccasins. Going strictly for comfort.

On the ride here, I-87 wasn't too bad; it's been a little while since I've been to White Plains. The last time I was here I met with a potential client at her home, not sure why that one didn't pan out. If I recall, she and I just weren't a good fit. Way too needy for me.

Driving up you can see the grounds are exemplary; it's definitely a golfer's paradise, acres and acres of plush green grass that looks like if you step on it, your feet will get lost. The parking lot wasn't designed to meet the requirements of a mother to be. If I could have, I would've requested a caddy as I first drove in, beyond that this place is beautiful.

I'm greeted by a lovely woman at the front concierge, where she has me sign in, then directs me to where this soiree is being held.

I get to the entrance and the doors are closed, there's a makeshift wooden knocker on the door. Once I'm inside this utopia, there's no one here I recognize. I can't get past the décor, there are ceiling to ceiling white streamers dangling overhead, with different sized white balloons covering the floor. There are beautiful white calla lilies in extremely large glass vases towering the tables that are centered on pure white linen tablecloths that host gorgeous place settings of white porcelain dishes, exquisite glassware; nothing I've ever seen.

I continue to take in the magic of this airy place that feels like something right out a storybook. It's like they left nothing to chance, there's even a royal chair for me to be seated in with a crown to be placed on my head, that's actually real with encrusted jewels. The tone of the room is soft and sweet; everything here is decorated in all white, even the guest, although there are some people here that still care that white after Labor Day is still a fashion faux pas, so some have chosen to do the winter white such as myself. It's said white signifies purity; I used to believe in that.

A man dressed in a white tuxedo comes to escort me to my seat of which shall I say my throne for the day. At this time the room slowly darkens, and on a perfect three count, the music softens and everyone faces the screen that begins with numerous counts of pictures displaying me as a baby. I soon notice the face of the woman that gave birth to me, sitting next to the man that took part in that. They're at a table set aside for them and other special guest, they look fabulous, but full of joy at the same time. I haven't seen them look this way in a long time.

The voice that comes over the screen is one I've heard before; it's a mixture of Chi Chi Rodriguez meets Dreuxilla Divine, with a bolder yet sassy tone. The slideshow is started with a fabricated fairytale in a land far, far away ... while Aladdins' *"A Whole New World"* begins to play. I can't move, goose bumps cover my skin. As the pictures continue, one by one I'm being encircled by the people that I've shunned away, its momma, its daddy, its Julian, it's Reese, and just when I don't think I can take anymore, I'm serenaded by Lucy, with tears streaming down his face. I'm totally caught by surprise, but one thing, Lucy knows me so well, it's as though we coordinated our attires down to the minute. He's draped in a tailored winter-white wool crepe suit, ascot, dawned with a pair of brown Prada suede boots, topped off with a crème Fedora. We hug as if time has never passed. It dawns on me this is my gracious host, who else would know me so well to pull off something this extraordinary. He whispers in my ear, "I got your favorite planner, Preston Bailey." I want to scream.

I make my way around the room to say thank you to everyone that has come to share in this moment with me. I don't know how they did it without my knowledge, but everyone is here. My wedding wasn't anything compared to this. All of my girlfriends from the old neighborhood are here; I stop at a table that even has my father's family all the way from N'awlins. Also there are a lot of my clients here from when I first became a financial advisor. I can't help but think if any of them know what has happened with me, if they know I'm no longer employed or if they know I'm POZ. These are people that have entrusted me to advise them on their life savings, better yet, help make decisions regarding their entire financial future.

I do a double back, for a minute I believe I see Malcolm standing in the door way, can't be, he wouldn't be here. But of course Nate, Aunt Colleen, and the rest of his family are on the invite list, and that's understandable; he is the father of my child. Even though he and I are no longer together, I realize they will still be a huge part of her life.

Now that I've made rounds, I can sit and take this all in. Never could I have imagined something as beautiful as this. Zoe and her mom are even here, and the good part is Zoe is not dressed like a rich homeless woman in white.

I know momma and daddy had to be responsible for this, because I know it's been a while since Lucy and I talked, but I don't think he's become a member of this club in that short time, but he does know a lot of people so anyone could have done this for him. Plus, if I'm mistaken daddy is no member of a country club, that's not his bag. He calls that the upward mobile boogie crowd.

Following the introductions, and the thank you's, I am so glad the food is on the way, and so is she. My stomach has been doing flips ever since the hike here, so therefore she and I will leave no plates uneaten. I'm beginning to see why they chose this place, the food is divine. A menu strictly geared toward pure royalty. It's also a good thing they opted for a sit down menu, because this is not a day for finger foods.

There are several meals to choose from, starting with a small salad, several choices of entrees, such as Prime Rib of Beef, with grilled asparagus, gratin potatoes, with a cabernet sauce, or even Roast Lamb Chops, with roasted potatoes, but my favorite will have to be the Pan Seared Salmon with grain pilaf, glazed with a rosemary lemon. One thing for sure is I won't be ordering any specialty drinks, too many eyes watching, so it looks like it's going to be a glass of lemonade for me, with the straw that says "it's a girl", because I would hate for it to quickly turn into a bad scene.

As I'm drowning myself into the abyss of sin, Lucy comes over to make sure I'm fine, and before they cut into the six-tier white chocolate cake with butter cream icing, he sashays his way over and softly says, "Vic, how's everything?"

While I'm trying to finish off this last bite I say, "It's beautiful. I just want to say—tha…"

He stops to say, "Don't mention it, why wouldn't I, diva you can thank me later."

I try to stop him again to let him know how sorry I am for acting the way I have been, but he doesn't take a minute to listen, either it's not on his mind, or he really hasn't missed me as much as I want to believe.

After a wonderful couple of hours I'm exhausted. I'm not sure if it's because I've put on the face of happiness for so long until I'm worn out, or because I can't stop thinking about what's going on in my life for one minute. If I'm not concentrating on the disease, I'm thinking it's a possibility I could spend my time in prison. It helps that Melissa is here, although it is a constant reminder that RBN is a low down firm that does whatever possible to use you and then abuse you. But I'll be fine. If God himself is so true, He'll make all of this go away.

With all of the fanfare, I'm relieved I came; we received some really great gifts. I think the best one is the hand-knitted outfit with booties from my mother. Next it would be the bassinet that's been passed to Julian and now me, but looks like he put a special twist on it; he had some extra fru-fru added to it. And hands down the cutest gift is the Valco Tri Mode stroller with bassinet included from Lucy. And, oh yes, the gift certificate from Bell Bambino's, given by the Kensington's; they have been one of my most faithful clients. It was Mrs. Kensington that first approached me while I was an intern, she said I had potential and she would wait until I was ready, and she did that, then convinced her then fiancé to come aboard. They've been with me since then. I'm sure Melissa is responsible for them being here. would give credit to for having them here; Also I'm very grateful to the tons and tons of pampers, along with the sweet little under shirts, and the necessary daily items I hadn't thought of. Zoe has decided to construct the cornice and crown in her room, as well as have one of her artist friends do the artwork on her wall. Lastly with all of the other gifts, wrapped in some sort of white paper there is this one gift that leaves much to be desired. It's wrapped in a plain brown box, with thin pieces of pink velvety ribbon around it that states, "To be opened on your birthday." There is no name or card attached.

After three great tiresome, but fun-filled, hours of laughter and tears, it's time I make my way back uptown. It has been decided the gifts will be shipped so that way I will not be bogged down with trying to haul them inside the house with no male figure present.

On my way out the door, I take a couple of souvenir monogrammed petit fours and truffles to keep as a sentimental value. A tear drops from my eye, because today has really turned out to be a good day.

Chapter Fourteen
Victoria

The seven hour flight was torture. I asked the doctor was it okay for me to fly this late in date. I assured her I would not be under any undue stress, but I didn't take into consideration the crowded LAS, not alone the walking. I think the layover was dreadful enough. There were several times I wanted to tell Zoe I change my mind; this is not going to work. I keep forgetting I'm as big as one of those planes, and that I can't move as fast as some of these people here on oxygen tanks that have come to gamble all of their life savings away. I'm glad the hotel is not too far from the airport.

The Four Seasons is by far better than that cramped airplane. Everybody and their mother was on there. I can't wait to get checked in, so I can take a long hot bath, and then get a nap before I can even begin to think about any shopping. Zoe has a meeting this evening at five o'clock, so I probably won't see much of her tonight.

I turn on the television and you would swear that there is no news, nothing just casino action galore. I may try and catch a couple of shows; I hear Jos Stone, Ledisi, and Chrisette Michelle are here. I may even try to see if I can press my way to see Maxwell, but to be honest, I'm in no mood to listen to some man croon about how much he loves you, and how much he wants to make you happy ... yeah right. That's only for those who care to believe in the magic of love. Anyway I look more like Shamu right now, a fabulous Shamu, but nevertheless it's Shamu, so who would give me a second thought?

I call momma and daddy to let them know I made it, even though they were dead set against my coming here. I'm sure if I didn't call that would set war back in motion, and not to mention even after the shower it seems like Lucy still hasn't gotten over our fall out.

I put a call in to room service to have them bring me up a sandwich and an order of fries, after putting on the extra five pounds I fight my sleep. But I'm slowly succumbed to my fate.

Later this evening I realize just how much I've needed the rest. Every time I convince myself I'm ready to get out and do something my body says no. This just may turn out to be a relate, relax, release kind of trip. Zoe calls to see if I'm breathing.

Screaming on the other end, she hollers, "Lady, what's up?"

Trying to get my bearings together I answer, "Nothing much, trying to get up."

"Girl you are in Vegas, what's wrong with you? You'd better get up, that baby is a trooper, and she'll be alright."

"We'll see how you act when you are knocked up and feel like you weigh a ton."

That makes her laugh. "In the next lifetime." She says.

"How was your meeting?"

"Still working on him, but it looks good. Once I get this deal we are going to have to celebrate."

"Have you called your mom yet?"

She gets quiet. "Vic, how many times must I remind you, I am 35 years old, I don't have to call my mother every time I make a move like some people I know."

"We'll see, when Mrs. Sinclair comes here and turns this place upside down. You know yo' momma is crazy."

She takes a minute and thinks about that thing, and finally says, "Well since you put it like that."

"I thought you would see it my way."

"Anyway ... you're still a daddy's girl."

That makes me blush, especially to know that I really have people that care about me.

"Call it what you want."

She continues to press the issue, "So are you going out tonight or what?"

What is it going to take for this child to realize I've settled into the comfort of this hotel bed, and I don't see myself moving anytime soon. She eventually gets the picture, and states, "Alright party pooper, I'll see you tomorrow."

I'm glad we're in separate rooms, because tonight I don't want to be disturbed.

It's eight o'clock and I decide the least I can do is go down to the lobby and see what the hotel has to offer. Lying here so long has made me a little bed sick, it also won't hurt to stretch my legs.

Looks like a party all by itself down here, people everywhere; I'm starting to have second thoughts. Glad I didn't just throw on anything, just because I'm three sizes larger doesn't mean I still can't look good, even if it is to go to the hotel lobby.

It's been said, you'll run into someone you know in Vegas, and this must be true, because before I can make it off the elevator here's my soror Leslie Edwards. It's as if we haven't seen each other in years, "Oop-oop," she says, and then we proceed to greet each other with full Delta honors. She still looks good, and just like a DST, she's draped in the crimson and cream, head to toe, and the red suede boots are a must have.

Somehow I've let her talk me into going to the Flamingo to see George Wallace, it's a no brainer, I need a good laugh. I know Zoe's going to trip, since she's been trying to roll me out of bed since we've gotten here.

By the time we make it, the shows about to start. At the last minute we sprang for the "golden circle" package, mainly due to the fact my not wanting to wait in a long line, plus as an added bonus I get an up close and personal with George himself.

When I finally decided I was coming, I changed clothes again, but it wasn't hard to find something ultra chic, yet comfortable, so I swung for the Tru Religions and a cute turtleneck sweater.

I must've made the right choice, because either the men here are too wasted, or so hard up, that a pregnant woman in a pair of jeans would turn their heads. Leslie has laughed the entire time we've been here because she makes jokes about going out with me still hasn't changed in all these years. She blames it on the hazel eyes, she says once their pulled in, there's no way they'll notice my forever growing tummy with a navel that greets them before I do. Which isn't hard to believe, because I don't remember the last time I've seen my feet, except when I'm elevating them to get them back to normal size.

After a while I'm glad I came, although just as he begins, the crowd is somewhat a little hesitant to break out in a huge burst of laughter, but he eventually gets it rolling. He lets us know up front that he doesn't have a lot of new material; he just goes with the flow. His style of humor still leaves a bit to be desired, he's definitely "old school", especially with the yo' mama jokes, and maybe it could just be me, because Leslie on the other hand has been cracking up the whole while.

In spite of some of the corny jokes he cracks, it really doesn't help that this theatre is a pretty old one, but you gotta love it when he brings out other acts; now this is hilarious. But the funniest part is where he does a joke where he gives this lady in the crowd a bell to ring at 11:15. He says he wants to get off of work like everybody else does, but for the most part the show keep it's energy, and my favorite part would have to be is the up close and personal. I get a sweet little autographed picture, then hear him say, "Oh looks like you don't have too much longer to go, what you got in there, a girl and a boy, or the whole kit and kaboodle?" On the defense, this is my cue to exit, but of course Leslie finds some strange way to turn even this into a come on, but in some funny kinda way, after all the free stuff, and the souvenir glass it's actually a nice show.

Scoping out the scenery, I remember I've been a single independent woman now for several months, and I still don't see the hype or the magic of finding a man to come in on his white horse and save you, like he's your knight and shining amour. That only happens to Cinderella. I look around and it's so many women here with their girlfriends, I guess no one does the couple thing anymore. I don't blame them, if you ask me , you're better off by yourself than having to deal with whether or not he's going to be the same person you first met, then one day you wake up and you're like, "isn't it somewhere you need to be?" or better, having to deal with the fact that he has all the qualities of a thoroughbred, six pack, fresh goatee, gorgeous smile, clean nails, and you think he's looking at you, but instead he's checking the brother out over in the corner that looks just like him. Then they wonder why so many of the women have chosen to do it all by themselves. It's because we don't know what we're getting, but later for that, for me anyway. Those days are long gone. Even if I wanted one, I couldn't get a man to come within five feet of me, unless he's asking me when I took my medicine last.

It's not too much longer before I'm headed back to the hotel. My phones been vibrating like crazy, once I got a chance to check it, only one of them are from Lucy, and the rest are from Zoe. It's past midnight, and it's my guess she's just getting started. Leslie and the others are headed to the casino, it's likely I won't make it, I give Zoe one last call, and of course she's already at the casino, and from the sounds of it, either she hit, or she's just excited to be in the company of someone who did. I decide to call it a night.

Wow, I didn't realize how tired I was. After a long night of tossing and turning, I lie in the bed looking at the ceiling. I had a great time last night, but the thought of dealing with this case is way more than I imagine. I haven't heard anything from them in a while, I'm kinda nervous. I talked with Grant the other day, and according to him, there's nothing to worry about, but that's easier said than done; it's all I can think about. It really doesn't matter, just as long as I'm proven innocent.

Once I get some breakfast on my stomach, I do the usual routine to get prepared for the day, I glance out of my window and notice today is truly a day for shopping. Zoe says she'll catch up with me after her meeting and that's fine by me, because if it's one thing I can do alone, its find my way to the nearest shopaganza.

My first stop is all about the baby, a little boutique where they have the sweetest baby clothes ever. I walk around a couple of times, but I don't see anything that jumps out at me, just on my way out, I look back over at this adorable bling pacifier, it's just one thing that I can't pass up. Every baby needs a pacifier adorned with Swarovski crystals, if not for every day usage, at least to have for a special day. At the counter they have some special items for me as well, but one thing I don't have to worry about is breastfeeding, can't take any chances, in saying that I'll pass on the nursing covers.

On my way to my next stop, I see a marquee at the Mandalay where my favorite show is playing, *"The Lion King"*. I've seen this at home I know six times already, and every time I see it, it gets better. Oh well, haven't seen it in Vegas, so my mind is made up. I know what I'm doing tonight, but getting Zoe to go may not be that easy, she doesn't strike me as the musical type.

The phone rings several times before she answers.

"What's up sleepy head?" she says.

Yelling in the phone I say, "On my way to Nordstrom's."

All she says is, "That's sad, you've been here not a full twenty four hours, and you're already hitting up the malls."

"You know me."

"Yes I do, but I didn't think it would be so early, even though I'm glad you're doing it now, shopping is the last thing I want to do."

"What time do you think you'll be done?" I ask.

"Around three."

"That's good."

"Why what's up?"

"The Mandalay is playing my favorite show?"

"What, Phantom of the Opera?"

I'm laughing so hard I can't bring myself to tell her that's not the show.

"No Zoe, the Lion King."

She doesn't say a word.

"Did you hear what I said?"

"I heard you; the thing is I don't believe you."

I snap, "What's wrong with that?"

"Nothing, if you're into the whole animal kingdom thing."

"You're crazy."

"No you're crazy if you come all the way to Vegas to sit in a theatre, only to have some animals sing to you, you can get back at home on Broadway."

I'm a little embarrassed to let her know I have "special" VIP seating on Broadway. If I could sing, I would have auditioned for the part of Nala a long time ago.

I step out on a limb and ask, "So I'm guessing that's a no?"

"And you would be right." she says.

Disappointed I say, "Well, I'll see you next time."

Relieved she says, "You know where to find me, Caesar's Palace."

"Just don't give them all your money."

Laughing she says, "You know my motto, I work hard, but I also play hard."

That even makes the baby laugh.

Finally she says, "Just make sure you leave the stores with some shoes."

On that note we end our conversation, and by this time, I've arrived at the place where dreams come true. I'm trying to keep in mind what Zoe said about the shoes, that was the last thing momma said to me before I left, "don't bring another pair of shoes back to the city," but ... it's my weakness.

When I catch a glimpse at my watch, several hours have already passed and I'm still here. I only have enough time to get back to the room, freshen up, and make it to the show. I've been like a little girl all day ever since I found out it was playing here. Believe it or not, after I called to purchase my ticket, shopping wasn't really on my mind. Not sure what it is, but it's something that makes me feel so much better once I leave the theatre. This time it's going to be even more special, because it'll be the baby and me. Last time I saw it, I was by myself, after the first time Malcolm said he wasn't going anymore, so after that, it's been just me. I really didn't expect Zoe to go, but I gave it a try anyway.

I'm sooo excited you would think I was going on a date. I pull out this gorgeous gown I bought while I was out; I wanted to look extra special tonight, so I spared no cost.

Even though I'm carrying the baby weight, I take one look at myself in the mirror, and I must say both me and the baby look good. First and foremost, I love this dress because it's black and strapless, with an empire waist that has a big satin ribbon around it. I fell in love with it at first glance, from the way it fell right below my knees. I do my little girl spin that makes me feel like a princess. Momma always told me no matter how bad you may feel, or whatever it is you're dealing with, to always look my best, and with everything I've got going on, tonight I need this, I need to escape to Pride Rock.

Continuing to make myself feel like a million bucks, I throw on the freshwater pearls, and although I'm sure I will pay dearly for this later, I slip into the jeweled sling back Jimmy Choo's and cover myself in the vintage mink bolero.

It's a wonderful thing the hotel is located on the same property because if I had to go any further, I would have to hail a cab for a two minute ride. Somewhere between getting dressed and the stroll here I convince myself tonight I'm Katherine Chancellor. I think back to my finishing school days where Mrs. Johnson taught me to walk with books on my head, so I imagine she's here with me, and walk in back straight as possible considering I have a serious case of lordosis going on; but if she could see me now.

I was lucky to get such good seating on the spur of the moment. I'm just glad I was able to get an end seat for two reasons; one, I can't wait for the cast to come down the aisle, there's nothing like it, gives me the feeling I'm right there with them. Especially when the tall huge elephant makes his way to the stage, the next reason is because if I have to make a mad dash, there's no climbing over anyone, or saying, "excuse me please," all the while I'm knocking them in the back of their heads with my belly, so this is a win-win situation for everyone.

From the beginning of *"The Circle of Life,"* I'm completely mesmerized. I sit here in a daze, because no matter how many times I see this show, each time is different. By looking over the super bill doesn't look like this is the same cast as NY, but nonetheless it's awesome.

I love it how the producer recreates this to look like the real thing, from the actors' headdresses, to the animals themselves; pure genius. My first tear jerker is where Mufasa takes Simba to the top of Pride Rock and shows him the pride lands, stresses to him that he's not to go too far beyond the place he knows in fear that something bad will happen to him. But of course he does like me and others ... what we're not supposed to do, in spite the fact of Zazu giving the morning report that the hyenas are out. It's funny how when you look back over some of the things your parents have tried to show you because they love you, we don't take heed, and we have to learn the hard way. I guess its called experience. Lately, I've also come to find out that we too have family and friends such as Uncle Scar that pretend to care for us, smile in our faces, but setting us up to fail. Too bad Simba's too young at this point to understand that everyone that says they love you doesn't always mean it. I could stand to learn a lesson from that as well.

Before the first act is over I'm reminiscing over my estranged relationship with Lucy. As funny as it may be, we were thick as thieves just like Simba and Nala, but due to life's circumstances, in reality I've let Scar trick me into thinking Lucy doesn't care, so as everyone else around me. Now when I think about it, just when Mufasa finds out Simba has done the opposite of what he was told, he explains to him how being reckless, making poor choices leads to even worse destruction. Sounds similar to what all of them have been trying to tell me these past few months.

By the time Simba meets Timon and Pumbaa, I'm already singing my theme song the loudest, Hakuna Matata, and before I know it, I'm lost, and it's time for a break. I've tried to hold my water for as long as I could, so I make my way to the nearest restroom, lo and behold a lady feels mercy for me, sees that I'm on my last leg and allows me to go ahead of her. I guess there are still some nice people in the world after all.

On the way back to my seat, I hear a deep male voice that calls my name; an accent like none other.

He says, "Hello Victoria Diamond Jean-Pierre Cartiér."

Because I'm in a rush to get back before the next act begins, I hurriedly turn around to get a closer look at who this could be calling my entire name. Just as the lights dim, there he is standing in the middle of the aisle, it's Marcel Bouviér. Since its dark I can't tell whether or not the suit he has on is grey or black, either way, he looks nice. He sees I'm only focused on making my way to my seat so he doesn't force it, he smiles and gently says, "Enjoy the show."

Normally any other time I would be zoned in on Scar flirting with Nala, but now I find myself wondering what he's doing here. I slowly resist the urge to turn around to see if he's alone.

For the first time, I can honestly say I do not remember anything from the time Rafiki realizes Simba's alive 'til Nala and Simba tumble and wrestle, before he realizes it's her he's fighting with, and she convinces him to return to Pride Rock to take his rightful place as king. I really shouldn't have drank so much water earlier, because I'm fighting the urge to get up and move. Just as Simba and Scar fight to death, my bladder suddenly alerts me it's time for another run, which now means I have to get up and disturb the aura that's in this place, and it also means I get a chance to see where Mr. Bouviér is sitting and who he's sitting with, without being so noticeable.

Maybe it's a good thing I didn't see him, now I don't have to worry about answering any questions about the office. Just as I return the battle is over, Simba is just about to be crowned the new king of Pride Rock. Another tear falls as the cast all gather to celebrate as Rafiki lifts Simba and Nala's newborn baby in the air. True Love conquers all.

After the final curtain call, tears flooding my face, I realize I'm the only one in left in the theatre, so I think. I look to the right of me, and Mr. Bouviér hands me a handkerchief to wipe away my tears. I am so ashamed, a grown woman crying over a story where a lion triumphs and finds happiness in a place he calls home.

I look at the clock, and it is well past one o'clock in the morning. Marcel and I are still talking about everything from the opening act, to the color of my eyes. It's strange how we both are here at the same time, just on different occasions. He says he's been here since Wednesday of this week attending an expo. I've tried everything I know to avoid having to discuss what's going on in my world. Somehow he already knows.

We go out to eat, and it's hard for me to concentrate, because this is, well ... it was my client. Now I'm sitting here explaining to him the details from the time they called me into the office to accuse me of those ridiculous charges, up until the point where they let me go. I've told him everything minus the bogus HIV/AIDS accusations. I haven't thought about that for the last couple of hours.

All the while we've been here I can't get past how much of a gentleman he is. I thought chivalry was dead until tonight. It's been so long since I had a man, besides my father, pull out my chair for me to be seated, nevertheless have a gentleman pay for dinner and leave the tip. Even before Malcolm and I divorced that had long faded. We were almost at the point of going dutch.

Before he drops me back off at my hotel, he once again reassures me that if I need him for anything, he's only a call away. I walk up to my room thinking about the first time I went to the prom. By the time I get undressed, gently fold up my prom gown, take one last look in the mirror at the girl who was the prettiest of them all, I lie down with a smile on my face the rest of the night.

I haven't woke happy in a long time. This morning I jump up, wash my face, and do something I haven't done in a while I take my medicine. By judging the pill counter, I have way more than I should have, which only means I have time to catch up. My mother calls just to see how I am, and as much as I don't want her to, she still says a prayer before she gets off the phone. Daddy asks if I've won him enough money for him to retire in the morning, we both laugh, because he knows if I did that would be a miracle.

It's ten in the morning; I've just finished eating an omelet with a glass of orange juice, and the room phone rings; must be Zoe, she's the only one who knows my room number. I answer and to my surprise it's not her. It's Mr. Bouviér, calling to see if the baby and I survived the night.

He asks, "So how are your feet?"

I burst into laughter at the thought of that being the first thing on his mind. By the end of the night my feet were hurting so badly, I could no longer hide the fact my stallion days are over.

"They're better. Thank you for the slippers."

"No problem, didn't want you to hurt yourself any more than you had to, not to mention you were probably putting a strain on your back more than you know."

If he only knew, how much I need to be rubbed down with a jar of Ben-Gay, along with my feet soaked in a big round tub of Epson Salt, but I play it off as if all is well.

"Thanks, we're fine."

He asks, "Are you up for doing anything today?"

I follow with a brilliant answer, "Any other time I would have to check my schedule, but looks like I'm free."

"Great, if you have no other plans, can we make a day of it?"

"Aahm, a day?" I ask.

He must sense the hesitancy in my voice, because he rushes to clear it up so I want think he's a kidnapper.

He boldly says, "I have several events that I'm attending, and I would love it if you would be my guest for the day."

I say, "I have to ask, but what is the attire for the day?"

He says, "The event at one o'clock is business attire, but the event at five is Red Carpet."

I'm like what ... obviously he must not realize my clothing selections are limited, and also my feet have not recovered from last night, I first have to decide what to wear to the first event, nevertheless a Red Carpet event.

He continues, "No need to stress over that, it's on me. I just need your sizes."

Oh no he didn't, is that his way of trying to find out just how big I really am? Quickly I remember this is not my normal size, so that gives me comfort, therefore I begin to call out my new sizes.

Softly I say, "Dress size 10, shoe size, 7."

He goes on to say, "Wonderful, I'll have them sent to you, and I'll be there to pick you up at noon."

I rush to call Lucy, and I remember today's Sunday, he's in church. I hear he has really become involved in the church. Guess that's a good thing, but me I still haven't gotten to the point where I can go there. He is going to have to do something miraculous for me to believe again.

I wake Zoe to see how her night was; I know she's the last person I want to share this with, because she's the other scorned woman of this friendship, which reminds me, I'm moving too fast with him. In the wake of emotions with the show and all I forget my situation. How can I go anywhere with this man? I can't lead him to think that there may be any possibility of us becoming more than friends. It just felt so good to have someone treat you as if you matter for a change. I immediately call him back to get out of the day's events. I call the number that's in my cell phone, but I only get the voicemail. I leave a message saying that something has come up, and I'm sorry I want be able to go.

After an hour I try to convince myself I made the right choice in hopes that he received the message in time. Just as I'm pulling myself off the bed, there's a knock at the door, I answer it and it's a delivery man carrying three boxes in different sizes wrapped with gold paper topped with the most beautiful gold metallic bow. I thank him, and turn to pay him for his services only to find out, that's all been taken care of. What do I do now? I feel obligated to go at this point. It's my thought he didn't get the message. I look at the time, and its eleven fifteen so I proceed to get ready for the day.

Once I began opening the box on the top, I see that it holds two pair of shoes; one is the cutest pair of black ballerina flats, and the other a gold encrusted ballerina flat. It's my guess he doesn't want the feet to become an issue. Next I open the second box, which holds the most adorable black wrap dress, accented with a pearl neckline that says on the top 'Wear me first'. Glad I have an extra pair of tights for back up. Now for the huge box, once I get through the lightly folded tissue paper I come across a simple, yet elegant long gold sheath dress that flows at the bottom, that simply states bring along for the ride. Once I'm done, I have only twenty minutes to finish getting ready.

12:00 sharp he knocks at my door, dressed to the nines. I only wish I knew where we were going. He kindly takes my things and we head for the car. This may seem a little facetious, but I feel like the Vivian in Pretty Woman walking through the lobby, big, pregnant, but fabulous, with my version of Edward Lewis.

This has been a wonderful day thus far, I am totally surprised, I have been his advisor for a while, yet I didn't realize one of his business ventures was his ownership of five jewelry salons. He was awarded today as one of the top 50 retailers. What's so important is that one of his top selling stores is here, located right on the strip. He has invited many of his family members to celebrate with him in this special ceremony. I actually get the chance to meet his mother, who is a very charming and brilliant woman. I love her accent, reminds me of my fathers'. I would love it if I could have a little more time to talk with her, but she's only here for the ceremony, she and his brothers will be leaving out going back to France in the morning.

We're running a little behind for the evening event; needless to say I'm glad this one is held right here at the hotel where he's staying. He asks that I go up to his room where I can change, in what happens to be, of course, the Penthouse Suite. It's so beautiful in here; it's like having your own house right in the hotel.

While getting dressed I get a glance of the invite to the Red Carpet

Revue to be held in the Level 4 ballrooms. Looks like this may be a pretty nice affair, who would've thought the Venetian really knows how to throw a party. In spite of everything I'm really glad he invited me.

A couple of hours have passed and I am beginning to notice how much this little girl requires both of us to sleep, because out of nowhere I yawn, which is so embarrassing, but Marcel doesn't seem to think anything of it. The one time I get to attend a jewelry fashion show I get a case of the babyitis.

On the way back to the room my phone vibrates, I look at it and it's a New York area code number I don't recognize. The call hangs up, but they immediately call back, I answer it, and it's the call I have dreaded.

I pull the phone away from my ear to see exactly what time is it, and by the time on my phone it reads 6:20. A masculine voice on the other end asks to speak with a Victoria Cartiér. My heart flutters, and I eventually say, "This is she."

In a fast dry tone he says, "Hello Mrs. Cartiér, this is Laurence Thomas the investigator with the District Attorney's office in reference to the case in where you have been charged with several felony counts. We are asking that you report to the 22nd precinct by 5:00 tomorrow to turn yourself in, or else there will be a warrant filed for your arrest."

I hear nothing else. I'm sitting in the car frozen still. Marcel is trying to ask questions to which I have no answers. All I know is that I want my daddy! I'm miles away, and he can't save me.

Marcel comes upstairs with me to ensure I make it up safely, because he knows just how distraught I am. I must admit the last day or so, he has done everything he can to help me forget about what's going on, but even now he can't help me. I have come face to face with my fate. He waits for me to get undressed so that I can be more comfortable to situate myself in a more relaxed setting. It's good I had already begun packing my things in preparation for tomorrow's flight, because I was scheduled to leave out around six o'clock in the evening but in light of this, it looks as though I'll be leaving a lot sooner.

I'm having the hardest time getting to sleep, once again I try Lucy, and this time he answers.

Rushed he says, "Hey Sweetness, how you enjoying Sin City?"

I answer in a suttle yet disturbing tone. "I'm having a nice time."

He goes on to ask, "So when will you be home, knowing you, I hope you haven't been dragging my niece all over that place."

I can tell he's in a hurry, so I don't waste any time. I say, "Lucy the investigator called tonight, I have to turn myself in tomorrow no later than five."

I hear him drop whatever is in his hand, and then he asks, "Do I need to pick you up from the airport?"

I say, "I'm not sure yet."

"What about Zoe?" he asks.

"She's not leaving out until Tuesday, and I haven't told her yet."

He doesn't seem amused.

"What time will you be here?"

"I really don't know, the earliest I can leave for New York is 7:45, and that plane is full, but I'll call you."

He can sense the nervousness in my voice, so he tells me to get some sleep. Next, I make sure all my things are ready so that there will be no hold ups. Just as I close my eyes Marcel calls, and I answer the phone in hopes he has better news.

His voice tired, he says, "If you can, try to sleep tonight, tomorrow is a brand new day. I know it seems dark, but there is a brighter day ahead. You will have a three thirty wake up call, and you will need to be prepared to leave for New York at five o'clock a.m. Sweet dreams, and remember, no worries."

I muster up a smile, and say, "Hakuna Matata."

I'm just about ready to go. I take one last look around this room, thinking and hoping one day I will get the chance to return, and then maybe I can fully enjoy myself, without the stress.

It wasn't made clear of how Marcel was able to get an earlier flight for me, but I'm glad he did, which was very noble of him. I don't want him feeling sorry for me in any kind of way, that's why last night after he left I came to the conclusion if and when we cross paths again, I will not give any impressions that I would like him to do anything else than what he's already done. Although he stresses he's willing to help, I choose not to put myself in a position to ever be hurt again. It's better that way.

There's a knock on the door which lets me know it's my time to make it back home. I gently pick up the gown he gave me, place it over one arm as not to induce one wrinkle, because I want to remember it just as it is, perfect.

I'm told there's a car waiting to take me to the airport, I insist on giving the bellman his gratuity, but he tells me that would only be an insult, from there he proceeds to assist me into the car. Once I'm inside and I'm comfortable, I look to the left of me, and there he is, Marcel Bouviér. I'm speechless, because I was under the impression I was taking this ride by myself.

He says, "Good morning Victoria."

As I try to regain my composure without looking like a love struck teenager I say, "Good morning to you too."

"You look a bit surprised." He says.

Not wanting him to know just how surprised I am, I answer and say, "Actually, just a little."

"Well you didn't think I would let my best financial advisor go back home to face this all by herself now did you?"

"I thought you weren't scheduled to leave out until Wednesday."

"Plans were made to be changed." He says.

"Well thank you for coming with me."

"Like I said, no worries."

I turn to look out of the window not really sure what or how to feel. I can't think of anything else except what is ahead of me. I've left messages for Grant but he hasn't returned any of my calls. I've been blowing him up ever since I got the call. I vaguely remember him telling me he was going out of town, but I wasn't sure if it was this weekend or not. There is no way I can go in there alone to face them without my attorney by my side.

He gets a message on his phone, and he turns to me and says, "I've reached out to one of the best attorneys I know, he will meet us at the station, I've already briefed him on the charges, and he has been working nonstop through the night to ensure that you will not have to stay in anyone's jail."

At this moment I want so badly to ask him why he is being so nice to me. This is killing me on the inside to know that his man is going over and beyond for a woman he knows nothing about, and I am sure that is not all for nothing. From life's experiences I have learned no one does anything for you for nothing in return.

Just as I fix my mouth to tell him thank you, we're pulling up on the runway of LAS, and there is a G-IV 13 passenger jet waiting for us to board. By far this is the last thing expected. Lucy wouldn't believe this if I tried to tell him. This is far more than I could have ever asked for. As Marcel proceeds to get out of the car, it dawns on me that I have been so preoccupied that I have not taken notice that I've been wisped away to the airport in a Rolls Royce Phantom, not to mention, this man has chartered a Blue Star, to get me home so that I can turn myself into the authorities, and become another statistic. This is all so nice, but the fabulosity of all of this, doesn't compare to what may lie ahead.

Walking up the stairs, I turn and look out over the rising sun, and how beautiful the skies seem even in the midst of the fog. If I had to recall a time of beauty of the GOD I used to know, it would be now.

Chapter Fifteen
Victoria

This was the longest four and a half hour ride, although I'm so grateful to Marcel that he would go this far for me, but I don't want to think about how comfortable the flight was, because I actually could've slept the entire way. It wouldn't have been so bad, but I couldn't make myself relax long enough to take in the luxury.

Once we land, it becomes crystal clear of the fact that once I enter the doors of the precinct, I will forever have a blemish on my record. I wonder how it will read. Will it have stamped across it the words FELON, or better yet CRIMINAL, I don't think I can go through with this, its all so overwhelming, and in spite of Marcel's pleas that I calm down, it seems like the more I try, the harder it gets. This may be the hardest thing I've ever had to do.

On the ride here I call my parents, and naturally they're already one step ahead of me, they're on their way to the station as we speak, and so is Lucy. I believe Zoe is a tad bit upset with me that I didn't let her know I had already left, especially because today is the day we both have tried to put out of our minds. I assured her that I would be fine, and there's no need for her to rush home. Besides it's not much she could do from this point anyway.

I realize this will be an awkward situation being this will be my father's first time meeting Marcel. I just hope the attorney that he has really knows what he's doing, Julian offered to get someone for me, so did Reese, but at the time I felt Grant would be here and he would handle all of this. I guess none of us thought today would be that day.

Marcel is taking no chances getting me there. It was sort of strange that once we landed we were taken to his car. I would have thought he'd have some limousine pick us up, or at least we'd ride in the Range Rover, yet we pull up to what looks to be an older model Audi, that you can tell definitely has it's share of miles. Though after everything he has done, my questioning his choice of transportation right now seems less than shallow.

I overhear Marcel talking over the final details with the attorney he calls Lance, just before he hangs up he hands me the phone so that I can at least become acquainted with him before we arrive.

First he says, "Mrs. Cartiér, we will do everything in our power to make sure you are vindicated of these charges, but this is normal procedure. I ask that you don't be afraid, because I will be there with you every step of the way."

I can't help but ask, "Have you ever been involved with a case such as this?"

He replies, "Yes, several times, and to calm your fears, our firm has a 99% success rate. I only want to stress to you to answer all questions truthfully and to the best of your knowledge. If for some reason you can't remember a certain event, don't worry about it, that's why I'm here, and also it's their job to try to get you to mix up as much information as you can, but just remember always answer with your first thoughts."

By the time he and I end our power chat, I look up, and we're here. I would love to say that what we've talked about has made me feel a lot better, but if I said that it would only be to convince me and the baby, and from the way she's kicking it may take a lot more convincing. I'm rubbing my stomach in hopes of calming her, even though I know with every heart beat she feels it.

Pressing my way past the relentless media, I take the very first steps into the front door, and this place is not quite how I pictured it. All this time I was under the impression this was the actual jail, but Marcel informs me this is what is known as police headquarters. I'm not really sure of how, but in some way, now that I know this is not the jailhouse persé; it helps take the edge off. I get a glimpse at the man who is now my attorney. He introduces himself as Lance van Derbilt. I shake his hand with a strong confidence that says, "I'm depending on you."

Once I approach the desk, there's a lady sitting here with a smirk on her face as if she already knows who I am. I look back at my parents seated on the second row, give them the see you later wave, and then turn to let them know I'm here. A man resembling a younger version of Tom Selleck comes to the window, and asks that I come around through the double doors. Out of nowhere, Marcel belts out three words, "Just have faith."

I turn and say, "I need a lot more than faith."

The room is a lot different from the way I envisioned it, the lights are normal, not dark and drab like it's portrayed in the movies, although one thing remains the same ... the table. Nothing fancy, just a regular woodened table with several chairs that look like they have been worn a long time ago. I'm guessing they don't make it a priority to do any upgrades, wouldn't want the hardcore criminals getting too comfortable now would we? First he asks me if I would like a glass of water, and just because my throat is in dire need of water I take him up on it. Lance and I take a seat, and from there the questions begin. I take a look at the clock, and thanks to Marcel I'm here four hours earlier than originally scheduled, so hopefully this want be too long.

(4:05)-Investigator: Mrs. Cartiér, how long were you employed with Rucker, Banks, and Norris, LLC.

(4:05)-Victoria: Over ten years.

(4:06)-Investigator: What was your position with the firm?

(4:06)-Victoria: I've had several positions, at what time are you speaking of?

(4:07)-Investigator: The entire time you worked for the firm.

This will not be too hard to answer, being that this is the place I've been since I graduated college.

(4:07)-Victoria: I originally began with the firm as an intern; from there I received a position working in the mailroom. I held that position for two years, until I was offered a position as runner, and I held this position for almost three years. From there I worked myself to the position of Junior Partner Status, in which I held this position for the last five years, up until the point I was offered the opportunity to become one of the Senior Partners.

(4:09)-Investigator: While working in the mailroom, did you have access to your client's personal information during that time?

(4:10)-Victoria: Well ... yes and no. If I did it was already enclosed in an envelope.

(4:11)-Investigator: But you did have access to their information correct?

Right now I'm beginning to get a little disgusted.

(4:12)-Victoria: Being that I worked in the mailroom, I guess you can say I did.

(4:13)-Investigator: Was there ever a time you opened any of the mail that would come through the office?

Lance leans over to me, and says, "You don't have to be precisely accurate, just try to remember if there were any times where you had to open the mail."

(4:15)-Victoria: Yes, there were times where I was asked to open the mail.

(4:15)-Investigator: Did you open the mail by yourself or were you in the presence of someone else?

Now how am I supposed to remember every time I opened mail by myself, or if someone was around? But I answer anyway.

(4:16)-Victoria: There have been times where I've had to open mail myself, as well as in the presence of others.

(4:17)-Investigator: What is your relationship with Tyler Darwin?

(4:18)-Victoria: We have a business relationship.

(4:18)-Investigator: How long have you and Mr. Darwin known each other?

(4:19)-Victoria: Since college.

(4:19)-Investigator: So you would say you've known him long enough that if you both wanted to plan something of this nature, then it wouldn't be a problem?

(4:20)-Victoria: No! I am not saying that ... I'm saying I've known him since college, we both went to NYU, and—

(4:22)-Investigator: What Mrs. Cartiér? Did you take the same classes; hang out at the same parties, what?

Lance senses my frustration and reassures me that he's only trying to upset me enough that I might say something that they can possibly use against me. The investigator must sense the same thing, because all of a sudden the questions switch.

(4:25)-Victoria: No, Mr. Thomas we did not hang out, he went to classes, and so did I, whatever he did on his own time was his business.

(4:27)-Investigator: What was your annual salary Mrs. Cartiér?

I snap ... what does this have to do with anything. Again Lance tells me this is all a part of the investigation, just to answer the questions to the best of my knowledge. I hesitate.

(4:29)-Victoria: If you must know, my base salary was $500,000.

He whispers something in the other investigators ear.

(4:30)-Investigator: This is what Investment Advisors get these days; I must be in the wrong business.

I say nothing. He walks around the office as if he has a vendetta against me or something. His tone of voice changes dramatically.

(4:30)-Investigator: What about your personal assets, how many homes and cars do you own?

What! By this time, I'm beginning to feel like this is all about me. This has nothing to do with why I lost my job.

(4:31)-Victoria: I currently own two homes, and if you must know, I own one car.

(4:32)-Investigator: If you don't mind Mrs. Cartiér, may I ask what is your remaining mortgage, as well as what is the type of car you currently drive?

(4:33)-Victoria: First of all, both my homes, I own outright. I also own a 2007 Mercedes S550.

(4:35)-Investigator: Did you pay for the car outright?

(4:36)-Victoria: To be exact, no I didn't, my father is the owner of a Mercedes dealership, therefore I received dealers cost, at which this allowed me a huge discount, for the first year I agreed to pay a note, but after my d-d-vorce, I made final payments.

The second investigator mumbles under his breath, "Are you sure it wasn't from the client's fund that you paid off your car?"

(4:37)-Investigator: Mrs. Cartiér, you're divorced?

(4:37)-Victoria: Yes, what does that have to do with anything?

(4:38)-Investigator: How long have you been divorced?

Tapping my fingers on the table, I began to think this is pure harassment.

(4:38)-Victoria: Almost six months.

He pauses, stares off as if he's calculating dates in his head.

(4:39)-Investigator: So you were married during the time the charges were brought upon you?

(4:40)-Victoria: No I was not. I recently found out about these incriminating charges against me.

He moves on, good ... but not for long, he quickly comes back asking all of these questions regarding my finances, my investments, off shore accounts, retirement options, he practically questions my entire portfolio. He questions the places I go on vacation, how long to take vacations, the amount of money I spend on vacations. Do I pay for my purchases with cash, or do I opt to use credit. He goes so far as to ask what I do in my off time. Besides trying to make more money, everyone knows that. I shop! He asks do I have any supplemental income as far as alimony. This actually makes me regret that I refused to have Malcolm pay anything in the divorce decree. I should have held him liable to at least pay something, because this only gives this man another reason to think I need to steal someone else's money. I've been called a lot of things, but never a thief.

(5:00)-Investigator: Moving to the day at hand, Mrs. Cartiér, do you recall speaking with a Mr. Bailey Coleman in regards to him investing any of his portfolio in a hedge fund?

(5:01)-Victoria: Yes I do, but I didn't—

Lance has to calm me at this point, because I know for a fact I didn't make him do anything out of his own will.

(5:03)-Investigator: Mrs. Cartiér, can you tell me exactly what happened when you spoke to the client?

I ask to be excused to take a restroom break; this little girl has been very patient with me. The entire time he's asking me questions, she's kicking like crazy, I wonder if she knows her mother is couped up in some grungy room where the floors look as though they haven't been cleaned in days, not to mention the walls could stand a little Ralph Lauren Premium, at least two coats.

I never pictured myself trying squeezing into a stall in a police precinct, I guess they're all the same, but it's just something about this one, nothing special. You would think they would spring for the Charmin, instead of **tis-sue**, it really doesn't give any hope to someone like me going back to sit in a chair that truly wasn't made for comfort. My first mind is telling me to bring along some "tis-sue" just to sit on, but I'm hoping I want be here much longer.

Walking back inside, I think of how much my life has changed in the last few months, here I am being questioned for something I didn't do, trying to help out a fellow colleague. I think of my parents, I feel I have let them down so much. I know Marcel is being very nice to help me, but I'm not sure if he has enough pull to get me out of this.

(5:15)-Investigator: Now where were we?

(5:16)-Victoria: You were asking me what took place between me and Mr. Coleman, well ... to my recollection, both Tyler and I were scheduled to meet with Mr. Coleman at 1:00, but he arrived half an hour late. It was agreed by both Tyler and me that I would be the first advisor since I've had more experience in hedge funds and how they work. I was the first to speak with Mr. Coleman in regards to the consultation, because he had been a previous client, and I worked with him on some other business.

(5:17)-Investigator: Was he aware that there would be two advisors?

(5:17)-Victoria: Yes, I explained this to him during out initial phone conversation.

(5:18)-Investigator: Is there anything else you explained to him at that time.

(5:18)-Victoria: No, but during the day of the consultation, I explained that first he would need to be established as an accredited advisor, and once that was established there would be necessary paperwork involved, and that it would be best that if he was serious about investing into a hedge that he would need to have an attorney draft the necessary offering documents. Although we already had the ones needed to begin the process.

(5:18)-Investigator: What makes him an accredited advisor?

(5:19)-Victoria-An accredited investor is any individual with a net worth greater that $1 million, and has also has an income in the past two years that exceeds $200,000 a year, and expects to remain that way, or holds assets greater that of $5 million.

(5:19)-Investigator: Did Mr. Coleman meet those standards?

(5:19)-Victoria-Yes, when I last worked with him his total net worth was $20 million.

(5:19)-Investigator: What documents are involved?

(5:19)-Victoria- The subscription agreement, and more importantly the Private Placement Memorandum, also known as the PPM.

(5:20)-Investigator-What does the PPM entail?

(5:20)-Victoria: This is an extensive document that's created individually for each hedge fund. It basically explains all relevant trading strategies, along with the risk associated with trading. It has bios of all involved, namely attorneys, accountants, and the partnerships compliance with blue sky laws.

(5:22)-Investigator: On the day of the meeting, did Mr. Coleman seem at all interested in signing up for the hedge fund?

(5:22)-Victoria: At that time it was hard to tell, although he did take time to thank me for the information.

(5:23)-Investigator: What did you stand to gain from this fund? What was the fee charged to manage Mr. Coleman's fund?

(5:23)-Victoria: The normal management fee is 2%, but because we were splitting it, it was settled at 4%. With 20% charged as a performance fee, but also you must know I had to spend approximately fifty thousand dollars in legal and administrative fees, before any trading was ever to be done.

(5:25)-Investigator: So if he invested $1million, then his fee would have been $40,000, to be split between you and Mr. Darwin?

(5:25)-Victoria: Yes, and whatever his performance was then we would gain 20%.

(5:26)-Investigator: So basically you were standing to make a killing.

What did he think I went to school for nothing. Money is all I know, and I am not settling for anything.

(5:26)-Victoria: That's my job; it's what I get paid to do.

(5:27)-Investigator: At anytime, was there a point that anyone was excused from the meeting?

(5:27)-Victoria: Yes, after about an hour into the meeting, my assistant informed me my previously scheduled client had arrived for our meeting. Therefore I explained to Mr. Coleman that Mr. Darwin would be responsible for handling any other questions and concerns at that point. If he wanted to follow up with me then he was free to contact me.

There's a knock at the door, and a lady with long blonde hair sticks her head in the door and hands him a manila folder, then he stops to read over whatever is inside of the folder.

(5:32)-Investigator: So how long would you say you were away from Mr. Darwin and Mr. Coleman?

(5:33)-Victoria: Over an hour, because my meeting lasted longer than I had expected.

(5:33)-Investigator: Then what?

(5:33)-Victoria: About a couple of hours later, Tyler comes into my office very excited with papers in hand, saying Mr. Coleman is ready to move forward, but he would need my sign the signature pages. So I signed and that was that.

(5:35)-Investigator: Did you notice if Mr. Darwin's signature was on the agreement?

(5:36)-Victoria: No I didn't, I took Tyler's word that Mr. Coleman was ready, so I didn't feel I needed to check behind him especially since I was only helping him out anyway. It was fine with me that we shared the fee.

(5:36)-Investigator: So you trusted him that much.

(5:37)-Victoria: Yes, and being that Mr. Coleman had done business with us prior, I figured Tyler would do the honest thing. Later it was clear that Mr. Coleman had chosen to subscribe to the Hedge Fund, which that was my understanding from the beginning.

Again he and the other investigator whisper in each other's ear, exchanging ideas, jotting down thoughts. I have always despised that, maybe because you never know what the other persons are really saying. You're only left to your own imagination, and just like now, my imagination is telling me this is not looking good.

(5:40)-Investigator: Alright Mrs. Cartiér, going by the phone records we've received, it clearly shows where you and Mr. Darwin have talked on several occasions after work hours, and your credit card statements show where you've made substantial purchases that line up with the time where Mr. Coleman has made these accusations against you. According to this, looks like you spend most of your time spending other people's money at Saks, Neiman's, and Bergdorf's, not to mention Barney's. Do you ever shop places that the average working person can only afford to go?

The second advisor laughs out in the background, "Is Payless even an option for you? No that's probably beneath you." Then the first investigator runs down my bank statement laughing, "There's a purchase on here from Target on Flatbush. Let me guess ... Bloomingdales doesn't carry Evian?"

Hearing them laughing and making fun of me is beginning to upset me even more. I'm not as shallow as they are trying to make me out to be. I've been known to shop in other places besides department stores, I've even gone to a local Wal-Mart a time a two. Then he continues.

(5:44)-Investigator: It would be one thing if your signature wasn't the only one on the agreement besides Mr. Coleman's.

(5:44)-Victoria: So you're telling me Tyler never signed the paperwork?

He shows me a copy of the agreement where I signed, and Tyler's signature is no where on it. He tricked me!

(5:45)-Investigator: As you can see Mrs. Cartiér yours and Mr. Coleman's are the only ones present.

Like I said this doesn't look good.

(5:45)-Victoria: So what does that mean?

(5:45)-Investigator: It means that since we have a great deal of evidence against you, mainly the subscription agreement where you signed, along with other documents we have no other choice but to formally charge you.

I start screaming and wailing.

(5:46)-Victoria: But I didn't fill out the documents! Tyler had to be the one to transpose the client's information, not me. He had to get it off of the New Account Card …

Lance tries to calm me, but this is way more than I thought. Tears rush to my eyes. I do not realize it, but I'm crying even harder.

(5:48)- Investigator: By this, you are the one responsible for the clients' information.

My heart drops, and suddenly the room comes to a standstill. I feel faint, and of course Lance is here to help me, but I can't believe what I'm hearing. I thought I would come here, they would ask me a few questions and that was it, now they're telling me, they want to prosecute me. God where are you when I need you, you've let me down once again.

He tells me that I'll need to go across the street so that I can be booked in. What! I take one look at my mother as I head out of the door; she looks like she's lost her little girl forever. Looking at Daddy makes me want to break down, but he has a don't worry, daddy's got you look on his face. Oh and Marcel, standing right here at the door waiting for me to take the next step. If it was a puddle of water under my feet, I believe he would wipe it up just so my feet wouldn't get wet.

With the noise of the traffic, and sirens everywhere, firmly Marcel tells Lance to call him ASAP, let him know what the outcome is. As if he doesn't know. The outcome is that I'm going to deliver this baby in jail.

I'm so displaced from this whole thing, and I still can't believe the media is still out here, scrimmaging to get cruel snapshots, only to be sold to the highest bidder. The SEC is going to have a ball with this one. Now I guess you can add me to the list of with Bernie Madoff, and the McKelvy's.

There are cameras flashing everywhere, I never thought that a walk across the street would take this long. One lady even has the nerve to ask "Do I expect to spend Thanksgiving behind bars?" which only makes me even more nervous, because with everything going on, I forget this will be my first holiday alone.

Lance keeps reassuring me I'll be able to bond myself out, but one thing … we aren't sure of the amount as of yet, the closer I get, the more afraid I get. All of the times I've made fun of the people on COPS, now I see how they feel. This is nothing I would wish on anyone, not even Noëlle.

Escorted by a police officer resembling Ponch from CHIPS, I take a breath and realize this could be my last walk of freedom. It doesn't take me long to notice this is a far cry from the tour my eighth grade class took as an attempt to scare us straight. Until this point those vivid memories were what has kept me from this place all along. Never got past the hideous and grotesque looks of the women that looked like they hated you, just because you were on the other side. Not to mention the attire that is worth enough tickets, that the best of the best fashion polices would shy away from, and last I checked, the equation (Fashionista + an orange pair of scrubs with numbers written across the back, DOES NOT = my idea of a trendsetter), translated, that is a bad fashion statement.

As I enter the doors they already know who I am, and first is a big boned lady takes me aside where she has me place both of my hands in a concoction of black paint so they're able to get a carbon copy of my fingerprints. Next comes the most awful thing that could ever happen, my picture is being taken on the one day I wear a multi color striped polo sweater, with a ponytail in my hair! And let's not talk about the bags under my eyes from having a few hours of sleep; needless to say this is not the snapshot I'd planned to give her as a memory of her mother. It's killing me to know this will be the image plastered over all airwaves on this evening's six o'clock news.

I'm told my bond is $500,000, and there is no way I can get my hands on $50,000 in such short notice. This goes down as one of the worst days of my life.

Forty-five minutes later I'm released, somehow my bond has been posted, and I'm told I can walk out of this world that's inside of a world. Once I make it outside, the first faces I see of course are my parents, and somewhere in between my exclusive photo shoot Lucy's made it here, and Marcel … yep he's waiting patiently for me to get myself together. I guess he say's what has he gotten himself into. I feel like this is all happening so fast. Knowing my luck this would be the day I give birth to my angel.

It's now seven thirty, all is calm, and for a while I was beginning to think people would never leave from in front of my door. I never knew just how relentless those people were. They'll do anything for a story. My parents stayed as long as they thought they should, which translates to, I made them leave. I need to be or shall I say I want to be alone. I hope I didn't offend Marcel, even though I understand he was the one who posted my bail, for which I am very grateful. I offered to pay him back, but he refused. I only wish I knew what his intentions were. No one does these kinds of things for you, just because.

As usual around this time, she gets a desire for a McDonald's chocolate sundae with extra nuts, and what kind of mother would I be if I didn't oblige her. Before we head out, I take one look out the windows just to make sure no one is hiding around the corners, or behind any cars anywhere; they've already gotten me one time today looking a hot mess. I can see it now, all over Monday's newsstands there will be a copy of the latest edition of Star with a caption of me in a long maxi dress, baby doll slippers, trench coat, and to top it off, I've thrown on the close fitted hat that reveals the real me although my objective is to be strictly incognito. The caption will read "What Not to Wear."

This must be the longest drive thru ever, I only wanted a sundae, but instead it's a car full of teenagers ordering up the entire place. For some reason, my hand pushes the button for 1190 WLB, and suddenly I hear Kirk Franklin's voice saying, "I know they hurt you, they saw you stumble but didn't help you, now they left you. They were quick to pray, but slow to move. Then it says ... now your empty, too tired to run, you walk away, but in the night there's a voice, if you listen He sweetly says, come back to your first love, come back home where you belong ... "

Sitting here this long is causing me to think about this day in general. It's so hard for me to imagine that this could play out in the worst way. Just the idea of my having to stand before a judge and make a plea is driving me insane. I tried to play the cool, calm, and collective role around everyone else earlier, but I really don't think I can handle this too much longer. It's like my life is flashing before my eyes. At this time he's saying, "...you didn't make it; you thought your love would last forever, ain't it funny how a chapter can change a story. Cold and lonely, you never knew hurt could feel this way, understand there's a plan if you're patient, just hear the savior say."

Before I notice, my face is soaked with tears. I take a trip down memory lane reminiscing about my life as a once happily married woman with everything at my feet. It was as if everything was right with the world. My marriage wasn't an imitation of the Cosby's, but we had good times. I don't like to think about it, but sometimes I wish we could have worked it out. I believe Malcolm and I could have began to go to church, and maybe, just maybe things would have turned out different, and I wouldn't be here pregnant, HIV positive, and most of all, I would probably still have my job. There are other times where I think about my relationship with Noëlle, I can't believe it, but one day I actually wanted to pick up the phone and make amends with her, but ... I can't bring myself to do that just yet. It still hurts too much.

After waiting for almost thirty minutes to get my sundae, I find myself stuck at a stoplight between 145th and Broadway. It's like my mind is playing tricks on me. I'm thinking back over my life, and I remember there was a time when God loved me, I would pray and He would answer but now ... I think of the times my mother telling me growing up that God will never put more on you than you can bear, but I can't help but ask where He has been all of this time. It's like I've been in this whirlwind for a very long time by myself. I've had no one to call on. I have to ask, does He really love me, or does He plan for me to live the rest of my life like this?

I get so caught up, until I totally forget I'm behind the wheel. Just as I begin to do what momma has always told me to do; call on the name of Jesus, there's a loud crash, and a jolt through my body like never before. I don't realize it, but I've been hit from the side by a car driven by a woman with the alcohol level well over 0.08%.

Next thing I know there are ambulances, fire trucks, sirens sounding, and more importantly, I can't move. My legs are bound, there's an airbag pressed against my face, blood on my steering wheel, front windshield cracked, and most of all, there's a puddle of blood in my dress! People are coming from everywhere. A man with an EMT uniform on tries to rescue me from my seat, to no avail, I'm trapped. I hear them saying the wheel has popped and broken causing my legs to become crushed, therefore they need to call in reinforcement. My breaths are becoming more and shallow. The pain, oh the pain, is nothing like I've ever felt before. I tell myself to hold on, but it's getting hotter and hotter, I don't think I can do it. My chest is hurting, everything on me is hurting, and I try to force myself to wiggle my toes, but I can't. Then I hear this loud and excruciating noise at the top of my once beautiful car tugging and pulling. The top is gone! I feel myself slowly drifting away, but I think about my baby, I can't leave her now, not like this. We're all we have!

I look and people are surrounding me; all I can see is up. I try to turn my head, but I'm restricted by the brace that's been placed on my neck. The kind man, as I know him, continues to ask me my name, and I'm drawing a blank. I can hear him, but I can't speak. I can only feel the tears running down my cheeks. I can't stop thinking of my baby; I pray she's alright, because I haven't felt her move. Before I go into shock, the last thing I do, is say to myself, "Lord, if you hear me, please help me."

Chapter Sixteen
Victoria & God

An entire day has gone by, and I'm just now awaking. For as much as I can see I'm inside of a room with enclosed windows, a small television, and I'm lying in a bed that is nothing compared to the luxurious queendom I'm accustomed to. I hear a machine that alarms, notifying a woman oddly dressed in a pair of grey scrubs that has a nametag attached to it which reads Rita. She comes in to see why the machine keeps beeping, there's a chance it could be related to the needle in my vein, but I try to get a glimpse of her to say thank you, but I'm confined to this bed with what looks to be an oxygen mask covering my face. She comes over to adjust the mask to make sure I'm getting it all in. I look at her and give her a smile that lets her know I'm very grateful to her at this point.

About a half an hour after she leaves out, my parents come in with some bags that holds some of my intimate apparel, along with other items, such as a toothbrush, deodorant, along with some more personal things. There aren't many words said, I'm just glad they're here. I rub my stomach to make sure my baby is okay, but ... I suddenly notice it's not as large as it once was. Where is my baby? Oh my God, where is she? I take a look at my mother, and she looks as if she wants to get in the bed and hold me for as long as she can. My father comes over to the side of the bed, and whispers in my ear that they had to deliver her by cesarean because her heart rate dropped so much. I can see the tears swell in his eyes, it's like he has so much he wants to say, but the words won't come out. He holds my hand to comfort me, and to let me know no matter what he loves me.

He says, "Baby she's going to be alright, God's watching over her."

There's a confused look on my face, I look at him to say, "Is she—

"No baby, she's alright, she made it, by the grace of God, and so did you."

I look over at momma, and she's putting up the cards people have obviously given her, but to settle my mind I need to see her face to make sure my baby is alright.

She must have sensed that because she says, "Your father is right, the baby is wonderful."

She walks to the opposite side of the bed, and gently says, "Because I lost so much blood, her lungs are not performing as they should, so she's on a ventilator."

I burst into tears, but the pain is so horrible it hurts to cry. My father says I have two cracked ribs, and also because of the things I have done lately such as the partying, and constantly drinking, there are other factors at stake. Right then my stomach is tied in a knot. I maneuver the mask from over my face long enough to ask my mother, is she really okay. I know she knows what I am asking, because she has this strange look on her face. At this moment the doctor comes in.

"Good afternoon," he says.

I nod my head, because the pain in my chest is unbearable.

Looking over the chart, he says, "Mrs. Cartiér, looks like you have suffered a severe concussion, along with your having severe internal bruising, which was completely due to the seatbelt, and the pressure of your airbag deploying, but looking over your scans everything else looks normal, but there is still more test I would like to order."

The only thing I want to know is what about my baby. When can I see her?

He goes on to say, he wants me to have more lab work done, because my viral load can't be correct, he says it's now 150,000, which means I'm no longer undetectable! He says he's put a call into my ID doctor to compare these results against my last labs. My stomach is doing flips; I get the sudden urge to vomit. For the last couple of visits the doctor has told me I've done well, can it be all the drinking? When I think about it, I have been doing a lot of things out of the norm lately.

"Victoria, before I order another set of labs is there anything you would like to tell me?" He asks.

I feel so bad, because I never thought that having a few drinks would do this much harm, and again what about my baby? How will this affect her?

Because my parents are in the room there is no way I can't tell him.

"Yes it is, for the past few months I've been doing a great deal of drinking, and could this be the reason." I say.

He continues to look down into my chart, while making notes. I hope he's not making note of how bad a mother I am.

"About how long has it been?" he asks.

The only thing I can say is, "Over two months."

My mother looks so disappointed in me, as if she wants to say, "I told you so." The doctor writes down a little more information, and then he says, "We will have to make sure the baby has had her first dose of AZT." He closes the chart, and says he will get back with me when the rest of the results are in.

Before he leaves, I force myself to ask, "What about my baby?" He turns around to say, "Dr. Johnson, the pediatrician will be in to speak with you in regards to the baby. She will be able to give you more information than I can." Again tears fill my eyes. I've heard it said before that the fear of the unknown can be hard to deal with.

I feel myself getting sleepy; maybe it's my body's way of saying it needs rest. My parents have decided to get something to eat and allow me to rest; it's not too much longer that I find myself slipping into a deep sleep. I can say by far this is the most peaceful sleep I've had in a while.

Obviously my subconscious mind takes over and I dream I'm in a place where for once there are no distractions; it's quiet, calm and most of all its peaceful. To my knowledge I'm here alone in a huge field of nothing but acres and acres of grassy lands, symbolic of plush emerald carpet spread out over the earth. The flowers look as though they were planted just before I arrived, the sweet smell in the air is a fragrance that I long to stay with me forever. The skies are heavenly, with the sun making an appearance, shining ever so brightly. The wind that wraps itself around me blows gently across my face, and finally the sounds from the streaming rivers that flow past me just to reassure me of its beauty.

This day, I have an encounter with a man that says he knows me, although I'm not sure if we've ever met before. He walks past me in hopes that I would notice him, his voice is soft and pleasant, not too harsh, just the right tone. His presence demands my attention. Eventually he asks would I mind if he and I talk for a while. I tell him I don't mind. As he begins to speak, the earth shakes from the sound of his voice. At first he tells me things about myself I never knew. He even goes as far as to share with me my hopes, desires, inner most thoughts, and dreams.

I ask, "How do you know these things about me?"

He simply says, "I know each and every one of your thoughts, the good and the bad, even before you think them."

The more he talks I began to sense I've heard his voice somewhere before. I continue, "How do you know me?"

He responds, "I knew you before you were formed in your mother's womb."

My voice begins to tremble, because now this is beginning to get a little scary. One minute I'm walking by myself, and out of nowhere this man appears telling me things that only I should know. He reaches to grab my hands, and suddenly the feeling of heaviness in my chest is lifted, I feel free and light. He senses my hesitation, but doesn't move.

I turn to face him, look him in his eyes, and at this moment everything is clear to me. I see myself as the innocent little girl I once was.

He says to me, "I'm here."

I take a step back out of fear, and before I can ask a question, all of a sudden he asks me, "Do you believe me?"

I'm thrown for a loop. He asks me again. "Do you believe me?"

I reply, "I 'm not sure what to say, because I really don't know who you are."

"Who do you think I am?"

"Well ..."

In my life I've heard this asked before, but it doesn't take long for me to realize this is God. I'm having a conversation with God. I immediately jump to defense mode and began asking him a number of WHY questions. He doesn't flinch. Every question has an answer. I began to tell him of all the things I've gone through these past months, and how I'm at my wits end, to the point where I'm tired, I'm weary, I don't think I can go on. My heart is broken, I've had family and friends to walk out on me, even my best friend failed me.

Angrily I ask, "If you loved me the way you say you do, and you being the good and loving God you are, why you have allowed all these things to happen to me?"

He answers, "I love you, because you are my child, and there are times when I allow my children to suffer, because this is how I'm glorified, but please know it all works together for good, and in your suffering there is a divine purpose."

I turn away, but still ask, "What is that purpose?"

He replies, "My ultimate purpose is for my children to grow into the likeness of my Son Jesus Christ, and the suffering you have endured is a part of the process of your being sanctified; where I will ultimately get the glory."

I continue to ask, "But why me, why have you caused me to suffer like this?"

He says, "Because suffering will produce perseverance, and perseverance proves your faith in me, and remember through all of your struggles, pains, and heartaches, you still have victory."

I go on, "But even in that you still allowed me to have a rich life, full of success."

He tells me, "One thing you should know, is yes I allowed you to become successful, but your idea of success is not my idea. I never said that I wouldn't give you things of the world, but I never meant for my children to become a part of the world. Having nice cars, large homes, the initials behind your name, the high rise office, these things do not equal to success, they are a part of it. Success in my eyes is living my Word, doing what I have asked of you to do, but somewhere down the line you forgot all about me, you became puffed up, it became all about you, you felt you were ultimately responsible for your success, and as far as them taking it away, I am the only one that has the power to give and to take away. I have the power to open doors no man can close, because I am God."

Right here is where I began to feel very badly, because there were times where I had no time for Him, it was all about me. Momma calls it, penciling Him in to my schedule.

Although it's over and done I really want to know the answer to this question, "My relationship with Malcolm, and then the divorce, why did this happen?"

He says, "First let me say, I do not condone divorce, but I do realize it consists of two sinful beings, so there's a chance it's going to happen. But one thing you must keep in mind, I designed marriage that the two would be equally yoked, and I did not choose Malcolm, you chose him. So there are times when my children tend to hold on to things I want to set free. I know he hurt you, but there are just some things you have to experience in order to know I am that I am."

"But what about the HIV?" I ask.

"His response is, "What about it? It starts at the beginning, from Adam and Eve. Before they sinned, there was no sin, and when I placed judgment on Adam, this is where death entered the world. And at that point all sickness became a part of this cursed world, and they that live in this world shall be subject to death. Although I'm aware that you were on the receiving end, but as you know all choices bear a consequence, but if you do as I ask you shall live."

"But why me?"

He looks me in my eyes, and says with a fiery passion, "I chose you, just as I chose Job; for different reasons, but the same outcome. I knew Job was a perfect man and he would not curse me. Yet you on the other hand, I know you are weak, I know you have an anemic faith. Therefore I needed to test you, to see just how much you really love Me. In that you have cursed me, you have said horrible things about me, but still I love you, in the end I know you will endure."

At this moment, I'm speechless, because I think about all the cruel and nasty things I've said about Him. I've doubted His love for me, I even thought of taking my life. Who am I to do these things, to a man that loves me so unconditionally that He would go to the ends of the world to find me? I feel less than the crud on the ground.

He continues, "Victoria, my daughter, for so long I've waited for an invitation to come into your life. And yes I recognize you've put me on the back burner, but I still love you, you're my child. I will never leave you nor forsake you."

"So where have you been all this time?" I ask.

He simply says, "I never left, I've been here all the time."

We've been talking so long; I can't believe I forget to ask about my baby.

"Can you tell me if my baby will live or die?"

His response is not what I expected, it's plain and simple.

He asks, "Do you believe I am who I say I am? Do you trust me to do what I say I will do? She is a heritage, the fruit of your womb, she is a reward."

With my face full of tears, I only say, "Yes."

I'm not sure where this is coming from, but I can't pass up the opportunity to ask about Marcel.

He laughs, and says, "You're a curious one aren't you? Also know, he's my beloved, I picked him especially for you."

I get goose bumps because for so long I've wanted someone to love me for me, to love me through the ups and the downs, the good and the bad.

"Should I trust him?" I ask.

"Do you trust me?" He asks.

Before we end, I need to know how will my life turn out, will I live long enough to see my child graduate, get married, and have children of her own.

I ask, "What about the accident, will I live?"

He ends by asking me, "Why are ye fearful, O ye of little faith."

By this time I am on bended knee, praising him from the pit of my soul. I'm crying out to him, as I call on his name.

Father forgive me for not believing you, forgive me for not trusting you, Lord please give me the courage to stand against the devil, where as he may attempt to make me believe your love for me is not true. I want to live for you; I want to be an example so that my child may see you through me. I love you, and I give you all the praise even in the midst of my storms. I say thank you, for you are El Shaddiah, my God almighty. You have been my strength and my power. You are, Jehovah Shalom, you are the peace that passes all understanding. Lord, you are Jehovah Nissi, you have protected me through the fires, and the storms, and Father you are Jehovah Jireh, my provider. I continue to cry out ... Lord I will not die, I will live! And I claim it in your name that by your stripes I am healed, because you are my Jehovah Raphe!

It's seven o'clock, and it seems like I've been with Him all day. I awake with tears still falling. Sitting next to me is Marcel, my parents, Lucy, and Malcolm. Next, in comes the nurse with the most beautiful creature on this face of the earth; a seven pound, eight ounce little girl. She has the striking features of her father. Her skin is a warm caramel color. She adorns fine curly hair, with bright and wide green eyes, taken from her mother, and the hint of a smile. She appears to be a replica of mine. She's gorgeous, nothing I've ever seen. A little girl I named Gabrielle Grace Cartiér. My mother asked, "Of all names why Gabrielle?" I smile and say, "Why not Gabrielle? Of course, she's named in honor of my favorite designer to ever grace this planet, Gabrielle "Co-Co" Chanel!

Chapter Seventeen
Victoria & Gabrielle

It's hard to believe it's been almost two weeks since I've officially been a mother. I'm so excited, because today my baby comes home. I think they've poked and prodded on her enough for her to want to get up and walk out of this place on her own.

I don't know what made me think otherwise, but Malcolm's been here nearly every day she's been in the nursery. I look and I'm so proud of her, because she's really been a brave little girl through all of this.

According to the doctor's she should be fine. She was term and otherwise there weren't any other major complications. She's now breathing well on her own, which that's very good to know; at least that removes some of my worries. I'm still nervous about her having to be tested over the next eighteen months. The doctor did explain to me that babies born to HIV mothers tend to carry their mothers' antibodies, and this is why remaining calm is easier said than done.

Her initial DNA test was negative, and she will be tested again at 2 months, then again at four months. At that time if all of those test have been negative I have been assured it's safe to say she doesn't have the virus, however there is one last test that will need to be done at eighteen months, in which he again assures me that more than so this should come back negative as well.

The hard part is she's received AZT three times a day since birth, and she will also have to continue the same regimen for the next four weeks, of which I have been told is standard. What scares me is that I will need to give 0.65 cc's, but thanks to the nurse who has shown me the tuberculin syringe needed as well as she's shown me how to draw the medicine correctly. I'm so afraid I will do something to mess that up too. Knowing this, it would be much easier to say that everything is fine, but because of my irresponsibility, missing doses of my meds weeks at a time, also drinking as if there was no hope, I just only pray that I haven't done anything to further harm her.

I thought I chose the perfect coming home outfit for her, but Lucy has shown out once again. He's had one of his "Diva" friends create the most beautiful antique crocheted layette with silk underlay, with the booties to match; he says only the best for his little niece. He even saw to it she was camera ready, and that would explain the pair of hired photographers here to capture this moment, as if my Canon is not good enough. Not to mention you would think he's the "mother in waiting", because he's here in all of his fabulousness. Except if you ask him about changing diapers, there's a sudden rush of amnesia. The one thing I love about him though is that he didn't forget about me, he's made sure I have enough help since it's going to be rather difficult lifting her; I'm still pretty sore from the injuries. It'll be a wonderful day when I can shed the bandages, and the next to go will be this horrific wrap that hugs me so tight. I know I should at least loose ten pounds.

The only wrap I really would love to be in is a seaweed wrap at the spa, nothing better than that right now. I'm imagining at this moment, the lights are dimmed, and of course Beethoven's Moonlight Sonata playing in the background, and then a therapist named Kingston comes in and prepares me by first giving me a rejuvenating brush massage, and next he smoothes on seaweed paste all over my body, and then wraps me with those most relaxing warm thermal sheets, and to finish it off eucalyptus oil giving my body the essential nourishment, it most definitely needs. Uum, uum, uum! It's like I can taste it. Hopefully it'll help rid me of some of these stretch marks I've noticed in the last few months. Now that's surely a no-no! But one things for sure, after forty-five minutes of that, I should have the most supple and smooth skin ever. As a matter of fact I need to make it a point to call Mandisa to get me on the schedule at least once a week for the next six weeks, which to some may be a little pricey, but who cares beauty is not cheap!

Unexpectedly, Malcolm asks to take us home, but Marcel's made arrangements for that already. Right now I really don't care who does it as long as Gabrielle and I get home; I've waited so long for this. The past couple of weeks have been long for me, waiting and waiting. Yet Marcel has done nothing to pressure me, he's only been the perfect gentleman, by attending to me as well as making sure Gabrielle is taken care of, without overstepping Malcolm in any way. But I can't focus on that, my only concern is to make sure my baby is okay.

On the ride home Marcel doesn't say much, he just allows me this time with my daughter, although I do catch him peeking in the mirror once or twice. I even think I see him smile, especially when he realizes he's flying over a bump in the road, but it's not that bad today, we're not riding in the Audi. He decided to pull out the Range Rover, in which this is one smooth ride, if I must say so myself, and the leather, the smell of the leather, which only reminds me of my baby ... MY CAR! It brings tears to my eyes just to think of it. The worst part is the thought of having to ride in a 'courtesy car' that my father recommended until I can decide what I want to do. But I'm sure he knows, I've had my eye on that S600 for some time now, major supremacy, metallic majestic black, cashmere leather, walnut trim, custom package just for me ... oh yes ... and Gabby. But that's a fantasy right now, I have no job, and I'm one foot in, and one foot out of the concrete walls of fame, but the good thing is at least her first ride will be in luxury.

It hasn't been quite a month, and I'm still having a hard time piecing together how this man has come into my life just when everything is all wrong. My entire situation is complicated, and he acts as if it's nothing, even though I haven't gotten around to "that" part of my life yet. I keep telling myself to relax, but I'm not sure if it's because I'm more afraid that he will no longer want to hang around, or is it just that I'm afraid that he may want to stay, and then that will mean he really cares for me, and I'm not sure if that's what I need now. Lucy keeps hinting around how much I should give him a try, because he's so sweet, he's so this, and he's so that. I think his decision is only based on the things Marcel has done. Even Zoe talks him up, and come to think of it, not sure of their relationship, I just know they've worked together in the past. I tell both of them, it's not all about the things, (oh my goodness, I sound like my mother!), because with Malcolm I've had that, and look where that got me. Besides, one thing anyone who knows me, should know, I don't have to have a man based on finances, I can buy my own Prada shoes, and the bag to go with them. If and when I ever fall in love again, it will be different. He must have all the qualities Malcolm didn't have, a FEAR of God! F: Faithful, E: Enduring, A: Annointed, R: Redeemed.

Before I realize it, we're home; I think he felt the scenic route was a good idea. I've lived here for some years now, and I'm sure the ride from North General to home isn't that long. If you ask him, he was only giving me the royal treatment, he says, plus he thought it would be great for me to take it all in. Everyone knows after today I won't be getting out that much, but my mind tells me, he took a longer route to throw off the media. I noticed them way before we left the hospital. Lately, I've been in the news more than Michael Vick, and the doggy drama.

Everything looks so differently, from the frost on the ground to the "what were you thinking Christmas tree," sitting directly in hinds view of my neighbor's stoop. Not sure of the theme she was going for, but it's a cross between the ever so beautiful Macy's tree, with a hint of Pic-n-Save. Speaking of that, these last past weeks have flown past me, Thanksgiving was a blur, and now it's time to decorate. Don't think I'm up for the caroling, the egg nog, or even trimming a tree. Baby and me will have to miss out on that this year.

It's hard to think the last time I left this house my only concern was to feed my face with a sundae I didn't need, and come to think of that sundae ... I wonder what happened to it anyway?

Once I'm inside, I head straight for the couch, take a seat, make sure she's comfortable. Momma keeps telling me to "make sure I'm holding her head in my hands upright, so that it doesn't lag." This couch never felt sooo good. It's a little chilly in here; I've got to get in the mindset of another human being sharing this space with me, because if it was up to me, it would be ice cold. First thing Marcel does is make sure all of the blinds are closed, in case the lurkers are working overtime, then he asks where is the temperature setter, I point to the right, in the same direction as the television, which I kindly ask him to turn on so that she can get used to a little noise. A tip from Julian he said helped with Melanie once she was home. He says, "if they get used to noise, then you want have to worry about tip toeing around the house, and then that way they can sleep through anything," which will be a blessing in disguise!

All I want to do is sit here and hold her forever, she's whimpered maybe ... three times. If this is how it's going to be, bring it on, I'm ready! The phone has been ringing nonstop, people from my parents' church, the few neighbors I've recently befriended. I even got a call from Marcel's mother, which comes as a surprise, although we didn't talk long I really connected with her spirit. She's a pleasant woman, very soft spoken, she doesn't have much to say, but when she does, it has powerful meaning. She told me something that will stay with me awhile. Before we ended she kindly stated "God presses us to make us stronger, because in that our tears become our testimonies. You will never have a testimony without first having been tested." Sort of similar to my dream I had while lying on that hospital bed; after I woke it was as though I had been through something for sure, and there was no one or nothing that could make me feel bad ever again. I've been apologizing everyday to God for the things I've done, as well as I've been thanking Him daily for bringing us home safely. Looking back, I know it was no one but God that did that.

Although Marcel's presence is great comfort, I'm going to have to ask him to leave. I don't want to make him feel uncomfortable in any way, but if he really knew, he would know I need to be alone with her. I can tell by the look on his face, he seems happy to be here, but right now at this moment, I need to enjoy my baby. Just us two.

One thing I've stressed is her nursery. My fear was that it wouldn't be complete, and I was right, although Lucy's assured me he has it taken care of, that's still important to me.

After what seems like a lifetime since she's been in my arms, all of a sudden, Marcel asks to hold her. My first reaction is to say no, but I take a slow deep breath, and release hold of her. He takes a seat next to me, and I hand her over to him. I still can't believe she has hardly cried. He looks like a natural holding her, it's like he's done this before. He even holds the back of her head like a pro. He doesn't flinch at all, and neither does she. Immediately I realize this is another area of his life I know nothing about, as a matter of fact; there are many areas of his life I know nothing about.

Just when I reach out to get her he says, "She's beautiful."

I want to agree with him, but I can't bring myself to take my eyes off the way he gently holds her as if he could do this forever.

I say, "Thank you."

Looking her over, he asks, "Did you ever think that God could create such an angel?"

"No, I didn't."

In my mind, I'm thinking ... not for real. She's a portrait of perfection. I couldn't have imagined anything greater.

"Babies are a gift from God, their sinless, faultless, they are priceless, and the closest to God anyone will ever be." he says, as he continues to rub the crown of her head, calming her even more. I take a look, only to see she's asleep, as if this is the place she was meant to be ... home.

I reach to grab her, but instead he slowly stands as not to awaken her. He asks to lay her down, and I point him in the direction of my bedroom so we can place her in my bed. He heads down the hall towards my room, but immediately takes a detour to her room. Opens the door where the light is off, he mustn't know this is as unfinished project, but no sooner that he presses the switch I am in a state of shock. Her room is complete and it's way more than I ever expected! It's everything I wanted.

Softly he asks, "Do you like it?"

I'm at a loss for words.

He goes on to say, "Between, Lucy, Zoe, and myself, we had to make this thing happen. We knew just how much it meant to you, and so you know, it was Lucy who planned it, Zoe who called in her connections, and I only sat in as the overseer."

I laugh. "What does that mean?"

"I gave the orders." He says, laughing himself, while trying not to wake her. "Lucy would have it no other way." He adds.

I take a long look at what used to be a room that once upon a time had so many plans for it, an office, a get-a-way spot, "the girly room," or better yet maybe even the junk room, who knew.

While still holding her, he walks over to her bed and gently places her down, but not before pulling back the gorgeous pink silk taffeta sheets, and not waking her at all. She's sleeping like a princess. Just before he reaches to turn on the mobile, he leans down and kisses her on her forehead, and of course I'm thinking where did he really come from?

Both of us walking to the front he turns and asks, "Would you like for me to stick around so you can get some sleep?"

Aahm, I think about that thing, but quickly I'm reminded of the fact of this is Gabby and me; this is how it's going to be, so I nicely tell him no thank you. I kindly thank him for bringing us home, and being so sweet, and oddly he only says, "It's the God in me."

"What!" If he could only see, my knees are in buckle mode. This man is straight out of the Cinderella story, only that he looks a lot like me, just not with the excess swollen belly.

"What are you planning to eat?" he asks.

"I'll put something together," I say.

"Look in the refrigerator, and you can thank Melissa for that, but she had to fight Lucy for that."

I burst out in laughter, because let Lucy tell it, he's Mrs. Chef Boy-R-Dee.

He gathers his things, and heads for the door, again I say thank you, and he then says, "You're welcome." Right as he turns to close the door, he asks, "By chance, did you ever get a chance to open that envelope?"

Perplexed I respond, "What envelope?", and right at this moment I remember the envelope from the shower, the one wrapped in a brown bag with a ribbon. I say, "As a matter of fact, I didn't because it stated—"

"To be opened on your birthday, yeah I know," he says.

Once again, I'm shocked, because now I have so many questions, but my mind is tired, I don't think I can handle the answers.

Again he turns to head into a world that awaits him, and says, "I will see you later Diamond, sleep tight."

I gently close the door, standing there breathing in the scent he has left behind. I take in an aroma that fills this place with both a sweet and exotic fragrance. If I had to guess, it would be Michael Kors, but whatever it is, it smells good. My heart gives a flutter, and I notice there's nothing between us except this woodened hand carved door, then suddenly I come back to reality, and it hits me, he called me Diamond.

I'm quickly thrown into culture shock, because no longer than fifteen minutes has gone by, and she belts out the loudest cry ever. I'm sure everyone on 125th can hear her. OMG! Now what? What happened to the sweet little baby that just layed there smiling, without a care in the world? Where is she? The first thing that comes to mind is I haven't fed her since we've been here, and the way she's crying my first instinct is to whip out the God given food, but because of the HIV I have been heavily warned against breastfeeding, so ... looks like I'm going to have to make my first bottle. Where do I start? Where are the bottles?

My father must know me, he told me he stopped by to check on the house yesterday, and by the looks of it, he not only checked on it. He must have known this would happen because all of her bottles are nicely washed, and ready to go. All I need to do is figure out how to mix this stuff up.

As I'm trying to read the instructions on the can of Enfamil, the phone is ringing, she's screaming at the top of her lungs, and I'm about to loose my mind, and this is just the first day. Lord help me! I'm spilling powder everywhere, this isn't making any sense to me, it has to be a better way. What baby would want to drink a boring bottle of a mixture of formula and two parts water? I think that's what it said.

Within five minutes I manage to put together the best milkshake made by a new mommy. Once she gets a taste on her tongue, she's in heaven, she's at peace. She takes it down as if she was seated at the table with the disciples and Jesus partaking of the Lord's Supper.

I finally get her settled down by rocking her to sleep. I never thought it was possible to feel love like this. There's something about the way she looks at me, it's as if we've known each other forever.

Right as I head to put her down, the doorbell rings, and if I go with my first mind, they'll be standing on the other side of the door until I wake up, but there's a softer side of me that tells me to open it. A distinguished man no older than fifty stands there holding a box addressed to baby Cartiér. I sign my name, and give him a tip. Then I slowly turn, because with all the excitement I'm reminding there are at least ten staples keeping my insides together from the surgery where she was delivered. I catch myself in midstride, and breathe, because this pain is becoming increasingly unbearable, but I make my way to counter to open the package, and by the way it's wrapped, it'll take an army of fifty men to pry this open. Once I get it open after what feels like a decade, I automatically notice a red bag with the words written in gold that houses the sweetest little red box, and holds the most adorable Cartiér engraved tri-colored rings on an adjustable black silk cord. It even comes complete with the certificate of authenticity papers included. The card so eloquently reads: To my beautiful princess, wherever you are, there I will be also. Love Daddy. Just as I begin to place the gift on the counter an envelope falls out. On the out side it says please read to me. Now I'm a little perturbed, what is he trying to accomplish with all of this? I admit the gift is a nice gesture, but ... this is going a bit far.

I walk back towards her room to see she's still asleep, hopefully this means I can too. I didn't take into consideration just how badly my incisions would hurt. Since I've been in the hospital, it's been all good; they would give me meds when I needed them. Maybe I should have asked Marcel to get my prescriptions filled, but since I didn't I'm going to have to bear the pain.

I take one look at my bed, and never has there been a time that I wanted to become acquainted with a mattress and pillow as I do right now. The only thing I can think of is plopping down, but that's not happening, I forget for one minute, that I have more bandages than 50 cents did in Get Rich or Die Trying. I try to remember the best way the nurse demonstrated of how I was to roll-ll in the bed, and all of that goes out of the window. I take one good roll-ll and that's it! I'm sore from head to toe, but right at this moment; all I need is my bed, and whatever way I make it in is fine with me.

NO-SHE-DIDN'T! I know I have not been in this bed any longer than thirty minutes and now she wants to do this to me again. I just staggered my way into the bed, now I have to figure the best way of how to get out. I thought climbing into this monstrosity of a bed when I was big and pregnant was bad enough, but this is a whole new ball game, she is relentless, where did she get those lungs from? I take one roll to the right, that doesn't work, one roll to the left, that is definitely not right, now I'm caught in between the top of my shirt, and this dangling chain I had to put on before I left the hospital, therefore I would look like the "dazzling diva," and now I can't breathe. I'm just stuck here, arms stretched open wide, if this was how Jesus looked on the cross, I feel even sorrier for him.

I finally tussled my way out, and I make it into her room, as soon as I am near the bed she stops all of a sudden. Unn-uun little girl not today ... it doesn't last long, she starts all over again. What can it be this time? I've fed her, I even tried to sing a tune or two that worked this time, maybe it'll work this time. I pick her up only to find her entire back is soaked and wet. Ugh! Thank heavens for Lucy and the gang, because I don't have to scramble to find any pampers, there all stacked on the wall. I grab one as soon as I can as not to keep her airing out too long, don't want any surprises. Too late! This can't be happening. All I asked for was one hour of sleep. And now I'm covered in baby sprinkle. I grab the powder, the baby oil; even spray a little perfume in the air to give a feeling of love. I'm beginning to think I should have taken that class after all. I just thought once you've done this before, it comes natural. Momma even said so, but looks like I should've signed up anyway. This only makes me mad all over again that Malcolm is not here, but nooo he feels as though cutesy little expensive gifts will do. He needs to be here to listen at this. I shouldn't have to go through this alone. Just then I remember there is something I need to read to her. She and I walk back to the front, I get the envelope, and we walk back to her room, where I try to sit as soft as possible in her chair without disturbing the incisions, or better than that without dropping her. I open the envelope and there is a letter written to her, I began to read the words:

To my baby Gabrielle,

Where do I begin? First let me start by saying I am your father, my name is Malcolm Tyrell Cartiér. When I first found out you were on your way, I was terrified, but I have loved you even before I knew you were going to be apart of my life. There are so many things I want to share with you, but because I only have so much paper I'll try and say as much as I can.

In your life there will be many people that will say bad things about your father, but I want you know that I'm not a bad person; I just decided to make bad decisions that have caused me to be away from you, although you are not, or never will you be the cause of those decisions. In my life there are many things I regret, and I know that's a big word for you, so I will tell you what it means. Regret means: to feel sorry for, to be saddened, remorseful. Guess that doesn't help any huh? But as you get older and you begin to experience life you will understand then.

I have loved your mother every since the first day I saw her. Back then we were so young, we had the whole world at our feet. I never meant to hurt or harm her in any way. I only wanted to make her happy, but because I chose to go outside of our marriage and do things that were not pleasing to God, I have paid a huge price. I have lost your mother; I am missing out on special moments being with you, and most of all I have put all of our lives at risk, and this is why I write this to you.

Your father has to take medicine because I am very sick, and I have spoken with my doctors, and they've told me I am doing fine as of now. I have a disease called HIV which is a type of virus, and once it gets into your body it can make you very sick, anyone can get it. It doesn't matter if you are rich or poor, young or old, black, white, straight or gay. It's not who you are, it's the things you do that can cause you to get it. There are several ways you can get it, for instance, you can be born with it, or by sharing drug needles, also you can get it by blood transfusions, but the way I got it, was by having unprotected sex with women other than your mother, and for this I am more than sorry, because I have hurt so many people.

I have also been told by my doctors that if I take my medicines right, keep my viral load down, my CD4 count up, then I will live to be as healthy as you. That way I can be around to see you grow into the beautiful young women I know God desires you to be. Although I have this disease living inside my body it doesn't take my love away from you or your mother. I have apologized to your mother, and I want to apologize to you, but more importantly I want you to know I have asked God's forgiveness, and I believe He has done that. I pray you will one day in your heart grow to forgive me, and to love and accept me. I know your mother will soon find someone to love her and care for her in the way I should have, because she deserves it. She didn't deserve the embarrassment and shame I have put her through, and neither do you. I also hope and pray that God will allow me to live so that I may see you accomplish all of your dreams, but I promise as long as I am alive I will never miss out on any important events in your life. I plan to be there for every birthday, piano recital, if that's what you choose, or any other activity you decide to do. The one important thing I will not miss out on is making sure you know who Jesus is, I plan to pray with you every night before you lie down, read the bible with you, and make sure I go to church with you. I've been going a lot lately and it has helped me deal with this.

Please remember no matter what, I will always love you, and I want you to wear your bracelet every chance you get as a reminder that your father is always there.
Love,
Your Daddy Malcolm T. Cartiér

I sit here in awe, and then I notice she's dozed back off to sleep. It's funny because I always used to say, he never ceased to amaze me. I really don't know what to say, I do know that he seems very sorry for what he's done, although it's too late for that now, life goes on, and in my heart I have forgiven him. I've made peace with that. I had to for her sake. It's best for all of us, because until I truly let it go I'll never be able to love again. Whew, the idea of me loving again is scary. I just can't get hurt again, it would have been a lot easier if Malcolm just cheated, but it's still hard to forget he gave me something that I can't change. The good news is I'm reminded of my dream, and in it God let me know He has all power, and He can change any situation if I only allow Him to do what He said He will do.

This has been one of the longest nights ever, it's the four o'clock feeding and I'm so ready for a venti Mocha Frappucinno, with a shot of espresso, and make it a double. I must say it hasn't been that bad, the worst part is getting in and out of the bed, but after the warm shower everything else was good. I've already taken notice that she's real fond of the Duke's *"Satin Doll"*, but I think her favorite is Louis Armstrong's *"What a Wonderful World,"* She gives me the sweetest smiles when he says 'I love you.'

What's today? It slipped my mind, today is December 1st, World Aids Day, how can I forget. Lucy has reminded me for the last two weeks. I want reach him today, because he'll be busy with the march and everything. I remember Zoe mentioning something about taking part this year which comes to me as a shock, because she doesn't even take her meds properly, if at all. So I'm sure there will be a lot of people being tested today, and there will be a lot of red ribbons today as well. Some people will get good news and others ... I only can pray for them, because this is not anything I would wish for anyone, but if it can save one person's life, then that's a good thing.

Too bad I want be marching, because today is also the day I'm scheduled to for the preliminary hearing. They changed the date due to my being in the hospital, therefore today is the day. I guess Marcel didn't think about it either, he probably felt I already knew. Not long before these words escape me, I look over and see the red light flashing on the Blackberry. I listen to all ten messages; most of them are from my mother. I chose to turn the ringer off in hopes I wouldn't be disturbed, instead I've missed some very important calls, as my father would say, *J'ai manqué quelques appels trés importants.*

There are two messages from Lance that I need to be prepared in the morning, well ... today, to appear before the judge at nine o'clock. This is crazy! We talked about it several times in the hospital, I thought I was prepared, but now I don't know. I just didn't realize this day would come so fast. I've been praying daily they would find evidence proving my innocence, although I've been warned because I pled not guilty this can lead to a lengthy trial, in which I am not ready for, but if it will show that I had nothing to do with Tyler and Mr. Coleman's saga, it'll be worth it.

Recently I've gone through my bank statements, and for now I'm good. I have a pretty good nest egg saved up for a rainy day, but I don't think my bank account can handle the cost of a lengthy trial. I haven't told anyone, but I've dipped into my savings more than I would have liked. I've been rather careless lately, so now ... I've got to be mindful of how I spend. I didn't take into consideration if you're not working you feel obligated to keep your standards of living up, (according to society's standards), but not to mention a new baby. It's a blessing that the house is paid for, but I can't forget the cost of the HIV meds. I just realized, my insurance ended yesterday, and now I have to pay for it on my own. Most private insurances will not cover my meds, and over my lifetime this will mount to be a substantial burden, and the sad part is that some insurance companies have already denied me because it's considered as a preexisting conditions. The last thing I don't want to do is worry my parents, because that's one more thing on their mind.

It seems like everyone is thinking of me this morning, Marcel left a message to remind me. From his message, he didn't want to stress me, but he felt I should know in case I was somewhere buried under a pile of baby clothes. That makes me smile to know he's very thoughtful that way. He asked to take me, but I'm wondering is it because he somehow knows I'm still very nervous about driving. I believe this is why I haven't chose another car as of yet. I am afraid, and to know I'm traveling with precious cargo at this time makes me even more afraid.

Almost three hours later, I'm up and at it, I've got this bottle thing down, so she's smelling good, her belly is full, and she's dry! I love to see her on her back with her little legs in the air as happy as she can be. It's hard to believe it's been almost three weeks already.

I can tell my mother must have gotten the memo, because she has not let up on the phone at all. Everyone knows this isn't easy for any of us to deal with; it's even harder when it's blasted on Good Morning America's headlines. I immediately turn off the television, because they've been talking about it since six o'clock, and honestly I care not to hear about it anymore, but it continues everywhere, Today, New York's Financial Guru faces a court hearing on Fraud charges to ultimately learn her future, as well as her newborn baby with now ex-husband Malcolm Cartiér. Guilty or not guilty?

Isn't anything sacred anymore? You would think they would let people remain innocent until proven guilty; it's awful that he media convicts you even before the judge is chosen; their response is that they owe it to the viewers.

Momma says quietly, "Good morning baby."

Worn out, I say, "Morning momma."

She giggles, "How was your night?"

No giggle from me, "It was good, exhausting, but good."

"This is only the beginning." She comes back.

We both laugh. It's my thought she senses my brain is in overload.

"Did you get the reminder?" She asks.

"Yes I did."

"Good, because I'm on the way over to watch the baby while you're at the hearing."

Now how did she know I didn't have plans for anyone else to do this? I guess this is why she's momma, she wouldn't have it any other way.

"Victoria, I don't want to ask, but—"

"Yes momma, I've taken my medicine."

"That's good."

"You're right, and you don't have to worry about that ever again, I think if anything, I have been shown what can happen if I don't. Momma I have another call on the other end, can you hold?"

"No, I'll see you in a bit."

I switch the call, it's Marcel.

"Good morning sleepy head. How was your night?" He says.

"If I said everything went well, and I have it all under control would you believe me?"

He laughs, "Yes I would, because I know you are resourceful like that, you can handle anything that's thrown your way, and this is just another loop in your belt. You got it, you're a big girl."

"Well thank you I needed that."

"So are you ready for today?"

"Just about."

"Great, because I'm not too far away."

"You know I have the—"

"Yes I'm aware of that, but that's the last thing you need is to deal with the New York drivers today."

'That's sweet of you, but you don't have to—"

"I know, but I want to."

"Thanks."

"See you in about ten minutes."

I'm glad I'm almost dressed; he doesn't seem like the kind that likes to be kept waiting. Right as I hang up with him, there's a knock at the door.

"Hi momma, where were you, around the corner?"

"You can say that, I've been up pretty early, and I knew you would need me, so I wanted to be here in time for you to get there without any delay. By the way how are you getting there? Your father wanted to come with me to take you, but we figured if need be you could drive my car, or take the—"

"No ma'am not the courtesy car, I noticed it out there. When did Daddy have that sent here?"

"He told me it was arranged when we found out your exact discharge time. He wanted it to be here if you needed it."

"Well thank you Daddy, but no, Marcel has asked to take me."

"I'm beginning to like that gentleman day by day. It's something about him. I never involved myself in any of your men friends, but he's different. You can see God all over him, and it's not a pretend thing either."

"Momma stop it, if it was up to you, any man that talked about God would seem that way to you."

"No, not really. Some things I just know, but ... where's my sweet grandbaby this morning? She should be lying in her newly decorated nursery."

"You knew too?" I ask.

"Honey, you know much doesn't get past me. Your father and Marcel put the bed together, and who do you think took the time to wash all of her bottles, and make sure they were right where you needed them in case of an emergency."

I think back to last night, and then she looks around the kitchen and notices remnants of formula on the counter top and floors.

She points towards the floor, "Could this be an example of an emergency?"

We both let out a thunderous laugh, forgetting she's asleep.

A strong but respectful knock comes across the door, but I have momma get it so that I can put my shoes on and get my things together.

"Hello, Mrs. Jean-Pierre."

"Good morning Marcel, it's a good thing you're here, now she won't have to worry as much."

"Yes, I'm honored to take her."

"Thank you."

Momma heads in to give Gabby a sweet kiss, and we are on our way.

"You look very nice as always." He says.

"Thank you, and so do you."

I also want to say, and you smell good too. I give momma a hug, and the last thing she says to me is, "God has it all in control."

Traffic spares us no mercy, but I still wouldn't want to be in the Holland Tunnel right now, but Malcolm X Blvd is back to back; hopefully it's not a repeat. Manageably he gets around it, and we're able to press through the rest.

At first the car is quiet, except the eclectic tunes of Sade' flowing through the speakers. I don't talk much; I don't want to let on again how nervous I am. The first time he and I were headed to this, I thought it would turn out totally different, I didn't expect I would wind up in this position.

"I never got the chance to tell you thank you for posting my bond."

"Consider it an early Christmas gift."

"I'll get it back to you."

He turns down the stereo, and his voice masculine but caring says,

"One thing you will learn about me is I never do anything I don't want to do. You may have already guessed it, but I grew up in an affluent family, but I have been very fortunate to make my own way. I never wanted to be defined by what my parents had. I give because God has been good to me. I was taught at an early age you reap what you sow, and when I became a man I decided that with every dollar I earned, I would give a dime back to God, and he has never failed me. So when I give, it's out of love, not to be confused with recognition."

What do I say after that?

"I guess the only thing for me to say again is thank you."

"And for the very last time, you're welcome."

"I know I may regret this, but do you mind me asking you, what is it about me that peaks your interest."

"That's not hard. Do you remember the day we met in the elevator, and I told you I had also done my research on you?"

Laughing, I say, "Oh so you were stalking me?"

He also laughs, "I wouldn't say that, but if you must know I was referred to you by a long time acquaintance that you had done a piece of business for in the past. So I began to search you, I read articles, I followed your success, I even sent a couple of clients your way, because I had that much faith in you as a business woman. Your business savvy is incredible."

"But why did you wait so long to acquire my services?"

"I needed to grow some more, as a man."

"I'm confused."

Here we are caught by a light, and I take a look at my watch, and it is already 8:15. Please God don't let us be late.

"No need to look at your watch, Lance is very capable of doing what we've hired him for."

Do I seem that uncomfortable?

"As you know I was with a great company before I petitioned RBN, but before I came I needed to make sure that I was in good hands, and being that I would be specifically your client, I would need to have everything right."

"But money is no problem for you—"

"That's it; it's never been about money with me. I needed to get my spirit right. I've been taken advantage of so much in the past by the people that you would never think would hurt you."

"Who is that?"

"The church, I've been turned away; I've been looked to as a financial breakthrough for some, but never as a human being."

Just as we get into the conversation, we're here. After we park, I gather my things to open the door, but before I can get my hands on the door, he's already at my door. And some women say chivalry is dead.

"My father always taught me to always make sure a woman's foot never touches the ground before you're there to help her."

Why do I feel as though if there was a roll of red carpet at the door he would make sure it was unrolled far enough for me to walk across the street?

He kindly lets me walk beside him, but not before he ensures I'm on the inside. I notice this. This is how my father told me a man is supposed to walk with a lady.

"Did your father teach you this too?"

"No my mother did. My father died when I was ten years old, and from that moment on, everything I learned about women, she taught me."

I knew it was a reason I liked that women. A class act.

Once we're inside the butterflies start all over again. I notice Lance is already inside speaking with the District Attorney, and by the way it looks, doesn't look good.

"Don't be afraid." Marcel says.

Lance comes over to me, explains again the procedure that the prosecuting attorney has to establish probable cause, and hopefully there is none then the case can be dismissed, and then I will be free of all charges.

"Hi Lance, how's it looking?" I ask.

"As far as I can tell, everything is going according to planned. We're just waiting on the judge."

"Will Tyler be here?"

"No there is no reason for him to be here. From what I gather, he has had his own court date. Today is all about you, but you shouldn't worry, I'm still confident there will be no trial."

"I hope so."

I can't wait to set eyes on Mr. Tyler Darwin, it's funny how he has caused so much trouble, but I have yet to see him. I wonder what my baby is doing at this moment. It's almost time for her to eat again, if it's up to momma she's already feeding her. She says the book mother's go by nowadays we are nothing like they used to be. I look up and here is Daddy coming through the doors. You can tell he's been rushing by the way he walks in. Like a lion protecting his cub, much like Mufasa and Simba.

Marcel and I must were thinking the same way, because by the way he walks in, all heads turn, and we say to each other, "Lion King."

The judge comes in, and I am asked to stand before the court, Lance comes right behind me, while my heart is beating a mile a minute. The judge says the prosecuting attorneys do have enough evidence to proceed with the case. Just my luck, there is evidence, and what is it I wonder. He calls both Lance and the District Attorney to the front, which they stand there for what seems like an eternity. After talking back and forth, Lance comes back over to me, and told me there was a witness at the last minute; therefore the case has been turned over to the Grand Jury! It's taking every fiber of my being to stand up straight. Lord what else is it that you have for me? A tear makes it's way to my eye, but I look back at Marcel, then my father, and they both seem so strong, then Marcel mouths to me, "Have faith."

Chapter Eighteen
Victoria & Marcel

It's only a couple of days before Christmas and I still haven't gotten all the gifts on my list. If it wasn't for Marcel encouraging me to get in better spirits, no one except Gabby would have gifts this year. At first it was very hard, especially because I still don't know much about what's going on with the case, so it's hard for me to focus on anything outside of that.

Zoe and her mom stopped by to give us gifts, and I must say Mrs. Sinclair is like Mrs. Claus of the eastside. She asked that I open my gift today, but I chose not to. That was one thing Daddy was adamant about; we wait until Christmas morning to open gifts, even though he would always insist he pass them out. Maybe it's because he wanted to see just how many gifts belonged to him. Those were real special times. When I think of how Julian and I would always try to see who would go to sleep first so we wouldn't get soot in our eyes. Daddy had us so afraid that I think I would stay up most of the night before so that I could fall asleep early on Christmas Eve. I never really found out who ate the cookies, because as I grew older I discovered Daddy really was never fond of chocolate chip, and that was a must have for Santa. That and a Café Brûlot, and come to think of it, Daddy tricked me, because that's coffee with Brandy, but who knew then, all I wanted was for Santa to be happy.

I've really gotten the hang of this mommy thing. We're on a much better schedule now. It was looking rough at first, but now it's become a lot easier. It wasn't long that I realized Mylicon was the best thing since sliced bread, ¼ tsp in her formula and its sweet dreams from then on out. The cutest thing is when she gets a taste on her tongue and she starts smacking as if she has had the best meal yet. I can't even begin to think that in a few days she'll go to get her first set of immunizations, now I'm not sure who's it going to hurt worst, her or me.

There is still so much I need to do before Melissa's wedding, the invitation states it begins at six o'clock, therefore that'll give me time to get Gabby settled at Julian's'. He and Reese have asked to keep her for me tonight, and that's right up Mel's alley. Every weekend she's called to "babysit" her little cousin, so she gets her chance tonight. First I need to make sure her things are packed in case there are any emergencies. Julian laughs at me; his new nickname for me is "Perfect Patty." It's hilarious seeing Janet Jackson in that kitchen screaming, "Perfect Patty messed up!" To be honest there are times I really feel like that.

For so many years I've felt the need to be in control of everything, because I knew there were so many people who looked to me for advice, guidance, and direction, so for me to lose control was out of the picture. Even though I'm not at the point to totally relinquish that control factor; I'm thankful for Marcel, he's been a great support. Just the other day, he sent me an inspirational message that helped get me through the day. It said, "Just when you're at your lowest, that's when God is up to something." Its simple things like that, which makes me want to know even more about him, and in return I've been pondering when will be the best time to disclose my status. Zoe and I have talked about it, and she agrees that if I am going to continue to have him around I at least owe it to him to be honest. She also thinks he's the type to take the good with the bad. I've also noticed she's loosened up a lot lately, I'm starting to think she doesn't hate men as much as she used to.

It's a good thing my doctor cleared me this week. Now that I'm over the six week hump I'm free to come and go as I please, and that means I can now drive a real woman's car, and not the loaner Daddy gave me. I'm so glad he took the little car back, later for that ... I need my own car now. Marcel has asked if I needed him to go with me, but I think I can do that by myself. He's been nice enough. It was him who helped with the tree, and if I must say so myself, he did an awesome job. My favorite touch this year is the sentimental ornament for Gabby.

Time is flying faster than I thought, its two-thirty already, and I'm now getting finished with laundry. I've never seen so many little blankets, washcloths, and onesies in my life. It's an all day job getting it all done, and if I'm not mistaken, it's time to eat-eat. She likes it when I say that, matter of fact she likes it when I do anything that's out of the norm. I never thought being a mommy would bring out your inner child, because between the silly little songs, and the goofy little dances, I've become a regular American Idol contestant.

The phone rings, and if I had to guess, it would be Malcolm or Lucy. One thing I will say is Malcolm has never been so dedicated to one thing than he has this little girl. If he doesn't call in the morning, he calls at night, just to check on her. He came by the other day, and it was a little strange having him here for that time, but he wanted to make sure he gets his time in as far as rocking her. He sings this song that cracks her up! Something he says his mother used to sing to him. While pulling her little toes, he sings, "This little piggy went to market, this little piggy stayed home, this little piggy had roast Beef, this little piggy had none, this little piggy cried wee-wee-wee, all the way home." Really doesn't leave much to be desired.

"Hello Victoria, how are you?"

"Hey Malcolm, I'm fine, and you?"

"I'm good. How is she?"

"She's doing well, I'm about to feed her, I can tell she's hungry."

"Is she crying?"

"No not yet, but she will in a minute. She warns you first, but if you don't have it within a couple of minutes—"

We both laugh and say, "Apollo look out."

"Just wanted to check on her, and see when is a good time to bring both of your gifts."

I pause, "Like I said, she's doing well now, and ... I'm going to Melissa's wedding this evening ... so ... I won't be home."

"So when would you say? I can bring them tomorrow after church."

Just then I'm reminded Marcel has invited the both of us to church in the morning.

"Well, I'll let you know, because we're going to church tomorrow also."

You would think I told him I hit the lottery.

He says, excitedly, "Are you going to Brooklyn Tabernacle, because I can—"

I regret to inform him but, NO!

"Actually no, we're going with Mar—"

He promptly says, "Marcel."

Hesitating, I say, "Yes, it'll be her first church appearance."

At this moment I hear it in his voice, it's sad, hurtful. Oh well!

"Alright then, hopefully I'll see you girls on Christmas."

"That sounds good."

Just before we hang up he has to say something to change my mood.

"Oh and Victoria, aahm, although she and I have decided to just remain friends, but ... Noëlle brought a gift by for her as well, and she would like it if I gave it to her. No strings attached. Are you okay with that?"

The Victoria six months ago would have told him something I would have later regretted, but the me I'm trying to be is looking at things out of clearer eyes.

Calmly, I say, "Malcolm, if you should know, I have forgiven her for what happened in the past, and this is not about me, it's for Gabby."

Relieved, he responds, "Thank you, and I know that was hard for you to do."

I end by saying, "Not really, because I've come to understand that as far as forgiveness, as long as I don't do it, I'll never free my heart to be loved again."

There is total silence, and then he says, "Okay I'll see you later."

Marcel will be here shortly, and I'm putting the final touches on this hair. It has grown so much over the time I was pregnant. Those prenatal vitamins were good for something; my nails are even looking healthier than before. This is the first real outing I've had since being home, and I'm having withdrawals from Gabby already. I thought I was going to have to put on the boxing gloves when Lucy found out Julian and Reese was keeping her. I think he has gotten her every color Robeez that there are, and she isn't even wearing shoes yet. I think he is going to put Baby Juicy Couture out of business.

I open the door, and I tell you there are times when I just want to ask this man, do you have any regular clothes, because there has never been a time where he wasn't dressed to impress, and this evening is no exception. I love it because he stands like a man that just demands respect. His skin a replica of Hershey's milk chocolate, and he even has the nerves to have dimples. When he smiles, my heart flutters, although I can't let him know that just yet. And I would have to say whoever his dentist is, must have a special place in their heart for him, because of his beautiful teeth. I have never seen a mouth full of teeth where every one of them is sparkling white. I was almost tempted to ask him the night at the show in Vegas were they his, or porcelain veneers. Makes me want to ask my dentist for the VIP treatment.

Tonight, he must be in a playful mood, because he picks me up in what he calls his toy, a silver vintage Aston Martin convertible. Now, he has to know it is December in New York City, and there isn't a drop of sun nowhere, and my name is definitely not Muffy, of Mitsy, and his name sure ain't Skippy or Biff. And last I checked I didn't graduate from Andover, although I did once own a copy of "The Official Preppy Handbook." You couldn't tell me that I was not a member of the Elite socialites.

The Essex House, where Melissa and Harrison chose for their wedding, is all but beautiful. I specifically love her choice in colors. Lavender has always been a calming, peaceful color, a great way to start off the marriage.

We arrive where we are welcomed by a host of greeters that direct us towards our seats. I do recall Melissa telling me she had a hand in the programs because she wanted to have her own stamp on them. She did a wonderful job. Marcel even makes note of the monogrammed 'H' on the front. Everyone looks so beautiful, and I can't help admiring the little people, it's something about the children in a wedding that makes it even more special. I can't pass up getting a sneak peek at the bride to be, just before the wedding starts. I have to give her a kiss, because she has no idea of just how much I love and appreciate her. I don't get the chance to tell her that often, but hopefully she knows it. She looks absolutely stunning. I remember her looking through the books, sneaking on the internet, while she was supposedly doing client referrals, but it was worth it, because tonight she is a picture of elegance; and oh yes Harrison looks good too.

I wish I could say I could stay here dancing all night, but I keep thinking of the little person that's waiting for me, so I know this is not going to be a very long night, and we've got church in the morning. I've called to check on her I know three times already. Marcel gets a kick out of it that I have lasted this long. He doesn't realize it, but I actually caught him looking at his watch a couple of times. Gabby is really beginning to grow on him.

Three hours later, we are headed to Brooklyn, this is one thing I don't miss that much. Lately it's like the ride here is so exhausting although it's not as far as one would think, but at nine-thirty at night, when you're tired, it seems like an entire day's journey.

When we get to Julians', all the lights are out. I'm afraid to knock on the door. I call to give him heads up that I'm outside, but he sounds like he's been asleep for hours. By the way they have made their own little makeshift baby bed. I'm almost skeptical of waking her. It's so cute how they've bundled her up, she's sleeping so peacefully, but I have to do what I have to do. The funny part is her "babysitter" Melanie is knocked out too. Reese tells me she was no trouble, and anytime I need them to call them. Momma and I tend to think wedding bells are not too far away from them. She's really a good woman. He's blessed to have her, because I have noticed a huge change in him. It could also be due to the fact they go to counseling. If she can accept my brother after having had a relationship with a man, and still love him, there has to be hope for me after all.

One thing he or I didn't take into consideration was the size of this car! We're barely able to get everything in this you would call a back seat. It's small enough for a Samoyed, but we make it work. Hopefully we don't get pulled over, because right now I don't need to cross the street the wrong way.

With much prayer we escape NYPD, and all is well, she's still sound asleep, even while Marcel gave me a brief review of his wild side. I thought I would holler when he pushed the player to #4, Andre 3000's *"Prototype."* I never pictured him as a fan of Hip-Hop, and this was one of my favorites, he puts me in the mind of more of a Gershwin lover, but I guess this another aspect of him I love ...Whoa, did I say that?

The snow has begun to fall a bit harder right as we make it home; thankfully it held up this far. Once I get her settled in, I do a double take because I know it's not going to be too much longer before she wakes for the eleven o'clock feeding. We're almost on a regular schedule, but that depends on the day.

He doesn't waste anytime, once he makes sure we're all in, and all is well, he says he's going to call it a night. There's a big day ahead of him, and I remember the same for us. He kisses Gabby goodnight, then as we head for the door he tells me how much he enjoyed himself tonight. He says he hasn't had this much fun in a very long time, and I say the same. He leans in to kiss me, but instead he gives me the warmest hug, and oh my goodness he smells so good. Every time I'm around him I leave with a scent on my clothes that has me acting like a love sick teenager, even though I knew this time he would at least give me a kiss on the cheek, guess I was wrong. He closes the door, and says to me again, "Goodnight Diamond."

Before he's at the light good my phone rings, he's calling me to tell me sweet dreams, and that he can't wait until in the morning. He reminds me that we need to be ready by nine-thirty, for the 10:45 service. What no one has eleven o'clock service anymore, God knows I'm going to need that extra fifteen minutes. It's been a while since I've been to church and I need to look cute for Jesus.

Going through my phone, I see that I missed Malcolm's call. I really think it's sweet that he makes sure he doesn't miss a beat, but he must also realize that there will be times where I'm unavailable. Therefore, he's going to have to get used to the idea that a message will suffice. Being nice I call him back just to settle his nerves, and thankfully I get his voicemail.

"Hi Malcolm it's me, I saw I missed your call, but Gabby is fine. She was with her Uncle Jules tonight. Everything went well, and she's home now asleep. I will talk with you tomorrow."

Just as I am leaving the message my phone is beeping and the screen flashes "Adulterer," which I've been meaning to change, but as of now it is what it is.

"Hey, you called?"

"I was returning your call from earlier."

"How's Gabby?"

"Fine, she's asleep, you should listen to your message."

"I will, sorry to disturb you."

"Unconcerned, I say, "You didn't but I was on my way to bed."

"Late night?"

I take a long deep breath before I speak, "Remember I told you I was going to Melissa's wedding?"

"Oh yes, I forgot, how was it?"

What is this ask a million questions night?

I stammer, "It was good, she looked beautiful."

"That's good; you were beautiful on our wedding day too."

That's it!

I loose it. "Malcolm, what are you trying to prove? I get it, you're sorry that we're not together anymore. I'm over that, and so should you. I appreciate and respect the fact you want to be a part of Gabby's life, but as far as you and I that's as far as that goes. I'm in no mood to take a stroll down memory lane."

He comes back, "Vic, I only wanted to let you know that was what I thought, and I'm sorry for upsetting you. I thought we could at least be friends."

I say slowly and deliberate, "We can, but that's all we can do."

"Thank you, that's all I want. For my daughter's sake."

I want so badly to tell him off right now, but I'm trying so hard to be nice, but he is the reason we're where we are now, and if he had any common decency he would hang up now.

"Well I can sense the frustration in your voice, so I will let you go. I hope you have a good night."

"You too."

This is not how I planned to end my night, arguing with him. Just as I get my bearings together she wakes up. Time to eat! This is one night she and I may go to sleep together. I take a look out of the window, and by the looks of it the snow has increased a lot. I put on her favorite CD, the one I made for her that has the Top 10 selections that gets Gabby to sleep. I change her, but as soon as I think that's over, I get a warm feeling in the palm of my hands. If this isn't the poopiest baby ever, but I guess just as sure as it goes in, it's gotta come out. And she has no limits to how much she puts out at one time.

I didn't get a chance to take my evening med, so I take the missed dose. Can't be messing up anymore, too much is at stake. I try to pass the urge to send Marcel a text, but I'm overcome with emotions, so against my better judgment I do.

11:30pm-Victoria: Hope you made it home safely. Again I had a great time. Sleep tight.

At first I'm a little stunned because there's no response, but after several minutes, my message alert alarms.

11:38pm-Marcel Bouviér: Thanks, I did but the snow is rough

though. Glad you had fun. Laughter is good for the soul, but you can call next time, I don't mind.

This is the first time I've texted him, because we always call each other, maybe he doesn't like it.

11:39pm-Victoria: Sorry! But I didn't want to disturb you.

11:40pm-Marcel Bouviér: You didn't.

Right then my phone flashes from a number I'm not aware of, my first instinct is not to answer, but I do, and it's him. The sound of his voice takes me to a place that I once remember as happy. I've been in the company of many people that has accents, but his is different, with every word it's sends a feeling of warmness through me.

"What took you so long to answer?" he says.

I'm smitten for the moment, but I catch myself. "I didn't recognize the number."

"Were you expecting anyone else?"

"Not as I know of."

"Well I guess you answered the right call."

Blushing I say, "Guess I did."

Hurriedly, he asks, "What's up with the text?"

"Nothing, wanted to be respectful of your time and space."

He cracks up laughing. "Where did that come from?"

"Nowhere it's the truth."

"Just so you will know, for future references, YOU don't have to text. There should never be a time where I'm that busy that you have to deduce me to an encrypted script sent through a phone. I save that for business."

"I got it."

"Good. So Ms. Lady why are you not sleeping, it's almost Christmas Eve, and you wouldn't want Santa to think you haven't been good would you?"

That gets a girly grin from me, because although this year by far hasn't been one of my best, excluding giving birth to Gabrielle, but lately I'm beginning to look at things differently.

"Yes, you're right; I should be sleeping, because I have to get up early in the morning. Don't want to be late."

"Be sweet."

For the first time in I don't know how long, I lie in my bed with the biggest smile on my face. I kinda feel like that little girl waiting for Santa, but I pray these feelings I have are not just make believe, because as the saying goes, all that glitters ain't gold. I close my eyes; lay my head on the pillow, and doze off into a sleep as at this moment I have no cares in the world.

Six-thirty on a bright and beautiful Sunday morning, and I wake singing like a blue bird. This morning the sky is as clear as ever, although the weather channel has predicted a forecast of rain, but as of now, there are no clouds in the sky, the snow has even come to a calming halt.

I haven't felt this good in a long time, as soon as my feet touch the floor I place a Fred Hammond CD in, and that's when I remember the song "*This is the Day*" happens to be on it. Once I put it in for some reason I loose my mind, I began dancing, singing, praising Him like I never have before. I don't realize it but tears are falling from my eyes like buckets of water, and I don't even know why. It's like the place is filled with a divine presence that's almost frightening, I can actually feel the Lord's presence right here in this house. It's not long that I totally forget it's a baby in the house so instead of me getting quiet, I pick her up and we dance together in the middle of her room like it's our last time. I believe we have sung everything from, "*Go Tell it on the Mountain*," to "*Away in a Manger*," and if I could think of anymore it would suit her just fine.

Once I get her things together, it dawns on me that I need at least three outfits just in case there's an accident on the way, and another for if she has an accident in church. I didn't think about all of this, so I'm just hoping it will be a quiet day, but if not, she's well packed.

Now that I've gotten her squared away, it's time for me to get my ensemble together. I can't decide between the Carolina Herrera grey wool dress with the metallic Jimmy Choo sling backs, or should I swing for a little more comfort, by choosing the cute little ivory Dior dress with the low neckline and gathered bow, accompanied by a pair of red patent peep toe pumps? Thinking over that for a minute, it doesn't take a rocket scientist to know that I'm going to the House of the Lord, and not Club 1221. So looks like Carolina gets the golden ticket! It's my guess the plunging neckline was the deciding factor, and of course it has been some time that I've been to church, but I don't have to show *all* my goods, and anyway, I don't want Marcel to think I have no "church" clothes.

A knock at the door lets me know he's here. Once again the man is spectacularly dressed, not too much, very easy on the eye, just enough to make Jesus proud. Almost three hours later we are on our way to Sunday Service. When he picked us up I have to admit, it all felt kind of strange, maybe it's the whole Christmas Eve vibe going on. No matter what happens in my life, every year around this time I get so excited, it's something about the Gift. For so long I would get caught up in opening manmade gifts, but when I became older and began to understand what Christmas is all about, my outlook changed. It's not about how many material gifts you get; it's about the greatest gift of them all. It's about Jesus! But I've never found anything wrong with opening a delicate wrapped box with the most beautiful 2-carat princess cut diamond earrings inside that shine so brightly you can see your reflection.

During the ride Gabby begins to cry, so I ask Marcel if he'll pull over just so I can sit in the back with her, as soon as I'm riding side by side with her she's as calm as a mouse. Right as he pulls off he turns the volume on the radio up, and the entire car gets quiet, and Yolanda Adams comes through the speakers saying, "According to society, everything has to be okay, bills have to be paid, everybody has to be happy, husband and wife should always get along, but Our Word says that even in the midst of out trouble He will hide us. Everything that concerns us concerns Him, also He puts angels in charge of us, and the world is filled with promises that we can depend on now, not just when it's alright, but if we bless Him, He will keep us in the midst of all." Then the music begins playing, and immediately tears fill my eyes, because listening to the words makes me think over my life, because I too have been through so much, and God is still keeping me. He has never left me or never has He let me fall, and in my heart I believe He will protect me.

As the song goes on, but I can't seem to control the tears, especially when it gets to the place where she sings, "I thought I could do it on my own, but Jesus, Jesus, Jesus, kept me, even when I purposely did wrong, when I thought I was going to loose my mind, Jesus kept me!"

Oh my goodness, this song is so powerful ... It's so amazing how the word to a song can comfort you at the right time. Between the burning sensations in my eyes, I try and notice if Marcel sees my tears falling, but it seems as if he is just as caught up as I am.

"I love this song." he says.

"So do I."

"I've seen her in concert several times." he adds.

"Really?" I ask.

He continues, "Yes, a couple of times at my church, then another time when I was in Houston for a convention, I caught her while I was there, and ohhh yes, she is a powerhouse, and she has a beautiful spirit."

"Did you meet her before?"

Laughing he says, "Yes, but it was through a mutual connection. It was after the concert in Houston, and it's funny because I didn't realize she was that tall!"

Too bad I can't relate to this, the only time I've ever seen her was on BET during one of the gospel shows, and she didn't look that tall to me.

As he pulls on the grounds of the church I take a look around, and suddenly I'm shocked, because I just knew we would pull up on some magnificent plantation that houses a mega church which seats no less than 15,000, but to my surprise we are facing a smaller size church that resembles the ones I'm used to growing up. Oddly enough there isn't a fleet of Benz's, Lexus', or Bentley's parked in the "special spots," just everyday cars driven by everyday hardworking people, but not to say people who own extreme luxury vehicles, namely myself, aren't hardworking ... well ... right about now, I'm not either a hard or soft worker. I'm just plain ole' unemployed, although the other day I heard Marcel said to me, "You're not unemployed, you're just in between jobs." so there it is. I'm a person that chooses to drive a luxury automobile that just so happens to be in between jobs.

I can't believe how much being here makes me feel welcome. I don't remember a time where I was in a church that made me feel they were happy to have me there. Some churches I've gone to have been so cold to where I wasn't sure if it was the air that was blowing so, or was it the actual atmosphere in the church itself, from the Pastor down to the ushers.

I look down at Gabby with her eyes wide opened captivated by the bright lights; it's as if she's and the angels are playing. It does my heart all the good in the world to see the twinkle she gets when she zones in on a particular object, she seems so happy and at peace. I also take notice that Marcel obviously attends on a regular basis, because as soon as we hit the door everyone we pass speaks to him. Just as I'm thinking about this, an older grey haired lady comes over and whispers in his ear, and at that time he asks to excuse himself, in which I'm fine with it.

We're already one hour into the service, and people have been praising the Lord non stop. I look over at Marcel, and I don't think he has sat down once. A feeling of excitement comes over me because going to church with Malcolm was different. He was into the service and all but ...with Marcel this is a whole new experience. I like it. I like it that he knows the Word, and most of all I really believe that he loves the Lord.

The Pastors sermon really hit home for me, he asked the question, "Do You trust Him?" I don't think I've shed this many tears in church since the time Julian and I were caught passing notes in church, and momma decided to show us just what "spare the rod spare the child" meant. I think I cried the rest of the service, and it wasn't because God had been so good to me either. I also think Gabby liked his message too because she hasn't gone the whole time we've been here. God is so good!

What really moves me is that during the Call to Worship the Pastor asked if there is anything that you would believe God for to do for you that you know is beyond any humanistic trait, to come to the altar, and as much as I want to remain seated, there is something inside of me that won't let me stay here. With the tears pooling in my eyes, I look to the left of me and Marcel is standing reaching his hand towards me to walk with me to the altar. My heart is pounding, and I'm not sure if it's out of embarrassment, or is it that what I've prayed for in Malcolm for all this time. Marcel is really the man that God has for me.

By the end of service I am persuaded to tell him about my status. After the ladies testimony today of how God has blessed her in spite of her having AIDS, helped me get over the fear. I sat and listened to her talk about how she has lived with this disease for over twenty five years, to where at first there was no hope, but now since she has been blessed through the Pastor, and other members of the church who has helped her emotionally, physically, and more importantly they have reached out to her to help her pay for her medicines through the HIV/AIDS ministry they have in the church. I'm in total disbelief, this is unheard of. I can't believe that there are churches that actually talk about it nevertheless deal with it.

As we prepare to leave, Marcel says he would like for me to meet someone, but just then I get a whiff of Ms. Gabby's stench, I'm guessing she couldn't hold it any longer. I find the nearest restroom to relieve her. Once I'm done Marcel is patiently waiting for me to meet the Pastor. In that this is a nice gesture, although I hope and pray that I don't have any left over residue of baby poop. He walks up to him as if they've known each other for a while.

"Pastor Stephens, great message today, you truly blessed me." Marcel says.

He laughs, "Brother Bouviér, I'm glad you felt the spirit."

Laughing Marcel says, "I want you to meet someone."

All I can think of is Gabby don't spit up on me now.

He reaches out to shake my hand. "Hello Msss ..."

Marcel jumps in, "Ms. Cartiér, Victoria Cartiér."

"It's a pleasure, Ms. Cartiér." He adds.

"Same here Pastor Stephens. I really enjoyed the sermon today."

"Again I'm glad that through Him I could touch another soul."

I can't get past the fact that here I am talking to a Pastor that doesn't quite look like the typical Pastor. He's not dressed in a three piece suit, tie, and handkerchief, nor is he wearing the typical Sunday gear a Pastor would wear. He has on a nice sports coat, with a button down shirt, and a pair of JEANS! OMG my mother would have a fit! I can hear her now, she would say, what Pastor would even have the audacity to wear a pair of jeans in the pulpit, and if she was here I would look at her and say, "mommy this one."

Nevertheless meeting the Pastor was good for me, it made me feel even more welcomed than I did at first. He seems like a very humble man, but I couldn't help overhearing that he asked Marcel if he was free to help out with the ministry this week. Of course, he says, "Yes, anything I can do, I'll be glad."

Later this evening I am still floating on cloud nine. Ever since we left church I've felt this way. After church, Marcel invited us to his home, he has given the invite before, but I didn't feel ready just yet.

When we pull up to the Highrise Park Avenue condo, I didn't expect to walk into a mansion such as this. I always imagined him living in luxury but never to this magnitude. The doorman greets us as we head up to both the 27th and 28th floors to what I would say is a townhouse in the sky, my mouth falls open. Thank heavens Gabby has fallen asleep on the ride here, so I get her settled in her carrier just as we walk in. He takes my coat, and offers me a glass of water, and since it's on the New Years resolution list that I drink more water, I gladly accept.

While I wait for him to change clothes I take a look around the spacious family room that sits the softest pure white leather chairs, along with a sectional in an "S" design, with the most gorgeous silver ball pillows in between, seated on top of the most luxurious carpet your feet would ever want to stand on. Directly under the glass coffee table is a round Peruvian White Alpaca rug. His style is timeless, and also eclectic. So many geometrical glass vases I'm afraid I may accidentally knock over something, and there goes my income for the next five years. I take notice of framed black and white pictures displayed of different people; I love the one of him and his mother that is situated just over the mantle. He has several pictures of notable celebrities all over the world, and as I get a good glance at the picture in the silver frame, I see he has one of him and Sydney Poitier, that's signed to my beloved nephew, Love Uncle Sidney, and right above it it's engraved with the words. "We all suffer from the preoccupation that there exists ... in a loved one, perfection." My heart comes to a standstill. Simply beautiful, and yet I'm still impressed with the wall to wall bookcases that house all books from Spiritual, to Inspirational, to Motivational, also Historical, but he also has a huge Financial gallery of books, such as "*The Total Money Makeover,*" "*The Millionaire Next Door,*" "*Rich Dad Poor Dad,*" to name a few, but the most impressive is he has his first bible obviously given to him when he was a child.

Ten minutes later he steps out in all but a Black and grey track suit with a pair of socks, no dressy clothes, just a regular sweat suit.

"You look surprised to see me dressed like this." he says.

I giggle, "Is it that obvious?"

"Yes, you look like you've seen a ghost."

"I wouldn't say that, but ..."

"But what, you didn't think I had clothes like regular folk? Just because I wear nice expensive clothes doesn't define who I am. They don't make me, I make them. Not to sound as if I'm bragging, I just realize that it doesn't matter if you wear a nice pair of pants from Saks, or a H&M as long as you feel comfortable. Don't get me wrong I love the quality of the clothing. I love how they feel, but it doesn't stop there, I'm more than the clothes. To be honest, I feel better sometimes in just a track suit rather than a stiff neck tie with the full four button suit."

A puzzled look comes over my face, not that I don't agree, but I never thought of him as a regular man, every time I've seen him he's been in a well …

Out of the clear blue sky he asks the dreaded question. "So you don't own any everyday clothing?"

I'm guessing he can tell by the look on my face, that that is a no.

"I only have two pair of sneakers, and they are both for when I'm working out, and as far as jeans, I never thought about dressing them down, the ones I do own I manage to pair them as dress attire."

He comes back, "Food for thought: you should take inventory of the things that matter most to you. Is it the clothes or the things you buy, or is it the one that gives you the resources and makes ways for you to buy those things?"

We look at each other, and suddenly Gabby awakens. Therefore I know it's time for her to be fed, in which he kindly reaches over to remove her from her place of comfort, and begins to search her bag for her bottle. Once he locates them he so nicely says you can change her clothes, and then I will feed her. Did he fall straight from heaven to earth?

As he feeds her he proceeds to give me a tour of this city he calls home. First I can't imagine what one man would need a home with 6 bedrooms, 6½ bathrooms, that houses a library, state-of-the-art kitchen, with top of the line appliances. I thought the family room was enough, but to my chagrin this house even has a staff/guest room and bath that adjoins to a double laundry room, and extra storage space on the 27th floor. I begin to get dizzy, but this is not the half, a glorious stairway leads to the 28th floor with a media theatre, play room, and GYM! There are four bedrooms up here with marble baths, and an awesome master suite with a sitting room, dressing area, and to top it off Marcel has a divine pale green onyx bath, that has its own separate elevator entrance.

Once I'm done with the tour of Disney World he can tell I'm a bit overwhelmed, and so is Gabby. He's fed her the entire time. For a minute I thought I was going through a home you only see on CRIBS.

I take a seat on the couch where we begin and out of breath as I may seem, I somehow gather up the nerve to ask him, "Why a home so big?"

He looks at me with so much fire and passion in his voice, and says, "I need a home to be shared with the jewel in my life."

Chapter Nineteen
Marcel & Diamond

New Years Eve is finally here. I'm so excited because I'm looking forward to everything next year has for me. I'm ready to put the past behind me and press toward the future. This time I am burning bridges, cutting ties, and taking inventory. I'm saying goodbye to turmoil that was never mine! Even though I still haven't heard from Lance yet I'm remaining positive that I will come out of this better than before.

It's still early and Lucy's here to make sure so we perform our ritual. On the last day of every year for the last fifteen years; we given each other a token to take into the upcoming year reminding us of the old and the new, some years it has been sentimental, some have been comical, some have been just plain ole' tacky, but ... this year is different, this year he didn't go way out he just came straight from the heart. His old token to me is a picture that we all took way back when the "get fresh crew", namely Malcolm and Noëlle, amongst others that are no longer apart of our future. The new token is a picture that he insisted the photographer take in the hospital of all of us including Marcel, and of course it's in a pretty pewter frame that displays the words, Live, Laugh, and Love. I think Marcel has really begun to grow on him ... a lot!

He says, "Now don't you come with all that crying honey, it's like ever since you've taken on the title of "mummy," you've been nothing but a pail of water."

Trying to wipe the tears away I respond, "Whatever!"

"Now where is my token, I know you got me something good."

I go to the closet and pull out a bag that has two gifts wrapped. I look at his face and it's not the usual expression I'm used to. I watch him as he opens the first token, labeled "2 Corinthians 5:17, Therefore if any man be in Christ, he is a new creature: old things are passed away."

He burst out laughing, "No you didn't! Where did you get this from, it's my book of thoughts of how I wanted to become the fiercest diva alive. It's my blueprint. All of my hopes and dreams of meeting Mr ... oh well."

He stops in the middle of his sentence and turns to pick up the other gift, labeled "…behold, all things are become new." As he picks it up, he realizes it's a bit heavier than the first. He slowly pulls back the paper as if he's expecting a very expensive gift, but to his surprise. Tears stream down his face, like it's the greatest gift of all; well I guess you can say it is.

At a loss for words he somehow gets it out, "Vic, never would I have thought—a bible, it even has my name engraved in gold, Luciano Andrés Martinez."

He can't stop crying. I have never seen him this vulnerable before. He's always the one that has so much to say, never backing down, but now, nothing.

I say, "Now who's the one that needs a pail?"

We both laugh, and hug as if this is our last time, but it doesn't last long. Immediately he hammers in on me about how I need to stop being so hard, how I need to let Marcel love me. I'm starting to think Marcel is giving him a cut. Of all the men that have been in my life, Lucy has NEVER shown this much liking to.

"The old me, would have wanted to keep him for my self, but thank God for change…"

"Boy you are crazy, so you're telling me that you no longer need the love of a man?"

He blows me by saying, "This year if I haven't learned anything else I have learned that no man will ever compare to THE MAN. Don't get me wrong, there are times that I'm still tempted, and I know it's not going to be easy, but He promised me that if I would just trust Him, He will do the rest. I used to think that I would never want intimacy from woman, but lately that has changed, and look at Jules, he's a great example. He and Reese are getting married soon, and if God can change him, He surely can change me."

He looks like Lucy, and he sounds like Lucy but where is my friend?

He goes on to say, "When I tell you that Marcel is a good man, believe me. I know Malcolm hurt you, I know Noëlle hurt you, but that's what it is, it's hurt. We are going to have hurts, and pains, but now that I have been spending time at the clinic, I see so much that we take for granted,

231 Chizellé T. Archie

and I realize that we may not have all we want or need, but He has never forsaken us, so I know that all things will work together for our good. And as far as the people that are no longer with us going into the New Year, its okay, let them go! Sometimes that's what God is trying to do, he's trying to tell us to say bye-bye to people that never meant us any good in the first place. I once heard the Pastor say, some people you have to love from a distance, because they don't deserve a front row seat in your life. So Vic, trust God, and let him love you, like God loves us. People are going to talk, let them talk, if they find out your status so what! For all we know, they could be just as positive as you, but too afraid to say so."

And on that note preach boy! If Daddy was here he would say "Ushers will you come."

I can tell Gabby is up from her morning nap; therefore my schedule is likely to change. It's a good thing Lucy's here to help. Hopefully he's learned enough in the past month of how to at least change a diaper. I don't care what he says; some things are harder to change than others. All of a sudden I remember I haven't taken my medicine, I must have been caught up in I and Lucy's conversation.

Being around Gabby really makes him happy, although he's not too happy about having to go to work, but the good thing is everything will be closing early. I'm sure by now Times Square is completely flooded with people from all over the world wanting to see the ball drop. This year it's been said it's bigger than before. Marcel even suggested we go down, but I opted for a quieter night. I've seen that ball enough times in my life, so I don't think missing it this year will hurt anything.

I had so much planned to do today, but it doesn't seem I'm going to get it all done. I never intend to go into the New Year with things undone. Growing up Momma would always stress to me how I should never have any unwashed clothes once the New Year comes in. I've been killing myself to get all of this done before tonight. Marcel and I have dinner plans, so I want to make sure that I get everything taken care of before he gets here. Momma and Daddy have asked to watch Gabby, and at first it sounded like a good idea, but for some reason I just feel an urgency to bring the New Year in with my baby.

Time has gone by so fast, it's already four o'clock, and I'm still knee deep in cleaning. I can't help but think of how much Lucy has changed though. I never would have thought in a million years, that he would be saved and talking about the Lord the way he is, it's like he's been around someone that has been talking in his ear. Whoever or whatever it is I'm glad. I didn't realize that he had been going to church so long now. I've been so entwined in my own life until I haven't taken the time to notice my best friend has changed right before my eyes. Come to think of it, I haven't seen him with anyone, namely a man in a while. I'm also excited that Zoe has decided to make a few changes. She invited me to go with her to a group session. Something about a survival group sounds good, but I still have reservations. I will probably feel a lot better once I talk to Marcel.

It's becoming clear to me what Marcel and I talked about as far as my having so many clothes. Again, here I am standing in the room I call a closet that's large enough to fit inside another bedroom. I'm looking at all the shoes I have accumulated just this year alone. I began to count them one by one, including the ones I have on now, and it's even a shock to me. I own 237 pairs of shoes, everything from Gucci to Guisseppe. A wall filled with high heels, low heels, round heels, skinny heels; I even have ones with no heels. Lucy once said I needed a shopaholic's intervention, and now I'm thinking I should have taken him up on it. I continue to look around, and the more I do, it becomes apparent to me that I have spent entirely too much time and money trying to impress people that weren't worth impressing anyway. It's been a while since I've taken notice of everything that's in here. I never realized there were suits and dresses here with tags still on them; I guess I'm still waiting for that special occasion. I have no idea what to do with all the "special occasion gowns" I have, especially the one custom made for me by Donatella, when I was honored at the Financial Advisors of America's Banquet. Oh my goodness, to think of the money I spent on this dress, one I've only worn one time!

What really gets me is that once I'm done counting the shoes; I look up and see that there are almost as many bags, as there are shoes. I think Louis Vuitton himself owes me a check. I can give ten away, give some to Poochie to sell in the village, and still have one for every day of the week. I know I have one from every collection, but my all time favorite is the Monogrammed Vernis, pure genius, I love the glossy leather ... Not to mention the orange crocodile Birkin bag, I HAD to have, even waited for it to come in. It was one of the most selfish purchases I ever made. $37,000, what was I thinking? I saved up a couple of my bonuses to get that one, why, because Oprah had one of course. Looking at the Chanel bags neatly placed in a glass case made for me by "Designed with You in Mind," sort of makes my head hurt. It's a good thing Daddy took on that cost, because the case alone—was a car note. I understand a lot of these were impulse buys, but most of them were make up gifts from Malcolm, in which I'm not mad at him at all, actually I thank him very much.

Right as I stand here I am led to do something I have never done. I scramble to find the last six months of bank statements, so I can compare the last time I bought an expensive item against the last time I gave anything to God. I felt compelled to give an offering last Sunday just because, but I honestly can't say when was the last time I tithed. Makes me think really where my priorities have been, better yet I don't think it's anything wrong with me being fabulous, but I think it's time I revamp some things. The lady from Sunday crosses my mind, and as a matter of fact, I think I will donate some of these items to the ministry at the women's ministry. I'm sure it's some women there that may need these way more than I do. Now I know Lucy has changed but ... he is going to die when he hears this.

Thank goodness my parents are here to watch Gabby. Momma somehow convinced me to enjoy myself tonight; only because she says she wants me to have a great time, and as much as I hate to admit it, I need to, and I want to. Any other New Year's it was understood I would have to be the best dressed woman in the room, everything from my hair to my nails had to be on point, but I'm going to switch it up this year, instead of being so dressed up that I can't have fun, or in constant fear of spilling something, I'm going for strictly comfort, therefore I won't be inflicting any pain on these feet tonight.

Its seven o'clock on the dot, and he's here. Strangely enough I still get goose bumps in my stomach whenever I'm around him. The last time I felt like this I just knew I had found my soul mate, but later for that. It's a new man in town, and his name is Mr. Bouviér, and he loves me. I take one last look at myself dressed in all things Ralph Lauren, there's the grey cashmere turtleneck with the poncho wrap, and a blue pair of Black Label jeans ... paired off with the RL loafers, but ... pray for me, I can't leave home without the Hermès bag.

In the living room where everyone waits, with his back towards me, I stop to look at all 6'3" of him, and if I didn't know any better I would have thought he was in my closet. Inside I'm laughing so hard because he's wearing a green/rose argyle sweater vest, crisp white shirt, and a pair of relaxed fit jeans, and to finish it off a pair of shearling boots. You would think we were the new faces of Ralph Lauren, but he didn't forget the corduroy blazer ... It's nice that I get to see another side of him, for the first time I see him without the suits, and ties and I have to say, he looks real nice. Daddy even notices, he makes the statement to Momma, 'D', you've got to get me a pair of those boots girl."

She laughs and says, "Not in this life time."

He laughs himself saying, "Well I guess I'll be the sharpest dressed man in heaven, huh?"

"If I have to pay for some boots that cost more than a hundred dollars, I guess you will."

He looks at me, and winks, "That's why God gave me Diamond."

The only thing I can do now is shake me head, because if Daddy only knew.

She gives him that girlish grin I love to see. Knowing how happy these two are has always been my strength; it gives me hope that true love is attainable. The love I have for my father is incomprehensible, and I'm so grateful for the things he has taught me, even though I didn't always adhere to his teachings, I'm still thankful, just as am thankful to Malcolm, because by looking at Marcel tonight, if Malcolm would have never treated me like he did, I would not know what it was like to be treated like the queen Daddy always told me I was.

Finding a parking spot anywhere in New York tonight is almost impossible. After walking three blocks we come face to face with the restaurant, in which it wasn't all that bad. It's been a couple of years since it rained on New Year's, but the parties have yet to stop.

I know Marcel really hoped we would make our eight-thirty reservation, but from the looks of it, things may take a drastic turn. This place is packed, so much for a romantic evening. He tries to see if there is anything available, and the hostess kindly lets him know it will be at least another forty-five minute to an hour wait.

He asks, "Is this okay with you? You know we can find somewhere else to go of you'd like?"

"I'm fine waiting, because I'm sure everywhere we go will be like this tonight."

I can sense the hesitancy in his voice, and I know he wanted tonight to be special but believe it or not I'm not tripping out, I'm actually okay with anything he decides.

Next thing I know he tells not to worry about anything he has it, so we go to the car, however with the traffic we're at a standstill. It's been a long time since I just hung out like this; I'm just enjoying the ride. Watching everyone scramble to get to their destination puts me at ease that I'm not on the outside. It also reminds me of how happy I am that I chose not to where the four inch platforms, because by the looks on some of these women faces, they don't look too excited having to walk in the rain for miles in shoes that was only designed to make their feet look good.

He sets the disk player to track three, and all of a sudden Ella Fitzgerald comes over the speakers singing "*The Man I Love*", and I think I'm in another world. Oh my goodness, where has he been all this time, and on top of that I catch him trying to scat, and that cracks me up! We both break out together in an awful rendition of Ella's song ... that's why she recorded it, and not us. We both laugh together saying, "Now come on man ... what you say ... he's out of sight my man ... dadada ... that's my man ... I'm waiting on my man." Then we debate on whom did it best, Ella of Billie? We both settle on Ella hands down.

I glance up at the roof, and the panoramic view from the top of the truck only adds a sweeter feel to what is already turning out o be a great night.

We make our way to Almond, in which this is not one of my regular dining establishments. Marcel says he comes here on occasions when he just wants to get away from the hoopla of the day. He assures me this is a good spot, especially because it's French, and in saying that I already have an idea what I plan to order. I like the feel as soon as we enter, and I can tell Marcel is a regular by the way a waiter named Chaz greets him instantaneously as if they've known each other for years, and from there he rushes a to a secluded area and immediately places our order. Impressive service I must say. One good aspect to this is I am pretty hungry. I've anticipated this meal all day and obviously so is Marcel.

It doesn't take me long to decide on the Frittatas and the Nicois salad, and Marcel orders the Cavatelli Shrimp Sausage, with a glass of Long Island Iced Tea. Looks like it's later for the appetizers!

As we wait for our meals, a funny feeling runs through me. A nervous yet calming feeling, and out of nowhere I ask him what's my favorite color.

Without any hesitation he says, "I'm going to have to say pink, although you have a great deal of grey in your wardrobe, but you look beautiful in pink."

I find that to be a good guess, even though he's right, I have been wearing a lot of grey lately. I've just told myself it's the new black.

In an attempt to get his reaction, I say, "You would be correct."

He doesn't seem moved.

Keeping a makeshift scorecard he says, "One for me, none for you."

"Okay, you got the first one, lucky guess, but what is my favorite gemstone?"

He finds this amusing, but again he doesn't think twice. "That's a given, a Diamond."

I answer by saying, "That was an easy one."

"You're right it was, but the question should be why a diamond is your favorite?"

I sit here in a bit of a daze, and the warm and cozy atmosphere doesn't help. I ponder the question because all of these years I never thought about that. I just felt it was my name so I might as well like it, and it never dawned on me to like any other jewel.

He switches the script and asks, "What do you know about me? What's my passion?"

Shifting in my seat, I jokingly say, "The love of money."

Chaz brings our meals, and as he places the food on the table, I catch a glimpse of how he tucks his napkin inside his clothes the way they taught us to do in Finishing School, I didn't think anyone, and especially a man did that in the real world.

When he's set everything in front of him just as he would like it, he continues, "Where were we? Oh yes, you were saying how much I loved money, and if I thought you were serious I'd have to say yes, but ... no, that's not my passion."

"So what is it?"

"Its gemstones, and their entire composition, their make up, I love their beauty, their rarity, and most of all durability. How they can withstand anything. I'm intrigued with the way the light plays off them as the gems diffract, or better yet reflect waves of light."

As I began to cut into my salad, I realize that this is something that is very dear to him, from the intensity he gets in eyes when he talks about them.

I have to ask, "Which is your favorite gemstone, and why?"

He takes a break from his meal, and says, "Of course the Diamond. Growing up as a young man, my parents thought I was strange. Everyday I would come home with all these rocks in hopes to one day create the perfect diamond. Needless to say I never did, but I think my mother is proud of me, and so would my father be to have a son that owns and operates five salons across the world. With a new one scheduled to open mid-summer next year."

My mouth all but wants to fall open! It all makes sense, this is why when he first met me, I'll never forget how he noticed the ring on my finger first, not because he was watching another man's wife, but because he was intrigues with the diamond itself. Just the though of that makes me blush.

He asks, "If you were a diamond in a jewelry salon, what type of diamond would you be?"

I stutter, because I'm thinking the most expensive one, but if I know Marcel that's not what he's thinking.

Taking a sip of his tea, he takes his time and enlightens me on diamonds 101.

"All well and good, but my seeing you in the natural eye, I would say you were a (FL) or an (IL) grade, which is flawless, with no imperfections. This is a very rare diamond. It's the one that want be on display inside the case. This one I would keep for myself, hid and tucked away in a vault, and if anyone wanted to view it, they would need permission to gain access. This is what I would say drew me to you."

With my head buried in my plate, I ask, "Why such a high quality?"

He replies, "I see you this way, because this is how God sees you. Perfect!"

WHAT YOU SAY! You better go boy ... here I am trying to be the one for the world to see, but all along I don't realize I'm more than that.

He continues, "If I never say this to you again, you are special, and remember if you were the diamond being showcased daily then everyone namely your enemies, or your haters some would say, would see you as no more than a (I1) visible flaws seen by the naked eye, or even worse (I2), (I3) these may even have black spots, they may be bruised, broken, or even cracked. And this is how the enemy sees us, for all of our imperfections.

Before I know it, I'm overcome with emotion, but somehow I ask, "Do you love me?"

"Yes," he replies.

I take it a step further, "Would you love me if I wasn't like everyone else you've ever dated?"

Again he says, "Yes, and also I would hope you weren't like everyone else."

There's a long pause, and as hungry as I may be, I say, "I love you too, but you should know these past months have been very rough for me."

I look into his eyes that have so much care and love in them; it makes me want to tell him even more. I have to.

I go on, "You never asked why Malcolm and I never divorced."

"It never mattered, I wasn't drawn to him."

My heart thumping in my chest I continue, "He was very unfaithful to me, and because of that I'm now faced with something I will live with forever, and it not only affects me, but all of us."

The more I try to finish my dinner, the more choked up I become.

"Go on." he says.

"Six months ago, I was told I have ...uum, God this is so hard for me—"

"You can say it."

Breathe, Victoria, breathe. "I have HIV."

As soon those words escape me. I suddenly feel liberated, but I can't figure his take on this. He gets real quiet, and continues to eat. After the last bite he looks up and says, "Is that it? I thought you were about to tell me you were guilty and you stole those people's money, and now both of us are about to go to jail."

I laugh until I can't stop. It slowly turns into a misty cry, because now I get it. This man was truly sent to me by God. Even in my weakest moment, he lifts me up, and says, "God is in control of all things, all we have to do is trust Him."

Half an hour later we're on our way back to the car, and it looks as though the rain has let up. On the way we pass a group of tourist that apparently has been partying all night. We can't but overhear them counting down to the New Year, Marcel stops, and looks me deep into my eyes, and we act as if its only us. We began yelling, 10,9,8,7,6,5,4,3,2,1, Happy New Year! He pulls me close to him and plants the sweetest kiss ever, then turns and says, "Next year, we're going to church." I grab his hand; take a long breath and say, "Fine by me." After all there is no doubt in my mind this will be a great year for me.

I am having Gabby withdrawals, I've tried not to call so much tonight, but I can't help it, it's New Years, and I want to tell it to my baby.

Quiet as I can be, I say to Momma, "Happy New Year."

"Same to you baby, how's everything?"

Excited I say, "Momma its good, its real good. How's Gabby?"

"She's fine baby, don't worry about her we have her, you just enjoy yourself."

Marcel snickers in the background, "Tell your mother Happy New Year, and your father too. Oh and Gabby, give her a kiss for me."

Just as I finish the conversation, I notice my alerts are going off nonstop, every second, it's another wish one right after the next. I didn't think so many people had my number. To save myself time and heartache, I compose a generic message for all to see.

"I pray that this reaches you in the New Year. May God's blessings be with you. Diamond."

One press of the send button and it goes to the worthy recipients somewhere in cyberspace. Marcel makes the joke that it's been New Years in France six hours ago, so he's late on the text messages.

After cruising the city like a pair of teenagers, we decide to stop by an all night jazz gallery, but just as we come to this decision, my body reminds me that I can't hang out like I used to anymore, so we make a detour and head for the house.

He says, "I hope you enjoyed yourself tonight."

"I did."

"I'm glad."

"So am I."

Then he says something I would not have expected. "Are you taking your medicines?"

For the first time since Lucy and I fell out over someone asking me that, I realize this time, I don't mind.

I answer, "Yes, I am."

Then he asks, "Have you opened that box yet."

Once again, I'm reminded that I have failed to open Gabby's shower gift from all this time. I looked at it the other day and told myself I'll get to it. Between the feedings and diaper changes it slipped my mind.

He tells me, "Next week I will be in California for about a week. I have to go out and take care of some business matters, tie up some loose ends, but I will be back after that."

I grin and say, "I think I can handle that, although I'll be glad when we hear something from Lance."

He says, "Wait, I say, on the Lord."

We pull in front of the house, and he rushes to open the door for me. I invite him inside, but he decides against it.

"It's late," he says, and being my parents are here, he doesn't want to disturb them, or Gabby. He walks me to the door, makes sure I'm settled in, and again he tells me how much he loves me, and that there is nothing to be afraid of, because he's not going anywhere. We give each other a warm hug and kiss. I say, "Call me when you make it home." He smiles, and says, "I will." I stand on the other side of the door thanking God for this day.

Everyone is asleep so I tip toe into Gabby's room, give her the best night- night kiss, and make my way to my room. One I am so glad to see. Tonight was fun, but I know that I'm not the young girl I used to be. I didn't want to let on to how tired I was because I know he wanted tonight to be a good one in that it was.

3:27a.m. Hello my Diamond, I made it home. Sleep tight. Hakuna Matata. I love you. Marcel.

3:28a.m. I'm glad you're home. Love you too, Diamond.

I take a long hot shower; prepare myself for what lies ahead of me in this year to come. Before going to sleep I run across some things I could never bring myself to go through from the job. It's a box I placed under my bed, that I said I need to get rid of.

There are so many certificates, amongst other credible papers I received while at that office. I still can't believe they let me go like that. I was a great asset to the company. I notice that I threw the gift Melanie gave me for my birthday in the bottom of the box. I never learned how to use it. Some of these gadgets they have today are way too technical for me, but she was dead set on getting her Auntie Diamond an iPod Touch.

I sit and try for the longest to figure this thing out. I remember the last time I used it was the day Tyler came into my office, the day I signed the papers, we talked about Mr. Coleman's uum ... wait. I scramble to get it on. The last thing I was doing when he came in was trying to set up voice memo recording. I had it until he interrupted me.

I desperately try to understand the logistics of this handheld toy that's the latest craze. As soon as I connect the microphone, I get a message that that ask me to select voice memos > recordings. Once I select it I hear a low grade static, so I try to transfer to the computer. It's a good thing I purchased the additional software.

When he came into my office, I was learning how to record, and I must did not realize it was going the whole time, but most of all neither did Tyler. All of a sudden I hear the conversation between Tyler and me!

It's not as clear as I would want it to be, but it's audible. Got ya!

I immediately rush to call Marcel, and once he hears this, we both say it at the same time, "Thank you Jesus!"

This is enough evidence to clear my name of these hideous charges, as well as it proves Tyler was the one who coerced Mr. Coleman into signing his name by fraudulently misrepresenting documents, and passing the subscription agreement, and PPM off as a New Account Card.

I hear a voice in my head saying, "If you have the faith of a mustard seed."

"Again, Happy New Year!"

Chapter Twenty
Diamond

Four months later ... and things couldn't be any better. Today I turn another year older, and it's hard to think last year this time I was on top of the world. I had it all planned out, but Marcel said something to me the other day that made me think once again. He said, "If you want to make God laugh, tell Him your plans." That took me way back, because that reminded me of my grandmother Belle.

She died when I was fourteen years old, and growing up my mother was pretty strict on me. Now Daddy was a different story, looking back, I had him wrapped around my finger, but no matter what, when momma would discipline me in the way she felt was best, I would someway make decide to run away; right to Grandma Belle's house. I would get so fed up, because Daddy was working late, momma was trying to finish her degree, and Julian oh; he only had time for the books. What about me? I would ask. I'd pack my bags with a few clothes, but enough shoes to last weeks at a time. I figured you could change the outfit, but as long as you have a banging pair of shoes, who would realize you had the same out fit on Monday that you did Thursday.

There were times I couldn't take it. One day my parents refused to give me an addition to my allowance, so I decided to pack up, go over to Grandma Belle's and ask her to take me to the bank so that I could cash in all the stocks and bonds my father had given me every year on my birthday, to me which probably then equaled up to about $5500. I had already calculated it. I was determined that if someone would rent me a room for $25/week, plus the money I had saved up equaling $1200, I would have enough for room, board, food, that would last me until I was 18 years old. I would even have enough to buy myself some sharp clothes, that way I would be fine, because I would still have the money my parents were giving me towards my regular allowance, so I was set! So I thought ... I was looking good too, because Daddy always taught me whenever you walk into a bank you look like you've got the money that's in that bank, and you're coming to get what belongs to you. So I convinced Grandma Belle we were going to the bank, and she even got dressed up herself, she put her lipstick on, and her favorite hat, and we both were the cutest things in Brooklyn. We walked in the bank, as if we owned it, Grandma Belle explained to the Bank teller what I was planning to do, so she got out the necessary documents in order for me to cash in my stock and bonds. To my surprise ...All that time, they were only worth $2500. Where was my money! When Grandma saw the look on my face, she looked up at the teller, then at me and smiled, and immediately said, "Baby if you want to make God laugh, show him what you've got planned." Shall I say I was stuck at home for the next four years, and I never asked for an increase in my allowance either. I'm not sure if Grandma even told Momma and Daddy about that. She was sweet like that. Its times like this I miss her like crazy.

Preparing to head over to my parents, I peek in on my sweet baby, and I can't help think how fast she has grown. She's getting so big; she's even starting to pull up! I'm still praising God that all of her blood work has come back negative! I would have to say, it's the best birthday gift I could ever ask for.

Everyday I look at her, I'm so thankful that I did not make the choice to abort her. I admit there were nights where I felt I couldn't do it. But looking back over that now, I don't think I would have been able to live with myself, but God knew best.

Several months ago, I didn't think I'd live to see another birthday, and yet God has spared me. I am so glad that Zoe talked me into going to the support group, because I feel so much better. I have now learned to accept that what happened to me is not my fault. I did the right things; I never cheated on my husband, although he felt he needed to do that to me. I can't take back what has happened, I can only try to make the best of it, and live it as though I've been given a second chance.

Marcel has been wonderful too, not a day goes by that he doesn't forget to tell me he loves me. He even invited me to go with him to the Annual Jewelry Conference next month, where he's the featured speaker.

I keeping trying to find something wrong with him, but I can't. He has done everything to make sure that I'm happy. He's miles away now, and even when he goes out of town, he always calls and says good night, and that he loves me. Last month we flew to Beverly Hills, the home of the flagship salon. I believe he knew it had been a while since I ... well I lost it! I went crazy on Rodeo Drive. Until you've been there, it's only pure imagination, but now they know me on first name basis. When there, I only have three words; I'll take that! I even shopped for my ladies at the church that might explain the look on Pastor's face Easter Sunday. It looked like a Hat Extravaganza. Round ones, tall ones, small ones, I even got Sister Luella one covered in Rhinestones. By the time I left out of there I had the owners personal address, cell phone number, he even gave me his wife's cell phone number.

The best thing I have come to love about him is he's an ordinary man, although he has a multi-million dollar empire, he is still regular. His love for God is immeasurable, and everyday I wake up, I thank God for sending me someone like him. From the bike rides in Central Park, to the quiet movie nights at my house, it's like he's too good to be true. If I didn't know any better, I'd think God released one of his angels just to protect me.

Zoe finds it hard to believe we haven't been intimate at all ... she makes the joke that it's something wrong with him. I even thought that myself at one time. I felt it was because of my status, but he doesn't stress over that; it's as if he could care less. Lucy gets a kick out of it too; he calls it "the waiting to exhale moment". I just say he has his grown man on, and everything is not about sex. At least that's what I'd like to believe this time.

It's still so hard to believe that after all that time I'm a free woman. Turns out, after I gave the iPod to Lance, he then in turn gave it to the District Attorney, and everything else is history. The case was thrown out, and I was free to do as I please. Yet and still, I'm having a hard time figuring out how Tyler was able to get Mr. Coleman's signature on the documents. He must have had that planned all along. He's even tried contacting me a couple of times to apologize, but I feel there is no need to go there. The best thing I can do for him now is pray for him.

Earlier when I spoke with Marcel he asked me for the one hundredth time have I opened Gabrielle's shower gift yet? He's asked me that on more than one occasion and my answer have always been "not yet." I don't want to give the impression, I keep forgetting, but I do. Every time I go to open it, something has always come up. In an attempt to show him I'm appreciative, I promised him I would get to it today, and since I have a few minutes before I head to meet Mrs. Richardson, I would say now is the best time.

In my nightstand where I have kept it this long, I gently untie the pink ribbon in fear of destroying some nice gift wrapping customer service rep's hard work. In one hand I 'm holding the box, and the other I use to dial his number.

On the second ring he picks up, *"Bonjour mon amour*, I was just thinking about you."

Smiling as if Michael Jackson had just picked up the phone, I ask, "Were you?"

Even the sound of his voice gives me chills. Sometimes I hold the phone just to hear him speak, and when he talks in French, I'm gone ... it never fails, my mind runs away with all kinds of pure and unholy thoughts, but just like now I bring myself back to reality.

"How are you love?"

"Great, about to open Gabby's gift."

"Finally, I was beginning to take it personal." he says.

"So where are you now?" I ask.

"When you called I was about to meet one of my partners—"

As he's talking I'm trying to make sure I'm seeing correctly.

"Hello ..."

Somewhat distracted, I respond, "I'm here."

I sense his excitement, "Have you opened it yet?"

Hesitating I say, "Yes, I have but—"

"So ... ?"

In total awe, I slowly respond, "A million dollars?"

He gets quiet, and eventually asks, "Is there a problem?"

Right away I say, "There's no problem but ..."

"But what?"

Shockingly enough it's a document drafted where he has made arrangements to place $1 million in a trust for Gabby to be set aside at the predetermined age of 18, contingent I the trustee remain in total control.

Not sure what to say, still in complete amazement, I say to him, "No, it's not that, I've just never had anyone do anything like this."

Surely he senses my hesitation, although I don't want to seem ungrateful, because besides Daddy, there has never been any man in my life that would have ever thought enough to do anything like this, not even Malcolm, and he's her father.

He explains, "You know I have no children of my own, and it has always been my desire to leave behind a legacy that would be carried on for generations to come, and other than my nephew who's already working on his career path, I had no one else to leave my legacy to."

I interrupt, "Why Gabrielle?"

"Why not Gabrielle? When Melissa first told me you were having a baby I immediately began to think. At that time, I already had love for you, and who better else could I leave my legacy to, than to someone who was a part of you."

I asked him what made him do such a thing, were there any other motives, and of course being the man he is, he stated "I have no motives, my only motive was to love you, and whatever that's part of you."

I also wanted to know why did he not give it to me himself, again his response to me was, "It wasn't time, to everything there is a season." It must have been fate that Zoe and I were in Vegas when we were because I'm starting to think that was my season.

"You will get it after while." he says.

The only thing I know to say is, "Thank you."

"No, thank you. Sorry I can't be there today, but I love you. We will celebrate when I get back. *Bon anniversaire!*"

"Lord Have Mercy, even when the man tells me Happy Birthday, I get chills."

Forgetting that I'm supposed to meet everyone over to my parents, I realize I'm the birthday girl, and I'm going to be late as always. Well, it's been said a diva is entitled to be fashionably late.

Wow, I miss my baby the S550; we had so many good times together. Everything was personalized for me, although I believe I made a good choice with the R350, and of course it had to be black ... but Mercedes is all I know. Daddy made sure of that, and when it's in your blood, you take it with you everywhere you go. Gabby doesn't seem to upset riding in an upscale versioned Mini-Van. However, Melanie jokes that her Auntie Diamond, looks like the "fabulous soccer mom," and I'll take that. Daddy purchased it for me, us, as a gift, something about he wants me to be little safer now, especially since I'm driving around the newest heir to Jean-Pierre's Mercedes Benz of New York.

Turning the corner I can see the streets packed with cars, Gabby and I have to walk what seems like a mile up the street. Who all have they invited? It was understood this was supposed to be a small gathering. I just wanted to spend a nice quiet afternoon with my family.

Oh my goodness ... these people have flipped out. They have a makeshift dance floor in the middle of the living room, along with my fifty-something old Uncle Seymore as the dee-jay. As soon as you walk in, you can hear him over the speakers screaming, "Now wave your hands in the air, and wave them like you just don't care, if you really and truly love Diamond, everybody say Oh Yeah!"

Can you say embarrassed! I don't know whether to walk out, or first get a paper bag to put over my head then walk out. The sad part is that Gabby thinks it's funny; she lets out the biggest laugh ever. My baby laughed! Guess we're staying.

Everything from the food to the decorations is beautiful. My parents went all out for me, and I think what makes it this way is that everything is out of love, no fabulous frills or well known party planners, only my family. Daddy says this one was more special than ever, because God allowed me to see another year, a year I thought I wouldn't see. He calls it His Grace and Mercy. I call it Favour!

Mrs. Richardson, my mentor is here, and she's even brought along a couple of ladies from the group. Shelly says to me, "This makes her so happy to see that someone with HIV, that their family can still love them." She was diagnosed two years ago, and everyone she thought loved her turned their backs on her. Also Lilliana came to me with a tear in her eye, saying, "This is unheard of, to have people from the church that knows your status, and still they want to be around you." She almost committed suicide because the one place she thought she could go to, (the church) they treated her like she was an outcast. She hasn't been to church since. Lucy even brought a friend, Phyllis, a nineteen year old girl diagnosed last week. She waited so long, and when she finally gave in, the first time she got HIV, and the bad part is that he knew it!

As I look around everyone that's here are people I love. I couldn't imagine turning 34 any other way. I just hate that Gabby has fallen off to sleep. She's been passed around so much, I can see why. I just pray that tonight she doesn't feel the need to stay up and play until 2:30, because Mommy just may have to let her, but she'll be all by herself.

Today has really turned out to be so much fun. Once Mrs. Richardson and the others leave, Daddy thinks this is the "take a stroll down memory lane" moment. I don't know what we will do if anything ever happens to him, because who will be the one to bring up all the most embarrassing and forgotten moments in our lives. He even had the nerve to bring to remembrance my eleventh birthday, it was then I had begun to feel empowered, so he says. I felt I could do almost anything. Just so happened, there was a concert that same day, in the park, and I figured Lucy and I would show up at the party, but we would soon leave. No one would really miss us, because Julian was the favorite child anyway. Therefore, we went and we stayed way too long. That was the one time Daddy let me have it. Over all the noise, I could hear him calling my name, for some reason no one could call me Diamond like he could. All of my friends turned around, it was like Moses parting the Red Sea, and I'm not sure if I was able to sit down for a week. Lucy was even on fire. He claims to this day Daddy is the reason why he never pledged any fraternities, because after that night, he never wanted to be beat again.

"Victoria, I think I have some letters you wrote us while you were in college." Momma says.

"You still have those 'D'?" Daddy asked.

Julian makes the joke, that Momma never gets rid of anything.

"Have you been in the basement?" Julian asked my Daddy.

Daddy responds, "Not since the last time your mother trapped me. That woman has every letter I ever wrote her in school."

"All of them Daddy?" I ask.

Momma turns her head, as not to let us know just how much she hasn't given away.

He continues, "Yes baby, even the one where I first wrote. 'Do you love me check Yes or No'."

We all burst into laughter. I didn't think people that old wrote those kinds of letters. Back then, you would think everything was so profound, being that was the time of the Civil Rights Movement, and the Black Panther Era. Yes or no just seems so ... plain.

Momma insists I go to her closet to find the box where she's kept the letters. I go into her room, where she has made picture perfect bed made. I recall Daddy always asking why does there have to be so many pillows on the bed? One is enough. He would never sleep with me then.

As I reach up to get the box placed neatly behind a stack of books, the box falls over, and so does the books. A letter falls out of the book with my name on it. Maybe she forgot to give this to me. I turn and kneel beside her bed to open the envelope addressed to me.

My Sweet Victoria,

The day you were born, it was a very bad storm; it had been raining for twenty-four hours straight. I had been in labor for ten of those hours.

The entire time I carried you, I felt you were different, you only had one side you preferred, and you didn't kick until you really wanted something. I would sing to you, I would play all kinds of music so that you would have a love for that one day. I spoke words of encouragement over your life. I constantly prayed that no harm would come against you.

Both your father and I knew you would grow to be something extraordinary, because when we first saw you, it was something in your eyes. Your eyes at that time were hard to distinguish the color, but they were so bright, more greyish than anything, they looked like small diamonds. With one look we knew we were in trouble.

It was always the plan that you would know Jesus Christ as your Savior. Every night we'd pray with you and Julian. You knew the Lord's Prayer by age 2. We would take you to church every chance we got. We wanted to make sure you were involved in all that was going on, because we loved you, and we wanted what was best for you, and being close to God was the best thing for you.

When I first found out you were diagnosed with HIV, it was one of the worst days of my life, because for the first time I couldn't help you. For the first time I couldn't fix it, and it made me very bitter. I wanted to erase all the hurt and pain from you, but I couldn't.

I was so angry with God, but first of all I was angry with myself. I thought I had done something wrong, that I didn't take enough time with you to let you know how much you meant to me. I thought this was a punishment from God to me, because while you were growing up, I was so hard on you, but I thought I was doing the right things. If only I could have not gone to class for a night a two, and stay with you while you completed your work, or better yet, maybe I should have taken a little more time to explain to you about the birds and the bees. I didn't know what to do. I just felt it was my entire fault, and this is why I could not give you the support you so deserved. You may have felt I was there, but I wasn't. My heart was, but my mind was elsewhere.

Today I'm writing this letter because I have seen you become so strong in the midst of all your adversities; you have even been a rock for me. I know it has been hard, especially with having a new baby, and I want to tell you I'm so proud of you. I have seen you do things that I know I wouldn't have been able to do. You have come through so much in just these past months; you have even inspired me to join other mothers that have children living with this deadly disease. When I look at you, I see your beauty and your strength; it's like the first day I looked into your eyes. I now know why we named you Diamond.

Diamonds are rare and exotic; they are perhaps the most treasured gem on earth. They have been known to glitter and dazzle because of their exquisite beauty. They are pure, and there is no other that's as transparent. They are brilliant in color, actually they are colorless. They are the hardest substance known. You should also know that the only substance than can scratch a diamond is another diamond. They are fiery, they have the ability to reflect light in a rainbow of colors, and most of all they are priceless, and all of that is you.

Because you are all of these things, I want you to know that you can trust God and take Him at His word. With all the pain you have gone through there is still someone that loves you. Marcel is a wonderful man and I believe in my heart that God has sent him to be your mate. It may seem that He has come in an awkward time in your life, but God is a sovereign God, which means He can do what He wants, when He wants, and how He wants, because He's God. And all you have to do is trust and believe that He will do what He said.

So go ahead, and love again, its okay. God has your back and so do I. There's no need to worry, He's brought you this far and I don't believe He will leave you now. And to all of those people that have said things about you baby, all of the negativity that has been shown over the news, its okay, because God is the author and finisher of your faith. I want you to look them all in the eyes and tell them, look at me now!
Your Mother

Momma walks in and sees me reading the letter. It's a wonder how I even got through it. I bring myself to stand up, and then she gives me one of the best hugs ever. We cry together, and for the fist time since my diagnosis, I finally know how my mother felt.

By the time I'm back in the living room, everyone is singing and dancing, and it looks like Uncle Seymour has gotten a little tired because he's given it to the young'uns, so he calls it. He does give me a dance, a slow one, but nevertheless it's a dance.

Julian and Reese just let us know they are expecting a baby in the fall, and that's the best news yet. He looks so happy, and so does she. Mel is jumping from the chandeliers, although she insists this one must be a boy. The way she sounds would make you think Taylor and Leigh are a handful.

"Is everyone going to church tomorrow?" Momma asks.

"We have no choice 'D' do we?" Daddy says.

Laughing, she says, "Winston you always have a choice, it's if you make the right one is the thing."

Daddy rares back in his chair, and says, "It's a good thing Marcel ain't here, I believe between you and him 'D', somebody gon' be a preacher, because that boy quotes more scriptures than the disciples."

Momma shoots back, "Well we know who want be a preacher."

Out of nowhere Daddy says, "But we also know if they had cars in heaven God would be the first on my list I'd give a Mercedes to."

Everyone turns to look at me, I don't think that's what God has planned, but who knows. He is God.

I didn't expect to be at my parents this long. Zoe asked if I felt like doing anything, but I have no energy left. The only thing I want to do is get comfortable, and get ready for church in the morning. We've been going to church with Marcel since Christmas Eve. I feel so at home there. I'm glad Marcel invited us. I've learned so much in the time I've been there. Lucy has come with me a couple of times, so has Zoe, they both feel the same way. One thing I really love is that the Pastor is real, he doesn't sugar coat anything. He tells us what thus saith the Lord, and that's the truth. A lot of times he has stepped all over my toes, but I know it's only been to better me, to push me to a greater level, and for that I'm thankful.

Since it so late , it doesn't take long to get Gabby down, I think she's worn out from today in which I'm so happy, because if I do another round of Barney's "*I Love You*", I'm going to sleep myself.

I call Marcel and tell him goodnight. I can tell he's had a long day, because he sounds beat, but even in that, he musters up a lovely I love you. We don't talk too long, because we both are tired. Even though I've heard enough French to last me a lifetime, it's something about the way he says it, so I ask him to tell me something good in French.

"*La bonne nuit mon amour, mon sommeil tendu et je vous veux ne pas avoir d'inquiétude.*"

(Good night my love, sleep tight, and I want you to have no worries.)

"Whew! He has to be a fallen angel."

Just before we hang up, he tells me before I lie down tonight, there are two scriptures that he wants me to read, and that I need to read them in order.

First there is Joel chapter 2 in its entirety, focusing on verses 25 and 26, and then there is Psalm 139, in its entirety, focusing on verses 13 and 14. He assured me that once I read this *everything* I've prayed for will be answered. My heart beats fast, because never in my life would I feel I deserved a man such as he.

I smile, and say, "Hakuna Matata."

After my bath, I climb in the bed and remove my bible from the nightstand. First the words are a bit unclear, but the more I read, the clearer they get. After reading Joel, I reread verses 25 and 26 and they say:

And I will restore to you the years that the locust hath eaten, the cankerworm, and the caterpiller, and the palmerworm, my great army which I sent among you. And ye shall eat in plenty, and be satisfied, and praise the name of the LORD your God that hath dealt wondrously with you: and my people shall never be ashamed.

My heart is full, and to know that Marcel knew exactly where to tell me to go, is just another sign that God has sent him to me. I can't stop crying, because I know that God loves me just this much, and after all I've lost. He still plans to give it all back. I immediately turn to Psalm 139, and I read, and I read, and I come across verses 13 and 14, and the say:

For thou hast possessed my reins: thou hast covered me in my mother's womb. I will praise thee; for I am fearfully and wonderfully made: marvelous are thy works; and that my soul knoweth right well.

The only thing I know to do at this moment is fall on my knees and cry out to the Lord that has seen me through another year. Lord, I know there were times where I felt you left me, and I thought you were so far away. I questioned you, and asked where were you. There were nights where I couldn't feel you, nights I couldn't hear you, but I know now you were there all along. There is so much in my life that wants me not to believe you, thinking of the pain, the hurt, and the disappointments. Lord the devil wants me to think I can't make it, but Lord I now know with you I can make it. I know that you will never leave me, and you will always be here. You love me, and this is why I trust you. Lord, you have been faithful to me; I know that you would not have brought me to this not to bring me through this. Lord you have never failed me. Lord I'll trust you!

You asked me to believe you, and Lord I trust you, every tear I've cried I still trust you, I can, I will, I'll trust you, even when I can't track you or trail you, I know you will never put more on me than I can bear, and this is why I can trust you. I didn't always do the right things, and you loved me still, you watched over me when I ran from you, you kept me from all hurt and harm, and Lord, I say I trust you! My life is not over, and I'm praising you in advance for what I know you're going to do, I know you'll make a way for me, and I believe the best is yet to come. In the name of Jesus!

Chapter Twenty One
Victory!

The weather report stated to expect severe thunderstorms, and by looking at the rain pressing up against the windows I would say they were right. A couple of minutes left before we land at Dekalb Peachtree's Airport.

I've tried to think of everything I've brought with me, I'm hoping I didn't forget anything, because I really want to look nice for Marcel. I'm so proud of him; he's being awarded tonight as one of the top selling Jewelry Salon Owners in America. My dress is a one of a kind made by a local designer here in Atlanta, Michael Knight. I fell in love with his designs on season 3 of Project Runway, and since then, I've been a fan.

Hoping that some of this rain will pass over, Marcel has the driver wait a while and we stop in the 57th fighter to get something to drink. I'm not hungry, because I ate a little something on the jet, and of course I'm not getting anything to drink because now that I'm undetectable again, I wish not to have anything mess that up.

Marcel has a few things planned for us this evening; he's the perfect tour guide. Of all the places I've been, Atlanta has not been one of them. Julian says it's a beautiful place, he says it reminds him of NY, but just on a smaller scale. Both he and Reese made sure that we don't leave without eating at the famous Spondivits, and the historic Paschal's. Julian is not one to brag, but he says both of these are a must have.

I've heard many things about Peachtree Street, but I never knew there were so many of them! On the way to the hotel, we've past about three of them, Peachtree Street, Peachtree Road, not sure if I saw a Peachtree Avenue or not, but if I didn't there's probably one somewhere.

We finally arrive at the Georgian Terrace Hotel, and I'm so impressed. Valet is superb. I noticed one of the men in Valet asking for Marcel's autograph, you would think he was Bob Johnson, and the funny part is once we we're inside a greeter named Maya recognizes me, and asks. "Are you Mrs. Cartiér, Victoria Cartiér?"

I'm like ... how does she know me. She says she moved here about three months ago from Brooklyn, and she's seen me featured in *Black Enterprise Magazine*. She said how proud she was to see a sister doing her thing, and I also think its sweet what she asks as I walk away. She turns and asks, "If I had enough money, would you take me on as a client?" I smile and say, "If you had no money, I would take you on as a client." I think I made her day. I think I made her whole year.

The rain hasn't let up at all, looks as though we are going to order in tonight. I've caught Marcel going over his speech a couple of times; I believe he'll do fine.

I call Momma and Daddy to let them know we've made it safely, and to see how Gabby is. I miss her so much. The last time I left her like this we were in California, and I didn't think I was going to survive that, so hopefully I'll do good this time as well.

"Hey Momma, we've made it."

"Good, how is everything?"

"Everything so far is good, the room is nice, and well shall I say the Penthouse is nice. Of course there's enough room for all of us to fit in. How's my baby?"

"She's wonderful. I can tell she misses you though."

"Probably not as much as I do her."

"How's Marcel?"

"He's fine, working on his acceptance speech."

"Oh, he'll do just fine."

"Yes, I think so too."

"Your father says hello, and that he loves you."

"Tell daddy hi, and I love him back."

"Did Malcolm contact you?"

Shocked she asked, I say, "No ma'am he didn't. Why did he call you?"

"Yes, he called earlier, and said that it was important you call him."

"He doesn't want anything; every time I talk to him it's the same thing over and over again. He constantly tells me how sorry he is, and how he wishes things were different. I've told him there is no chance of us ever getting back together, and that's final."

"I believe he wants to tell you his Aunt Colleen passed last night, and since you were pretty close to her he felt you should know."

Aunt Colleen was one of the sweetest women I have ever known. She was always honest in her thoughts. She spoke her mind, and if you didn't like it, then oh well. She never took sides with Malcolm and I, when we both were wrong she'd tell us. I think she never has been able to accept Malcolm's diagnosis, nor mine. It was just too much for her to handle. The best thing is that she was able to see the birth of Gabby. She wanted so badly for us to have a baby, and that was her only wish. When she found out Gabby's test results were negative, that's all she needed.

I know Malcolm is torn up now; both he and Nate are going to be saddened by this. I should call him, just to let him know I've gotten the message.

"Hey, how are you?" I ask.

"I'm fine, about as good as can be expected."

"What about Nate, how is he?"

"He's taking it hard. He was there when she passed."

"What, was she in the hospital?"

"Yes, he had taken her last night, because she complained of chest pains. From my understanding, they checked her over, and sent her home about four hours later. Then Nate called me at 10:45 and said she wasn't breathing. He called 911 and they immediately took her back, but she was already gone by time they made it. The doctors say she died from a broken heart."

I hate to hear him like this. He sounds so broken. The last time I heard him like this was the time she had the heart attack three years ago. I pray they will get through this.

Trying to comfort him, I say, "I'm sorry to hear this, and I know she is in a better place, she's not suffering anymore. The best thing you and Nate can do now is be strong for one another. You both need each other now more than ever."

"Yes you're right. Thanks for calling." he says.

"No problem, I wouldn't have had it any other way. Momma told me you were trying to contact me, but I'm out of town, so I didn't get the messages. Let me know when the services will be."

"Okay, how's my baby, is she with you?"

"No, she's home with my parents. I'm in Atlanta."

His voice changes, a bit frustrated he asks, "Are you going to be gone long?"

Calmly, I answer, "No, I shouldn't, we're here on business."

"We, as in you and him?"

"Yes."

He rushes to get off the phone, but not before telling me we really need to talk. There's something he has to tell me. What that could be I don't know, and honestly if it's not about Aunt Colleen, or Gabby I can't worry about that now.

By the time I'm finished with my conversation, our food has arrived, and believe it or not, I'm starving. I didn't think I would be this hungry, but obviously I was wrong.

It hadn't dawned on me until now, Marcel and I will share a similar space. When we were in California, we stayed at his home that's even larger than the condo, so there were enough rooms for me to sleep anywhere I chose to, but being in here is a little close for comfort. I've noticed he's made sure that we have separate beds, but ... Lord help me!

About 10:00 Zoe calls laughing in the phone, "Hey you what ya doing?"

"Nothing silly, we're sitting here watching television."

"Yeah right."

"No, seriously, we're watching television."

"Okay I believe you. Just calling to check on you, and see how you enjoying the ATL."

"Actually, I haven't been out of the room all night—"

"See, I knew it ... you did it didn't you?"

"Did what?"

"I know it hasn't been that long, has it?"

"Girl you are crazy."

"No I'm just playing; I just wanted to test you. I believe you when you say that you're not doing anything, and I really believe Marcel is a good guy, I respect him highly. Glad you found him."

"Me too."

"Have fun lady, you deserve it."

"Good night, and hold it down in the NY."

"I got you."

By the time I'm done cutting up with her, it's late. Marcel and I turn it in for the night, we tell each other good night, and I go to my separate bed and so does he. "I love you Mrs. Cartiér." he says. "Good night, Mr. Bouviér." I say back.

The day is here and Marcel seems so nervous. I've reassured him that it's okay, and if he makes a mistake it's alright because I'm here. My first thought was he was in shock because I didn't go overboard at the mall. I don't have to shop everywhere I go, but mostly everywhere. I'll probably get something from the Versace store before we head back.

There's a knock at the door, and the concierge hands me a bag from Neiman Marcus, and surprisingly there's a box with a pair of Christian Louboutins' on the inside. I open the box and there is a note that says,

"Aren't we cute, I saw you eyeing them earlier, and you know you can't pass up a beautiful pair of shoes."

By this time I look towards heaven, and I tell God, "No you can't have him back, you sent him to me, now he's mine for the keeping."

I give him a big kiss, just to let him know how much I thank him and appreciate him. He so kindly obliges me, and then he says he'll be back, he wants to go down stairs for a while. I rush to call Lucy to let him know how much I'm enjoying myself.

"Hey Diva, how are you?" he asks.

"I'm good, I'm having sooo much fun, I can live here."

He says, "Whatever! Girl you aren't going anywhere without me."

Laughing, I say, "No honest, I can see myself living here."

He cracks the joke, "Please don't tell me you're on first name basis there as well?"

"Nooo, not yet. I don't want to break the city in so fast, but I just like it here. It seems like somewhere I could raise Gabby."

"Okay enough about that. I let the man take you to Atlanta one time, now you're ready to pack your bags and move. I wish Grandma Belle was here, she'd tell you about making plans, and you know she would."

Just the thought of that gets a laugh out of me. He always knows how to bring me back to reality. Although this place is nice, I really can see myself living here. I loved it when we drove through some of the neighborhoods, and the houses here are a lot different from home; there is so much space, so much land. It's a great place to raise a child, but I don't know what Marcel's take on that is.

I look at the time, and I tell Lucy I'll call him later, or tomorrow. Time is passing fast, and I need to start getting ready.

"How's your dress?" he asks. "Do you like it?"

"I love it, and I believe Marcel will too."

"Leave it to Lucy baby to hook you up every time."

When Marcel first told me of this I hurried and got Lucy on the line, he called some friends that knew some friends, and next thing I knew Michael Knight was at my door, we had the measurements and the design just like that.

An hour later, he returns with the most beautiful bouquet of red roses you'd ever want to see. When I think this is it, there's another knock at the door, and this time the concierge has another dozen red roses, this goes on for another ten minutes, and by the time there done knocking, ten dozen red roses stare at me. The fragrance fills the room, and the only thing left for me to do is stand here and blush.

The more I look at the dress, the more I love it. I've put on the final touches to my make up, and the final detail is my hair, after I curl it I don't care too much for the big hair look, in saying that, I think tonight I want to be as sensual as I can be, so I'm going with a nice little updo, with just a few tendrils pulled out. I haven't felt this way in a very long time. When I got my nails done today I even went a step further, stepped out of my comfort zone of the usual "French manicure," and I walked out of the nail salon with OPI's Louvre Me Louvre Not!

Just as I go to put on the gown I suddenly realize there's a zipper in the back, and who else is there to help me, but of course Marcel. I kindly ask him for his assistance, and by no means does he hesitate. He looks at me and tells me how beautiful I look. He says I will be the prettiest woman in the place.

Once I'm settled in, I turn and take one look at myself, and I'm even in awe. The purple silk sleeveless dress stopping right above the knee, accented with a jaw dropping detachable floor length skirt. I have to say he did his thing ... I had planned to wear another pair of shoes, but it's my guess Marcel knew the color of the dress, therefore this is how I would play up the lavender "Tahiti" patent leather pumps. Absolutely gorgeous! Before we leave I fix Marcel's tie, and I give him one last kiss, to say, I'm proud of him, and I'm glad I'm here to share this with him.

When we walk into the Grand Ballroom, I am stunned, because the room is amazing, and there are people already here and seated. Marcel too likes being fashionably late. It's either that or the times must have gotten mixed up. He originally told me six o'clock. If he doesn't mind, neither do I.

"Hello Mr. Bouviér," one lady says at the door, and she then takes us to our seats. Everything is so beautifully decorated, white linen tablecloths cover the round tables, and there's also each napkin is held by a diamond napkin ring, which only adds to the table's beauty. The glassware is immaculate, and so is the tableware. Whoever is the coordinator of this event, I would have to say they did a wonderful job.

We're seated across from another couple that seems very excited to be here. First, the lady leans in to ask me is this my first time being here, and I answer her by saying, "Yes". She says when she first heard about this, she was a little hesitant, but the more her friend talked her into it, she thought it was a good idea. She also says she was a bit nervous at first, because she didn't think people celebrated anything like this. I tell her I'm as excited as she is, especially because I'm with the honoree for the night.

Sipping on my water, I take a look over the program. It's even done to perfection. *The Elite Society of the Undetectables* must be a huge society, because they have such a large following. Just as I'm getting ready to order my food, a gentleman named Dr. Phillip Wilson goes to the podium and begins to speak about how people are living longer with HIV/AIDS today, how that the statistics show that more people who are taking their medicines as prescribed have been given opportunities to live longer and healthier lives. I look down to read over the program a bit more, because maybe the Jewelry Industry is a contributor to some of the HIV/AIDS foundations. But as I continue to read, I see that this entire program is filled with information about HIV/AIDS. We can't be at the wrong function too now can we?

Once Marcel is introduced by a lovely lady named Donna, he proceeds to go to the podium. He clears his throat, and thanks her for inviting him, and then he looks at me as to say, "Please don't kill me." At first I'm totally thrown off but as he begins to open his mouth, I slowly forget that I've been tricked into coming to an HIV/AIDS event that is known for celebrating people living with HIV/AIDS whose status is undetectable. After a while I get excited, because that's me! I'm undetectable, and I look around and obviously every one in this room is too. I love Marcel, because he loves me, and he would take this time to lend his voice to others such as myself struggling with this disease on a daily basis. He opens up with a heart felt poem, and with his voice bold and firm he says these words:

"Aspirations
The River running blindly to its greater destination.
The world dancing without reserve.
Red faces painted in observation of those that fell behind.
Flashing lights signify the motion of the open mind.
The needles eye reflects the focus-the door to creation is wide open.
Reach out towards your inspirations; look inside to grasp God's intuition.
Let go of useless fears and inhibitions, knowing there is so much more to explore.
Manufacture your dreams into vivid living, breathing reality.
Quantify your goals and chart the progression of your destiny.
Achieve your hearts desires ... obtain control of all your passion.
Success is only hostage in your mind."

He continues, "On July 19, 1968, a baby boy was born by emergency cesarean due to internal bleeding. At birth the baby weighed nine pounds and seven ounces. At first glance the baby appeared to be healthy, but to the doctor's amazement the baby began to bleed severely from the mouth, and initially the doctors could not find out where the bleeding was coming from. As a result, the baby lost an overwhelming amount of blood, which caused the baby to need a blood transfusion.

It was first thought that the blood transfusion would save the infants life, but so happens the blood that was given turned out to be tainted, and because of this the infant contracted HIV.

It wasn't until six years later that the parents were told this child had HIV, and during that time it was taboo to have such a thing nevertheless a child would be diagnosed. Because the little boy parents were considered to be classified in the upper echelon, there was no way they could risk anyone finding out.

The little boy's parents tried to do everything in there power not to let him know he was infected with a deadly disease, so they showered him with, money, gifts, toys, anything his heart desired. Until one day at the age of nine, the little boy became very sick, and he was given a lot of medicines to take. He could not understand why he had to take so many medicines, and then he finally asked his parents what was wrong with him, why was he constantly missing days from school, constantly getting infections that were taking forever to go away?

On the little boys tenth birthday his parents finally told him he was HIV positive and that he would have to take medicine for the rest of his life in order to stay healthy. They explained to him that the disease that was in his blood was there to eat all the good things in his blood that his body needed to survive, and because of this it would make him very sick.

The little boy cried out of fear, first of all because he really didn't know what it was, but he knew that no one would ever love him. He also cried because he knew that one day he would want to grow up and have girlfriends, and they would not love him because of this.

Well this little boy grew up, and he became a very successful owner of five jewelry salons across the country. Although, he never had a successful relationship with anyone because it was very hard for him to trust. Due to him being HIV positive, the women he dated never understood why he wanted to remain celibate until he found the right woman God had designed for him.

That little boy is me! But the good news is I have finally found the woman that God has designed for me. He sent her to me at a time in her life where she needed to be reminded that she too can trust Him, and this is why today I celebrate my life with the person I want to spend the rest of my life with …"

I'm no good right now. I have nothing. So many emotions fill my heart. I don't know whether to be shocked, angry, mad, or surprised. I don't know, but I do know that THIS man is truly the man of God I've waited for.

Just as he finishes his speech, the lights go dim, and all I can hear is Rafiki, and the cast of The Lion King! He has it so that the cast does a serenade from "*The Circle of Life,*" in my honor.

I am speechless, and just when I thought that was it, the lights come up and there is a man standing at the podium. He starts out by giving his name, and where he's from. The first thing he says is that he's here on behalf of the family of Cartier, then he gives a speech about the history of the company and how they came into establishment. Then all of a sudden he says, "I have been asked to represent your *past,* then he has me come forward so that he can present me with a token from the company. He gracefully reaches in the inside of his left pocket, where he pulls out the most beautifully crafted red leather box, and inside it sits a 2-carat round, single-stoned diamond.

I feel like Ma'Dea right now, "If only I could just drop dead for a little while …" Afterwards he proceeds to take his seat.

Next like clockwork, another distinguished man in his fifties approaches the podium, and he starts out by saying how a diamond is a girl's best friend. He is here on behalf of Charles Lewis Tiffany, he goes on to explain the significance of the "little blue box" and how Mr. Tiffany mandated that the one thing you can not buy from his company no matter how much money you may have, is one of his boxes. He then says, "I have come to represent your *present*, and then he pulls out the most adorable blue box, crowned with a crisp white ribbon, and once I open it, here sits a 5-carat princess cut, single-stoned diamond.

By now I feel my heart is beating at rate of 100 times per minute ... He then takes his seat.

Last but not least, Marcel heads to the podium, but just as he makes his way, I hear the whimper of a baby's cry. I look to see where its coming from, in walks my father with Gabby in his hands, also behind him is my mother, and then there is Julian and Reese. Oh my God, Lucy is even here, sharp as ever. Mrs. Bouviér has come all the way from France, and so has his brother. Zoe and her mother are here, Mrs. Richardson is here, Mr. LeFleur is here, and lastly Melissa and Harrison are even here. Everyone is here!

Marcel begins to say, my name is Marcel Armand Bouviér, and I am here on behalf of Armand. Our company has been in establishment since 1968. He goes on to say that he is here to represent my *future*, and if I will have him, he will promise that with every day he will be the best man God has prepared him to be for me. He also says that he promises to never hurt me, that he will always protect me. Then he pulls out a white leather box with gold trim, and in it sits a 10-carat pear diamond ring!

There is not a dry eye in the place. I think I see Mr. Le Fleur dropping a couple of tears himself.

After I take less than zero seconds to say yes, everyone cheers, and we all sit down together and reflect over just how great tonight has been. Later, as we are on our way out, a lady with a baby in her arms about no more than four years old comes up to me and says, "You're lucky, at least some of us survived." I turn to her and say, "I wouldn't call it luck, I'd call it favour!"

Before we leave, we find out there has been an anonymous donation left for the foundation in order for them to continue to help build others up that are presently living with the disease, striving to reach an undetectable status. Marcel even made mention that he one day sees this event far surpassing this place. He says that he can envision this becoming a worldwide affair, where people living with HIV/AIDS will come from all over the world, and fill the place with cheers in celebration of their undetectable status. Not just focusing on their present state, but the best part is they remain that way, while helping to teach others as well. When I close my eyes and picture it ... the thought of it is mind-blowing.

I still have so many questions of how and when, I could spend all night thinking about it. I found out that Lucy and Zoe were in Atlanta the entire time. Lucy even said he saw me at Lenox Mall earlier that day, and one time he thought I saw him, so he turned the corner very fast so that I wouldn't notice him. While Zoe was calling me, she and her mother were hanging out in Buckhead at the Houston's restaurant. Marcel had flown them in two days earlier. My mother even was in on it, when I was talking to her about Malcolm, she and my father were busy getting ready to catch their flight then. I asked my father when did Marcel ask his permission, and he cracked the joke saying, when he brought that R350 for you and Gabs. But he later admitted he asked him the day they put Gabby's bed together. Apparently this was the day it was all thought of. It's one thing when everyone knows something you don't, especially when it turns out for your good.

Monday morning and it's already 9:15, I would have thought the judge would be here by now. I got the call last night from Grant that I needed to be in court this morning. Marcel immediately came to pick me up, but we're the only ones here.

About five minutes later in walks Beth, Mr. Rucker, Mr. Banks, and Mr. Norris along with the company's attorney. To my knowledge this was a closed case, but...

As the judge walks in, she asks has there been any new evidence presented in this case. Suddenly, I notice all of them huddling together, and I'm looking at Marcel and Grant like what's going on. As it stands, once Beth realized that Grant was relentless in finding out who actually disclosed my status throughout the company, she began to get nervous, and then out of the blue, she confessed that she was the one who alerted the partners to my status. Also it is found that she was in on Tyler's scheme to get rid of me the whole time. So as the bible states, *For evil doers shall be cut off: but those that wait upon the Lord, they shall inherit the earth.*

I eventually won my case against Rucker, Banks, and Norris LLC, for an undisclosed amount on the grounds of discrimination. What they didn't know was, although it appeared I walked in that office alone the day I was let go, the fact is, He was there all the time.

And as momma would say ..."Now unto him that is able to do exceeding abundantly above all that we ask or think, according to the power that worketh in us."

For so long I've seen it, I've spoken it, and NOW I BELIEVE IT! It's my own firm, "Diamond Investments". In saying that, pray for me, because I'm about to shut Fifth Avenue Down!

Afterword

My Beloved,

    When I first set out to write this novel, I had no idea of the path it would take me, all I knew is I was given a vision by God, and He wanted me to share it with the world. I didn't know how, or where, but I did know that if I leaned not to my own understanding and acknowledge Him then He would direct my path, so I did, and this is where He led me.

    In my life I have met many people of various ethnicities, races, religions, cultures, and beliefs, I've even come into contact with some non-believers as well, and never have I been so sad to say how we as a human race have become so comfortable with the idea that if we live or die, it doesn't matter, because why? It's going to happen anyway, so why stress it, but never have I seen it as much as I have in the African-American community.

    I see it every day where our young girls grow up with low or NO self-esteem; never realizing their worth. They began as little girls thinking no one loves them, so in order to change that, they want to have a baby to "love," then later they start thinking in order to find a man they have to wear the revealing clothes that show every nick and cranny, or they need to make sure the thong is placed right above the low rider jeans so I and everyone else will know what color underwear they have on. I used to get so upset about this until I remembered these little girls have mothers, and more than so if you follow them home, you will see that momma and daughter are dressed exactly alike, except momma's thong sits right beneath a Chinese tattoo that is supposed to mean "Virtuous, "sitting under a pair of high priced jeans, coupled with a pair of 5-6 inch stilettos. I don't think this is the woman in Proverbs 31.

    So ladies, I ask, when are we going to stop devaluing ourselves? When are we going to realize that we are more than that? We are priceless, and we don't need money, popularity, or a MAN to validate that. Also when are we going to stop falling for a man because of the car he drives, or whose name he has on his back, or better yet how much money he has in his bank account? If you know that you are worth it in the first place, it wouldn't matter if he had $1,000 or $1 million in the bank, because you should be able to buy your own shoe collection anyway!

    To my men, I am not going to put you down by mentioning the "black men in jail syndrome," however I will say …there are many of you that lack a sufficient amount of self esteem, because why? Your father wasn't present and your mother raised you as a single mother. That's fine and good, but that was then and this is now.

There are too many of our young men that are growing up thinking its okay to abuse women (physically, verbally, mentally, financially, and most of all SPIRITUALLY) because that's what you were taught? It's been said that there aren't any good men; I don't believe that. I believe every man God made is good.

Though you may feel undervalued, and unappreciated, please know you're not. You are worth more than you know, and we as women, we love you, but we need you to love yourselves, we need you to be the men God intended you to be. We need you to walk and talk as men.

So men, STAND UP, LIFT YOUR HEADS UP, most of all, PULL YOUR PANTS UP! Once you begin to know who you are, and whose you are, then you will never want to inflict hurt or will you want to feel hurt again, because then on you will know you are worth it.

We all may know someone that has been diagnosed with HIV/AIDS, and if not you just don't know it. Look around you may be sleeping, eating, working, or praising God on Sunday's right next to someone. Guess what it may be you!

According to the Centers for Disease Control and Prevention, at the end of 2006 there were an estimated 1.1 million people living with HIV, of which almost half (46%) were African American.

In 2007, African Americans accounted for 51% of the 42,655 persons (including children) new HIV/AIDS diagnoses, also they accounted for 48% of the 551,932 persons (including children) living with HIV/AIDS, and for African American women living with HIV/AIDS, the most common methods of HIV transmission were high risk heterosexual contact and injection drug use. In African American men living with HIV/AIDS, the most common methods of transmission were sexual contact with other men, injection drug use, and high heterosexual contact.

What frightens me as an African-American woman is that so many of my sisters are the leaders of this epidemic, and we have continued to turn our heads as if it doesn't matter. African American women make up 61% of all new HIV cases among women in the U.S., and we also have an HIV prevalence rate nearly 18 times that of white women. It is the leading cause of death for us ages 25-34, and 80% of new cases are contracted through heterosexual contact, and the officials have said that the heterosexual black men with multiple sex partners, not the bisexual men who secretly have sex with other men, the ones we call the "down-low brothers," are responsible for the high rates of HIV among African American women.

This epidemic is a long way from being over, but we as a community, including the churches, not only the African American ones, but all of them, Pastors too, we must take a stand, not to be in fear that we will offend anyone for the sake of loosing a member. I know it's not a topic everyone wants to hear from the pulpit, because of the stigma associated with it, but we must be held accountable.

The good news is that today you can know your HIV status much easier, there are places you can get tested for free, you may be afraid, but don't be, go with a friend, it's fast, and prayerfully it can save a life. In learning about this disease

I have found out so much, and it is completely preventable if we start to become more responsible, take actions and not think about the few minutes of enjoyment, even if that means holding out. Ladies, if he doesn't want to strap up, remind yourself you are worth it, men, if she doesn't want you to rap it up, remind yourself you are worth it, and so is your future generation. Life is too precious!

To my brothers and sisters in the struggle, I applaud you. You are some of the strongest people I know. You have overcome so many obstacles that some people would never imagine. You've shown us that one can live a healthy and meaningful life, if only they do what's expected of them. I'm glad to see you looking as fabulous as you can look; I appreciate you for your determination, and your integrity. Although you may have a disease in your bloodstream that has been said to have no cure, but remember we all share the same blood, His blood, and in that we are all made clean.

One may ask, why I chose such a heavy topic, it wasn't me. I just realized although my status may be negative, it just as well could have been me, because I didn't always do the right thing, but, as I grew older, my mindset changed, and I began to realize I am a Diamond, I am a part of a chosen generation, a royal priesthood, a holy nation, a peculiar people. I have been called out of the darkness into His marvelous light, and for that I know I am fearfully and wonderfully made ...

Love,
Chizellé

Acknowledgments

Where do I begin? To all of you that have been an integral part to my writing this book. First, to my spiritual father, Pastor Craig L. Oliver Sr., for the last eight years of my life, I have been blessed to call you Daddy. You have taught me so much, you have helped me through some of the worst times in my life when I couldn't tell anyone, I would walk into the doors of Elizabeth Baptist Church, and it would be like you were in my business, but it wasn't you, it was Him! And I thank Him for sending me you. Also Mrs. Chi'Ira Oliver, I am so blessed to have you in my life, and I thank God for you, watching you has inspired me to be the Titus 2:5 woman. I love you!

My editor Reneé Crutcher, thank you. Mr. Nathaniel Dyer for hooking up the cover, the website, and the images, boy you bad! Clint Alexander for bringing the necklace that made its way all the way from Scotland to life. No one else could have done it. Brother Tshombe Roberts, the poem you wrote *"Aspirations,"* would have made Marcel real proud, because it made me cry! Thank you and I love you! Ms. Dee Stewart, my publicist, girl you are the truth, I thank you so much for enlightening me on the world of Self Publishing, I wish you total happiness. Ms. Kristie at M-A-C, you gave me exactly what was needed. You brought the beauty out that I already I had in me, and turned it into a portrait of pure fabulosity!

Ms. Jessica Cole,(AidAtlanta/Elite Society of the Undetectables) words can not say how much you mean to me, thanks for trusting me enough to take two chapters and turn it into this. I love you. Ms. O'dessa Nixon, thank you will never be enough. I love you! Dr. Melissa Osborne, you have no idea of how you helped me, you made me go back to my nursing school days. Also can't wait to get back to the Cheesecake Factory. Is it a date? Dr. Jeanette Leader, you know how much I love you don't you? You helped give me Freedom! I love and thank you. Hope I did you proud. Dr. David Melbranche thanks for introducing me to thebody.com, and also Mrs. Diedra Favors R.N. you are awesome! Dr. Steven Shore, thank you, who would have thought a phone nurse could go all the way to this huh? Dante McDowell, (Capitol Investments) the baddest Financial Consultant in the ATL Mrs. Lisa Poppell CPA, thank you, I know it was along time coming. Bradley T. Harris, thank you so much for teaching me all about the jewelry industry, along with Drew Anderson, one of the sweetest gemologists on this side of earth. Now, for my Law enforcement ... Lonnie Jackson of the Mobile Police Department, thank you for the info on the "white collar crimes," also Mr. Earl Adams, thank you, the streets are much safer with you out there. Kingsley,"Cheap Laptops

Atlanta" thank you for saving me. Mr. Bruce Assaf, thank you for your spirit, God Bless you! Jeremy Prince, the Apple Pro, thank you so much, and Tonya Allen, right in the nick of time, He always shows up! Mr. Carl "Buckethead" Jackson, what can I say, only that God knows best.

Now ... to the ones that made this entire book possible. My precious jewels, the one's living with this virus on a daily basis, but going at it hard, never wavering. The ones that say to us, I have it, but it doesn't have me, Praise God! Ms. Cynthia Boykin, thank you I love you, Ms. Sonja Williams, I love you my sister, Look at you now! Mr. David Duckworth, I know wherever you are you are somewhere enjoying LIFE, and Niceala thanks girl. I love you and so does God!

My Gemstones

My Pearl: My grandmother, Mrs. Hattie. M. Williams. Thank you for being the God fearing woman you are, a true example of how a Godly woman should live. I love you!

My Rubies: The woman who gave me life, my mother: Mrs. Catherine Williams Packer. Mommy, thank you for introducing me to Jesus, by going to church with me, not only taking me. For wanting me so badly that you and the George Washington Bridge could have made the headlines. The best mother I could've ever asked for. I love you immensely! My mother-in-law, Mrs. Queen "Estelle" Archie, thank you for accepting me seventeen years ago, as your other daughter, loving me just the same, and telling me to stay on my knees. Finally thank you for giving me the best part of me.

My Emeralds: Nanny Cynt, Mary, "Anie", I love you, my other aunts I love you all! My hosts of cousins thank you for your love and support. Melaine, my promoter! Keep my seat warm. Sonya, my God sister, thanks for listening. Mrs. Dukes, I love you dearly. Mrs. Tangie, 60 cents to the homeless can go along way! Dr. Vanna Jackson, Freedom and I love you. Hope I made you proud. Mrs. Cindy, I love you! Melissa, my partner in crime ... Mrs. Burkes, and my Elizabeth Baptist family, my First Baptist, St. Luke, and Mt. Zion families.

My Diamonds: Katina Seals, my best friend, thanks for everything. I love you sis. My sister-in-laws, Letitia, thank you for being there, Wendy we're in this thing together and I love you both. Katina Smith-Adams, girl you are the truth! I know you got me ... I love you. Lastly, Katrina Ann No-Moore Batain, my other mother, I took your advice, and found another gift. LOL! I love you! Jada, "Godmommy", thanks is not enough, you have been more than a friend; you've been my sister. Jadice, I love you! Danyale, I love you, cuz. To my other one hundred plus cousins, I love you! Nadia, I love you. Collirene: I got you, and I love you all! Camille, thank you for introducing me to Eastern Parkway, I love you! Chermine, love you just the same. Jana "Melissa", please know I love you and thank you for allowing me to invade your life! Ophelia my other sister I love you! Tameka, I love you! Trecia, thank you for believing in me. Stephanie H. I love you girl! Zelda, thank you, and I love ya! Darlene, love you. Tencie, love you! Stacey, love ya! Cassandra and Cheryl, I love you! Mrs. Kim, and Mrs. Stephanie, thanks for taking care of "Person". Bonnie, thank you, and I love you. The Girl's Night Out Crew! Tanya, Rhonda, love you! Ms. Nia, for finally setting me free! Lataunya, love you sis, Dana, Doris, Tan, my SSP, and my CCS Family!

My Sapphires: "Diamonds in Training," My daughter Johnna, I love you, and I'm proud of you. My nieces remember Auntie loves you. Sheridan, Godmommy loves you! And to the rest of my D.I.T's, I love you!

****

My Black Diamonds: My father: James Packer. Daddy thanks so much for loving me, and always encouraging me. I love you. My father-in-law, John Archie, thank you, and I love you. Uncle Hilliard, I love you always! Pastor Clark, thank you for preparing me to fly, thank you for the teachings that have stayed with me on this journey of life. I will forever treasure them.

My Onyx's: Eric, a one of a kind brother in-law, I love you! Terry. I love you, Goddaddy Ron, thank you so much, and I love you! Uncles, I love you all! Robert, the brother I never had, for so long I thought you were! To my other male-figure cousins, you are all the best ... I love you! Vince, your words of encouragement ... immeasurable! Tynelle, I'm very proud of you. Also Richard, thanks for always telling me like it is, also for listening, even when you didn't want to! I love you. John, "Clip", thanks for twenty-one years. I finally put down the fist, and picked up a new sword; the pen. I love you brother! Mr. Alex Dukes, Grandaddy, I love you!

My Hematites: My nephews, remember Auntie loves you. My cousins, I love you all! Kenny, I'm proud of you. Khalil, I love you, and the rest of my future men of Valour!

My Cubic Zirconia's: All of the ones that said I couldn't or said I wouldn't, to the ones that smiled in my face, and talked about me as soon as I left, the ones that gave me the inspiration, and the motivation to say I can! And I did! To the haters! You helped me press toward the mark of the prize of the high calling of God in Christ Jesus. So I say thank you, when you meant it for evil, God meant it for my good!

Finally, to the ones I have forgotten to mention, it wasn't intentional, please know you were on my mind, and I love you. Catch you in the next one!

R.I.P.

Reginald D. Mack

Cousin, you didn't make it to see this come to pass, but I know you're in heaven smiling down on me, and making God and the others look their best. I know God has the prettiest two strand twist there is. I'm guessing by now, you have introduced the girls to the Flat Iron! I love you ... and I pray that you save a seat for me at the table!

Resources

Where to get tested

If you or someone you may know would like to be tested for HIV and not sure where to go please call the National AIDS Hotline 1-800-342-2437

How to Prevent the Spread of HIV
Specializing in a wealth of information as far as prevention The U.S. Centers for Disease and Control National Prevention Network is a great outlet. They can be reached at 1-800-458-5231, or you can access their website at www.cdc.npin.org

Aid Atlanta Inc. is an organization that has been transforming lives since 1982, and since then has grown to be the largest and most comprehensive AIDS Service Organization in Southeast U.S. Located in Atlanta, Georgia, it's their mission to empower individuals living with HIV/AIDS to live independent, productive lives while delivering world class educational programs to help stop the spread of HIV by reducing at risk behaviors in targeted populations.

Please call 404-870-7700, or access their website at www.aidatlanta.org
Balm in Gilead is an organization that with its achievements have enabled thousands of churches to become leaders in preventing the transmission of HIV by providing comprehensive educational programs for those infected to seek and maintain treatment. Also the organization based in Richmond, Virginia, engages Black Churches to become centers for education, compassion, and care in the
fight against HIV/AIDS. Please call 804-644-2256 or visit their website at www.balmingilead.org

Helping Hand Ministries is a non profit organization that focuses directly towards HIV education and prevention. Based in Mobile, Alabama this organization aids in assisting with both referral and support services. They can be reached at 251-431-6842 or visit their website at www.helpinghandmobile.com

Overview of HIV

The Body is a commercial website run by the Body Health Resources Corporation; it has easy to understand terminology which provides a wealth of information of HIV/AIDS by having question and answer forums with HIV physicians. Access their website at www.thebody.com Also the Center for Disease Control provides information by gathering statistics about the spread of HIV in different populations by listing a numerous amount of articles, newsletters, brochures, along with providing question and answer sections. You can reach them at 1-800-342-AIDS, or by accessing their website at www.cdc.gov/hiv

Information about African American Men and Women with HIV/AIDS
The National Minority AIDS Coalition, which strives to develop leadership among all communities of color as far as HIV. Their website is www.nmac.org
 Also the National AIDS Treatment Advocacy Project includes summaries of conversations held by AIDS experts directed towards African Americans and HIV. Their website is www.natap.org
Again, the body.com has extensive resources reliable to African Americans with HIV/AIDS of all ages.

Living with HIV/AIDS
The Elite Society of the Undetectables is a social an educational network that was founded by a team of medical providers working at the Joye Bradley Health Services Clinic at Aid Atlanta. This society was formed as a ways and means to celebrate and acknowledge those who have reached undetectable status. They recognize it is a challenge to become adherent to the meds everyday, and a trend was noticed that 80% of clients that were on medicines was undetectable within 60 days of beginning medications. Because this society is heavily associated with celebrating life, the name was birthed as a tribute to those, being that they were an elite group of people, without the stigma of the name HIV/AIDS.
They can be reached at 404-870-7756 or through the website www.elitesociety.me

HIV Campaigns (Get Involved)

Rap It Up-is about taking a stand in your life and community to help stop the spread of HIV/AIDS. It's about protecting yourself and those you care about, being informed, by getting tested annually, talking openly with your partner, friends/family, and taking responsibility in your community. Sponsored by BET, to learn more visit www.rapituppresents.com

To my M-A-C DIVA's, in 2008 MAC launched its VIVA Glam VI campaign, and by the time this goes to print the next campaign would have debuted. This initiative is part of an ongoing effort by both the VIVA GLAM campaigns, and the M-A-C AIDS Fund to fight HIV/AIDS around the globe. The M-A-C Fund has been in existence since 1994, and since then they have raised over $100 million dollars. They have been very integral in providing financial support to organizations working with underserved regions and populations. 100 percent of the proceeds from both the Lipstick/Lipglass are donated to help fight this disease.

As a personal dedication I wore VIVA GLAM VI on the cover. Thanks M-A-C!

For My Book Clubs and Readers

1. Beginning with chapter one, what was your initial thought of Victoria?
2. Do you feel Julian's choice to began dating men was an act of rebellion, or to some, "a state of confusion"?
3. In your opinion, was Malcolm's behavior typical of a married man, functioning in an "I do what I do, because I can get away with it", mentality.
4. When Marcel was first introduced, did you feel he had a certain connection to Victoria at that time? If so was it physical, mental, or spiritual?
5. Do you feel Sydney represents many women today, seeking out ONLY married men for financial gain?
6. In your congregation, how many people do you sit next to Sunday after Sunday that are hurting, but afraid to say so because of the stigma of "church folk"?
7. Do you think Marcel was really chosen for Victoria, or because she had been hurt so ... she wanted to believe he was the one?
8. Why do you think Lucy decided to change his lifestyle? And do you feel he will remain changed?
9. Do you think Victoria's love for fashion was somehow due to a hidden insecurity of her own?
10. In the end, what do you think can be done to get more churches involved in assisting its members and those in the community that are affected by HIV/AIDS?

Sneak preview from ...

His Grace, His Blood, His Mercy!

One

Summer is almost over, and I can't wait to get back to school to see my friends. Everyone tells me the eighth grade is the best, because I get to say goodbye to my little girl days, and hello to becoming a young lady. Can't believe I thought about having sex so many times. I was the only one in the crew that hadn't done it yet ... maybe it's about time.

I did have a great time in France over the break. I got the chance to do and see so many things, but the best part was Fashion Week. One thing I will cherish forever was meeting Mrs. Bethann Hardison. I've read she now has her own modeling agency for girls like me; she had her son, Dwayne Wayne from "A Different World", and he still looks like that guy with the glasses turned up. I've been smiling from ear to ear, ever since she told me I have great potential in becoming a model, but ... Daddy and Momma say that they want me to become something more stable, whatever that means. The one thing that makes me happy is believing one day I'll be on the runway with all the top supermodels. Watch out Eva, because I'm America's Next Top Model!

I log on to my Facebook account, and I've got another friend request. This time it's from a boy that goes to my school. Not interested! I automatically click ignore, because Quinn tells me I need more mature boys to hang out with. Later for the boys that still have to get permission to drive the car. I want someone that has their driver's license already, so if we do get pulled over by the cops, he'll be old enough so that they want have to call our parents. There is a message from Drew; I haven't talked to him in a while. I've tried calling him a couple of times but he doesn't answer, so hopefully he's writing to let me know he loves me.

Andrew Harrison: July 16 at 9:52am - Got your calls, couldn't get back. What's up, can you get out later today? Don't be playn, I ain't about them games. Drew

I get a rush of excitement over me, because I have not seen him in a week. He was already mad that I went to France for a month. I kept telling him my Daddy wanted me to visit my cousins, and that I was not going to be with any other boys, but he didn't believe me.

Gabrielle Bouviér: July 16 at 12:10pm - Yeah I can, I have to ask my mom, and then I can get Quinn to come by and get me. Where you gonna pick me up? Lenox or Phipps? Your girl, Gabby

Oh and I have got to look fly, he loves the Apple Bottom's. He says baby got back. Just like Erykah Badu say's "get it from my momma." I call Quinn to see if she'll come over here to pick me up. Hopefully she's over her grandmother's house this week.

"What's up girl?"

"Nothing and you?"

"What you doing? Can you come by to take me to the mall?"

"Why? Don't tell me, you talked to Drew."

"Yeah sort of, he sent me a message on Facebook. He wanted to know if I can get out."

"What time?"

"Not really sure right now. I got to see if he hit me back."

"Well check right quick, then I can tell grandma I need to borrow the car."

"Hold on."

Andrew Harrison: July 16 at 12:23 pm - Phipps by the Versace store. At six, don't be having me waiting. And if you ain't planning on putting it down don't even bother coming. Drew

"Okay, he hit me back. Is 5:15 good?"

"Should be okay, you know grandma go to sleep at eight so it should be all good."

"Okay thank you. Now I just have to ... "

"You gon' do it this time?"

"I think so, because when I left he was mad at me, so I want to show him I'm all about him."

"We'll see. You said that last time."

"You tripping, I'll see you later."

She's right, I did say that the last couple of times, and I know he hasn't pressured me, but I know he wants to. I've thought a lot about it, and everyone else is doing it, so I don't want to be the last virgin standing. Tonight I'm loosing it.

Momma should be home around four. She and Daddy have a meeting tonight, so it shouldn't be hard me telling her I'm going over to Quinn's grandmother's house. I swear lately she has been tripping a lot. Ever since we got back, she's changed, and it has only been a week. I guess it is hard running your own firm, and it doesn't help that Daddy has to be gone so much, but I believe getting out tonight'll be piece of cake.

I choose the flyest outfit I've got. It's a little something-something we got in France. It's a cute little yellow peasant dress, with a pair of yellow sandals. I hope Drew likes it on me, but I hope he likes me better with it off. I would hate it if he cheats on me with another girl only because I wouldn't.

I love living in the ATL, there is no telling who you are going to see on any given day. I just saw Monica coming out of the Jimmy Choo store, and I didn't want to look like a star crazed fan, but I couldn't help it. I had to say hello, but the nice thing was that she said hello back.

There he is the finest man I've ever seen. I'm so glad Quinn hooked us up. As soon as he walks up, I give him the biggest smile just to say hello.

"What's up sexy?" he says.

Blushing, I say, "You what's up."

"Well, that's what's up then."

We stand there talking as if this is where we plan to hang out. I was hoping he would show me a little more affection, but I guess he doesn't want to ruin his precious image.

"You ready to go?" he asks.

Nervously I say, "Yes, where are we going?"

"You said you were ready right?"

"Yes."

"Well where else, my boys spot."

I hesitate for a minute, because I thought we'd at least go to a hotel. But we've waited this long so no need to make him wait longer, but I have to ask, "You do have condoms right?"

www.ingramcontent.com/pod-product-compliance
Lightning Source LLC
Chambersburg PA
CBHW030630110726
47901CB00002B/388